T. FRANK MUIR

THE MEATING ROOM

A DCI GILCHRIST INVESTIGATION

ACADEMY

CHICAGO

First published in the United Kingdom in 2014 by Constable
An imprint of Constable and Robinson Ltd
This edition published in 2017 by Academy Chicago Publishers
An imprint of Chicago Review Press Incorporated
814 North Franklin Street
Chicago, Illinois 60610

ISBN 978-1-61373-789-7

Library of Congress Cataloging-in-Publication Data

Names: Muir, Frank (Crime novelist) author.
Title: The meating room / T. Frank Muir.
Description: Chicago, Illinois : Chicago Review Press Incorporated, [2017]
Identifiers: LCCN 2016029765 (print) | LCCN 2016037317 (ebook) |
    ISBN 9781613737897 (pbk. : alk. paper) | ISBN 9781613737903 (pdf) |
    ISBN 9781613737927 (epub) | ISBN 9781613737910 (kindle)
Subjects: LCSH: Police—Scotland—Fiction. | Murder—Investigation—
    Fiction. | GSAFD: Mystery fiction.
Classification: LCC PR6063.U318 M43 2017 (print) | LCC PR6063.
    U318 (ebook) | DDC 823/.914—dc23
LC record available at https://lccn.loc.gov/2016029765

Cover design: Joan Sommers Design
Cover image: © iStockphoto
Typesetting: Nord Compo

Printed in the United States of America
5 4 3 2 1

1

Maggie Ferguson heard the car before she saw it. The sound of its burbling engine reached out to her through the morning darkness. At the age of sixty-seven her hearing was still good, although her eyesight was not what it used to be. And the haar that had drifted inland off the North Sea, shrouding the forest in a stirring fog, did nothing to help. She thought it odd that the car was parked in the clearing, with its lights off and its engine running, and her first thought was that it must be a couple of young lovers up to no good in the backseat.

She gave out a short shrill whistle and a "Here boy. Over here," and sighed with resignation when Fergie, her golden Labrador, ignored her call and carried on crisscrossing the ground, nose to the pine-needled carpet. Poor old Fergie, she thought, his hearing was now as bad as her own eyesight. But as she walked off toward the beach, the wind rose, and the haar shifted, and the shadowed hulk of the car revealed itself for a fleeting moment before settling once more into the fogged darkness.

She was no good with cars, never knew their names, although she did notice that it was one of these big posh ones, far too expensive for a pair of youngsters. Which made her think it must belong to someone older, and that he, or she, might be on the phone. So she ignored it, and strode on through the trees toward the sea.

But with that shifting of the wind, Fergie caught some new scent, and he tracked off, nose to the ground, in the opposite direction.

"This way, Fergie. This way."

But Fergie wandered on, oblivious to Maggie, until he noticed the car.

Later, in her statement to the police, Maggie would say that Fergie had seemed to know something was wrong, that he must have sensed death, for he stood there, his hackles raised like a fur fin on his shoulders, his coughing bark straining his canine vocal cords as if ready to snap. But in that early morning chill, Maggie was unaware of what she was about to find as she rushed to quiet him.

"Shush," she ordered. "Shush now, Fergie. That's *enough*."

But Fergie was as good as deaf, his hearing drowned by his own barking.

"Oh, dear," Maggie said, digging into her pocket. "We'll need to put your lead on."

Even then, when she leaned forward to clip Fergie's lead to his collar, and cupped her hand over his nose to stop him barking, she did not notice that the driver's window was just a touch ajar, a crack at the top. Nor did she notice the rubber tube that led from the window to the exhaust pipe. Only when she stood upright, tugged Fergie away, and gave the car a parting glance did she realize that the windows were steamed up, and that a scarf, or a pullover, or something woollen, was stuffed into the crack in the window, through which smoke seeped into the early morning air.

The driver, nothing more than a silhouette in the mist, took no notice of her—not on the phone but sleeping. Or maybe not sleeping but . . .

"Dear goodness," she gasped, and stumbled backward.

In her panic, as her mind struggled to compute what her eyes were telling her, it never occurred to her to open the door and check if the driver was alive or needed help. Nor did she think to switch off the engine or use her mobile phone to call for an ambulance. Her thoughts were clouded with the panic of the moment, intent only on putting as much distance as possible between herself and the car.

Fergie seemed to have found new life in his old legs, too. He tugged hard at his lead, as if chasing after some new, irresistible scent. Or maybe his canine senses caught the danger in what had gone before and urged him to pull his owner away from the scene—to the safety of her car and the drive back to Leuchars.

———

"Has anyone ever told you you're a gentle lover?"

Gilchrist held Cooper's inquiring gaze. Her eyes fascinated him. They always had. The lightest blue, sharp and clear as a winter sky. Even after the night before—one too many Deuchars in the Central and a bottle of Moët back home in Fisherman's Cottage to celebrate nearing the end of the week, any excuse for a session—her eyes looked fresh and alert. Or maybe, at the age of forty-one, Cooper was too young for him, and now it was showing. But he thought he caught a sense of wariness in her question, a subtle probing, and he pushed a hand through her hair. He loved the way her curls spilled onto his face, loose and long and shampoo fresh. He breathed her in, slid his other hand down the length of her back, heard her gasp.

"Why do you ask?" he said.

She leaned forward, settling deeper into him, pressed her lips to his. "Why do you always answer a question with a question?"

"Do I?"

"See what I mean?" She smiled, as if to make him think she was letting him off the hook, then said, "Well? *Has* anyone ever told you?"

"What do you think?"

"I think you're too much of a gentleman to tell me any secrets from your past."

"And what about secrets from *your* past?"

If he had to analyze her reaction, he might have thought it was a warning to back off, a silent *Just don't go there.* Instead, he chose to believe that her questioning, their back-and-forth banter, was a form of verbal foreplay. Which seemed to be confirmed when she leaned forward, her breasts against his chest, her lips at his ear, breath warm and rushing as she—

His mobile rang.

"Leave it," she instructed.

But he reached for it, read the screen—Jessie. "I have to take this."

Cooper flexed her thighs, slipped off him, and lay by his side.

"Jessie," Gilchrist said. "It's early."

"And it's Friday, and we've got a body."

"Keep talking." Gilchrist held Cooper's gaze as he listened to Jessie rattle off a sequence of events that began with a call from a Mrs. Ferguson in Leuchars. The name rang a faint bell, but he couldn't place it.

"We've run the registration number through the PNC," Jessie said, "and the car's a . . . hang on, here it is . . . Jaguar XJ8 Vanden Plas, whatever that is when it's at home, registered in the name of Stratheden Enterprises Ltd."

The company name rang a bell, too, but again Gilchrist couldn't pull it from his memory. Of course, Cooper's hand on him did not lend itself to clear thought, but a Vanden Plas was a top-of-the-range Jag, suggesting the company had money, or at least the directors did.

Jessie helped him out with, "Stratheden's privately owned and specializes in luxury development, mostly overseas, and mostly for the stinking rich. The two registered company directors are Thomas Magner and Brian McCulloch."

Gilchrist pressed his mobile hard to his ear. "Did you say Thomas *Magner?*"

"The one and only. But the dead guy in the Jag's not him, so I'm thinking it might be McCulloch. We're trying to contact both of them by phone, but we're just being dumped into voicemail."

"Tried the company landline?"

"Same thing."

"Well, it *is* early," Gilchrist conceded. "So, who's at the scene now?"

"Just me and the SOCOs. I've had a quick look but kept my distance, if you know what I mean. I think our suicide had some help, though."

"Murdered, you mean?"

"Hey, Boy Wonder. You're quick."

Gilchrist frowned. Everything Jessie had described had suggested a straightforward suicide. So . . . "What have I missed?"

"You need to see the body. But the PF can't get hold of the pathologist." A pause, then, "Is she there?"

"Why do you ask?"

"Other than the obvious, she's not answering her phone either."

Gilchrist noticed Cooper's mobile on his bedside table and had a vague recollection of her powering it down last night. At that moment, Cooper rolled over, her hand guiding as she settled on top of Gilchrist. She leaned back, curls spilling over her shoulders, falling on to his legs, the tendons in her neck stretching from the effort of keeping silent.

Gilchrist managed to stifle a gasp, then said, "I'll see if I can reach her."

"Well, reach her soon. It's cold enough out here to freeze tits."

Gilchrist ended the call as Cooper fell forward and nuzzled into the crook of his neck. Her lips found his left ear and nibbled. Her fingers gripped the pillow like talons.

"You can be a cold bastard at times, Andy," she whispered.

He put his arms around her, held her through the final moments. Then, when he felt her relax, he said, "But gentle?"

She pressed her lips to his mouth. "Regrettably," she moaned, "you can be ever so gentle."

2

They took separate cars—Gilchrist in his Mercedes SLK Roadster and Cooper in her Range Rover. Gilchrist reached Tentsmuir Forest first, arriving just after eight, and pulled the Merc into an open clearing. He parked alongside Jessie's Fiat and removed a packed set of coveralls from the boot.

Off to the side, the dark blue Jaguar stood surrounded by yellow police tape, its paintwork gleaming like a showroom model no one was permitted to touch. Three SOCOs in white coveralls were on their knees scouring the adjacent area, prodding through the pine needles, cones, and roots with latex-gloved hands. Two more stood by the side of their Transit van, mobiles to their ears, their breath a vivid white in the cold air.

Gilchrist caught the eye of one of them, who nodded to the beach.

He spotted Jessie beyond the tree line of the forest, alone on the dunes, staring across the North Sea, on the phone. Standing there in coveralls, the early morning haar as a backdrop, she looked as pale as a ghost. The wind picked up, lifting sand off the dunes like spindrift, stinging his face as he strode toward her.

She turned as he clambered up the slope to stand beside her, ended the call with an angry grunt, and slid the mobile into her jacket pocket. She zipped up her coveralls. "Why is it always so fucking freezing on the east coast?"

"You're exposed out here," he said. "It's not so cold in the woods."

"No, there it's just freezing. Here, it's fucking freezing."

"Bad day?"

"Don't ask." She glared at him for a frosty moment, then said, "Follow me."

In the three months since DS Jessica Janes had transferred to Fife Constabulary from Strathclyde Police, Gilchrist had come to understand that her considerable bark was worse than her bite. But the remnants of last night's alcohol, on top of not enough sleep, was pushing him to the wrong side of a hangover, and he was in no mood to put up with either today. Besides, it was indeed verging on the fucking freezing.

"Any further forward with the ID?" he asked.

"Brian McCulloch."

"Positive?"

"I didn't have all day to wait, so I checked his wallet."

Investigation of a dead body usually did not begin until the police pathologist had first confirmed life was extinct. But the PF—the procurator fiscal—ran the show, particularly when a death was suspicious. And where a body was clearly dead, the investigation often began with the arrival of the first on the scene.

"Anything else I should know?" Gilchrist asked.

"Don't think I've ever seen so much cash in a wallet. Stuffed, it was. All brand-new hundreds. I didn't count it, but it had to be well over five thou."

"What about his mobile?"

"Can't find it."

Unusual, thought Gilchrist, but there could be a hundred reasons why McCulloch's mobile was not on his person or in the car. "Let's pull his records. See what we can find." A pause, then, "So why don't you think it was suicide?"

"Come and see for yourself."

They reached the yellow tape as Cooper's Range Rover pulled to a halt alongside Gilchrist's Merc. The SOCOs seemed busier all of a sudden. Gilchrist unfolded his coveralls as Cooper's door opened.

"Christ on a stick. Does she never have a hair out of place?" Jessie said.

Gilchrist thought silence his best response. Cooper lifted the hatchback of the Range Rover and removed a set of coveralls. He found it oddly erotic watching her slide in one leg, then the other, and slip the coveralls over her hips while he was doing likewise. Eight hours earlier, they had gone through a similar process in reverse.

Cooper zipped up and walked toward them. She nodded to Jessie, then to Gilchrist, who lifted the yellow tape for her to stoop under.

"After you," he said to Jessie.

"So you can compare backsides? I think not."

They followed Cooper side by side.

Cooper reached the Jaguar and opened the driver's door, taking care not to pull the rubber hose from the window. Then she leaned inside.

Silent, Gilchrist waited and glanced across to Jessie. The tip of her fine nose was red, and her eyes were glinting from the chill. Early March in Fife could be bitter, but this winter felt as if it had been with them forever, and the wind seemed to be gathering ice from the North Sea and firing it into their faces. Overhead, branches shifted and swayed, like evergreen brushes sweeping the air. All around them the forest rustled and stirred, groaning, as if almost alive.

"Rigor's not fully come yet," Cooper said, "so I'm guessing time of death would be—"

"*Guessing?*"

"—around midnight," Cooper said, ignoring Jessie. "Maybe earlier."

Jessie hissed under her breath.

"Body temperature's low," Cooper continued. "But I'm thinking not as low as it should be for time of death."

"Why's that?" Gilchrist asked.

"From the settings on the controls, the seat heater's on. And if the engine was running, with the heating set as it is, it would have been warm—"

"Expert in cars, too, are you?" Jessie said.

"Cars, no. But Mr. Cooper only ever drives Jaguars. He has one just like this."

"Other than Mrs. Ferguson," Gilchrist interrupted, "who was first on the scene?"

Jessie said, "Mhairi," as Cooper returned her attention to McCulloch's body.

PC Mhairi McBride. Recently applied to become a detective, beginning to make a name for herself, and a significant asset to any team. "Did she get here before the ambulance arrived?"

"Apparently."

"You speak to her?"

"She switched off the engine, if that's what you're asking."

Gilchrist nodded. It would probably be the first thing anyone would do. And, knowing Mhairi, once she had checked for a pulse, she would have taken control of the scene and told the ambulance crew they weren't needed. But he had a few questions for her. "Where is she?"

"Sent her off to fetch some coffees. I think she's planting the beans, the time she's taking."

Gilchrist turned back to Cooper. "How's it looking?" he asked.

"Nothing so far that would suggest it's anything other than suicide."

Jessie smirked.

"Any bruises around the neck?" Gilchrist asked. "Signs of a struggle?"

"Nothing."

Gilchrist waited until Cooper pulled herself upright; then he leaned into the car to inspect the body. Jessie had obviously seen something Cooper had missed, and he did not want their ongoing antagonism to turn into something nastier.

The first thing that struck him was how trim and well dressed McCulloch was—black hair graying at the temples and cut short at the back and sides, white twill open-necked shirt, gold cufflinks, dark blue suit, black leather belt, trousers neatly pressed, black polished shoes. The second was the empty bottle of Grey Goose vodka in the passenger footwell. But as he tilted McCulloch's head from one side to the other, parted his lips, peered into his mouth, checked his hands, fingernails, and wrists, he found nothing out of the ordinary. He eyed the settings on the car's controls, confirming what Cooper had said. Then the sliver of an idea came to him.

He pulled back from the car's interior and turned his attention to the door lock.

"How did Mhairi get in to switch off the engine?" he asked.

Jessie glanced at Cooper, then smiled at Gilchrist. "It was unlocked. Odd, don't you think?"

Gilchrist gave it some thought. "You attach the hose, you take your seat, you switch on the engine, then you wait to pass out from carbon-monoxide poisoning, knowing there will be no coming back," he said. "But you don't necessarily lock the door . . . because . . ."

"Because someone put you there."

Gilchrist shook his head. "Because you have doubts. Maybe McCulloch didn't really want to go through with it. Maybe he was hoping someone would find him—"

"Except that he was unconscious when they closed the door on him," Jessie said.

"*They?*" Cooper asked.

"Figure of speech."

"We'll check for fingerprints on the bottle." Gilchrist glanced at Cooper. "And alcohol in his system. And any narcotics, of course." Then he turned to Jessie. "OK, I'm listening."

"Check the window."

Gilchrist stepped back and swung the door shut. It felt solid, smooth, and closed with an easy click. The rubber tube still led to the exhaust pipe, the window still open a crack at the top, the gap stuffed with a black scarf. A quick look confirmed that McCulloch was not wearing a tie, so the scarf could have been his. Forensics would confirm that, or not.

What was he missing?

He pressed the door handle, pulled the door open again, studied the window, but still found nothing. He was about to give up when his eye was drawn back to the scarf. It was stuffed into a gap that was no more than an inch wide, narrow enough to nip the rubber hose and prevent it from slipping, but wide enough to leave someone thinking it needed to be sealed.

He glanced at Jessie and she raised her eyebrows. "Agree now?" she asked.

He almost did.

"The scarf's been stuffed into the gap from the *outside*," she said. "See the way it's folded? Someone's pushed it in with their fingers. It would be impossible for it to lie that way if you pushed it in from the inside."

"That would indeed be impossible," he said. "I have to agree."

Jessie's smile hung for a moment, then faltered. "But . . . ?"

"But McCulloch could have set the hose in place by snecking it with the window, then stuffed the gap with his scarf from the outside, then got in the car and closed the door behind him. In fact, that's how I would have done it." Although he would have chosen the passenger window or one of the two rear windows—not the driver's.

He thought it odd the way Jessie's lips tightened, how she glanced at Cooper before lowering her zip, retrieving her mobile, and striding off into the fucking freezing cold, presumably to continue the conversation he had interrupted on his arrival.

Cooper said, "Not a good loser, is she?"

Gilchrist gave a quick smile. "She's a good detective."

"I'm sure she is." Cooper pulled the coveralls' hood off her head, raked her fingers through her dark blonde hair, and tossed it in that way of hers that always teased him. Then she nodded at McCulloch's body. "Is this a rush job?"

He shook his head. "After the weekend'll be fine."

"If I find anything untoward, I'll let you know." She strode away, then stopped and turned to face him. "Are we still on for this evening?"

It seemed such an odd thing for her to ask. Of course they were on for this evening. They had been on for every Friday evening since Christmas. "Like me to pick you up?" he said.

She grimaced. "It might be better if I come to yours instead."

He frowned, cocked his head, asked the silent question.

"Mr. Cooper's come back," she said. "No doubt to demand his conjugal rights."

It took Gilchrist a full two seconds before he could reply, "Ah. Right."

"I *am* still married," she said.

"You are indeed."

Another toss of her mane, then she turned and strode off to the Range Rover. He tried not to watch her, but they were still in the exploratory phase, and he found himself leering after her before he managed to turn away.

He had no right to be jealous. He knew that.

But it surprised him to feel how much it hurt.

3

Gilchrist found Jessie in the dunes again, walking toward the sea, head down, kicking her feet through the sand—and no mobile in sight. He followed her in silence, closing the gap with every step, until she heard him and turned on her heel.

"You hoping to catch me dropping my knickers for a pee?" she said.

"It's too cold for that."

"Watching? Or peeing?"

"Both." They stared at each other for several silent seconds, then Gilchrist said, "Can I help in any way?"

She shrugged, turned back into the wind, tilted her head as if to breathe in the ice-cold air. "I sometimes struggle with it all," she said.

He walked up to her, stood by her side, followed her line of sight.

Waves chased each other to the shore, their peaks rising, arching forward, about to break, but somehow carrying on, as if they were all rushing to see which of them would arrive at the shoreline first. There was a strange urgency about the scene, which pulled up memories of his son's late girlfriend.

Although Chloe had been a talented artist, she had refused to paint seascapes, arguing that she could never capture the ocean's beauty in its stillness.

"You have to see the ocean moving to appreciate its beauty," Gilchrist said.

Jessie looked at him. "You what?"

He shrugged. "Something someone once told me."

Jessie nodded, returned her gaze to the sea. "That was Lachie on the phone earlier."

"Still making a nuisance of himself?"

She snorted. "Useless fat fuck."

"Well, he is fat. And probably useless, too. Most chief supers are. As for the fucking, I'll leave that for you to decide."

She chuckled, then shook her head. "I mean, what is it with you guys? You'd crawl five hundred miles on your hands and knees for a shag, but when it comes to shopping, oh, bugger that, it's too much like hard work." Then her mood darkened.

Like flipping a switch, Gilchrist thought.

"I wish you hadn't made me look like an idiot in front of you-know-who."

"I didn't," he said. "It's called brainstorming. It was a good theory. Very good, in fact." He shrugged. "For all we know, you might be right."

"I just had a feeling about it, you know? You ever get that?"

All the time. But he said, "Sometimes."

"Business partner of alleged serial rapist Thomas Magner murdered in forest. It just made sense to me. I mean, McCulloch's loaded, drives a big, flashy Jaguar whatsit. Why commit suicide? I don't get it. Murder seemed like the right answer."

"It still could be."

Jessie's eyes squinted against the blank whiteness of the haar. "He's got a wife and two kids. No doubt he lives in a mansion—"

Her mobile rang, and she removed it from her inside pocket with a sleight of hand that would have shamed pickpocket Wee Jimmy Carslaw. She scowled at the screen for a moment, took a step away from Gilchrist, and pressed it to her ear.

"What's it now?" she snapped.

Gilchrist thought it best to give her some privacy and headed back to the forest. Just the act of walking with the wind killed some of the chill, and he increased his step when he noticed Mhairi had returned, cup of coffee in hand—it looked like a Starbucks—steaming in the frosty air.

He reached her. "Got another one of those?"

"There's one for DS Janes in the car, sir. Would you like it? I'm sure she wouldn't mind."

He grimaced. "What do you know that I don't?"

"She doesn't bite."

"You sure about that?"

Mhairi took a sip from her drink, then handed it to him. "Have some of mine, sir. Excuse the lipstick."

"I like lipstick," he said.

"So I've heard."

Gilchrist stopped midsip. "*Excuse* me?"

"Sorry, sir. Just a joke that came out wrong."

The coffee was far too sweet, but he welcomed the way its heat sank to his stomach. He handed it back. "Thanks," he said. "Is there sugar in DS Janes's coffee, too?"

"Too fattening."

"Good. I'll risk being bitten, then."

He walked with Mhairi back to her car and waited while she reached in and retrieved another cardboard cup. He enclosed it in his hands. "You chased the ambulance away?"

"I did, sir, yes." She nodded to the Jaguar. "The driver was clearly beyond help."

He eased back the lid, took a sip. Latte, no sugar—perfect.

"I thought he might still be alive, sir, so I opened the door . . . but . . . he—"

Gilchrist was surprised to catch a glimmer of a tear. Or maybe it was just the cold air nipping her eyes. Then a thought occurred to him. "Did you know McCulloch?"

She gave a long blink and nodded.

"I'm sorry," he said.

She shook her head. "My mum knew him. I mean, a friend of hers knew him. I think they went to the same school. I only met him a couple of times. He seemed a nice man. You know what I mean, sir?"

Gilchrist smiled.

"His name popped up from time to time. That's about it. But Mum'll be upset."

Although Gilchrist had not known Brian McCulloch personally, he had already heard enough about the man to know he was that rarest of breeds—a local boy made good, who had clawed his way out of the doldrums and made something of his life. By all accounts, he had started out as a bricklayer, moved on to general contracting, mostly small jobs—roofs, extensions, garden walls—and hit the big time after meeting Thomas Magner, an out-of-towner with stars in his eyes, as Gilchrist's father would say. A major contract with Fife Council fifteen years ago had been the first of many, with McCulloch keeping every project on schedule and budget and Magner drumming up ever more lucrative business. No one had a bad word to say about McCulloch. He had married his childhood sweetheart, never forgotten his roots, and given plenty back to the local community.

Gilchrist took another sip of coffee, then replaced the lid. It was Jessie's, after all. "When you first arrived," he said, "and had a look around, did you see anything suspicious?"

Mhairi grimaced, wobbled her head in a yes-and-no answer. "Not *really*, sir."

"Except . . . ?"

"Except that I don't understand why he would commit suicide."

"Did you mention that to DS Janes?"

"I did, sir, yes. We had a chat about it. And she agreed it seemed suspicious."

"So, who came up with the murder theory?"

"DS Janes, sir."

He nodded, caught a glimpse of Jessie emerging through the trees, and tilted the coffee cup. "I'd better give this back to her."

Jessie met them halfway back from Mhairi's car. She took the coffee and asked, "You leave me any?"

"Just the top half."

She peeled off the lid and peered inside. "Very funny," she said, and swallowed a mouthful as if trying to burn her throat.

"Everything OK?" he asked.

"Oh, sure," she said. "Jabba's on his way to St. Andrews tomorrow. Says he's going to take me out for lunch. Got something he wants to tell me. I'm on a diet, I tell him. I'm taking karate lessons. I don't do lunch. Don't worry, love, he says. We can walk it off on the West Sands." She gulped another mouthful. "*Love?*" she said, with a grimace. "Wanker."

"What's he want to tell you?" Mhairi asked.

Jessie glared at her. "That's the scary part. I think he's really gone and done it this time. Left the wife."

"Fucking hell," Mhairi said.

"Exactly," Jessie declared. "Fucking hell's exactly where Jabba's headed if he tells me what I think he's going to tell me." She shook her head, blew out a gush of air, then held the cup out to Gilchrist. "Want to finish it?"

He took it from her, more to keep the peace than for the heat or the caffeine, then said to Mhairi, "Would you arrange for a liaison officer to visit Mrs. McCulloch?"

"I don't think she's home, sir."

"Why do you say that?"

"Mum says they have a house in Spain, one of these luxury villas, and that she's there more often than she's at home."

"You think she's there now?"

"Mr. McCulloch didn't get home last night, sir, and Mrs. McCulloch never phoned the Office to report him missing. I've already checked with North Street and Anstruther. And we've left I don't know how many messages on their voicemail, so I'm thinking that's where she's at."

"Maybe he told his wife he's away on business," Jessie offered. "Maybe staying out all night is par for the course."

"I don't think he's that kind of a man," Mhairi said, which received a snort from Jessie.

But something far more troubling was stirring in Gilchrist's mind. "They've got two children, right?" he asked Mhairi.

"Yes, sir."

"Ages?"

"Not sure, sir. Teenagers, though."

"School age?"

"I think so, yes."

"We're not in the school holidays, are we?"

"Not that I'm aware of, sir. No."

Jessie said, "You got an address?"

Mhairi rattled it off from memory; the McCullochs' home phone number, too.

Gilchrist recognized it as somewhere on the other side of Kingsbarns. Or maybe he had heard about the luxury residence while having a pint at the bar. Not that it mattered. What did matter was that the nearest police station was Anstruther. "Do you think the children go to boarding school?" he asked, as he dialed McCulloch's home number.

Mhairi shot that idea down with, "Mrs. McCulloch's too down to earth for that."

Gilchrist turned to Jessie. "Can you get directions? We'll take my car."

Jessie passed her keys to Mhairi. "Have someone drop the Batmobile off at the Office," she said, then wriggled out of her coveralls.

Mhairi pocketed the keys without a word, her thoughts elsewhere.

Gilchrist got through, but after a couple of rings he heard the automatic recording—a woman's voice with a soft lilt to it—and ended the call. He unzipped his coveralls and slid his phone into his jacket pocket. "Get hold of that liaison officer regardless," he said to Mhairi. "In case we're wrong."

"Yes, sir."

"And call the Anstruther Office, give them the address, tell them to send a couple of uniforms round, to check up." Only then did he glance at Mhairi and realize how thoughtless he was being. He offered a short smile of reassurance. "I'm sure there'll be a simple explanation." Then he turned and strode to his car, Jessie by his side, still fiddling with her mobile. "You got those directions yet?"

"Hang on, nearly there. Got 'em."

He clicked his fob and the Merc's lights flashed.

Without a word, he slid in behind the steering wheel and stuffed his coveralls under the seat.

Jessie strapped herself in as the Merc bumped across the clearing, then accelerated onto the tarmac road. "You know what I'm thinking?" she said to him. "I'm hoping I'm right about it not being suicide."

As Gilchrist pressed down hard on the accelerator, his mind worked through Jessie's thought process. When the logic hit him full force, he gritted his teeth and hissed, "Christ. Surely not."

4

It took just over twenty minutes to reach McCulloch's home, a renovated farmhouse with a pair of barns-cum-extensions on either side, and a U-shaped paved courtyard with a raised pond in the middle. A hideous-looking statue in the shape of an angel spouted water from its mouth. Netting as fine as muslin covered the pond, to prevent marauding herons from taking the koi carp. The pristine farmyard overlooked acres of open fields that spilled downhill, beyond which the North Sea glinted like diamonds on a gray canvas.

A police car, its doors open, sat beside a Lexus SUV with a private number plate—one letter and two numbers. Clearly the McCullochs had more money than they knew what to do with. The main door of the house was open too, and not a uniform in sight. It seemed that Gilchrist's worst fears were about to be realized.

"I don't like the look of this," Jessie said, as she stepped into the courtyard.

"Call Anstruther. See if they've heard anything."

He strode toward the farmhouse and entered without announcement. In the entrance vestibule, his hopes soared when he heard voices. Had Mrs. McCulloch invited the uniforms inside for an early morning chat and a cup of tea? But a pair of school blazers hanging on a couple of hooks, and a phone on a corner table, its red light blinking to remind the McCullochs they had unanswered messages, dashed his hopes in the next breath.

He followed the voices, his footfall echoing on the parquet floor, and turned left into what he presumed to be the main lounge.

One of the uniforms—a young PC—was already on her way to intercept the intruder. In a firm voice, she said, "Step back outside, please."

Gilchrist flashed his warrant card. "DCI Gilchrist, St. Andrews. We called Anstruther. Is that you?"

"It is, sir, yes. Sorry, sir. PC Jennings," she said, and stepped aside.

The other uniform, another constable Gilchrist did not recognize, finished talking on his phone, then turned to face him, his back to a wide bay window through which Gilchrist saw Jessie speaking into her mobile. The PC introduced himself as Taggart and gripped Gilchrist's hand as if intent on crushing it. Gilchrist thought the man's face looked drawn and tired, too pale, as if he had not seen the sun in years or had a good sleep in months.

"What have we got?" Gilchrist asked.

"They're upstairs. Three of them. All in bed."

Gilchrist felt his heart jump and a lump choke his throat. "The children?"

Taggart grimaced. "And the mother."

Something in Taggart's haunted eyes and in the resigned finality of his voice told Gilchrist to expect the worst. "Show me," he said.

Gilchrist followed Taggart into the hallway as Jessie entered. "SOCOs have already been called," she said. "So it's not looking good."

Gilchrist nodded. He seemed to have lost the power to speak. His feet felt leaden as he mounted the stairs to the half landing in silence, aware of Jessie behind him, then around a polished newel post, and up another flight to the upstairs bedrooms.

Taggart stopped at an open door on the left and held out his hand—an invitation for Gilchrist to enter. Even from where he stood, the posters on the bedroom wall told him it was the room of a teenage girl with a passion for boy bands. A powerful sense of familiarity came to him—memories of his own family, Maureen and Jack as children, how he had missed so much of their growing up because of work, how he would come home late from the Office to find them both in bed, his only interaction with them being to kiss them good night when they were already asleep.

"So, what've we got?" Jessie asked, and brushed past him.

Gilchrist followed but managed only two or three steps before pulling up. The murder scene was not what he expected. No blood, no mess, no disturbance of any sort, just a young girl in her midteens, lying in bed, on her back, apparently asleep. He felt as if he and Jessie should be walking around the room on their tiptoes. The girl's eyes were closed, lips curled in the tiniest hint of a smile, as if she were enjoying a peaceful dream. It seemed the gentlest of shakes would wake her.

Jessie reached the head of the bed and looked down at the girl. Her lips pursed into a tight white line.

Gilchrist asked Taggart over his shoulder, "You touch anything?"

"No, sir."

"So the bedside lamp was on?"

"Yes, sir."

Jessie glanced at the lamp, then at Gilchrist. "Is that significant?"

Gilchrist shook his head. "Probably not."

Jessie leaned down to the girl's face, and for one confusing moment Gilchrist thought she was going to kiss her. But she sniffed—once, twice—and said, "Not a thing. But vodka's odorless." Then she took hold of the girl's chin, as if to turn her head to look at her. "Full rigor," she said, and stood upright. "Which puts death at some time between, say, eight o'clock last night and eight that morning."

"Cooper might be able to narrow it down," Gilchrist said.

"Her name's Eilish," Taggart said. "Siobhan's in the next room."

"You knew them?" Jessie asked.

Taggart nodded. "Most locals do."

Gilchrist closed his eyes for a moment's thought. Two girls. What on earth had driven McCulloch to take their lives? How bad could his life have been? All that wealth, the big house, the big car, and the big salary to go with it, no doubt. But Gilchrist also knew that success in business was often achieved with other people's money. Was Stratheden Enterprises in financial difficulty? Had investors in the company demanded back their money? Had McCulloch's dreams of pots of gold turned into nothing more than buckets of rust?

He turned away from the bed and saw that Taggart's face was even paler now, if that were possible. The PC nodded in the direction of the other bedroom. As Gilchrist brushed past, he found he could not look Taggart in the eye.

The second bedroom was smaller but brighter, with the curtains open. Other than that, the scene was almost identical. Boy bands offered white-teethed smiles from the walls. Their sparkling eyes and fresh-skinned energy were at odds with the scene before him. Another girl, smaller than her sister, maybe a couple of years younger, lay on her back, the sheets tucked neatly under her chin. Gilchrist thought she did not seem quite as peaceful, her mouth downturned a touch, as if she had gone to sleep and slipped away with a petted lip.

He scanned the room, then said, "The bedside lamp's not on."

"No, sir."

Was that significant? He couldn't say. But at least it explained the open curtains.

From the hallway, Jessie asked, "Where's the master bedroom? Is that it?"

Gilchrist felt the floorboards shift as Jessie moved toward the door. He heard the click of its lock, then a sudden stillness and an ominous silence before a voice said, "Jesus fuck."

Gilchrist left Siobhan's bedroom and crossed the hallway in three strides. Taggart was standing with his back to the master bedroom, his lips clamped tight, his throat and jaw working hard to keep down the bile.

Even before Gilchrist entered the room, his mind was analyzing the scene before him, telling him that it must be bad for Jessie to be standing with her hand to her mouth. But when he walked through the door, turned to face the bed, and saw what he thought must be the body of Mrs. McCulloch, he realized nothing could have prepared him for just how horrific it was.

His breath left him with a gasp, and he struggled to suck air back into his lungs.

Jessie recovered first, and said, "I need to open the window."

"Leave it," he snapped.

She stopped, but frowned at him.

"Just leave it. Don't disturb the scene. Don't touch *any-thing*." He glanced out the bedroom door, but Taggart was no longer there. A hard retching cough came from the bathroom off the half landing, and Gilchrist felt his own throat constrict. Christ, he thought, we could all be queuing at the door in a minute or two.

He clenched both fists, closed his eyes, took two deep breaths, tried to ignore the bitter tang of blood and the sweet stench of raw meat that was pervading his senses. It struck him that he had not smelled anything from the upper hall-way. The door must have been closed to keep the morbid guff inside. A chill ran through him, but then he heard a fan running and scanned the room. His gaze settled on the door to the en suite bathroom.

He knew he should go and check it out, but his feet were rooted to the spot as his eyes assessed the mess before him. If no one had told him it was Mrs. McCulloch, he would have been hard pressed to tell if the skinned meat was male or female. He was conscious of movement at his side, of Jessie easing away from him, edging closer to the bed, as if to study what lay upon it.

Although the bedclothes—the duvet cover, the folded blanket, the stacked pillows—were sodden with blackened blood, they seemed not to have been disturbed, other than the fact that a body lay on the bed, head missing, skin stripped to reveal bloodied musculature. And the body looked oddly slim around the waist, the stomach slack, which told Gilchrist she had been gutted. He also knew that the missing head was sure to be in the bathroom, along with the guts, the window open and the fan on full blast—he could hear it clearly now. The skin might be in there, too, laid out to dry in some kind of perverse, symbolic message.

"You think it was him?" Jessie asked.

"Who?"

"Brian McCulloch."

Gilchrist let out another rush of air. His mind was spinning, firing away at a subconscious level, telling him that some piece or other did not fit, that it maybe even belonged in a different puzzle. He could not say what was niggling at him, only that something was not right.

His mind continued to churn, desperate to figure out what he was missing.

The children were at peace, while their mother had been decapitated, disemboweled, and peeled back to the bone in the adjacent room. Surely they would have heard something. Unless they had been killed first.

But then, what mother could let that happen?

Jessie walked around the end of the bed, heading toward the bathroom.

"Don't go in," he barked.

She stopped and glared at him.

"Don't disturb the scene," he repeated. Jesus Christ. *Don't disturb the scene.* What were they supposed to do? Dance around on tiptoes to keep any clue intact?

Then a thought struck him. "Blood," he said.

"There is that," Jessie agreed. "Lots of it."

"Exactly."

She looked at him, puzzled, as if his ears had sprouted feathers.

"Did you see any blood on McCulloch?" he said. "Or in his car?"

She narrowed her eyes. "No."

He did not need to say that whoever had killed Mrs. McCulloch, and ripped her stomach open and pulled out her guts and hacked off her head and skinned her, must have been splattered in the stuff. The realization dawned behind Jessie's eyes.

On automatic now, his mind crackling with possibilities, he walked around the end of the bed. Clotted blood formed black trails from the bed to the bathroom, marking the path of the head, the skin, and the entrails. Together, he and Jessie stood at the door, facing a scene from a slaughterhouse in hell. Only then did Gilchrist understand that he had the trail of blood the wrong way round, that the skinned and headless and disemboweled corpse had been carried *from* the bathroom *to* the bed. Which was why the bedclothes were undisturbed.

He edged closer to the bathroom threshold, taking care not to stand on any blood spots or bloodied footprints, although it did strike him as odd that the footprints were noticeable by their absence. By the door frame, he noted one of the switches on the wall was in the ON position. Which would be the fan. None of the downlights was switched on, so he made a mental note to ask the SOCOs to dust the fan switch for fingerprints.

He leaned forward and peered inside.

The bathroom was as big as Fisherman's Cottage kitchen and dining room combined. The floor and walls were fully tiled, the ceiling covered with prefabricated panels as glossy as marble and riddled with downlights. A wet room, large enough for a party of six, filled one corner. Even from where he stood, Gilchrist could see that was where the slaughter had taken place. Its glass panels were streaked with blood. Scraps of skin, hair, and lengths of gut as thick as rope were scattered across the tiled floor, although some effort had been made to sweep them to one side. Other areas looked as if a bucket-load of blood had been spilled over them, and the walls—from floor to head height—could be a blood-spatter analyst's training room.

"Any thoughts?" he asked Jessie.

"Bring back the death penalty?"

"Do you see her head?"

"We should check the boot of the Jag."

Gilchrist grimaced. "I don't think he would do that."

"Why not? He's not left much to chance here."

"The SOCOs will let us know soon enough."

Gilchrist continued to scan the scene, trying to imagine how the events unfolded—from a killing to a disemboweling to a beheading to a skinning to a ritual placement of the body on the bed. And, as he studied the bloodied mess, he came to see some order, some logic, in the massacre. The shower had been turned on to full power in the wet room, no doubt to clear most of the victim's blood from the assailant. Skin and guts had been swept to one side as if in an effort to clean up the mess, and the tiled floor was streaked and smeared as if someone had tried to rub it clean.

He froze for a moment as he took it all in, then said, "Where are the towels?"

"In a cupboard?"

"No. The towel rails are empty. There's none in here."

He waited while Jessie eyed the full-length heated towel rail on the wall next to the wet room, those on either side of the double sink, the rim of the claw-footed bathtub.

"Which means what, exactly?" she said at length.

"Check the laundry basket, the washing machine, the kitchen. I'd like to see—"

"What, you're thinking he washed up after doing—"

"Just do it." The words came out louder than intended. "Bloody hell, Jessie, for once in your life do something straight-forward without challenging it."

Her lips tightened and she said, "Yes, sir," before walking to the wicker laundry basket at the side of a wardrobe. She flipped back the lid, let it drop, then left the bedroom without another word.

Gilchrist stepped away from the bathroom door and walked to the window.

He pulled out his mobile and got through on the second ring.

"Missing me already?" Cooper said.

"It's a mess, Becky. An absolute hellish mess." He breathed in, knowing she would not break the silence. Cooper was like that—someone who would listen to the entire story, hear every word, before casting judgement, good or bad. "He's taken out his whole family. Wife and two girls, in their beds—" Another gush of air. Christ, it was difficult to breathe. All of a sudden, he was aware of the body on the bed behind him, the thick, stale air in the room. He reached forward and flung open the window, ignoring his earlier instruction to Jessie.

"Andy?"

"Sorry, it's . . ." He shook his head, struggling to stop tears nipping his eyes. Christ, what would he have done if this had happened to his own family? How could he have lived after that? But Brian McCulloch had not lived, of course. He had simply taken his own life, unable to live with the crushing burden of what he had done. As that logic fired through Gil-christ's mind—his subconscious challenging, ideas flickering, fading, then resurfacing—he came to understand what he had failed to see earlier.

He turned to stare at the skinless corpse.

"I need you over here," he said to Cooper. "I need you to establish how the children were killed. I suspect they were drugged. Maybe injected. Maybe spiked drinks. And I need you to check McCulloch's system for drugs."

"Are you all right, Andy? You don't sound—"

"No, I'm not all right." He paused, aware that he had raised his voice, and tried to pull himself together, squeezed a thumb and forefinger into his eyes. "I'm sorry, Becky. I'm sorry, I . . . it's just . . . I'll get back to you."

"*Andy?*"

He caught the urgency in her voice, sensed her desperation. "I'm OK."

A pause, then, "You're not telling me everything."

He eyed the skinned carcass and realized he had missed something in the bathroom. He strode to the door and had another look. The wet room where the murderer had showered himself clean; the blood-streaked floor that he had wiped with towels to erase his bloodied footprints; the clean corner by the full-length mirror where he had dried himself and dressed; the absence of towels that might have contained traces of his DNA; and . . .

"There's not enough skin," he said.

"*Skin?*"

"She's been gutted, decapitated, and skinned." Another deep breath. He had never fully understood how his subconscious mind worked, how it chewed through sensory information and spat out an answer. Nor did he understand how his sixth sense—his instinct—worked. All he knew was that they did work, more often than not. Mhairi's voice came back to him—*he seemed a nice man.* Then he recalled the neatness of the crisp white shirt and well-pressed trousers.

"Brian McCulloch didn't do this," he said.

"So why did he commit suicide?"

"Maybe he didn't."

"You're saying he was—"

"I need blood and toxicology results before I'm saying anything. How soon can you get them to me?"

"Twenty-four hours. Midday tomorrow," she added.

"How about today?"

"I'll do what I can."

He stared at the red, raw body, ran his gaze along the stripped limbs, and realized for the first time that the fingernails were missing, too. And the toes were little more than bloodied stumps. He had to turn away.

Back by the window, the March air felt cool, fresh, clean. He breathed it in, stared out across the open fields of the Fife countryside. It was the missing head and the lack of skin that sealed it for him. But he had one more question to ask.

"How long is a human intestine?"

"It varies," Cooper said, "but the small intestine is six or seven meters, and the large about one and a half. Why?"

"He's taken trophies."

"Intestines?"

"And the head, skin, fingernails, and toenails."

He heard her gasp, then realized he was probably telling her too much. After all, this was all a theory. But his instincts were so strong that he couldn't stop himself. "The worst of it is, I think he knew what he was doing."

"Someone in the medical field?"

Gilchrist gritted his teeth before taking another deep breath. "No," he said, offering a silent prayer to a God he didn't believe in that he was wrong. "I think he's done it before."

5

By midday, Anstruther Police had erected a barrier across the gated entrance to the McCullochs' driveway, with squad cars, forensic teams, uniformed officers, and detectives on one side and a baying media circus on the other. Within the space of a few hours, news of the "Massacre at the McCullochs'" had gone viral. Every radio and TV station was carrying it as breaking news, and a distraught local MSP interviewed on Sky News had said how devastated she and her constituents were at the tragic loss of such a philanthropic man and his young family.

In the front lounge overlooking the paved forecourt, Gilchrist stepped away from the TV and looked outside at the melee gathered at the front gate. He shook his head in silence as a Land Rover, its roof spiked with what had to be a dozen radio antennae, broke away from the line of parked vehicles and lumbered over the adjacent fields, as if the driver were trying to find some opening through the McCullochs' boundary fence.

Assistant Chief Constable Archie McVicar pressed the remote to mute the TV and said, "McCulloch doesn't appear to fit the profile of a multiple murderer. What's your take on it, Tom?"

Chief Superintendent Tom Greaves grimaced, as if giving it thought. "Our prisons are filled with people you'd be happy to introduce your daughter to."

"So you think McCulloch murdered his wife and daughters?"

"I'm only saying that you can't judge a book by its cover."

McVicar harrumphed. "How about you, Andy? What's your take on it?"

Gilchrist turned from the window.

McVicar stood side by side with Greaves. Six officers from headquarters—four he barely recognized—stood behind them in a group intermingled with familiar faces from St. Andrews and not so familiar faces from Anstruther. At the back, the tall figure of Stan Davidson, Gilchrist's former sidekick but now promoted to DI and in charge of a team of his own. McVicar was pulling out all the stops on this one.

Jessie was absent because Gilchrist had instructed her to locate McCulloch's business partner, Thomas Magner. As Gilchrist scanned the room, he worried that he had shared his suspicions that the killer might have killed before only with Cooper. But he thought it prudent to keep his thoughts to himself, at least for the time being. Jessie had found no towels from the master bathroom, so the conclusion was that the killer had wrapped the various body parts in them for removal from the house. Gilchrist had already phoned Jackie Canning in the North Street Office, St. Andrews, and asked her to research the MO, get onto HOLMES—the Home Office Large Major Enquiry System used by all UK police forces— and see if she could find similar killings in the past. If anyone could dig through the demented detritus of psychopaths' files and records, Jackie could—best researcher in the world, Gilchrist often told her. And he meant it.

He returned McVicar's unblinking stare and said, "I'll be in a better position to answer that, sir, once we have the toxicology results."

"I hear you, Andy, but what's your gut feeling on this one?"

Gilchrist knew he was one of McVicar's most respected DCIs, although he also understood that his maverick approach to a number of earlier cases had been noted with disdain. But he had always found McVicar to be a man of integrity, someone who kept his word. Not how he would describe Greaves. Gilchrist and Greaves had torn into each other before, and it would not take too many more arguments before the DCI told the CS where to shove it.

"It doesn't matter what my gut feelings are, sir. We can second guess ourselves until we're blue in the face. What matters is that we have four dead people, three of whom have been murdered. I believe we need to speak to Thomas Magner as a matter of urgency."

"Quite," said McVicar.

"I wouldn't trust that man as far as I could throw him," Greaves added. "God knows how he manages to look himself in the mirror every day. Where is he anyway, for God's sake? Why is it taking so long to find him?"

"DS Janes has located him in Stirling," Gilchrist said. "I believe he's on his way to St. Andrews as we speak."

"What's he doing in Stirling?"

Gilchrist ignored the question. It was time to leave. He caught McVicar's eye again. "I think we need to play this close to our chests for the time being, sir." He glanced at the window, saw the mob at the main entrance, which seemed to have swelled since he last looked. "We shouldn't disclose any details relating to Mrs. McCulloch's death. Nor the girls."

"Agreed."

"And I would also suggest we delay the media conference until we talk to Magner."

McVicar nodded. "I'll put them off for the rest of the afternoon; tell them we'll hold a press conference at Glenrothes HQ later today. That work for you?"

"That should at least help quiet this place down, sir." He tilted his head at the window to make his point.

"What time, Andy?"

"I'll arrange for daily debriefings at five. So . . . no later than six, sir?"

McVicar nodded.

"And it's early days," Gilchrist pressed on. "Until we have something more definite, if any of us can't get past the media with a 'No comment,' we should stick with the story that we're looking into why Brian McCulloch committed suicide."

"Is that wise?" Greaves asked.

"Don't know if I'd call it *wise*. More like playing it safe." He addressed McVicar. "If you have no more questions, sir, I'd like to get on with it."

"Of course." McVicar turned to Greaves. "Tom?"

"I want to be personally debriefed at close of play today, Andy. And I mean *today*."

Gilchrist barely acknowledged the order and strode out of the lounge.

Stan slipped from the rear of the gathering and caught up with him as he reached the front door. "What's eating Greaves, boss?"

"I've stepped on his toes once too often, I think." Gilchrist already had his mobile out by the time they reached the forecourt. Together they walked toward the fountain, where Gilchrist made a point of turning his back to the media scrum at the entrance gate. He did not want some overeager journalist trying to lip-read his call.

"Any luck, Jessie?"

"I'm almost at North Street. Magner and his solicitor should already be there. How soon can you get here?"

"Fifteen minutes," he said, then glanced at the reporters. It might take him all of fifteen minutes just to work his way past that lot. "Don't start until I get there."

"Spoilsport."

Gilchrist ended the call, then turned to Stan. "We have the ACC's approval to use all resources available. That won't last forever, so jump on it. Coordinate the investigation with the Anstruther Office. Visit Stratheden Enterprises, find out if the company's in trouble, what their financial status is, who owes who what, any bad debts, big bills, threatened legal action, failed contracts. Maybe it's all about money. And talk to the staff. Find out what kind of a guy McCulloch really was."

"You think he's two shades of gray, boss?"

"Maybe a dozen shades. He seemed too good to be true. An upstanding member of the community. Went to church with his family every Sunday. Never missed a day's work. Gave regularly to charities. Two daughters top in their classes at school. I mean, if you wanted the perfect family, you wouldn't have to look any further."

"I'll have someone check out the school, too, boss."

"And find out what's on the girls' computers, who their friends are on Facebook, who they're twittering—"

"Tweeting."

"What?"

"It's tweeting, boss."

"Oh, right. Who they're *tweeting*, messaging, e-mailing, calling. Do the same with the landline and Mrs. McCulloch's mobile. And if we can't locate McCulloch's mobile, pull the records from the network. Use the Anstruther lads to talk to the locals, find out who McCulloch hung about with, who he last had a pint with, who he last had round to dinner. You know the drill." He grimaced and shook his head. "We need to find out why this thing happened."

"Could be something to do with the ongoing Magner investigation, boss."

Gilchrist stared into the distance. He'd been thinking exactly the same thing. Fife Constabulary were currently investigating Thomas Magner over allegations of a series of rapes. As best he knew, eleven women had come forward since the beginning of the year, with each claiming that Magner had sexually abused her back in the late seventies or early eighties. The accusations themselves raised some serious questions, such as why now? And why all at once?

It was hard to see a link between that investigation and the massacre of the McCullochs, aside from the fact that Brian McCulloch and Thomas Magner had been business partners. McCulloch was clearly the prime suspect in the slaughter of his family. But Gilchrist just couldn't see it. Why would he commit such a brutal murder, kill his daughters, and then get dressed up to the nines before taking his own life? Gilchrist had seen more dead bodies than could be considered good for his health, as well as a fair number of suicides. But one thing did strike him. Of all the suicides he had seen, McCulloch was certainly the best dressed.

He faced Stan. "The ongoing investigation might be the what," he said, "but we need to work out the why."

"Boss?"

"Magner's the answer, Stan. I'm sure of it."

He turned and walked to his Merc.

———

Gilchrist entered the interview room and took the seat next to Jessie. He introduced himself as DCI Andy Gilchrist of St. Andrews CID, then noted the time for the record. Across the table, Thomas Magner faced them with arms folded. His black suit looked freshly dry-cleaned, his shirt white and straight from the packet. A red silk tie matched the tip of a handkerchief peeping from his chest pocket. He looked heavier than he seemed in media photographs, and harder, too—face lightly cratered with the faded remnants of acne, short hair more white than the blond it used to be, and more crew cut than styled.

He could be the poster boy for a bouncer's agency.

Seated next to him was a younger man in a dark blue pinstriped suit, hair and skin as slick as any male model's. He slid a business card across the table.

Gilchrist glanced at it—Thornton Pettigrew, of Jesper Pettigrew Jones Solicitors, with an address in Edinburgh. He said to Jessie, "Has Mr. Magner been advised that his attendance is voluntary and that he can leave at any time?"

"He has."

"I would remind you that my client has taken time away from his busy schedule to assist in any way he can," Pettigrew said.

"Yes," said Gilchrist. "I can see how the murder of his business partner and his family could be a bit of an inconvenience."

Magner raised his hand to silence Pettigrew's objection and said, "I've known Brian for most of my professional life, Mr. Gilchrist. I knew his wife, Amy, a lovely woman, for many years, too. Their two daughters, Eilish and Siobhan, were like daughters to me, too."

"Do you have any children of your own?"

"I've not been blessed in that way."

Gilchrist returned Magner's innocent look. Rather than ask for more personal details—he could always get them later—he decided to change tack. "It took us a while to locate you, Mr. Magner," he said.

"I was in Stirling at a developers' convention in the Highland Hotel last night. Most of these affairs are boring and can drive you to drink. So I obliged and had a few too many at the bar." He flashed a white smile, which had Gilchrist making a mental note to count his fingers if he ever shook hands with the guy. "I took advantage of having no appointments this morning by sleeping in later than usual, so I never caught the tragic news until midmorning. As soon as I realized it was Brian and Amy, I contacted the local police station in Anstruther to offer assistance."

"Extremely busy schedule?" Jessie said. "Drinking in the bar? Sleeping in?"

"Most of my business is done at odd hours," Magner said. "I was talking business until well past midnight last night, and I'm scheduled to be in meetings in Aberdeen this evening. They will have to be postponed now, of course."

"Of course," Jessie concurred. "And do the late hours you keep explain why you don't return phone calls?"

"I almost never return calls from numbers I don't recognize."

"Even when they leave an urgent voice message?"

"Indeed."

"What my client is saying," Pettigrew reasoned, "is that he contacted the police at the very first opportunity afforded him."

"And how did you first hear of the tragedy?" Gilchrist asked, in an effort to get them back on track.

"In the hotel. When I switched on the TV this morning. It was all over the news."

"And your convention? Was that held in the same hotel?"

"It was."

"Many people at it?"

"Two or three hundred, I'd say."

"How long did it last?"

"From seven in the evening until eleven."

"Straight through?"

"With ten-minute breaks on the hour."

"Were you with anyone?"

"Brian was supposed to meet me, but of course he never made it." Magner tightened his lips, shook his head.

Not a tear in sight, Gilchrist thought. "Did you try calling him?"

"No."

"Why not?"

"He's busy. I'm busy. We meet up when we can."

"Not even to arrange a meeting?"

"No."

"So, you attended the convention by yourself?"

"As it turned out, yes."

"Were you seated at a table with other attendees?"

"No, we were in rows, like in a theater."

"Preassigned seats?"

"No, it was informal. You could sit wherever you liked."

Jessie leaned forward. "So where did you sit?"

Magner shrugged. "I was near the back, but I couldn't tell you the seat number or row."

"All night?"

"Excuse me?"

"Did you return to the same seat after each of the hourly breaks?"

"I did, yes."

Jessie pressed on, "And who did you sit next to?"

Magner raised his eyebrows. "I couldn't tell you his name."

"*His* name?" Gilchrist said.

"Yes, it was a man."

"Singular, only one man. Did you sit at the end of a row?"

Magner stared hard at Gilchrist, as if seeing him for the first time. "Yes, I was next to the aisle."

"And was this man on your left or your right?"

"Does it matter?" snapped Pettigrew.

Gilchrist kept his eyes on Magner. "Left or right?"

"Left."

"So, you sat near the back row, in an aisle seat. You must have been one of the last to arrive."

"I missed the start of the conference, yes."

Gilchrist sensed Jessie shifting by his side, so he held up a hand to tell her to keep out of it. Vehicular access to Tentsmuir Forest was closed from 8:30 PM, but the exit barrier was never locked, so visitors could leave any time. And it took an hour and a quarter, maybe an hour if you pushed it, to drive to Stirling. So if McCulloch's death was not suicide, Magner conceivably could have killed his business partner, then driven to the convention, arriving at around 9:30 to establish his alibi. Well, it was a weak theory, he supposed, but at least worth a shot.

"How late were you?" Gilchrist asked.

"Minutes only. The first speaker was already at the podium, so I took the nearest available seat."

Gilchrist nodded, deflated by the answer. Still, he could check the hotel's CCTV footage to determine whether Magner was telling the truth. "And before that, where were you?"

"Stirling. I've been there most of this week."

"*Most* of the week?"

"I drove to Glasgow for a meeting on Wednesday."

Gilchrist persisted with his line of questioning, poking, prodding, but gaining nothing, going round in circles. He could check CCTV footage of every bar and restaurant Magner said he visited, but that would be man-hour intensive. Besides, he was beginning to sense that discretion was essential when dealing with someone like Magner—not the sort of man you arrested at the first opportunity.

Fifteen minutes later, he sat back and nodded to Jessie to take over.

She obliged with, "You said you knew Amy McCulloch for a long time. How long?"

Magner shrugged. "Twenty or so years."

"Before or after she married Brian?"

"Before."

Jessie nodded, waited a couple of beats. "Did you ever go out with her?"

Pettigrew jerked upright. "What's that supposed to mean?"

Jessie said, "I was asking if your client ever dated Amy McCulloch, before—or after—she married Brian McCulloch."

"On the grounds that my client is currently under investigation after a series of rape accusations—"

"That is precisely why I'm asking the question—"

"—which he continues to deny *vehemently*, I will have to advise my client not to answer that."

Gilchrist said, "You should also advise your client that we are investigating a multiple murder, so any answers that seem evasive could encourage us to reconsider your client's supposed innocence."

Pettigrew scowled but sat back, as if considering his options.

Jessie turned to Magner again. "So, did you date Amy McCulloch?"

Gilchrist sensed that Magner was sorely tempted to ignore his solicitor's advice, but instead he let out a heavy sigh and said, "No comment."

"How well did you know Amy?" asked Jessie.

"What do you mean by *that*?" Pettigrew again.

"Was your client intimate with Amy McCulloch?"

"My client has never been intimate with—"

"I'm not asking you," Jessie snapped. "I'm asking him. So sit back and shut it."

Pettigrew reclined in his chair with an almost unnoticeable shake of his head.

Magner repeated, "No comment."

"Not even a peck on the cheek when you met up at some fancy event, or went round to dinner and shared a Grey Goose or two with them?"

"No comment."

Jessie smiled, but Gilchrist could tell it was forced. He also noted Magner's lack of reaction to the mention of Grey Goose vodka, so he took up the questioning again. "What car do you drive, Mr. Magner?"

"Aston Martin Vantage."

"Company car?"

"Yes."

"How many company cars does Stratheden Enterprises have on its books?"

"Only two. Brian's and mine."

"Only two?" Gilchrist frowned in disbelief and glanced at his notes. "But Stratheden's turnover was in excess of sixty million last year."

"We broker the development side of the business to subcontractors and consultants. They have their own cars. We have in-house administration and accounting sections, a staff of about thirty, but they're salaried—no cars or car allowances. Strictly speaking, and legally speaking, too, Brian and I are the only executives of Stratheden Enterprises."

"And now it's only you."

Something shifted behind Magner's eyes. He unfolded his arms and gripped the edge of the table, as if to prevent himself from accidentally reaching out and throttling Gilchrist. "Brian and I were in business together for many years. We were close friends. I adored Amy, and I loved Eilish and Siobhan. I volunteered my time to help you investigate the deaths of my friend and his family, and you talk to me as if I'm some kind of—"

"You've been accused of sexually abusing eleven women," Jessie barked.

"Which my client categorically denies," said Pettigrew, pushing back his seat to let them know the interrogation was over. "Now, if you've no further questions, my client herewith revokes all voluntary assistance—"

"Just one more," Gilchrist said.

Pettigrew's face contorted into an irritated scowl. "What is it?"

Gilchrist leaned across the table, pressing closer to Magner. "How did you get that cut on your right hand?"

6

Magner's scowl turned into a smile, and he held out his hand.

The injury was on the right palm, at the base of the thumb, and taped with a Band-Aid streaked with the rust-colored stain of dried blood.

"It looks fresh," Gilchrist said.

"I cut myself in the hotel room last night, slicing fruit."

"What kind of fruit?"

"An apple."

"Don't you bite them like a normal person?" Jessie again.

"I prefer to slice off chunks."

"You must be left-handed," Gilchrist said.

"I am."

"So you held the apple in your right hand and sliced a chunk off with your left?"

"Exactly."

"And the knife slipped?"

"It did."

"You didn't need stitches?"

"Thankfully, no."

"Where did you find the Band-Aid?"

"I always have some in my toilet bag."

"I bet you do," Jessie said.

"What's that supposed to mean?" Pettigrew snapped.

"That your client gives the impression of always being prepared." She glared at Magner, anger shimmering off her like heat from rock. "I bet you spent a fortune on johnnies in your heyday—"

"Right. That's it." Pettigrew pushed himself to his feet. "This charade of an interview is now terminated. I am instructing my client not to utter another word. If you wish to speak to Mr. Magner again, you will have to find some reason to detain him." Pettigrew gripped Magner by the elbow and pushed him, rather unceremoniously, Gilchrist thought, toward the door.

Jessie announced, "Interview terminated at thirteen-eighteen."

Gilchrist waited until the door closed behind them, then let several more seconds pass before he turned to Jessie. "Want to talk to me about it?"

She grimaced, shook her head. "I hate cunts like that."

"Like what?"

"Cocky, arrogant, thinks he's God's gift to women."

"He's handsome, in a rugged sort of a way," Gilchrist tried, looking for a reaction.

"If you plastered over the pockmarks, maybe. You should have seen the way he looked at me when I walked in. Stripped naked and screwed by the time I'd sat down. I'd bet a year's salary he's guilty of raping every one of these women. I can see it in his eyes." She shuddered. "Gives me the creeps just thinking about him touching me."

"And his involvement in the McCulloch"—he almost said *massacre*, but settled for—"case?"

"His alibi seems solid," she said. "But I don't know. His answers were too quick, like he'd prepared them, particularly about the cut on his hand. I mean, who cuts their hand eating an apple, for crying out loud?"

"If you hadn't been so determined to rile him, he might have agreed to give a DNA sample—"

"Like hell he would. That slimeball solicitor would never have allowed it." She scraped the business card from the table and stared at it. "Thornton Pettigrew. I mean, what mother would ever call her child Thornton?"

"Pettigrew's mother?"

Jessie glared at Gilchrist. "You're such a smart-arse at times."

Gilchrist pushed his chair back. "Come on," he said. "I'm not sure I believe Magner. I want you to find out who was at the convention last night. Check CCTV footage, establish who he talked to, who he had a pint with, who he shared his bed with—"

"So, you're thinking he spent the night with someone?"

"Well, he's divorced, isn't he?"

"As if that makes any difference. Husbands screw behind their wives' backs all the time."

An image of his late wife, Gail, having it off with her lover Harry flashed into Gilchrist's mind, thankfully replaced by a picture of Cooper settling onto him. And wives do the same to their husbands, he thought.

"Maybe he's looking for wife number two," he said.

"I doubt it."

"How old is he?"

"Same age as McCulloch, I'd say. Late forties, early fifties."

"Check it out. See what you can find out about his past. And have a talk to the PF about the rape allegations. Maybe we need to set up a meeting. Then ask Stan about McCulloch's phone records. He must have something by now."

"And while I'm trying to cram a week's work into a Friday afternoon, what exactly will you be doing, sir?"

"Checking up with Cooper."

"Typical." She left the interview room, flashing a wry smile.

———

On the drive to Dundee, Gilchrist took a call from his daughter, Maureen.

"Hey, Mo," he said. "Long time."

"It's only been a week, Dad."

"But we live in the same town now," he complained. "Shouldn't we be seeing a bit more of each other these days?"

"OK, what are you doing tonight?"

"I can't tonight. I've got a major case on the go . . ." He let his voice trail away as he realized she was winding him up.

"I *know*, Dad. It's all over the news."

"How about tomorrow night?" he suggested, trying to change the subject.

"I'm working on my final thesis. You know how busy I am."

Three years earlier, Maureen had been involved in a terrifying incident that almost claimed her life. And after her mother's death, Gilchrist had managed to persuade both Maureen and his son, Jack, to return to St. Andrews from Glasgow. Maureen now lived alone in an attic flat in South Street. But rather than hide in the shadow of her horrific experience, she had tackled the devil head on and applied for an Open University course in forensic science. She expected to graduate in the summer and was always on the lookout for firsthand experience of crime scenes.

Which was why Gilchrist gritted his teeth. He knew what was coming.

"Any chance of being shown around?" she asked.

Shown around was Maureen's way of asking for access to a crime scene.

"Not this one, Mo. It's too high profile."

"But that's exactly the kind of case I need—"

"I can't, Mo. I've got to play by the rules this time. McVicar and Greaves are all over it. The press are camping out by the front gate. If you showed up, I'd be fired on the spot."

For a moment he thought she had hung up, but then she said, "OK. If that's what you want."

He felt a hot surge of irritation flash through him. This was Maureen at her worst. Just like her mother, she could twist his words to make him feel guilty. "It's not what I *want*, Mo. It's what I *have to do*. There's a difference." He waited a beat. "Why don't you join us in the Central tomorrow, and we can have a chat about the case?"

"Won't you be too busy for that?"

Gilchrist bit his tongue. "It doesn't matter how busy it gets, princess, we all have to eat. The Central's convenient, and it serves a great pint. We'll be there around one."

"I'll think about it."

He knew from experience that Maureen would not show up. "I can come by and pick you up, if you like." But the line was already dead.

He threw the mobile onto the passenger seat and cursed under his breath.

———

Gilchrist arrived at Bell Street Mortuary just before 2:00 PM.

He stepped from the Merc and called Stan before entering. "Anything?" he asked.

"Early days, boss, but it looks like Stratheden's not as successful as we thought it was. They're making money, which I suppose is some measure of success, but it looks like they're making it at the expense of their subs."

Gilchrist pressed his mobile tighter to his ear.

"I've been talking to Bea, their bookkeeper. Apparently they owe over six million quid in disputed billings."

Gilchrist grimaced at the amount. "Six *million?*"

"Listen to this, boss. One hundred and seventy-three thousand to MTT3 Architects—"

"One bill?"

"An aggregate of ten invoices dating back over a year. Then there's ninety-five thousand due to MacksiWorks Contractors. They specialize in earthmoving. You'll have seen their equipment around."

Gilchrist wouldn't know a MacksiWorks earthmoving machine from a lawn mower, but he mumbled his agreement.

"Another contractor is owed two-fifty thousand. A few more just under a hundred grand each. And on and on."

"Any idea what part McCulloch played in all of this?"

"Haven't had a chance to grill many of the staff yet. Some are still in shock and in no state to talk about it. But according to Bea, the general gist is that McCulloch and Magner's relationship was on the decline. They didn't see eye to eye on a ton of stuff, including the financial side of the business."

"Is Stratheden going under?"

"I'm not the man to ask, boss. But a number of subs have already taken legal action, which Bea says has never happened before. She had a meeting last week with McCulloch and Magner and some others from accounts, and she reckoned you could cut the atmosphere with a knife."

Gilchrist felt a spit of rain and looked to the sky. Gray clouds were rolling overhead. "So what's her take on McCulloch versus Magner?" he asked.

"McCulloch was definitely the more pleasant of the two—a bit aloof sometimes, according to Bea, but at least he took the time to listen. As for Magner, Bea says she can't stand being in the same room as him."

Well, there he had it—Jessie's summary of Magner had just been confirmed by someone who had known him for years. It never failed to amaze Gilchrist how some women could see straight through a man's false facade, while so many others seemed blind to it.

"What are they saying about the Magner rape investigation?" Gilchrist asked.

"As yet, no one's been willing to talk about it. Bea showed me a copy of an office memo sent by Magner when the press first got wind of the allegations two months ago. It said he would terminate the employment of any member of staff who discussed the matter during office hours, and that if anyone spread rumors about him outside the workplace, then that would be just cause for instant dismissal, too."

"What did Bea make of that?"

"She said six of them handed in their notice that day, and Magner told them to leave immediately. No compensation, nothing. Bea said she couldn't afford to lose her job, or she would have walked with them."

"Doesn't make for good employee relations," Gilchrist said. "And McCulloch? Where was he when all this was happening?"

"Up in arms, apparently. Bea said she'd never heard him swear before, but he and Magner went at it big time."

"This was two months ago, you say?"

"And again, last week, boss."

Gilchrist blinked as a spot of rain hit his forehead, then another. He shielded the mobile and strode toward the entrance. "It seems to me, Stan, that Magner and McCulloch did not have the warm relationship their corporate image liked to portray."

"Bea said I should talk with Janice Meechan."

"Who's she?"

"Stratheden's chief financial officer and—get this, boss—Amy McCulloch's sister."

Gilchrist sensed that more was coming. "I'm listening."

"The talk in the steamy is that Magner's been giving Janice one."

"Is she married?"

"Happily, allegedly, with three kids."

"Did McCulloch know about the affair?"

"Bea says if he didn't, he must've been blind."

Gilchrist picked up his pace as the skies opened. "OK, Stan. Get hold of Janice and find out if there's any truth in it. We might just have uncovered a motive."

"I hope so, boss, because McCulloch's phone records have given us nothing."

"Define nothing."

"Nothing to connect McCulloch with Magner."

Gilchrist almost stopped. "Nothing *at all*? Are you saying they never spoke to each other?"

"I'm saying they never *phoned* each other."

"Keep looking, Stan. There must be something." He killed the connection and ran inside.

7

Gilchrist found Cooper in the postmortem room, leaning over a hollow carcass—the lump of flesh that had once been the living, breathing body of Amy McCulloch. Two smaller bodies lay on gurneys locked on to the sinks, ready for their own PM examinations. The PM room could handle only three bodies at a time, so Brian McCulloch's corpse would still be in cold storage, the forensic examination of his murdered family having taken priority.

The sight of the smallest body—Siobhan's—had Gilchrist's throat constricting. Life was far too short for fathers to fall out with daughters, so he resolved to phone Maureen, tell her he'd had a change of heart. He would swing by her flat, take her out, answer all her questions about the McCulloch massacre, maybe even show her some crime-scene photographs. He was in Greaves's bad books anyway, so what difference would it make? He was about to make the call when he caught Cooper signaling to him to come to her office. Once there, he thought Cooper looked tired, as if the morbid task of confirming causes of death for an entire family was too

56

much to bear, even for a pathologist. Or maybe too much bed and not enough sleep had finally caught up with her.

"Anything?" he asked.

She raked a hand through her hair, then tossed it. No sexual innuendo in sight. "I'd put time of death between three and six yesterday afternoon," she said.

"After the girls got home from school?"

Cooper nodded. "Initial blood results on the girls show high levels of benzodiazepine. Not enough to kill them, but it would have put them into a state of unconsciousness. I suspect they were then simply smothered. I'll be more certain once I've examined them."

All of the date-rape drugs—Rohypnol, GHB, Dormicum, Hypnovel—contained benzodiazepine. Cheap, easy to find, easy to administer. Slip one into a drink and the girls would simply have fallen asleep.

"What about the mother?"

"No benzodiazepine," she said. "Different story entirely."

"Alcohol?"

"Not sufficient to suggest she was anywhere near incapable of defending herself."

Gilchrist thought for a moment. "Did he want her to feel pain?"

"Even if he did, I don't think she would have lasted long."

"Maybe he was in a hurry."

Gilchrist had a mental image of Magner's Aston Martin speeding from Fife to Stirling to establish his alibi. But could anyone really walk into a conference and act normal after doing *this*?—smothering the girls and beheading, gutting, skinning their mother, then killing their father to make it look like suicide?

"So far, I've identified five knife wounds in the chest, all apparently from the same blade. Any one of them would have been fatal. Considerable force was used," she added. "One of the wounds was deep enough to nick the spinal cord."

Gilchrist grimaced as a cold frisson coursed through him. "So . . . strong man, not woman?"

"That would be my guess." Cooper looked away for a long moment, as if her mind were elsewhere. Then she faced him again. "Almost all of her internal organs have been removed."

"*Almost?*" he heard himself say.

"The kidneys have not been touched. They're retroperitoneal, so would need to be taken out separately."

Gilchrist felt his breath leave him. An unhealthy spasm gripped his chest. Head, skin, guts, fingernails, toenails, and now most of the internal organs. He sucked in air for all he was worth. What drove someone to kill another human being, then violate their corpse in such a cruel fashion? If the force used to kill Amy McCulloch had been sufficient for one of the knife blows to pierce her body all the way through to the spinal cord, the killer must have exhibited monumental fury.

"I've never seen anything like it," Cooper admitted.

"No," was all Gilchrist could think to say.

"You thought he might have done it before?"

"I haven't heard back from Jackie yet," he said, "so she's likely found no other cases with a similar MO. Which means it's new and I'm wrong." He frowned. "What about surgical competence? Whoever removed the . . . the . . . must have had some idea what he was doing, don't you think?"

She shook her head, blue eyes creasing at the edges—tiredness from next to no sleep last night or horror from the job today, he could not say. "If your purpose is simply to remove the internal organs for the hell of it," she said, "then no surgical skill is necessary. A saw to cut the ribcage, a rib spreader to hold it open while you cut through the esophagus, trachea, and rectum, then lift the whole lot out in one. Lungs, too."

Gilchrist felt the bile rising. "And *was* a saw used?"

"It was."

"And the ribcage clamped open?"

"Yes."

"Any medical expertise evident at all?" he asked.

"The walls of the abdominal and pelvic cavities are scarred in places. So it was a bit ham-fisted. I'd say the killer has some postmortem experience but no medical training."

"But if he *is* a medical professional, he might have scarred the cavities deliberately to make it look like an amateur job."

"True," she said. "So, what are you suggesting?"

Gilchrist rubbed his temples. His mind was buzzing. He had no idea what he was suggesting.

The phone on Cooper's desk shattered the silence. They both stared at it for four rings; then she reached over and picked up the handset. "Yes?"

Gilchrist caught the metallic resonance of a man's voice, but when Cooper's gaze darted his way he took it as a silent request for privacy. He walked to the door and was turning the handle when he heard Cooper replacing the handset.

"That was Mr. Cooper," she said.

"You didn't have much to say to him."

"I ran out of things to say to him years ago."

Silent, Gilchrist waited.

Cooper returned his gaze for what seemed like minutes, then said, "I'm sorry, Andy."

Since her comment in Tentsmuir Forest that morning, he had been expecting her to bring their relationship to an end. After all, she was still married, and now her husband had returned from his overseas and out-of-town philandering to *demand his conjugal rights,* as she had so bluntly put it. Still, he'd hoped for one more evening, maybe another weekend, maybe even two.

"I understand," he said.

She shook her head. "You don't understand at all."

He returned her hard look. He seemed to be good at saying nothing.

"I'm sorry for getting you involved." She closed her eyes slowly, and her lips tightened to warn him that she might be about to say something she would regret.

He stepped toward her, touched her arm.

She opened her eyes, and he caught the faintest sparkle of tears. But two quick blinks and they were gone.

"Do you love him?" he asked.

She shook her head. "I used to think I did. But I see now that I was only in love with what I thought he could provide: security, companionship, intellectual compatibility. God, how wrong was I?" She seemed to recover. "And I'm starting to find out just how spiteful he can be."

"Ah," said Gilchrist, worried about what was coming next.

He was not disappointed. "He knows about you," she said.

"I'm sure he does. We talk on the phone—"

"Don't minimize me, for God's sake. Christ, I hate it when you do that."

He decided not to retaliate.

"He knows about you and me. He knows about *us.*"

"He *suspects*—"

"No, Andy. He *knows.*"

Gilchrist waited a couple of beats. "Does that worry you?"

She looked stunned. "You're missing the point."

He most certainly was.

"Mr. Cooper has thrown down the gauntlet."

"Pistols at dawn?"

She cast him a nasty glance that warned him to be careful. "He phoned to remind me that he is an important man. And that an important man should be seen in the company of a professional woman—not one who is reputed to be putting it about town like the local slut. I think those were his exact words."

"Reputed?"

"He's had us followed, Andy."

"Ah," he said, sensing the manifestation of something unpleasant.

"He has photographs of us together."

"Doing *what*, exactly?" He smiled at her. "Unless he has an X-ray camera that can photograph through stone walls, then all he has are photographs of DCI Gilchrist of Fife Constabulary talking to Dr. Cooper in her professional capacity as—"

"Oh, come on, Andy. I stayed over at yours *last night*."

"Well, there is that, of course."

Something seemed to shift within her, and she almost smiled. "Aren't you worried about losing your job?"

"Two consenting adults showing an interest in each other and developing a mutually respectful relationship that does not interfere in any shape or form with their professional responsibilities is hardly grounds for a sacking."

"Even with Chief Super Greaves in the sacking seat?"

"You know about that, do you?"

"That you're not his favorite DCI?"

"Ah, well, there you go."

She shoved her hands through her hair, tilted her head back and shook it. If he did not know better, he would have said they were back on track.

"Why don't you just leave him?" he asked.

Her blue eyes danced with his; then she said, "I'd better get on." She brushed past him and gripped the door handle. "I'll try to get the PM report to you by this evening."

He shook his head. "The day will be done by the time I debrief His Lordship Greaves. Tomorrow's fine." Then, realizing he had forgotten to ask earlier, "Any benzodiazepine in Brian McCulloch's toxicology results?"

She nodded. "He had no intention of being saved."

"So you still think it's suicide?"

"I think you're asking the wrong person. Isn't that your job?" She held his gaze for a long moment, then turned back to the door.

"This might not be an appropriate moment," he said.

She froze, her hand on the handle.

He hated himself for asking, hoped he did not sound desperate. "By the time Greaves is finished with me, I'll be ready for a pint," he said. "Why don't you come along? We can talk about Mr. Cooper, if you like."

She gave his words some thought. "Yes, you're correct."

He felt a flutter of hope.

"It's not an appropriate moment."

Then she turned and left him to fester in his self-inflicted misgivings.

8

As Gilchrist pushed through the Central's double swing doors, he was hit by the chaotic hubbub of a Scottish Friday night in full swing. The end of the working week—if you were not a DCI with a triple murder and another suspicious death to solve—was typically heralded by alcohol being quaffed as if in fear of a global shortage the following day, maybe even the following hour.

Students, rich and poor; couples, young and old and in between; red-faced caddies, wind-blasted after a day on the golf courses; groups of tourists, many from overseas, looking stunned by the sight or deafened by the noise—it was difficult to tell—filled the seats or swarmed in thirsty groups around the rectangular bar.

Gilchrist had always been intrigued by the name—the Central. Was it because of the pub's location on Market Street, which was more or less in the center of St. Andrews, or because the bar itself—behind which bartenders glided past each other in the tight aisles with the skilled grace of dancers—was situated in the center of the room? The conundrum usually lasted a pint or two before it faded to nothing.

Gilchrist located Stan seated in a corner booth with Mhairi, Jessie, and Jackie, and signaled to the barman for a beer. Either the others had left early or Gilchrist was arriving late. He glanced at his watch—8:20—and decided the latter.

With a pint of Deuchars IPA in hand, he waded through the crowd. "Room for one more to squeeze in?" he asked.

Jackie looked up in surprise, her eyes wide behind her black-rimmed specs. Then she reached for her crutches, which were resting against the wall.

"I've got them," Gilchrist said, and held them steady as he worked his way past and sat next to Mhairi. "And never a drop was spilled," he said, then took a mouthful that turned into a gulp.

"Thirsty, boss?"

Gilchrist returned what was left of his pint to the table. "Was I ready for that or what?"

"So, how'd you get on with Greaves?" Jessie asked.

Gilchrist nodded at his beer. "Can't you tell? He told me to work the teams twenty-four seven until we solved the case. I reminded him of his budget and our overtime rate."

"Ouch."

"The word *apoplectic* springs to mind." Another gulp had his pint close to the bottom. "Anyone fancy another?" he asked.

"Heh, slow down there, big boy," Jessie said. "Are you on a promise or what? Talking of which, where is Veronica Lake, anyway?"

Gilchrist pretended not to hear her and caught the barman's eye again. He circled the group with his hand and mouthed, *Same again.* "I'm getting a receipt for these, which I'll present to Greaves. That should test his heart valves for him."

Stan reached for his pint. "In that case, I'll have another two."

Jackie laughed and tried to follow the quip with one of her own, but her stutter beat her every time, so she ended up just clapping her hands.

"Right, Stan," said Gilchrist. He did not intend to stay long. He had a busy day—and probably another week or more—ahead of him, and he wanted to hear their thoughts on progress so far. "What's Janice like?"

Stan raised his eyebrows. "Mutton dressed as lamb, if you get my drift."

"Yeah, but is she boinking Magner?" Jessie asked.

"Well, she denied it. Said she'd heard the rumor within the company and was in the process of taking legal advice."

"Who's her solicitor?" Gilchrist asked.

"She wouldn't say, so I pressed her a bit, and she confessed that she hadn't exactly started the process yet."

"Lying trollop." Jessie again.

Gilchrist said, "I'm listening," then sipped the last of his beer.

"I told her that if she was in any way prevaricating—"

"That's a big word," Jessie said. "Did the bitch know what it meant?"

"She also knew what complicit meant."

"So she coughed up?"

"She certainly did," Stan said. "The pair of them have been at it since Christmas."

Which had Gilchrist thinking about Cooper. Christmas was when their affair started, too. "How long has she been with Stratheden?" he asked.

"Says she was offered a job just before McCulloch and Magner hit the big time, but turned it down. Decided to stay where she was—Robertson McKellar, an accounting firm in Cupar. Better job security."

"And Magner persuaded her to change her mind, when, exactly?"

"Ten years ago. Almost to the day."

"An anniversary boink." Jessie nodded to the bar. "They're up."

Gilchrist pulled himself to his feet and pushed in at the counter. Something did not compute. If Janice had been with Stratheden for a decade, why had she only recently started an affair with Magner? His gut told him she was holding something back.

He thanked the barman, pocketed the change, carried the small glasses back to the table—Drambuie on the rocks for Jackie; Bombay Sapphire and Slimline tonic for Mhairi. Another trip to the counter for his and Stan's pints of Deuchars—he'd persuaded Stan to quit Foster's—and Jessie's half of Belhaven Best. Again, he managed to squeeze in without spilling a drop.

"You're getting good at that," Jessie said.

"Plenty of practice." He gripped his glass. "Here's to Greaves."

"Long may he choke," Jessie said. Gilchrist had the IPA to his lips when her eyes lit up and she announced, "You've got company."

He turned, expecting to see Cooper, then felt his heart stutter at the sight of Maureen.

Her face, which had once been full and attractive, now looked haunted and drawn, with eyes that stared from hollow sockets. Her dark hair no longer bounced thick and glossy by her neckline but was tied back in a tight ponytail that only accentuated how thin she had become. Three stone she had lost in total, but from a body that had been slim in the first place.

Jessie rose to her feet and offered Maureen her seat. "Here you go, Mo. I'm going outside to make a call. I'll be back in five."

Gilchrist stood, as Maureen nudged his cheek in a half-hearted peck and whispered, "Sorry for hanging up on you earlier." Then she squeezed past him, nodding hello to every-one in turn. And in the passing, he sensed the lightness of her body, even though she was cocooned in a woollen scarf and thick anorak that hid her emaciated frame. She sat, black jeans slack on too-thin legs.

"The usual?" he asked her.

"I'll just have one," she said. "Then I'm heading back to the flat."

"Anything to eat with it?"

"I've already had a bite."

Gilchrist doubted it but did not have the heart to chal-lenge her in front of the others. Instead, he returned to the bar, caught the barman's eye again, and asked for a Cabernet.

"Large or small?"

Gilchrist wanted to reply "small," but Maureen would only down it in one to remind him she never drank small measures. "Large," he said.

When he returned to his seat and handed Maureen her drink, the conversation had already shifted to her Open Uni-versity studies.

"Can't wait to get the exams out of the way," she said, in response to a question from Mhairi.

"And then will you apply for a job with Fife?"

Maureen lifted the glass to her lips, then shrugged, giv-ing Gilchrist his first hint that she might soon be leaving St. Andrews again.

"I guess you wouldn't want your old dad as a slave driver," Stan joked.

Jackie mouthed a laugh, then clapped again.

"I'm not that cruel," Gilchrist said, but that only encouraged Maureen to hide behind her wine, letting him know that the topic of her postgraduate employment was off limits.

And so was his investigation. An early debriefing with the teams, followed by almost two hours with Greaves, most of which had been a waste of time, meant that Gilchrist had scarcely discussed the day's events with Stan and the others. Although he trusted Maureen, and had shown her details of previous cases, for some reason he did not want her involved in the massacre of the McCullochs.

He gripped his pint and asked, "So, how's Jon?"

"Wouldn't know. I hardly see him these days."

"I thought you liked him."

"I thought so, too," she agreed. Her next sip of wine almost drained the glass.

Well, that put an end to that. Like father, like daughter, he thought. Or maybe like father, like family was more correct.

In the several years leading up to their separation, Gail had cut back on her alcohol intake. He had since wondered if her sobriety had contributed to their breakup. Maybe through sober eyes she had seen what a failure he had been as a husband and father, which in turn had encouraged her to have the affair with Harry.

He almost felt relieved when Jessie reappeared.

"I tell you what," she said. "I'm ready to chew nails."

"Ouch," said Mhairi.

"There are never enough stools when you want one," Jessie said, looking around.

"That's 'cause it's Friday and the bar's busy."

"Who's a clever Stan? Can I squeeze in beside you, Andy?"

Gilchrist took his chance and said, "My turn." He stood, mobile already in hand, and left Jessie to take his chair. Without another word, he threaded through the crowd and exited by the side door onto College Street.

Outside, the air felt raw, as if the temperature had plummeted ten degrees. A bitter wind brushed the cobbles, and he turned his back to it as he made the call. A gull screeched from the black skies above Church Street as he counted five rings, then six. He was about to hang up when Cooper answered.

"I'll give you a call back," she snapped.

The line died before he had time to respond.

He returned the mobile to his pocket and eyed the entrance to the bar. If Maureen had not been inside, he would have walked to the Merc and driven straight to his cottage in Crail. As it was, he returned inside with a heavy heart, saddened by the knowledge that Cooper would be sharing her bed with her undeserving husband that night.

9

Morning hit Gilchrist with the sickening pain of a thudding headache. He lay still for several seconds, struggling to pull his mind from the dark cobwebs of sleep, before daring to open his eyes. The familiar twin skylights assured him he was at home in his own bed. He flapped an arm to the side, felt only cold emptiness. He rolled over and stared at the pillow.

No Cooper.

Memories of last night came back to him in fluttering moments of clarity intertwined with clouds of emptiness as dark as space. He remembered the others departing—Jackie with her crutches; Jessie leaving with her, and helping her to the door; Stan and Mhairi not long after, trying not to look like a couple but failing comically.

Then it had been just the two of them, daughter and father.

He closed his eyes and counted two more pints of Deuchars, followed by two—or was it three?—Glenfiddichs, while a carefree Maureen kept easy pace alongside, downing four large glasses of wine, maybe five. So much for having only the one. He cursed himself for being too lenient. Just like her mother, once Maureen started, she did not want to stop until the bottle was finished. Gilchrist tried to convince himself that she was just a young woman with a tortured memory who liked the mental release that a hefty dose of alcohol gave every now and again. She did not do drugs—or so she told him, and he chose to believe her—so he reckoned the occasional heavy session was not all that bad.

As his memory peeled back the previous night's events layer by misted layer, he remembered dropping Maureen off at her flat—he escorted her upstairs, made sure she got inside safe and sound—then driving back to Crail rather than abandoning the Merc and taking a taxi.

But it had not ended there.

Once home, he tried to make sense of what they had achieved so far and made a list for the following days. But like the fool alcohol often made of him, he opened a bottle of the Balvenie and poured himself a double Doublewood, or maybe a triple, and maybe even more than one.

Then came the recollection of calling Cooper, which had him groaning at the memory.

"I said I would call you back."

"I know, but I thought you might like to—"

She hung up, and that should have been that. But, on impulse, he dialed her number again, only for it to be answered by a man's voice telling him it was late and to stop calling his wife. Gilchrist did not hang up. Instead, he held on to the call in silence. The stalemate lasted all of ten seconds, after which Gilchrist took drunken pleasure from the fact that Mr. Cooper ended the call first.

Christ, just the memory of it brought a hot flush to his face.

He dragged himself from bed and just about managed to make it to the bathroom without throwing up. A scalding shave and a shower long enough to flood the bath did little to ease the headache, but he was able to keep down a mug of tea and a half slice of unbuttered toast, followed by four paracetamol that dulled the edge of the pain.

On the stroll to the Merc, it felt more like midwinter than early March. An icy wind, cold enough to bite the fingers off you, blasted in from the sea as if in advance of a hurricane. Or, as the Scottish meteorologists tended to say, gusty winds and scattered showers. They could be broadcasting hurricane alerts around the globe with winds as strong as these, but in Scotland it was business as usual.

He waited until he drove through Kingsbarns before calling Jessie.

She answered with, "Are you *never* late?"

"We've a meeting in Glenrothes this morning, remember?"

"I know, Andy. You reminded me fifty million times last night. Talking of which, how's your head? When I left, you looked as if you'd settled in for the night."

"My head's fine," he lied. "But I'd feel a lot better if Jackie had been able to find an MO that at least bore some resemblance to the . . . the . . ." He let the words die.

"Do you ever think," she said, "that we might have got it wrong? That it doesn't necessarily have to be a serial killer?"

"Sometimes."

"Or that we don't know we're dealing with a serial killer until the MO shows up at least another two times."

"So you're saying this might be a first?"

"Serial killers have to start somewhere," she said. "If there was an identical MO out there, Jackie would have found it. So, if we don't have anything similar from any other case in the country, then, yes, it probably is a first."

The first of a serial killer's victims? It was a plausible theory, but why did he not believe it? This killer had killed before. He was sure of it. But with nothing more than gut instinct, he knew he had little chance of convincing others.

He stared at the road ahead. In all his thirty-odd years with Fife Constabulary, he had never witnessed such a brutal crime scene. He had seen some horrific deaths in his time, but an image of the bloodied bathroom floor hit him with such clarity that he almost had to pull over. He tugged the steering wheel as a gust of wind buffeted the car. Away to his right, windswept surf painted strips of white on a blackened sea. The horizon flickered gray and blue, dangling the promise of a calmer day before his hurting eyes. For all anyone knew in Scotland, it could be warm enough to barbecue that evening.

"I don't get it," he said. "It's too . . ." He struggled for the words, then found them. "It's too thorough. Too targeted. Too precise."

"The girls, you mean?"

"Yes. Not a hair out of place. All tucked up like he's put them to bed."

"They *were* in bed."

"You know what I mean," he said, irritated by the speed of Jessie's tongue. "He's telling us that we're looking for a man with a hatred of"—he was going to say *women*, but that was wrong—"one particular woman. Amy McCulloch."

"So it's a revenge killing. Is that what you're saying?"

"Could be."

"But revenge for what?"

"Therein lies the problem," Gilchrist said.

"Listen, you're keeping me back. I need to put my face on."

"I'll be with you in ten—"

"Make it fifteen, unless you want a scare."

"Do you fancy a Starbucks?"

"Now you're talking."

"Latte in fifteen?"

"And no sugar."

With that, she hung up.

———

It was closer to twenty-five minutes by the time Gilchrist pulled up to the curb outside Jessie's semidetached in Canongate. Her little Fiat, brand new and hardly used, sat parked by the back door. For the first two months after joining Fife Constabulary and moving to St. Andrews from Glasgow, Jessie and her son, Robert, had lodged with a friend of hers, Angie, in Forgan Place. Their move to a home of their own three weeks ago seemed to have done wonders for Jessie's spirits. Or maybe it was Robert's imminent cochlear implant operation and the promise that her boy would finally hear, after being deaf from birth, that had pulled her out of the doldrums. Confirmation that the operation would be covered by the NHS had been the icing on the cake.

No sooner had Gilchrist shifted into neutral than the back door opened and Jessie scarpered down the drive, hand at her neck, head tucked into her chest, hiding from the wind.

The door opened, followed by a rush of ice-cold air and Jessie saying, "Fuck."

"Good morning to you, too." He slipped into gear. "Coffee's in the holder."

She removed it, peeled back the lid, and said, "What are you waiting for?"

"A morning kiss?"

"Just drive, will you?"

He waited until he turned left at the West Port round-about and was accelerating along Argyle Street before asking, "How's the coffee?"

"Wet and hot. How's the head? You look like shite."

"Surprised you noticed."

"With dog's balls for eyes? Who wouldn't?"

"I'm getting too old for it all now."

"Men never learn."

Gilchrist could not fail to catch the venom in the word *men*. He kept his speed at a steady thirty as he eased onto Strathkinness Low Road. He thought he knew the reason for Jessie's change of mood and edged into it with, "So, Lachie called?"

"Fat prick."

"Maybe he should go on a diet."

"Maybe he should jump in the Clyde."

"Want to talk about it?"

"How about we talk about Veronica Lake instead?"

"I don't think Rebecca looks remotely like Veronica Lake—"

"No, Veronica Lake's dead. With Jabba on the hunt, I could be so lucky."

Gilchrist thought silence was the best option, so he took a sip of latte. It was still warm and did wonders for the turmoil in his stomach. His hangover was diminishing, and pangs of hunger nibbled at his innards. Beyond the junction to Strath-kinness, he depressed the pedal and nudged the speed to sixty, then seventy, and held it there.

"Penny for your thoughts?" he said.

"You can have them for free if you promise to take Jabba for the day."

"Ah," Gilchrist said. "So he's going to spend the day in sunny St. Andrews?"

"Not just the day. The whole bloody weekend, so he tells me. Jesus, Andy, what the hell is it with men?"

Once again, he chose silence. Chief Superintendent Lachlan McKellar of Strathclyde Police—or Jabba the Hutt, as Jessie preferred to call him—had a thing for Jessie. As far as Gilchrist knew, they'd had a brief fling, which Jessie immediately regretted, ending their affair before it started. But Lachie did not know the meaning of the word *no* and pestered Jessie until she finally transferred to Fife, which did little to dampen Lachie's ardor. His recent threats to leave his wife had finished it for Jessie, and now she wanted nothing more to do with the man. End of.

Five minutes later, Gilchrist tried again. "Has he left his wife, then?"

"She flung him out, more like."

"So, he's up for grabs?"

"Grab hooks, I hope. Then over the side with the fat blob."

"What does Robert think about all of this?"

"What is it with you this morning? Robert's off-limits. You know that. I don't go asking about your family, so don't go asking about mine. Why don't you just stick to driving the car and getting over your hangover?"

"I'm feeling better, I have to tell you."

"Well, it must be contagious. I feel like shite now."

"You'll perk up once you get your teeth into Chief Super Whyte."

She chuckled and shook her head, which had Gilchrist frowning at her, wondering what the joke was. Chief Superintendent Billy Whyte was the SIO in the Thomas Magner rape investigation. He worked out of Glenrothes HQ and was scheduled to meet Gilchrist and Jessie at 10:00 AM.

"I forgot to tell you," she said. "Well, actually, I remembered last night, but I didn't want to spoil your evening." She tried to tease him with silence for five long seconds, but he refused to bite. "Chief Super Whyte asked me if the meeting was really necessary."

"Why would he say that?" Gilchrist asked. "Billy and I go back years."

"That's what he said."

Maybe he was still hungover, his brain too befuddled from its recent dose of alcohol to work out the obvious, but he could not think of any reason why Billy Whyte would not want to meet him. "You've lost me," he said.

"Does the name Logan mean anything to you?"

Gilchrist shot a glance at Jessie.

"Well, that brought the color back to your cheeks," she said.

"Don't tell me . . ."

"Afraid so."

Gilchrist gritted his teeth as he waited for Jessie to confirm his fears.

"DI Carol Logan," she said, "is assisting Chief Super William Whyte in the Thomas Magner case."

"Ah, shit," Gilchrist said, tightening his grip on the wheel.

"That's what I thought," Jessie said. "A fucked-up weekend for both of us."

10

Gilchrist drove on in silence, the memory of *that* evening flickering back to life.

Lafferty's on South Street, and deep into a Saturday night. It had seemed such an innocent comment for him to make: "Are you coming on to me?" Well, Logan *had* bumped into him and caused him to spill his drink, and he had meant the question as nothing more than a bit of banter between colleagues. But the flash of anger on her face warned him she had missed the point.

So, he apologized. Mistake number one.

"I seen what you done."

The voice from behind surprised him, from a woman he had never seen before.

"You touched her up. I seen you."

"I'm not that desperate," Gilchrist said, regretting the quip the instant it spilled from his mouth. Mistake number two.

He retreated to the corner of the bar with his pint and tried to catch Logan's eye when she and her friends left for the evening. But she was having none of it. And that should have been the end of that.

But it wasn't.

Logan had witnesses—four women who swore they had overheard Gilchrist's sexual innuendo and seen him brush his hand over her breasts. Gilchrist was interviewed—more like interrogated—by Complaints and Discipline for over two hours, and it took the intervention of Chief Superintendent McKay from HQ, and the promise of a recommendation for promotion to DI, to persuade Logan to drop her complaint.

Since then, Gilchrist had not set eyes on her.

He pulled the Merc into the car park at Glenrothes HQ at 9:50, in plenty of time for their 10:00 AM appointment.

Chief Super Whyte welcomed Gilchrist like a long-lost friend. A tall man with white hair cut as short as bristle, Whyte looked all of his fifty-plus years. Folds of flesh as loose as chicken wattles were tucked into the neck of his shirt, evidence of the five stone he had lost over the past two years.

Once introduced to Jessie, Whyte said, "DI Logan has been warned but, as she pointed out, she is involved in an investigation of her own."

Gilchrist gave a smile of reassurance. "The past is the past."

Whyte raised his eyebrows, then said, "Right. This way."

Gilchrist and Jessie followed Whyte into an office that overlooked the car park. Two detectives were seated at a center table—Logan and a man Gilchrist did not recognize.

Whyte announced Gilchrist and Jessie by their titles, then introduced his team as "DI Carol Logan and DI Mac Smith, assisting in the investigation of Mr. Thomas Magner."

Gilchrist reached forward, shook Logan's meaty hand, then Smith's. Jessie did likewise. Then they all took their seats.

"Right," Whyte said to Gilchrist. "You asked for this meeting."

Gilchrist placed both hands flat on the table, then eyed Whyte, Smith, and Logan, one by one, his gaze lingering on Logan a tad longer than the others. But if he was searching for any sign of discomfort or forgiveness, they were nowhere to be seen.

"Yesterday," Gilchrist began, "as you are no doubt aware, we found the bodies of the McCulloch family. The father, Brian, was the business partner of Thomas Magner. We know that the mother, Amy, and her daughters, Eilish and Siobhan, were murdered. But the jury is still out on Brian. His death may or may not have been suicide."

Gilchrist went on to explain the history and business relationship between Magner and McCulloch, the fact that Stratheden had an unusually high number of contentious billings, and his assumption that the company was in financial difficulty. He talked of the deepening rift between the two directors, the fallout with staff and the threat of dismissal, but chose not to mention Magner's alleged sexual relationship with Amy McCulloch's sister, Janice. In conclusion, he gave details of their interview with Magner and of his seemingly watertight alibi.

"Got a transcript?" Logan asked.

Gilchrist knew that Logan did not want or need the transcript, only for Gilchrist to spin his wheels. "I do."

"Let's have it."

"It'll be uploaded onto the Command and Control STORM system soon."

"When?"

"This afternoon."

"What's wrong with this morning?"

"Nothing's wrong with this morning. But it'll be available this afternoon." He waited until Logan slumped back into her chair, then held Chief Super Whyte's inquiring gaze. "The reason why we're here is to ask if, in the course of your investigation, you have come across anything that could conceivably be a motive for Magner to murder Amy and her—"

"Sounds like you're looking for straws to clutch," Logan said.

"Exploring all avenues is how I'd prefer to put it."

"*All avenues?* What are you now? Traffic Division?"

"From the look of things," Jessie cut in, "we wouldn't catch you speeding."

"That cuts both ways, Slim."

Whyte raised a hand like a referee.

Logan sat back, tried a smile, but the fire in her eyes gave away her true feelings.

Whyte said, "The short answer to your question, Andy, is: no, we haven't." He eyed Smith, who shook his head. Then he gave Logan a warning glance. "You're welcome to have a look through our files, of course, but we're still building our case, and I'd ask you not to use anything relating to it without checking with me first. Does that work for you?"

In front of Logan and Smith, Whyte was playing it by the book. But if Gilchrist came across anything critical to his investigation, he knew that Whyte would assist him in any way he could.

"That works perfectly."

DI Smith cleared his throat. "Do you mind if I ask a few questions, sir?"

Gilchrist was aware that Smith was putting the request to Chief Super Whyte, not himself, so he waited for Whyte's nod of approval before answering, "Sure."

"Do you have anything concrete that leads you to suspect Magner?" Smith asked.

"No. But until we identify a prime suspect, we're suspicious of everyone."

"From what you've said so far, it seems highly unlikely that Magner would have had the means to commit the crime, in terms of time and place, sir."

Gilchrist found it hard to disagree. Jessie's journey to Stirling yesterday afternoon to check the Highland Hotel's CCTV records had confirmed Magner's story. He had arrived at the conference a few minutes after seven and taken an aisle seat—verified by Gilchrist during a short five-minute review of the tapes, with Magner powering down his mobile before entering the conference hall. The room number also checked out with Magner's car registration, and his account had been settled with a Royal Bank of Scotland debit card in his name. The bank confirmed that the number and account did indeed belong to Magner.

"We're not ruling out that Magner could have hired someone to carry out the killings for him."

"Get real." Logan again. "Brian McCulloch did in his family, then topped himself. Plain and simple. It's an open-and-shut case. You're barking up the wrong tree again. It's not Magner's style. He's innocent . . . at least of murdering his business partner's family."

Gilchrist could sense Jessie stiffening next to him, so he lifted a hand off the table, just a touch, to signal that she should keep quiet. It pleased him that they had kept the brutal details of the murder out of the public domain, and from those in the constabulary not directly involved in the investigation. The tidiness of McCulloch's clothes, and the absence of blood on his body and in his car, strongly suggested that he was not the murderer. But few people were privy to those facts.

"You're probably correct," Gilchrist conceded, "but we'd still like to review your files. Just to be thorough."

"What're you up to?" asked Logan.

"I thought we'd explained that," Gilchrist said, and rose to his feet. He was through trying to reason with her.

Logan jerked to her feet. "I don't like it, Billy," she said. "He's fishing. I know him. I wouldn't put it past him to slip something into our files to make us look like pricks and—"

Whyte raised a hand to silence Logan; then he eyed Gilchrist. "*Are* you fishing?"

"Only trying to find a possible motive."

Whyte turned to Smith. "Show DCI Gilchrist and DS Janes our files."

"I'm telling you, Billy, I've seen this guy at work. He's up to—"

"I hear you, DI Logan." Whyte's sudden formality sent a message to Logan, who pursed her lips as if to stifle a curse. "But I've made my decision." He walked round the table and held out his hand. "If you need anything else, Andy, let me know." Then he faced Jessie. "DS Janes. A pleasure," he said, and shook her hand. Then, ignoring Logan, he said to Smith, "They're all yours, Mac."

Smith looked embarrassed as Logan walked from the room without a word.

"And then there were four," Jessie said.

"Quite," Whyte said. "The less said the better."

———

From what Gilchrist and Jessie could ascertain, Chief Super Whyte and his team had left no stone unturned in their investigation of Magner. They'd even gone all the way back to his primary school records at St. Cyrus—about fifty miles north of St. Andrews—where he was brought up as a single child to churchgoing, disciplinarian parents. He completed his secondary education in Mearns Academy in Laurencekirk, leaving at the age of sixteen with just two Highers—an A in art and a C in English.

Magner then headed north to Aberdeen to work on the oil rigs, first as a roustabout, then graduating to assistant driller, working two weeks on and two off. It was during one of these two-week spells ashore that he first got into trouble with the law—nothing serious, just a drunken brawl outside a bar in Aberdeen city center on a Saturday night. The incident was reported to Grampian Police, and both Magner and his assailant—Magner maintained he had been hit first, although witness statements suggested otherwise—spent two nights in custody. They then received identical fines on Monday morning at the Sheriff Court.

Throughout their search, DI Smith answered every one of Gilchrist and Jessie's questions, led them to names and places in the files, pulled out witness statements, and let them take notes, all with the patience of a saint. He confirmed that eleven women in total had filed complaints of sexual abuse against Magner. All the alleged assaults occurred within an eight-year period—1979 to 1986—after Magner left the rigs to work as a salesman in the construction industry, but before he started Stratheden Enterprises with McCulloch. Gilchrist theorized that the itinerant life of a salesman lent itself to overnight stays away from home and plenty of opportunities for short-term sexual liaisons that were readily forgotten or, as in Magner's case, came back to haunt him.

Of the eleven women who had come forward, eight still lived in Scotland, from Nairn in the north to Eyemouth in the Borders, and three had moved to England—York, Birmingham, and Manchester. Each had accused Magner of rape and forced penetration and, to a woman, declined to file a complaint at the time of the assault for fear of retaliation. Interestingly, all eleven complaints were made in the space of just forty-five days at the beginning of the year. It seemed as if they had all made the same New Year's resolution, and made a pact to see it through.

"And there were no complaints against Magner before 1979?" Gilchrist asked.

"We're thinking that the regimented routine of working on the rigs kept him pretty much on the straight and narrow up to then."

"Getting into a fight in Aberdeen on his shore leave, you mean?" Jessie said.

"And his new job as a salesman opened up opportunities for new relationships."

"That's one way of putting it."

"Any other way?"

"Women to rape whenever the mood struck him?" Jessie scratched her temple. "Why didn't they fight back, or at least report him?"

"A big strong lad like that?" Smith said. "After five years grafting on the rigs? With a few beers pumping up the testosterone? None of them would have been able to stand up to him during or after the alleged rapes."

Gilchrist glanced at his notes. "The first woman to file a complaint was a Mrs. Vicky Kelvin. What can you tell us about her?"

"Née Smith. No relation," he added with a smile. "She lives in Dundee. Recently divorced. Three adult children."

"What prompted her to file the complaint now, rather than back then?"

"Her divorce, she says. Apparently, that incident with Magner all these years ago got her hung up about sex. That's what her ex-husband thinks, anyway. His grounds for divorce were incompatibility. Read that as frigid."

"How old is Mrs. Kelvin?" Gilchrist asked.

Smith flipped through some files. "Fifty-four."

"Divorced recently?"

"Last year."

"And when did Magner allegedly—"

"August 1980."

"So she would have been, what, twenty-eight? And Magner was . . . twenty-four? When the incident took place. Allegedly," he added.

"Give or take a year."

"And once Mrs. Kelvin filed her complaint, the next to do so was . . . ?"

"Lindsey Seaton."

Gilchrist checked his notes. "And she did that on the very next day." He ran his finger down the printed list, mouthing the names, checking the dates. "Then nothing for a few days, then a flurry of activity until, in the space of six weeks, all eleven women had filed their complaints of sexual abuse—"

"Rape."

"Rape . . . against Magner." Gilchrist sat back. He would put Smith in his midthirties. Liquid brown eyes conveyed a calm confidence that told him Smith was an honest man, someone who had perhaps joined the constabulary with the idea of bringing justice to the world. He found it incredible that he had once felt the same way. But years of being ground down by a system flooded by criminals who thought prison was just a roof over your head and three free meals a day, until they let you out to commit another crime, had killed his idealism. Now the job seemed to be just a matter of tackling whichever case they shoved your way.

"Isn't it strange that they all complained in short order?" Gilchrist said.

Smith shrugged. "Once the first complaint is filed, it kind of frees up the others to come forward. They might have been intimidated or frightened when they were younger, or thought it had only happened to them." He gave a tight smile. "But if they learned that the same thing had happened to someone else, they could have taken strength from that and come out of the shadows."

Gilchrist gave Smith's comments some thought. There had to be a ringleader, he was almost certain of that, someone who initiated the complaints, which then persuaded the others to step forward. "So every one of them just walked into her local police station and filed a complaint in person?" he said.

"All but one." Smith flipped through the files. "Here she is. Charlotte Renwick. Lives in Perth. Said she wanted to file a complaint only if she could do so in total anonymity. As an upstanding member of the local community—churchgoer, charity organizer, etc.—she did not want to risk damaging her reputation."

"Is she prepared to go to court?"

"Provided she can maintain anonymity."

"Or she'll withdraw the charges?"

"Apparently."

Gilchrist asked, "How did the others know about that first complaint by Vicky Kelvin?"

Smith shrugged. "Read about it in the newspapers. Saw it on TV."

"So Mrs. Kelvin's complaint made it into the *Courier* and beyond?"

"Not at first. She said she felt bitter after her divorce and hated everything to do with . . . she hated men. The memories of that incident apparently haunted her to the point where she blamed Magner for everything that had gone wrong in her life, and in particular the end of her marriage. Then, one night, something clicked, and she realized that if Magner had raped her, then maybe he'd raped others. So she decided to find out, and through social media and Internet requests she managed to locate Lindsey Seaton. The two of them made their statements one after the other, then the rest heard and followed suit."

"Did she appear vindictive?" Gilchrist asked.

"Wouldn't you?" Jessie snapped.

Gilchrist bit his tongue. But it troubled him that a vengeful woman might muster damaging support against any man if she went out of her way to convince others. He could never condone rape, or abuse in any shape or form, but he had seen how claims of violence or abuse were often exaggerated to strengthen a case. His own experience with DI Logan was proof of that sour-tasting pudding.

They spent the next forty minutes reading more statements, taking more notes, but made no progress in establishing a potential motive for murder. It seemed that the deeper they looked, the more Gilchrist came to understand that Magner couldn't have killed the McCullochs.

Maybe Logan was right. Maybe they were barking up the wrong tree.

By two o'clock, Gilchrist's head had cleared and a worrying thirst for a pint was settling over him. He pushed himself to his feet and told DI Smith, "I think we've gone as far as we can for now. If anything unfolds, or springs to mind, let me know."

"Likewise," Smith said, his grip firm.

Gilchrist waited while Jessie and Smith shook hands; then he turned to the door and said, "We know the way out."

"Regards to DI Logan," Jessie said, unable to resist a parting quip.

"And watch yourself with her," Gilchrist advised.

But Smith already had his mobile to his ear, and Gilchrist's words of warning passed unheard.

11

"I'm feeling kind of peckish," Jessie said to Gilchrist.

"Thought you were on a diet."

"Only when I'm not eating." They drove on in silence for another couple of miles before Jessie said, "Do you never eat?"

"Only when I'm hungry."

"Do you never get hungry, then?"

"We can have a pint and a pie in the Central if you like. Once we've spoken to Vicky Kelvin," he added, and eased the speed up to seventy.

Jessie seemed to sulk at his response, and powered up her mobile. "Christ on a stick," she said. "How many messages can one useless fat prick leave in a day? Listen to this: 'In St. A where r u?' Then, two minutes later, 'r u not talking?'" She let out a cursed hiss. "No, I'm not talking. What part of N-O don't you understand?" She worked her mobile some more, still cursing under her breath. "A total of six messages. In fifteen minutes. I mean, if you don't hear back after the first two, you're not going to hear back from any more, are you, no matter how many you send, the useless twat." She tapped the keypad. "Delete, delete, delete."

"Sounds like he's making a nuisance of himself."

"Par for the course."

"Like me to have a talk with someone in Strathclyde?"

"I can handle it," she said. "If he continues to pester, I'll threaten him with my brothers. That should scare some sense into him."

"Aren't they locked up?"

"Only Tommy. But next month he's due for early release for good behavior. Read that as didn't kick someone to death inside. But he's still got time to take somebody out."

"Right," said Gilchrist, deciding to abandon the topic of Jessie's criminal family.

They found Vicky Kelvin's home, a two-bedroom apartment on the third floor of a high-rise complex that, at a stretch, overlooked Dundee's waterfront. As they stood outside, Gilchrist about to knock the door, Jessie said, "Next time we use the lift, all right?"

"Climbing stairs is good exercise for your karate lessons."

"I get enough exercise running away from Jabba."

"Isn't Jabba too fat to run?"

"Smart-arse."

Gilchrist pressed the doorbell and caught the melodic chime from somewhere deep in the apartment. It took five seconds before the door peeled open to the sticky snap of wood tearing free of painted weather stripping.

A worn-looking woman with dyed black hair peeked out from behind the safety chain.

"Mrs. Kelvin?" Gilchrist held out his warrant card. Jessie did likewise. "Do you have a couple of minutes?"

"What d'youse want?"

"To talk."

"Oh, aye? What about?"

"Thomas Magner."

The door eased shut for a moment, then reopened to a gruff, "In youse come, then."

"Tea would be nice," Jessie said, which received a glare from Vicky.

They strode along a dark hallway, past a kitchen that reeked of burned toast and something more unpleasant. Gilchrist caught a glimpse of dishes piled high in the sink. The small living room was crowded with two clothes horses packed with women's underwear—knickers, tights, bras, vests—that had long since lost their washday freshness. The whole place carried the stale smell of cigarette ash; the wallpaper yellowed at the ceiling line.

Gilchrist walked beyond the guddle and faced the window. Through glass smeared with bird shit and city grime—not been cleaned in months, maybe longer—the River Tay slid toward the sea. From the kitchen came the sound of a kettle being filled, dishes clattering, cutlery chinking. All they needed were a few chocolate biscuits to round off the afternoon.

He turned his back to the Tay. Jessie had finagled her backside on to the arm of a sofa that looked as if it doubled as a spare bed. In the corner, a muted TV flickered some old movie at them. Vicky made her way into the living room, carrying a tray with three mugs, the string of a teabag dangling over the rim of each. "I hope you dinnae like milk and sugar, 'cause I've no got any. And I've nae biscuits either. Ran out two days ago."

She presented the tray to Jessie and waited while she removed one mug, then turned to Gilchrist, who did not have it in his heart to decline.

He took a sip as a matter of courtesy, then said, "You recently filed a complaint against Thomas Magner for indecent assault."

"Rape's indecent. Aye."

"Why?"

"Well, it's no right, is it?"

"No, I mean why did you wait all this time before filing the complaint?"

She narrowed her eyes, then looked at Jessie, then back to Gilchrist. "What's this about, eh? I've already told them all this." Her look shifted from irritation through mild anger to full-blown suspicion. "Who're you with again? Here, give me another look at them cards."

Gilchrist showed her his warrant card.

She squinted to read it.

"We're with Fife Constabulary. St. Andrews CID. We're not involved in the investigation into the allegations against Thomas Magner, but we'd like to ask you a few questions relating to your complaint."

"Like what kindae questions?"

Gilchrist took another sip of tea. "I'd like you to think back to when you lived in Aberdeen, and tell us how it happened."

She screwed up her face, as if deciding whether to answer or tell them to leave. Then she said, "We was out for a bevvy, me and a couple of friends, Sheilagh and Morag. I've no seen them in ages."

"How old were you?"

"Twenty-seven." She ran a hand under her nose, then wiped it on her skirt. "We used to go to the city center. The Caledonian Hotel was my favorite. Right upmarket, so it was. At the weekend you could meet up with the crews coming off the rigs. There was loads of money back then, all they men with two weeks off looking for ways to spend their dosh. We'd let them chat us up, and they'd spend the evening buying the rounds, then trying it on. But we were wise to them, so we were. We'd let them pay for everything, then pretend we were going to the bathroom and make a run for it. Leave them standing." She laughed at the memory.

"Were you not worried about seeing them again?" Jessie asked.

"If we did, we'd chat them up like, then tell them we were married. Most of them had birds of their own to go back to anyway. They were just there to get pished. But we could go out and have a good time without spending any money. No like nowadays. Price of stuff would scare you shitless, so it would."

"And was that how you first met Thomas Magner?" Gilchrist asked, nudging her back on track.

Her eyes narrowed again. "He was different, so he was. He'd look you up and down before coming over for a chat. Fancied himself rotten."

"Sounds like you were familiar with him," Jessie said.

"After a while you get to know who goes to what pub, who to stay away from and who to let chat you up. So I'd seen him around, yeah. We all had."

"Did you see ever see him with a regular girlfriend?"

"No really. Just chatted some up like."

"Did he chat up Sheilagh and Morag?"

"He'd chat up anyone, really. He was just there with the crowd."

"So he was always with his friends?"

"No real friends, if you know what I'm saying. Just riggers on the same shift."

"But the night you say you were attacked, when he tried to chat you up, was he by himself?"

"Aye. Although I seen him earlier with someone who looked a bit like him. Same kindae hair, same build. I thought he was working with his brother. He'd chucked the rigs and was wearing a suit. They both were."

"Magner's an only child."

She shrugged. "I wouldnae know."

"Got a name for the other person?"

"Are you joking?"

"So, what happened later that night?" Gilchrist asked.

"This Saturday night, me and Sheilagh and Morag started out at the Caledonian as usual. We'd chip in to buy the first drink, then nurse it until someone chatted us up. Well, this particular night, Magner was over in a flash, so he was. I remember that. And there was something different about him—"

"Different? As in wearing a suit?"

"Naw. He was in a suit like, aye, but he looked like he was excited about something."

"On drugs?"

She shrugged.

"Did you ever indulge?" Jessie asked.

"Fags and vodka's my limit," she said, unfazed by the directness. "Talking of which, do you mind if I smoke?"

Gilchrist shook his head, sipped his tea.

Vicky placed her mug on the table, slipped a packet of Marlboro Lights from one cardigan pocket and a lighter from the other, and lit up with the expertise of a lifelong addict. She inhaled, her eyes closing with pleasure, then let out the smoke with a heavy gush. "I should gie this up," she said. "Save a fucking fortune, excuse the French."

Jessie shifted on the arm of the sofa, pushed herself to her feet, shoved her hands into her pockets. Gilchrist was always amazed how ex-smokers, himself included, became uneasy when someone lit up. Smoke curled in the air, giving him an odd flashback of the snooker club where his late brother, Jack, had first taken up smoking.

"So . . . Magner looked different that night," he said, nudging his mind away from the nicotine itch. "Then what?"

"We got chatting, had a few drinks, one thing led to another, and before you know it, I was on my own with him and heading out to some other hotel in a taxi."

"What one?" Jessie asked.

"Cannae remember."

Gilchrist almost spilled his tea. "Was that the hotel in which Magner allegedly forced himself upon you?"

"None of that allegedly anything shite. He raped me, plain and fucking simple."

"In that hotel?"

"Aye."

"But you can't remember its name?" It seemed such an extraordinary gap in her memory that Gilchrist found himself eyeing her with suspicion.

"I went back to check it out," she explained. "But it's been knocked down. There's nothing left. Just flattened."

Well, he supposed that might explain it, so he pressed on. "Do you remember what happened when you arrived at the hotel?"

"Remember?" She looked aghast. "How could I ever forget?"

Gilchrist could not fail to notice Jessie's disapproving stare, so he decided to take a step back and let her take over. Jessie seemed to sense this and led Vicky to the sofa.

"Why don't you sit down?" Jessie said. "Take your time. And once you're ready, tell us what happened."

"Aye. I'll do that. Just gie me a minute till I finish this off."

She sucked the Marlboro for all it was worth, then dowsed the dout into her tea. And with that action, Gilchrist set his own half-empty mug on the windowsill.

"He had this bottle of vodka," Vicky said. "I remember that. The Russian one with a red label and the funny name . . . Stollie-something."

"Stolichnaya?" Gilchrist offered.

"That's the one. We had a few of these, then one thing led to another, and before you know it, he makes his move. He rolls on top of me, then starts groping. I was pinned to the bed. He was too strong for me. I told him to stop—"

"Why?"

Both Jessie and Vicky looked up in astonishment at Gilchrist.

He tried to explain. "You were twenty-seven. You'd had a few at the Caledonian. You went back to his hotel room. Surely you must have known what was going to—"

"I wisnae a hoor."

"But what was to stop Magner thinking you were? You let him take you to a hotel. Just the two of you. Did you think he wanted to talk about the weather?"

"It wisnae like that."

"I'll bet it wasn't." He stepped away from the window and moved to the center of the room, until he was staring straight down at her. "Here's what I think happened."

She looked up at him, eyes widening.

"You went back to that hotel with the intention of having sex with Thomas Magner, and when—"

"No, I didnae—"

"—he came on to you, you said it would cost him—"

"No. *No.*" It sounded like a wail. Tears spilled from her eyes.

"—and when Magner realized he'd been duped by a prostitute, he refused to stop."

Vicky shook her head and put her hands over her ears.

Gilchrist waited for her to lower them. "What I don't understand is, why?"

She scowled at him. "*Why?*"

"Why did it stay with you for so long?"

"I was *raped*," she said. "*That*'s why it stayed with me. That bastard ruined my life."

"There's more to it than that," he snapped.

She looked up at him and shook her head again. "I don't know—"

"What is it, Vicky? What did he do to you?"

"I . . . I . . ."

"In your statement, you said it ruined your marriage. You blame Magner for everything that's gone wrong in your life. But after that night you got married, had kids. It wasn't all bad. So what are you hiding?"

"Please leave me alone," she pleaded.

"We're on your side here, Vicky. We're trying to help. But you have to tell us—"

"Please," she said, then looked to Jessie for support. "Will you please just go?"

Silent, Gilchrist collected the three mugs and carried them through to the kitchen, leaving Jessie alone with Vicky. A few minutes later, seeing Jessie standing at the kitchen door, ready to leave, arms folded, he knew he had pushed too hard.

He glanced at Vicky Kelvin as they walked into the hallway, hoping to catch some sign that she understood what he had tried to do, that he was on her side, that sometimes you have to be brutal to get to the truth.

But she just sat there with her head in her hands, shoulders heaving with misery.

12

Neither of them spoke until they were almost across the Tay Road Bridge.

"Why did you have to be so hard on her?" Jessie said.

"She wasn't telling us everything."

"She'd been raped, for crying out loud. She didn't exactly take notes about the guy's technique when he was sticking it to her. You're missing the point."

"Am I?"

"By a mile. Maybe a hundred miles."

He gritted his teeth and gripped the steering wheel. A reply seemed pointless. Maybe they were all missing the point. The entire day seemed to have been a waste of time. He had not heard from Cooper—no further PM updates. It was hardly surprising that she didn't want to talk to him after his performance on the phone last night. Still, he was the SIO in a murder investigation, and it was her responsibility to keep him up to speed.

He made a note to call her once he was back in the Office.

"What do you think?" he asked Jessie. "Wild goose chase?"

"What are we talking about?"

"Thomas Magner."

"He didn't kill the McCullochs."

"You sure about that?"

She let out a tired sigh, as if she'd had enough of his convoluted theories. Part of him felt the same way. The facts were piling up, telling him it couldn't possibly be Magner—he wasn't even in the same county, let alone the same town, when the murders took place. But his gut just wouldn't let it go.

Jessie said, "Tell me one thing that points to Magner, Andy. Anything. No matter how small. Just one thing."

"It fits," he mumbled.

"Is that it? It fits?" She shook her head. "Seriously, Andy, we can't continue with this line of inquiry. What are we achieving? Greaves'll be all over us like a rash, and so will the press if we don't come up with something soon. In the meantime, everything points *away* from Magner."

"But toward who?"

"That's the scary thing. It doesn't point toward anyone," she said, her voice rising with despair. "We've got sweet eff all and the day's almost over."

"OK," Gilchrist said. "Maybe I was wrong to put so much stock in Magner. But sometimes you have to push to the limit before you know when to back off."

"Like you did with Vicky Kelvin?"

"That's different. She wasn't telling us—"

Jessie's mobile rang, stopping their argument like an electronic referee.

She looked at the screen, muttered a curse, then made the connection. "Whatever it is, Lachie, I can't make it. OK?" But she held the mobile to her ear, strangely muted for once, listening in silence while the metallic echo of a man's voice fired at her.

She disconnected only when the echoes stopped.

Gilchrist glanced across at her. She seemed stunned, even scared. He looked back to the road ahead and waited, but Jessie sat in silence, her face to the window, as if searching for tell-tale signs of spring—she could wait a long time for these, he thought.

Just to break the silence, Gilchrist was about to call Stan when his mobile rang. He didn't recognize the number but made the connection regardless. "DCI Gilchrist."

"DI Mac Smith here, sir. You asked me to call if anything turned up."

"I'm listening."

"I thought you should hear about a turn in events. Two of the women who filed formal complaints against Magner— Eleanor McInnes and Laura Dewar—have both just retracted their statements."

Gilchrist recalled the names from their trawl through the paperwork, but his memory failed to pull up any specifics about either woman.

"Did they offer any explanation?" he asked.

"Only that they were mistaken."

"*Mistaken?*" He almost gasped. "Both of them?"

"It's strange, that's for sure."

Gilchrist's mind wrestled with what Smith had just said. *Strange* did not come close. Downright unbelievable was more like it. Someone must have persuaded both women to drop their allegations. Maybe Magner himself had gotten to them; or someone who knew him. But if that was so, and you took that logic one more step forward, with all that was happening, was it possible that whoever massacred the McCullochs also knew

Magner? If so, it pulled him right back into the center of the equation, no matter what the evidence—or lack of it—suggested.

"Do you think they were threatened?"

"Both are denying it, just saying they're having second thoughts."

"Are they saying they made it up? They were not assaulted?"

"No. Just that the assaults were not as severe as they originally claimed them to be."

"So the sex was consensual?"

"They're not saying that, sir."

"I don't get it," Gilchrist said. "They were either raped or they weren't. Do they know each other?"

"The information we have on file gives no indication that they do. But if you believe that, you believe in tooth fairies."

"Have they spoken to each other?" Gilchrist asked. "You need to check their phone records."

"With all due respect, sir, you're not my SIO."

"Sorry. Force of habit."

"We're already looking into it," Smith said. "And we'll be interviewing them again. I'll keep you posted."

As soon as DI Smith hung up, Gilchrist called Stan.

"Have Jackie run a check on two women for me—Eleanor McInnes and Laura Dewar," he said, then told Stan about Smith's call. "And see if Jackie can find something that links Magner, the McCullochs, and/or Stratheden Enterprises to one or both of them. Then have her look into their bank accounts—find out if any money's changed hands. Maybe we're dealing with a greasing of palms rather than a physical threat. You know, here's a couple of thou to drop the charges, that sort of thing."

As he ended the call, Jessie said, "You're caught up with Magner."

"He's the common denominator."

"Maybe we should stop spinning our wheels and talk to the one person who knows what he's really like."

Gilchrist frowned for a moment. "His ex-wife?"

"Right first time."

"Give Jackie a call," he said, "and get her to find out where she lives."

"A call? That'll be a bit one-sided."

"Just text her then, for crying out loud."

———

Thirty minutes later, they arrived at the North Street Office.

Jackie was in her office, seated behind her computer, crutches propped against the back wall, hair like a tangle of rusted steel wool. When she saw Gilchrist, she reached into her tray and handed him a printout of Magner's marriage certificate.

"Well done, Jackie," Gilchrist said. "What about McInnes and Dewar?" Jackie wobbled her head, and he helped her out with, "Still working on them?"

She nodded.

"Once you're done," he said, "just e-mail Jessie, Stan, and me with whatever you've got." He was about to leave the room when he heard her groan—Jackie's signal to wait a moment. He turned back to see her lift another printout from the tray.

Gilchrist took the sheet from her. "Looks like Magner's a widower," he said to Jessie, tapping the death certificate.

"Sheila Magner. Died September '85. Cause of death: heart failure from drug overdose."

"When did they get married?" Jessie asked.

"August '81."

"Only four years. And it's within the same window as the rapes." Jessie turned to Jackie. "Did Magner ever remarry?"

Jackie wobbled her head.

"So that's it? A big strapping lad in his twenties with muscles and gallons of testosterone and a sexual appetite that he feeds by raping women—"

"Allegedly."

"—and he marries only once? Let's see that other sheet."

Gilchrist handed over Magner's marriage certificate.

"Sheila Ramsay," she said. "Administrative assistant. A year older than Magner." She looked at Gilchrist. "I'd be interested to know if he got an insurance payout. Maybe that's how he started his business."

"Magner and McCulloch started Stratheden in '86," Gilchrist said. "His wife died in September '85. So if Stratheden was registered at the start of '86, the insurance money might have just come through—"

"We need to check that out."

Gilchrist turned to Jackie. "Find out if there was any life insurance on Sheila Magner. If there was, how much, when was it paid, and to whom? If it went to Magner, find out what he did with it."

Jackie scribbled on a notepad.

"Then pull Stratheden's records from Companies House. Find out from council records when they were awarded their first local-government contract and how much it was for."

Jackie looked up at Gilchrist, as if to ask, *Anything else?*

"Thanks, Jackie. That'll do for now," he said.

By the time he and Jessie reached the door, Jackie's fingers were already tapping the keyboard with the speed of a woodpecker.

———

Back out on North Street, the wind had pulled the temperature below freezing. The sky hung low, as gray as lead, and looked just as impenetrable. Spring could be months away. But at least the chill had cleared Gilchrist's hangover.

"Come on," he said. "My stomach's grumbling."

13

The Central reeked of alcohol and thrummed with the cama-raderie of a busy town pub on a late Saturday afternoon. They found a table in the corner and ordered their drinks: the usual for Gilchrist, a cup of coffee for Jessie. They faced each other in silence as the barman placed the glass and the mug on the table, then asked if they would like to see the menu.

"No need," Gilchrist said. "Steak pie, chips and beans."

"And for you, ma'am?"

"What the hell," Jessie said. "Make that two. But peas instead of beans."

Gilchrist sipped his Deuchars and watched Jessie stir her coffee. "Still trying to sober up?" he asked.

"Driving."

"Somewhere warm, I hope."

"Taking Robert to the pictures in Dundee tonight," she said. "I know, I know, Robert's deaf, but he likes to study the facial expressions of the actors." She shrugged. "Don't ask. It's all to do with his comedy writing. And besides, if he gives the film the nod of approval, then I can buy it when it comes out on DVD and he can watch it with closed captions."

Gilchrist had met Robert four times over the three months Jessie had been with Fife Constabulary. She had fought hard to raise her only child as a single mother, and he knew she would do anything for him. But as she fiddled with her mug of coffee, he sensed she had other reasons for taking him to the cinema that night.

"Jabba joining you?" he asked.

"No."

"Does he know that yet?"

Jessie lifted the coffee to her lips and rolled her eyes.

"If I could make a suggestion—"

"No, Andy, you cannot make a suggestion. It's my problem, and I'll deal with it."

At that moment Gilchrist caught movement at the swing doors that opened on to Market Street. An oversized man as wide as he was tall forced himself inside. "Well, you'd better deal with it quick, because he's just walked in."

"Bloody hell," she said. "Has he seen me?"

"He's on his way."

"I tell you, I'm going to have him for this."

Gilchrist had met Chief Super Lachlan McKellar several times before, and on each occasion he had been struck by how well dressed the man was. Marriage to a biscuit-manufacturing heiress must have helped to cover the cost of bespoke tailoring, of course, but even so, for a fat man he wore his clothes with remarkable swagger and style.

He had some difficulty squeezing past patrons ordering drinks at the bar, but he broke through and reached Gilchrist, skin glistening as if he had just stepped out of a piping-hot sauna. He placed a fat hand on Jessie's shoulder, and Gilchrist was surprised that she did not slap it off.

"Jessica," he said, "it's nice to see you again."

She tilted her head. "Give me a few minutes, Lachie, will you?"

He removed his hand. "I'll be outside," he said, then gave Gilchrist a half smile and the tiniest of nods.

Gilchrist waited until McKellar worked his way back along the bar before saying, "Is there anything you want to tell me?"

Jessie took a quick sip of coffee and returned the mug to the table. Gilchrist could not fail to catch a tremor that gripped her hand and seemed to be working its way up to her face. "I'll be back in a minute," she said, rising to her feet and following McKellar outside.

From his seat, Gilchrist watched the two of them face each other on the pavement, a couple of feet apart. Lachie lifted his hand to Jessie's cheek, as if to caress it, but she turned away. Gilchrist thought it odd that the fire in her seemed to have been dowsed, as if McKellar's sheer physical presence had suffocated—

His mobile rang. It was Cooper.

He made the connection. "Good afternoon, Becky."

"Where are you?"

"One guess."

"Are you free?"

"I can make myself available."

"I'll be with you shortly. I'll call when I'm closer."

"Any problems?" But the line was already dead. He thought of calling back and asking what was so urgent that she could not talk over the phone. Then he decided against it and returned the mobile to his pocket.

Outside, the conversation between Jessie and McKellar seemed more animated, with Jessie back to her spirited self, face flushed with anger, arms flailing. Something in the way McKellar stood—impassive, not rising to the heated bait of

Jessie's vitriol—told Gilchrist that whatever they were talking about, the big man had the upper hand. And he knew it.

Then, like a switch being flipped, Jessie turned on her heel and left him standing there.

McKellar seemed unfazed as he watched her return inside. A quick glance in Gilchrist's direction had their eyes meeting for an instant. Then he turned and strode across the cobbles, light gray overcoat flapping in the wind but not a crease in sight, black polished shoes reflecting a flicker of rare sunlight. Maybe the day was going to clear up after all.

Jessie eased back into her seat as their food arrived. She seemed unable to meet Gilchrist's gaze. Instead, she unwrapped the cutlery from the paper napkin, then wiped the knife clean with slow deliberation.

Gilchrist waited a respectful couple of mouthfuls before saying, "Cooper called. She's on her way."

"That should cheer you up."

"I was hoping she might throw some light on how Brian McCulloch died."

Jessie flashed him a look that he had difficulty deciphering, then stabbed her fork into the pie. The meat could have been as tough as gristle from the way she chewed it. Or maybe she was thinking it was McKellar's heart.

Gilchrist placed his own cutlery across his plate.

Two mouthfuls later, Jessie said, "You not eating that?"

"I'd like you to tell me what's going on."

"It's none of your business."

"If it interferes with an ongoing murder investigation, then it's very much my business."

"What's interfering? I'm here, you're here, Lachie's there, and Veronica Lake's going to join us in a few minutes, whoopity-do." She skewered another mouthful, then turned the full force of her glare on to the plate.

Gilchrist gave her another minute, then said, "I didn't like the way Chief Super McKellar talked to you."

Maybe it was the use of the formal title or the tone of his voice, but Gilchrist detected a softening in her attitude. Even so, she was not giving in lightly.

"Didn't know you had bat ears."

He smiled. "I don't lip-read, either. But Lachie seemed a bit . . . self-assured for my liking."

Jessie seemed to make a conscious effort to relax. She forked the next mouthful with care, then took a sip of water. "He's giving me a hard time."

Gilchrist held on to his beer. "In what way?"

She placed her fork and knife on her plate with resignation, then sat back and stared out the window. Maybe she was replaying the conversation with McKellar, trying to work out how she could have handled it better. Gilchrist didn't push.

After a long minute, she pulled her gaze back and said, "I suppose you'll find out eventually."

He scooped up a forkful of meat.

"You remember the resetting allegations against me?"

Gilchrist nodded. He had batted away allegations that Jessie had received goods she had known were stolen—not long after she joined Fife Constabulary. He had later learned that the allegations were true. But with the help of DCI Peter "Dainty" Small of Strathclyde HQ, they had managed to finagle Jessie out of a career-destroying situation.

"I do indeed," he said, "but we dealt with them."

"Well, Jabba's threatening to resurrect them."

"Why?"

"'Cause he can."

"If you don't do what?"

"Stop ignoring him."

"Well, that's easy enough. Answer his calls. Send him texts. Keep him sweet. He lives in Glasgow. You live in St. Andrews. The pressure of work doesn't give you time to—"

"It's not as simple as that."

"His wife?"

"Got it in one."

"He's left her? And now he wants a shoulder to cry on?"

"And the rest," she said.

Gilchrist took a mouthful of beer to encourage her to continue.

"He wants to set me up in a wee flat, he says. Well, me and Robert. So he can come up and stay over at the weekends. He's even got somewhere picked out for us, for crying out loud."

"Doesn't he know you've just moved?"

"It's not about moving. It's about control."

Gilchrist took a mouthful of chips and scooped up some beans, more to prevent himself from cursing than for epicurean pleasure.

"I told him I'd think about it."

"Sounds like he's given you an ultimatum."

Jessie nodded. "He says he needs to know by the end of the weekend."

"That's tomorrow."

"Clever you."

"What's the rush?"

"The agent's taken the property off the market to give him time to come up with the deposit. So he says."

"And if you don't agree, you'll be charged with resetting?"

"Again, it's not as simple as that. Lachie can be right sneaky."

Gilchrist read the helplessness in her eyes and could tell she was close to tears; maybe even close to giving up altogether. The echo of her words on Tentsmuir Beach the previous morning came back to him—*I sometimes struggle with it all*—and he thought he understood her dilemma. She had applied for a transfer from Strathclyde to Fife—Glasgow to St. Andrews—to escape the criminality of her own family and to end whatever relationship Lachie imagined he had with her. She had told him repeatedly that she wanted nothing more to do with him, but still he had come after her. If only they could pursue criminals with such vigor, he thought.

"So, what's he threatening to do?" he asked.

Jessie's eyes filled with tears, but she took a deep breath and wiped them away.

Then his phone rang. Cooper again. This time he scowled at the screen.

"Answer it," Jessie said. "I'm going nowhere. Not yet, anyway."

He made the connection. "Becky?"

"I'm in Market Street."

He looked out the window, his gaze scanning the passers-by, but he failed to see her.

"I'm about to step into Costa Coffee. We need to talk."

"I'm in the—"

The connection died.

Gilchrist rose to his feet.

"Problems?" Jessie asked.

He tried to make light of it by answering, "More than likely," but he knew it took a lot to ruffle Cooper's feathers, and from the tone of her voice she sounded plucked and ready for the stuffing.

He shuffled past patrons at the bar, stepped into the bitter chill of Market Street, and prepared himself for the worst.

14

Gilchrist found Cooper sitting on a sofa in the rear of the coffee shop.

She looked pale, her eyes tired, as if she had not slept, or perhaps been crying—which would be a first. He smiled as he sat opposite, and had to stifle a stab of hurt as she withdrew her hands from the table and placed them on her lap, as if defining a new boundary in their relationship, now that Mr. Cooper had returned—to claim his conjugal rights, no less.

"Have you ordered?" he asked.

She shook her head.

"Would you like something?"

Another shake of the head. Her hair was tied back in a tight bun that accentuated the blue sharpness of her eyes, the sculpted lines of her cheekbones. In an artistic sense, the look suited her. But he preferred loose curls, if ever asked.

Silent, he waited.

"I hate him," she said at length.

"So leave him."

"I wish it were that simple."

If only his own marriage had proved so difficult to terminate. An image of Gail in tears, storming from the marital
home, tugging Maureen and Jack behind her, arced across his
mind with a ferocity that caused him to blink. It took the
recollection of the front door slamming before he managed
to chase the picture away.

"It's as simple as you want it to be," he tried.

"You don't know anything about my relationship with
Maxwell," she snapped, "so please don't pretend that you do."

Well, there he had it. Back only one day and already
Mr. Cooper elevated to Maxwell. Did that mean her marriage
had entered a new phase? Or was she simply personalizing
her husband to distance herself from her forlorn lover? The
ensuing silence had Gilchrist thinking that the short outburst
had drained her.

"Ending my own marriage was painful," he said at length.
"But looking back, I only wonder why it took us so long to
reach the point of no return."

"I'll have that coffee now," she said. "Espresso. Hot milk
on the side."

At the counter, he contemplated texting Jessie to tell her
he would meet her later. But the way Cooper was behaving,
she could be on her way home to Maxwell before he even
delivered her espresso. When he returned with the tray, the
sofa was empty. For a moment he thought she had indeed
left, but then he noticed her jacket and scarf draped over
the arm. He laid the tray on the table, espresso and milk
in its center, and lifted his own latte. Better to share time
over a coffee, he thought, than to have her thinking she was
preventing him from returning to the Central to finish his
pint. Which had him puzzling why she had not wanted to
meet him there—they could even call it their local. Maybe

she had seen him inside with Jessie and felt a need to talk to him in private.

Movement at the back door caught his attention, and he was surprised to see Cooper pushing it open, mobile still in hand. Without a word, she reclaimed her seat and stared at her coffee. He thought of pouring the milk for her, then realized he didn't know how she took espresso. Until then, she had always ordered a latte with no sugar, the way he liked it.

Had she done that just to make it easy for him?

He reached for the milk jug. "Shall I play Mum?"

She said nothing as he poured and stirred. Then he sat back and lifted his latte to his lips. Cooper reached for her drink with both hands, her fingers squeezing the cup tight.

"Maxwell's going to talk to Greaves," she said, then took a sip.

"About what?"

"Come on, Andy, don't play dumb."

"Is he going to confess that he has marital problems?"

"You have this extremely irritating way of talking in questions."

"So what do you want me to ask?"

She glared at him, and for the first time since she had taken over from Bert Mackie as head of forensic pathology at Dundee University, he saw how formidable an opponent she could be. He had always believed that Mr. Cooper—man of the world, philanderer about town and overseas—gave out more than he got in that marriage. Now he was not so sure.

"OK. Tell me why you're worried about your husband talking to Chief Super Greaves."

"You don't know Maxwell," she said. "He doesn't do half measures."

Gilchrist was unsure what she meant by that but found himself reluctant to ask. "I'm already in Greaves's bad books," he said. "And I don't see me getting out of them any time soon."

"No. But *I* could lose my job."

"Ah." Now they were getting down to it. Nothing to do with what Greaves might say to Gilchrist but everything to do with how his affair with a married woman, Fife's foremost forensic pathologist, might have an impact on *her* career. Rather than rising to the bait, he decided to be awkward. "I could lose mine, too."

"After what you've got away with in the past?" Her lips creased into a wry smile, and she took another sip of coffee.

He waited until she returned the cup to the table before saying, "What are you not telling me, Becky?"

She hesitated for a moment, then said, "Nothing."

"Now who's acting dumb?"

Her eyes flared, making him think she was about to storm out. But she reached for her coffee again, clutching the cup with both hands as if seeking warmth. Well, it was chilly outside.

"Would you like another one?" he asked.

She shook her head, an act that looked strange without the benefit of long hair. He missed her curls and fought off the oddest urge to reach out and undo her bun. "One's enough," she replied. "I'll be twitching all evening if I have two of these."

He returned her smile, placed his hand palm upward on the table, but she still refused to reciprocate. He said nothing as she sipped her coffee and avoided his eye. He was starting to wonder why she had asked to meet him at all. For all she had said, a text message would have done just as well. The stalemate was broken by a call to his mobile. He removed it from his pocket, glanced at the screen—Stan—and rose to his feet.

"I'll take this out the back," he told her, but Cooper seemed uninterested, or perhaps resigned to perpetual interference from others.

Outside, Gilchrist tugged up his collar to ward off a gust of bitter wind.

"Does the name Jerry McGovern mean anything to you, boss?"

Gilchrist struggled to make a connection. "Any relation to Malky McGovern?"

"They're brothers."

"I'm listening."

"Malky was killed in a car accident on the A85 ten days ago, just outside Crieff."

Gilchrist pulled up a faint memory of something on the news—the TV camera zooming in on a mangled pile of metal that had once been a car. Then he realized Stan was waiting for him to say something. "Did they find anything in his car?"

"Driving license. Wallet in the center console. Files in the boot."

"*Files?* What kind of files?"

"Photographs," Stan said. "Lots of them. And we're not talking happy families here."

Electricity trickled the length of Gilchrist's spine. "What *are* we talking, then?"

"Young women having sex, giving blow jobs, getting licked—"

"Any way to ID them?"

"No chance, boss. Their faces have been blanked out."

"Inked out, you mean?"

"Pixelated is the technical term."

Gilchrist felt a surge of interest. He was beginning to understand why Stan had called. "So they're printouts from a computer, is what you're telling me."

"They are indeed. And this is where it gets interesting."

Gilchrist glanced back into the coffee shop and felt a flutter of confusion at Cooper's empty sofa.

"When the police contacted Jerry as Malky's only next of kin, they thought he seemed nervous. Not how you would expect a seasoned criminal to behave."

Gilchrist pushed through the door, eyes on the abandoned sofa—no jacket and scarf this time—then strode past it. He glanced at the counter, the main door, the seats at the window, through the glass to the street beyond.

No sign of Cooper.

"With Jerry acting like he was hiding something, the SIO applied for a search warrant, and yesterday they went over and confiscated his computers."

Gilchrist had worked his way through the coffee shop. He stepped into Market Street, but Cooper was nowhere in sight. "I'm listening," he said, scanning the thoroughfare, searching the pavements. But it seemed as if Cooper had just up and left.

"Well, in the process, they discovered some of Amy McCulloch's jewelry."

"What?" Gilchrist stopped in his tracks.

"Matching necklaces and earrings, that sort of stuff."

Gilchrist started walking again, faster now. He strode across College Street, heading back to the Central. "Had the McCullochs reported the items as stolen?"

"No. McGovern just came clean. Eager to get it off his chest, by all accounts. He served four years in Barlinnie for serious assault, which could have been murder if the victim hadn't survived. What do you think, boss? Think he might be involved in the massacre?"

"Serious assault's different from gutting, skinning, and decapitating," Gilchrist said. "No, Jerry's just shitting himself in case he gets mixed up in it." He gave it some thought, then said, "So how did he come by the jewelry?"

"Said he'd been staking out the mansion for a couple of weeks, boss, and broke in on Thursday morning."

"Jesus, Stan," Gilchrist gasped. "Was this before the family was massacred?"

"That's what he's saying. The house was empty."

"Where is he now?"

"Glenrothes Police Station."

Gilchrist reached the Central, rapped his knuckles on the window, loud enough for several heads to turn his way and the barman to frown at him.

Jessie heard, too, and jerked in surprise.

Let's go, he mouthed to her, then turned away.

"How long's McGovern been there, Stan?"

"Since last night."

"And when did they make the connection with the jewelry?"

"This morning. When he was interviewed."

Jessie interrupted with, "This must be serious. You've still got a pint to finish."

Gilchrist nodded for her to follow, and they entered College Street. "Call Whyte," he said to Stan, "and tell him we're on our way to talk to McGovern."

"I'll do what I can, boss."

"I'm talking to McGovern with or without Whyte's approval," Gilchrist said, and ended the call.

"Something I need to know?" Jessie said.

"I'll explain in the car."

Jessie had her mobile out. "Here, listen to this from Jackie." She read from the screen. "Confirm Magner married twice. Still married, question mark. PO in office."

Gilchrist stuffed his hands into his pockets to ward off the stiff wind. "PO?"

"Printout, I think."

"So, she's found another marriage certificate. Did she find any divorce papers?"

"I guess not. Nor a death certificate. Hence the question mark."

"When did you receive that text?"

"Just opened it."

Gilchrist tried to recall their interrogation of Magner, but could not remember asking if he was married. "Let's see what Jackie's got," he said. "Then we'll head to Glenrothes."

15

The door to Jackie's office was closed, her seat vacated, her computer switched off, and no crutches in sight. It was Saturday afternoon, after all, and civilian staff were less compelled to work overtime than members of the Force.

Gilchrist found the printout on Jackie's desk with an attached Post-it, on which was scribbled FAO: DS Janes. He picked it up. "Anne Mills," he said. "Married in February '86, round about the time Magner started Stratheden—"

"And within six months of his first wife dying," Jessie reminded him, as she fingered through more papers on Jackie's desk. "Anything here that tells us where she's living now?"

"Text Jackie back and find out." He headed to the door. "Come on," he said. "I'm in just the mood to tackle a piece of shite."

———

Once on the A92, Gilchrist called the Glenrothes Office and informed the duty officer they were on their way to interview

Jerry McGovern. He expected an interview room to be made available.

Arrangements made, he turned to Jessie. "We were talking in the Central," he said. "Where were we?"

"Can't remember."

From the way Jessie was staring at the passing countryside, Gilchrist knew she was regretting opening up to him about her relationship with Jabba, albeit for only a few minutes. Still, a bit of reluctance had never stood in his way.

"Chief Super Lachie McKellar," he said. "More commonly known as Jabba the Hutt. As fat and as annoying as they come. He wants to set you and Robert up in a flat in town so he can visit the Fife coast every other weekend for a little bit of domestic life—"

"Domestic life my arse," Jessie snapped. "Try domestic abuse. And it won't be me taking it."

"Ouch."

"Look, I don't want to talk about it," Jessie said.

"I think you need to air any issues you—"

"Please, Andy. Can we just leave it?"

Gilchrist tightened his grip on the steering wheel and concentrated on the road ahead.

By the time they arrived at Glenrothes, dusk was settling.

———

Jerry McGovern was already in interview room 2. He looked frail compared to Gilchrist's recollection of his brother, Malky, with bedraggled hair and a lantern jaw that aged him by at least ten years. He looked as if he had lived all of his life in the shadow of a bigger, older brother. Or maybe he was just the runt of the litter.

By his side sat a young woman, no more than thirty, Gilchrist guessed, with spiked blonde hair and black-rimmed designer glasses. She stood and held out her hand.

Gilchrist ignored it and took his seat without a word. Jessie did likewise. He switched on the recorder and formally introduced himself and Jessie, stated date and time, and added that they were interviewing Jerry McGovern with respect to the deaths of the McCulloch family. He then confirmed that Mr. McGovern was accompanied by his solicitor, at which point he looked across at the young woman.

"Ali McCrae," she said, "R. K. Leith & Associates, Dundee." She handed Gilchrist her card and slid another across the table to Jessie.

Gilchrist faced McGovern. "You've confessed to stealing jewelry," he said.

McGovern nodded. "That's all I done. I didnae kill anyone—"

"Just answer the questions one at a time," Gilchrist said.

McGovern pursed his lips, lowered his head. He could be a scolded child.

McCrae leaned forward. "My client has categorically denied any involvement in the murder of the—"

"So, he says," Jessie interrupted. "What else does he say?"

McCrae frowned. "Haven't you read his statement?"

"We're not interested in his statement. We're here to ask him—"

"We've already been through this."

"*This?*" Gilchrist said.

"My client's whereabouts on the night in question."

"And which night was that?"

"Please tell me you're not serious."

Gilchrist sat back in his chair and eyed McCrae. Anger and incredulity seemed to lift off her like heat from rock. "I'm serious," he said.

"If that were true, you would've made sure you knew all the facts before—"

"If we knew all the facts," Jessie cut in, her Glasgow accent as heavy as a punch to the gut, "we wouldn't be here asking questions, would we?"

McCrae glared at her for a long moment, then slumped back in her seat.

Jessie turned to McGovern. "Why don't you tell us where you were on Thursday evening?"

"I have to instruct my client not to answer—"

"On what grounds?" Jessie snapped.

"On the grounds that he has already supplied the police with—"

"You worried he might incriminate himself this time?"

"That's ridiculous."

"Mr. McGovern," Gilchrist interrupted. "I have to tell you that even though your solicitor will assure you that she is protecting your rights, she is doing you no favors at all here."

McCrae slapped her pen onto the table. "I've heard it all now."

"Do you understand?" Gilchrist asked him.

"Don't answer that."

McGovern swallowed, a hard dunking of his Adam's apple. When McCrae reached for his arm, he shrugged her off. "I've done nothing wrong," he said.

"Since when has stealing jewelry been legal?" Jessie asked.

"Aye, OK. But I've no killed nobody."

"Once again, my client denies any involvement in—"

"I've nothing to be afraid of," McGovern interrupted.

"You've plenty to be—"

"You're no listening to me," McGovern snapped at McCrae, who seemed surprised by his angry tone.

"Jerry," she said, "you need to—"

"Shut it, yeah?"

McCrae's eyes sparked with fury. "Look," she said, "you've—"

"Look nothing. I want to clear my name."

Give McCrae her due. She dropped the aggressive tone as easily as casting off a coat and said, "Fine. I'll take notes, Jerry." She raised her hand to ward off any complaint. "And I won't say another word, I promise. OK?" She could have been speaking to a temperamental child.

McGovern glanced at Gilchrist, then Jessie, then back to Gilchrist, and nodded.

Gilchrist was about to speak when McCrae reached for the recorder and switched it off. "I'm going to listen very carefully to everything you two ask my client. Be warned, I will take this further if I consider—"

"Where do you get off?" snarled Jessie, and switched the recorder back on. "Right," she said to McGovern. "For the record, you have instructed your solicitor not to intervene on your behalf. Is that correct?"

McGovern nodded.

"Please speak for the record," Jessie said.

"That's correct."

Gilchrist caught McGovern's nervous glance at McCrae and realized that the man was more frightened of his solicitor than he was of the police. As long as McCrae was in the interview room, Gilchrist doubted that McGovern would open up to them. So he said, "Would you like your solicitor to leave?"

"Now wait just a minute."

"I'm not speaking to you, Ms. McCrae," Gilchrist said. "But I'll repeat the question for your client." He waited a couple of beats, then said, "Would you like your solicitor to leave the room?"

A sullen shrug.

"Please speak for the record."

"Aye," McGovern said, shifting on his seat, as if distancing himself a crucial inch or two from McCrae.

"And, in the absence of legal assistance, would you like to continue with the interview?"

"I would."

"I can't recommend this, Jerry. You're making a big mistake."

McGovern cast another nervous glance in her direction, as if fearful that holding her gaze might petrify him. "You can listen to the recording," he said, then looked at Gilchrist. "She can, can't she?"

Gilchrist nodded. "She can."

"But by then you might have dug a hole too deep for me to be able to help you."

"I'll take my chances."

"It's your life." McCrae pushed to her feet and walked to the door.

Jessie lifted her business card and said, "Ali McCrae of R. K. Leith & Associates is now leaving the interview room." She glanced at the wall clock and confirmed the time.

McCrae left with a parting scowl at Jessie.

When the door closed, McGovern's eyes darted left and right, as if expecting McCrae to pop out of thin air and frighten him. Or maybe he was just a scared kind of guy, not someone capable of killing an entire family. But psychopaths rarely fit preconceived ideas of how they should behave, so Gilchrist knew he still had to tread with care.

"Where were you on Thursday night?" he asked McGovern.

"At home."

"Anybody with you?"

"No."

"Did you steal jewelry from the McCullochs' house?"

"Yes. But that's all I done. I didnae kill anyone."

Gilchrist folded his arms and sat back. "Talk us through it, Jerry."

Neither he nor Jessie said a word as McGovern explained that he had staked out the McCullochs' home off and on over a three-week period, noted who came and went, what time Brian McCulloch went to work, when Amy took the children to school, when they came home.

"All by yourself?" Jessie asked.

McGovern gave a tic for a glance, and Gilchrist knew the next words out of his mouth would be a lie. "Me and Malky."

Gilchrist watched McGovern's eyes dance after the lie. Roping in his dead brother was as good a way as any to cover up the involvement of others. "Malky's been dead for a wee while," Gilchrist said to him. "So I guess you did it all by yourself last week?"

McGovern nodded, a tad unsure. "Aye."

"So, why Thursday morning?" Gilchrist pressed.

"The cleaner works Mondays and Fridays."

"Which made Thursday morning the best time to break in?"

McGovern squeezed his hands together. "Look. I know youse dinnae believe me. But I swear I just done the house when she was out shopping. It's what she does—"

"Shopping?" Jessie asked.

"Aye. She shops a lot."

"How do you know she went shopping? You were staking out the house. She could have gone anywhere. Did you follow her?"

"No."

"Yet you knew she'd gone to the shops. So someone must have followed her."

Gilchrist watched confusion shift over McGovern's face like an illness. The man was truly torn. He could tell the truth and drop one or more of his thieving associates in the shit, or dig himself a deeper hole out of which his spiky-haired solicitor might not be able to pull him.

Gilchrist decided to offer a hand. "Would the others cover for you, Jerry, if they were in this situation?"

Jessie chipped in: "You owe them no favors, Jerry. None at all."

Still McGovern squirmed, said nothing; then Gilchrist thought he saw it.

"Who shifts the stuff for you?" he asked.

McGovern's eyes jumped.

Gilchrist waited a couple of beats. "He's let you down, hasn't he?"

McGovern tightened his lips.

"When your fence heard about the McCulloch murders, he didn't want to touch the stuff with a barge pole. And now he's dropped you right in it."

McGovern closed his eyes, and a high keening sound filled the room as he rocked back and forth. Tears rolled down his cheeks, giving life to another possibility. Gilchrist raised a hand to silence Jessie and waited until the keening subsided to a steady sobbing.

"What did you see, Jerry?"

McGovern's nostrils flared. He shook his head.

"You must have seen something, Jerry, to get yourself into such a state."

"Nothing," he gasped, his eyes wide open now. "I swear I seen nothing."

"You broke in on Thursday morning, when Mrs. McCulloch was out shopping?"

"Aye."

"And what about Mr. McCulloch?"

"I never seen him. He's away early and always comes back late at night."

"And we estimate the family were killed on Thursday afternoon, when the girls came back from school."

"I wouldnae know."

"Who's your fence?" Gilchrist asked, hoping the change of tack might trip up McGovern.

"I cannae tell you. I'll never get nothing sold again," he said—an open admission that he intended to continue stealing for a living.

And Gilchrist wondered that if McGovern had children, would he bring them into the family business, let them take over when he retired?

It didn't bear thinking about.

He pushed his chair back. "When you remember, Jerry, give me a call, OK?"

McGovern stared at Gilchrist, an unspoken question in his eyes.

"I believe you," Gilchrist said. "I'm sure you had nothing to do with the McCulloch murders." He paused.

McGovern twisted his hands, his rough calluses rasping like sand for soap, but he offered nothing.

Gilchrist stood.

Jessie said, "Interview terminated at six-twenty-one." She switched off the recorder.

Gilchrist removed a business card from his wallet, leaned forward, and slipped it into McGovern's shirt pocket. "If you can help us in any way, Jerry"—he paused until McGovern looked up at him—"I'd be grateful."

Silent, McGovern lowered his eyes.

16

Jessie spent much of the return drive to Andrews texting Robert or staring out the window.

"You see anything interesting?" Gilchrist asked.

"Just thinking."

"Has Robert written any new jokes lately?" he tried.

Even that failed to bring a smile to her face. "None that would interest you."

Well, there he had it—leave her alone.

It was almost seven o'clock by the time they passed the Old Course Hotel. "I'm going to check the in-tray," he said, "then have a pint. Interested?"

"I'm taking Robert to the movies, remember?" she said, and offered a wry smile. "If you're happy to give me the time off, that is."

They were involved in one of the biggest murder cases in Fife's history, and all hands were needed. But his staff were only human, and time away from the investigation could be just as important as cranking up the gears. Relaxation helped clear minds, focus concentration. The occasional pint helped, too.

He turned right at the City Road roundabout and drove straight to Canongate.

He pulled up outside Jessie's house. "Enjoy the movies. I'll be in touch," he said, his reminder not to switch off her mobile.

Jessie opened the door.

"Before you go?"

She stopped, half in, half out. "Yeah?"

"I can't help if I don't know what the problem is."

She held his gaze for two, maybe three seconds, then slipped from the car. Before closing the door, she said, "Later, Andy. OK?"

Gilchrist watched her walk up the driveway, past her Fiat— a car Jabba had helped her buy—and waited until she had the house key in her hand before he drove off.

In Bridge Street, he took out his mobile.

His call was answered on the third ring with, "Small speaking."

"Dainty. Andy Gilchrist here. Got a minute?"

"If it's quick."

Gilchrist smiled. Some things never changed. And DCI Peter "Dainty" Small of Strathclyde Police was one of them. Straight to the point. No messing.

"What can you tell me about Chief Superintendent Lachlan McKellar?" Gilchrist asked.

A hissed, "Fuck sake." Then, "What's he been up to now?"

"He's giving Jessie Janes a hard time."

"Be careful with him, Andy. I mean it. He's not someone you want to mess with. I know all about Jessie's reasons for transferring from Strathclyde. And I don't blame her. But walking on eggshells around Chief Super McKellar doesn't cut it. You burn your bridges with him, there's no coming back."

Gilchrist noted the use of Jabba's formal title. Not like Dainty to show uncalled-for deference. "If it was only personal harassment," Gilchrist said, "I wouldn't trouble you at all. I've been working with Jessie long enough to know she could handle that. But he's threatening to resurrect some . . . for want of a better term . . . past mistakes, if she doesn't come across with the goods."

"Fuck sake," Dainty repeated. "Jessie's a good cop. But with the baggage she's got with that fucking family of hers, the last thing she needs is to be hounded by some borderline-psycho cop."

Gilchrist felt his eyebrows lift. *Borderline psycho?*

"So, what's he threatening?" Dainty asked, his voice all business once more.

"Remember the resetting charge that reared up last Christmas?"

"We took care of that," Dainty said.

"McKellar's threatening to resurrect it."

"How?"

"I think the question is why."

"I know why. I want to know how he's going to do it. Has he got anything new on her? I buried the reports, remember? There are no witnesses. McKellar would need to find some, or come up with some new charges, and I don't see either of them happening."

"Could he fabricate something?"

"He could fabricate what the fuck he likes, but with no witnesses, or no one to come forward and talk against Jessie, he's on a loser."

An image of Jessie facing McKellar on Market Street lurched into Gilchrist's mind, and he wondered if he had overestimated the fat man's confidence. "Let me get back to you," he said, and ended the call.

———

Back in the Office, Gilchrist's mobile rang—a number he did not recognize.

He made the connection.

"DI Smith here, sir. Sorry to trouble you again, but I thought you should know that they're dropping like flies."

Gilchrist understood immediately. "Who is it this time?"

"Abbott, Warren, and Williamson. All by phone again."

"Reasons?"

"More or less the same. Jenna Abbott said she didn't want to go to court or even give her testimony anonymously."

"Did she say why?"

"Change of heart."

"So she's not saying the incident never happened?"

"But it's the same result."

"Go on."

"Kristie Warren withdrew her complaint, citing personal reasons. When challenged, she denied ever knowing Magner or being in his company."

Gilchrist exhaled. Someone was getting to them. "Has anyone spoken to them face-to-face?"

"We're doing that right now, sir."

"You gave me three names."

"Meredith Williamson. She called about an hour ago, in tears, to say she couldn't go through with it. Said she made a mistake."

"In her statement?"

"Said she made it all up. When she was advised that she could be charged with wasting police time, she said we should go ahead and charge her, then hung up."

"Christ," Gilchrist said. "So that's five now. How about the others?"

"Chief Super Whyte has already dispatched uniforms to interview them."

"Three live in England."

"They do, sir, yes. The chief has contacted the local stations for assistance."

Gilchrist gritted his teeth. Whyte's case against Magner was crumbling. How long would it take for the others to fold? He thought back to Vicky Kelvin's flat—the domestic disarray, the poverty, the hardship, life in general just grinding her down. It would not take much to persuade her to drop her complaint— a thousand pounds would go a long way to clearing up the mess in her life. Gilchrist thanked Smith and ended the call.

Sitting at his desk, he fired up the computer and checked his e-mails. Only when he read the last of them did he realize he had not heard back from Cooper. He checked his phone for missed calls—none—then dialed her mobile number.

After five rings he was expecting voicemail to kick in when a man's voice said, "You need to stop calling my wife."

"You need to stop answering her phone."

"Who the hell do you think you are?"

"I'm the senior investigating officer in charge of a multiple murder investigation," Gilchrist snapped. "And if you don't put me through to Dr. Rebecca Cooper *immediately*, I will have you charged with obstructing the course of justice."

The connection died.

Gilchrist dialed the number again. This time the phone was answered on the first ring.

"Andy, this is not a good time—"

"I haven't received any toxicology results yet," he said.

"I thought we . . . oh," Cooper said. "OK. Let me get them over to you."

"What can I expect?" he said. "In terms of the results, I mean."

But Cooper was in no mood for jokes and answered with, "Brian McCulloch had high levels of alcohol and benzodiazepine in his blood."

"Sufficient to kill him?"

"No, but enough to induce a state of unconsciousness."

"So he was not expected to drive home."

"That's one way of putting it."

"Any other way?"

"Suicide?"

Gilchrist grimaced. An image of the bloodied bathroom, the stripped meat that had once been Amy McCulloch, contradicted his image of her killer—McCulloch's pristine shirt collar, laundered suit, trim fingernails, neat haircut. He would have needed steam-cleaning before taking his life. And the SOCOs had found no towels or body parts in the Jag's boot. If McCulloch had not murdered his family, why would he have committed suicide?

Which brought Gilchrist full circle.

"Get those reports to me as soon as you can," he said, and ended the call.

Forcing Cooper from his mind, he returned his attention to the computer screen and opened the first e-mail from Jackie. It contained several PDF attachments. He clicked on one to reveal a copy of a Prudential life insurance policy for £250,000, with the beneficiary named as Thomas Magner in the event of the death of his wife, Sheila. Next a copy of a check for £250,000 made out to Thomas Magner and dated April 26, 1986—ample start-up capital to launch Stratheden Enterprises and to entice Brian McCulloch to join the company.

The next attachment was a Royal Bank of Scotland bank statement in the name of Anne Magner. Gilchrist frowned as his gaze rested on the £250,000 deposit for April 26, 1986, highlighted by Jackie. Magner must have transferred his first wife's insurance payout into his second wife's bank account the instant he received it. A quick flip through the following pages confirmed that a total of £265,433.47 was then withdrawn from Anne Magner's account over two weeks, to pay various vendors. A closer study revealed £47,405.83 paid to the Clydesdale Bank, and £125,000—the largest debit—to Property Management Ltd., a well-known mortgage broker in Fife at the time. One other debit stood out—£50,000—not only because it was such a round sum but also because it was a cash withdrawal.

The statements showed Magner to be not only a wealthy businessman but also a shifter of money, a facilitator of funds, someone who paid by cash, robbing his left hand to pay his right—including laundering dirty money? That thought conjured up an image of Jerry McGovern, and it struck him that he never asked Stan the value of Amy McCulloch's stolen jewelry.

He e-mailed Jackie, instructing her to find out what she could about the payments to Clydesdale Bank and Property Management. Then he opened her next e-mail, and felt a frisson of excitement. Magner's second wife, Anne, was still alive and living in Greenock on the south bank of the Clyde, west of Glasgow. He took a note of the address and slipped it into his pocket as his mobile rang. He looked at the screen—Greaves.

"Yes, sir," Gilchrist said.

"Where are you?"

"In the Office."

"Stay there. I'll be with you in five minutes."

Gilchrist disconnected as his mind powered into overdrive.

He had seen Greaves on the hunt before, as mad as a bull.

Maybe Maxwell Cooper had a greater reach than Gilchrist had given him credit for.

17

Gilchrist's mobile rang again, and an unfamiliar number flashed up.

He made the connection with, "Gilchrist."

"Billy Whyte here. Did Mac speak to you?"

For a moment, the first name threw Gilchrist; then he placed it—DI Smith. "He did."

"Then you'll be pleased to know we've found a connection. With the shit getting flushed down the toilet, we sent uniforms to the remaining six addresses and got a hit."

Gilchrist jerked alert. "Who is it?"

"Charlotte Renwick."

"The woman who insisted on anonymity?"

"Yes. Well, Amy Charlotte Renwick was Amy McCulloch's full maiden name."

Something cold and hard hit Gilchrist's chest. "Jesus . . ."

"Indeed," Whyte said. "When she filed her complaint, she said she had too much to lose for her past to come out. Part of her attempt to maintain anonymity was to give her sister's address in Perth. Her sister—Siobhan Renwick—never married, so Renwick was on the Council Tax records, and the phone number was registered under that name—"

"Which helps explain why no one picked up on it during investigation of the complaint."

"Exactly," Whyte said. "Although I'll be looking into that. It's not good enough."

"So did Amy/Charlotte claim she was sexually abused by Magner?"

"She did."

"Details?"

"Forcible rape, like all the others."

"And she kept this from her husband?"

"She must have, I'd say."

"What about the others?" Gilchrist asked. "Are they still pressing forward?"

"You tell me."

Gilchrist was puzzled by Whyte's comment and did not miss the chill in his voice. He did not have to wait long for an answer.

"You visited Vicky Kelvin," Whyte said. "Didn't you read her statement?"

"Curiosity got the better of me, Billy. But before we get into a personal battle, as Amy was murdered, and the others are dropping like flies, have you given consideration to providing protection—"

"What the fuck d'you think we've been doing?"

"I'm thinking of Vicky. She was the first to come forward, the instigator—"

"Listen, Andy, I've been more than fair with you, but don't go working behind my back. We're meant to be on the same side here."

Gilchrist pushed back his chair and closed the door. Then he turned to the window and almost cursed as he saw Greaves reversing his Hyundai into his reserved space in the Office car park below.

"How many sisters did Amy McCulloch have?" Gilchrist asked.

"Two. Why?"

"Siobhan Renwick and Janice Meechan."

"Yes."

"Any brothers?"

"No," Whyte said.

Outside, Greaves slammed his car door hard enough for the sound to reach Gilchrist. He turned from the window. "I haven't had this confirmed yet," he said, "but rumor has it that Meechan and Magner have been having an affair since late last year."

Whyte remained silent for several seconds, as if thinking through the possibilities. "That could be significant," he said at length. "The timing, I mean. Vicky Kelvin filed her complaint against Magner in January, but she'd been digging around for months beforehand."

Gilchrist smiled at Whyte's logic and cocked his head at the sound of a door slamming on the floor below, its hard echo reverberating along the empty corridor.

"Have you interviewed Janice Meechan yet?" Whyte asked him.

"Not personally. But DI Davidson did."

"What's his take?"

"She denied it at first but caved in the end."

"Did Magner ever assault her?"

"She didn't say."

"I'd like to talk to DI Davidson."

Gilchrist's door burst open, and Greaves pointed at him. "You. My office. Now."

Gilchrist cupped his hand over the mouthpiece and nodded. "I said *now.*"

Gilchrist turned to the window. "Can Stan reach you at this number?" he asked.

"Yep. Sounds like you've got company," Whyte said.

"Regrettably. Let me know how you get on," Gilchrist said, as the echo of another door slamming reverberated along the corridor.

Gilchrist killed the call. For one tempting moment, he contemplated just walking from the building, letting Greaves stew in his office. But the dragon would have to be faced at some point, so why not now?

He knocked on Greaves's door and pushed it open. "You wanted to see me, sir?"

Greaves stopped pacing behind his desk and stared at Gilchrist as if his question were a personal insult. "Close the door."

Gilchrist stepped into the office, the door shutting behind him with a firm click.

"I don't intend to beat about the bush," Greaves said. "Have you been screwing Maxwell Cooper's wife behind his back?"

Gilchrist raised his eyebrows. "I wouldn't put it that way, sir. I'd say I've been seeing Dr. Cooper, and yes, we've been sleeping together. But certainly not behind Maxwell Cooper's back. He's been out of the country for the last several months."

"For God's sake, man. Don't twist my words. Do you know who he is?"

"Dr. Cooper's husband."

Something seemed to settle behind Greaves's eyes at that moment—the realization that a less senior officer was making a fool of him. His lips quivered, as if undecided whether to scream or say nothing. They seemed to choose the latter, for he looked down at his desk, pulled out his chair, and sat down.

Then he glared at Gilchrist. "Sit."

Gilchrist obliged, taking one of the two chairs in front of the desk. For some strange reason, he almost felt sorry for Greaves, although prudence warned him to listen rather than offer sympathy. Greaves watched him with tight eyes that must surely hurt, and for a moment Gilchrist wondered if the man was just hungover.

"How long's it been going on?" Greaves said.

"What did Cooper say?"

"That you've been screwing his wife since Christmas."

"His exact words?"

"But with more venom."

"Which year?"

Greaves froze, except for his eyes, which danced in their sockets. "I'm in no mood for any of your lip, Andy. This is bloody serious."

"Why?"

Greaves glared, as if stunned. "*Why?*"

"Yes, Tom, why is my personal life anyone's concern—"

"You're the SIO in the biggest murder investigation to hit Fife since the Stabber, for crying out loud. Jesus Christ, Andy, we can't afford to have the press picking up on the fact that you're fucking around on the side, instead of working your bloody arse off."

"*Fact?*" Gilchrist pressed his hands on the desk. "The only people who know any facts about my relationship with Rebecca Cooper are the two of us." He sat back. "And that includes her husband."

Greaves stared hard. "He's had you followed."

"So he says."

"You don't believe him?"

"Do you?"

Greaves seemed about to explode.

Gilchrist tried to lower the temperature by saying, "I don't give a toss about Maxwell Cooper. And I couldn't care less about the papers. They print what they like anyway."

"Quite."

"And rest assured, Tom, that my personal life is just that. *Personal*. I don't go around kissing in public."

"Holding hands, then?"

"Too old for that," Gilchrist said, but a flurry of anxiety fluttered through him.

When Cooper and he first became involved, showing affection in public had been of no concern. Mr. Cooper had fled the matrimonial home, while Becky was toying with the idea of divorce. Then, as if in some silent joint New Year's resolution, they made a subconscious decision to refrain from affection in the open, for professional appearances. It now worried Gilchrist that if Mr. Cooper had known of his wife's affair since Christmas, then it was indeed possible that evidence of the pair of them cuddling up to each other did exist.

"You've been seen together in public," Greaves told him.

"We work together in public."

"In restaurants?"

"We have to eat," Gilchrist said.

Greaves pursed his lips.

"And I can assure you, Tom, that we've never ripped off the tablecloth and gone for it," he added, although it did trouble him that in the early days of their affair, they used to have the occasional grope under the table. He tried to reassure himself that they had always been discreet, but with alcohol involved you could never be sure.

"Do you intend to continue?" Greaves asked, one gentleman inquiring of infidelities of the other.

"Whatever I decide to do will not affect the investigation in any way, sir. Unless you plan to suspend me *again*."

Greaves flinched at the emphasis, then gave a tiny shake of his head.

Gilchrist had the best investigation record in the country. And ACC McVicar liked to make others aware that his blue-eyed boy was second to none. Greaves would not dare suspend him from such a high-profile case over something like this. He was just flexing his muscles, reminding Gilchrist who was boss.

So Gilchrist pressed on. "The investigation is making significant progress, with or without me screwing Cooper's wife on the side."

Greaves seemed to welcome the invitation to change the topic, if only for a moment. "So there's some good news?"

"It's early days."

Greaves nodded, temper on hold for the moment. "How the hell do we keep this out of the papers, Andy?"

"Don't tell them."

"Do come along. You know better than that. They'll find out everything. They always do."

Gilchrist waited several seconds, then said, "You've never told me, Tom, how you heard about Rebecca and me."

"Maxwell phoned."

"So you know each other?"

"That's really none of your business, Andy. But since you ask, yes, we golf together from time to time."

"Well, it seems to me that the simplest way to keep this out of the papers is for you to tell your golfing buddy to keep his mouth shut."

"It's not as simple as that."

"It's as simple as you want to make it."

Greaves returned Gilchrist's stare with a look that could chill blood; then he slapped a hand on his desk. "Oh, for fuck's sake, just get out of here and get on with it."

Gilchrist pushed his chair back and stood.

"And stay away from Cooper's wife," Greaves ordered.

"You're forgetting she's the forensic pathologist on my investigation."

"You're doing it again. Twisting my words. End it, Andy."

"Got it," Gilchrist snapped.

Greaves smiled up at him, as if at last seeing the funny side of an awkward situation. "You always seem to walk on thin ice, Andy. McVicar's on the phone to me four times a day, and I keep telling him you're on top of it." He shook his head, as if at the absurdity of the conversation. "As far as I can make out, the only thing you've been on top of is Cooper's wife."

"Cooper's wife has a name," Gilchrist said, struggling to quell a surge of anger that fired with a ferocity that troubled him. "And *Rebecca* doesn't need to see her private life spread across the pages of any newspaper. You tell your friend Maxwell fucking Cooper that if he ever mistreats her again, I'll come to his front door and arrest him personally."

"I'll pretend I never heard that, Andy."

"Pretend all you like, Tom."

"Get out."

Gilchrist closed the door gently behind him.

18

Night had fallen by the time Gilchrist left the Office. Black clouds dulled a leaden sky. A bitter wind chased him along College Street, compelling him to enter the Central by the side door.

The place was heaving. Bodies swarmed around the bar. Students dressed in look-alike hand-me-downs that probably cost as much as Gilchrist's leather jacket threw scarves and gloves to the side, as if preparing to get torn in. Tables and booths overflowed with spillage and bodies. He searched for a seat but ended up squeezing into a standing-room-only spot next to the bar with his back to the windows on Market Street.

He nodded to the barman, Phil, who was already pulling him a pint of Deuchars. "You're growing your ponytail back in?" Gilchrist said.

Phil nodded. "It's too cold without it."

Gilchrist's pint arrived creamy-headed. He passed over some change and waited while the IPA settled. He was about to lift it to his lips when a hand tapped his shoulder.

"Thought I'd find you here, man."

Pint in hand, he turned to face Jack, his son. "Where've you been hiding?" Gilchrist asked. "Do you only come out when you know your old da's buying a round?"

"This one's on me."

"Too late. Already got it."

Jack laughed and said, "Perfect timing, then."

"So, what's with the offer of a drink? You won the lottery?"

"Sold one of my sculptures today. I'm feeling flush, man."

"For the time being."

"There you go again. Mr. Negativity. You need to lighten up, Andy. Enjoy yourself. Let your hair down—"

"Have a pint?"

"Exactly."

"Well, get me another then," Gilchrist said, and took a swig that almost drained it in one. He wiped his lips. "You here by yourself?"

"No." Jack nodded to a table in the corner that was stuffed with young women—more girls than women, Gilchrist thought. "Want to join us?"

"If I did, I'd probably have to lift that lot for underage drinking."

Jack raised both hands in mock-surrender. "No way, man. I can vouch for every one of them."

"Right," Gilchrist said, finishing his pint.

"Thirsty?"

"Long day."

"You should be cutting back the hours, at your age."

"Try telling the bad guys that."

Jack handed Gilchrist a fresh pint of Deuchars. "This way."

Gilchrist followed his son, pleased that he seemed to have put on a bit of weight. Not that Jack was fat by the wildest stretch of the imagination, but he looked less skeletal.

His jeans, too, were less worn-in than usual. Maybe he was beginning to make some kind of a living from his painting and sculpting after all.

"Right, guys," Jack announced to the table. "I'd like you to meet Andy, the old man. He's joining us for a beer or two, but don't let him buy you any drinks, because tonight's on me."

The five girls, each with dyed blonde hair and grunge mascara, dressed in black jeans and tops that could have come from the same wardrobe—and probably did—nodded a half-interested hello. Gilchrist had the distinct impression that he was spoiling their fun.

Jack seemed not to notice and proceeded to introduce each of them by name—too many to take in. Gilchrist responded to each with a nod and a smile. He managed to squeeze in behind the table on a seat next to Jack, who lifted his pint and said, "Up yours," then tried his best to down it in one.

A barmaid materialized by Gilchrist's side and handed over a tray of drinks. Jack passed shots and tumblers filled with clear liquid—double Stollie on the rocks caught his attention—into eager hands. "Same again," said Jack before the barmaid had a chance to leave, and flashed over a fifty.

"You in a hurry?" Gilchrist asked.

"It'll take her half an hour to get another round," Jack assured him, "by which time we'll be gasping."

Gilchrist watched each of the girls throw back her shot, followed by a grimace and a swipe across the lips. "Expensive night," he suggested.

"It's worth it, though."

Gilchrist thought it best to hide behind his beer.

Jack lifted his shot and threw it back. "Whooee," he said, squinting. "That had a bite. Would you like one?"

"I'll give it a miss," Gilchrist said.

The next round came up in less than half an hour—more like ten minutes, by Gilchrist's reckoning. Jack paid for it and ordered another. As Gilchrist watched the girls knock back their drinks, he tried to recall if he had ever been as foolish with drink. With a surge of regret, he realized he had, and probably far worse.

Jack was speaking to him, but Gilchrist was barely listening—something about his most recent sculpture being sold for a cool five figures, with the likelihood of another three being picked up.

"What do you think about that, man?"

Gilchrist chinked his pint against Jack's and said, "Well done," while trying to catch the essence of a story one of the girls was telling. But he lost track of it in the ambient din of the busy bar.

Much more clear was the impression of how utterly vulnerable women can become once they've had a few too many. An ancient memory of a drunken Friday night in the days before he was of legal drinking age came back to him—an ex-friend, John somebody-or-other, who had long since left St. Andrews, round the back of the pub, trying to slide his hand inside his girlfriend's knickers. Gilchrist could not remember the girl's name, only his own hot flush of panic as he realized she was trying to fight off her boyfriend. Before he knew it, he was rushing in, pulling John back. Then came the shock and disbelief as they *both* turned on him. His parting memory had been one of muddled confusion.

"I said you're falling behind, man. Would you like another?"

Gilchrist shook his head. "Too much to do," he said.

"You need to change jobs, man. Find something that doesn't take so much out of you. I mean, at your age, you should be slowing down."

Gilchrist let out a laugh. "What do you mean, at my age?"

"If it's any consolation, man, I hope I look as good as you when I get that old." Jack laughed, a hard sound that came out like a bark.

Despite his son's ability to consume vast quantities of alcohol without any apparent downside, Gilchrist saw that the shots were taking effect. He knew any advice would be pointless—after all, next week Jack would turn twenty-four, going on fourteen. Christ, it didn't bear thinking about.

He finished the remnants of his beer and rose to his feet. "Got to go, Jack. Thanks for the beer."

Jack raised his hand, and Gilchrist was not sure whether to high-five it or shake it.

"Catch you, man," Jack said, grabbing Gilchrist's hand in one of those reverse shakes all the kids seemed to be doing. "Hey, guys," Jack said, "Andy's leaving."

Gilchrist freed himself from Jack's grip and said, "See you all."

But no one showed any real interest.

On Market Street, the quietness hit him with a muted buzz, as if his ears were still ringing from a night at a disco. He removed his mobile from his jacket, surprised to see two missed calls—both from Jessie.

"I've been trying to reach you," she said. "Where are you?"

Alert now, mobile hard to his ear. "Let's have it."

"I'm on my way to Pittenweem," she said. "Janice Meechan's been killed in a car accident."

The name hit him like a slap to the head. "Keep going."

"Hit-and-run on Pittenweem Road, just outside Anstruther. Jennings from the Anstruther Office called."

Gilchrist's memory pulled up the details—the young PC who had intercepted him at the McCullochs' home. "I'll meet you there." He disconnected and strode into College Street, heading for the Office car park, his mind crackling.

One possibility hit him, and he called Stan.

"Hey, boss."

"Did Chief Super Whyte phone you?"

"He did. Asked me about Janice Meechan. I told him what I knew. He said he wanted to meet her."

"With you?"

"No, boss. Why?"

"Just got a call from Jessie. Janice has been killed in a car accident."

A pause, then, "Jesus, boss, I don't know what to tell you."

"I don't like it, Stan. Find out where Magner is, where he's been, who he's spoken to." He blinked at the sky as spots of rain fell. From the darkness overhead he could almost smell a thunderstorm in the making. "Get back to me when you've got hold of him, Stan. And grill the bastard if you have to. I think we're stirring up a hornets' nest."

———

Jessie slowed her Fiat to a crawl and parked behind the ambulance—although, with the body covered in a plastic sheet at the side of the road, medical assistance was redundant. The skies opened then—unseen thunderclouds firing drops as large as marbles onto the roof of her car, bouncing off the bonnet, making her wipers useless. She switched them off but kept the radio on—soft music from Smooth FM, all the oldies. She was only thirty. How sick was that?

Rather than step outside—the body was going nowhere soon—she took out her phone. Robert would be upset, she knew he would—one more broken promise, one more night at home instead of at the pictures, which made four weekends in a row. Jessie had no idea what she would do without Angie; pay a fortune in sitters' fees, no doubt. Not that Angie looked after Robert for free, but she was happy to take payment in kind—a worry-free night watching the telly or one of Jessie's DVDs, with pizza or leftover Chinese, access to the occasional Boodles and tonic, or her head buried in a Mills & Boon. And Robert didn't need much looking after anyway—thirteen going on thirty. His time was spent mostly reading comics—*Judge Dredd* and *2000 AD* were two she could remember—playing his latest computer game, or writing new jokes. Angie was Jessie's only friend who knew sign language, so she was a good sounding board for him.

She typed the message—"late again no movies angie will order large pizza sorry mum xxx"— pressed SEND and hoped the enticement of a large pizza would appease him.

Earlier, she had phoned Angie and told her to take forty quid from the housekeeping purse at the back of the kitchen drawer, then make sure she helped herself to a few slices before Robert scoffed the lot. "Oh, and have a Boodles or three, and keep the change." Angie always drank in moderation, so Jessie knew she would not abuse the offer.

Two minutes later, the worst of the storm had passed. Jessie switched on the wipers again, turned up the radio on hearing an old Everly Brothers hit—"All I Have to Do Is Dream"—and eyed her mobile. Sometimes Robert texted her back right away, but he had not replied by the song's end, so she returned the phone to her jacket pocket. Maybe he was playing on his computer. Or maybe he was pissed off at being let down by his mum yet again. She cursed under her breath as she reached for the umbrella on the rear seat.

Then she gripped the door handle and made a silent promise to make it up to Robert next week.

In the meantime, she had work to do.

———

Gilchrist pulled in behind Jessie's Fiat.

Rain bounced off his windscreen, hard enough to have his wipers struggling.

Someone walked toward the car, umbrella up, and he realized it was Jessie.

She opened the door. "You stepping outside?"

"If I must."

"It's only water," she said. "But lots of it."

Gilchrist slipped from his seat and huddled beside her under the umbrella. "Thought you were going to the movies," he said.

"You know what teenagers are like. Feed them, then wrap them up for the night."

The sky let loose again at that moment, and rain bounced off the ground with a vengeance.

Gilchrist nudged closer, and Jessie said, "You'll be asking me out next."

"Just hold that umbrella steady."

"Spoilsport."

Blue and red flickering lights shivered through the downpour. The road had been closed off. Light spilled from the open back door of the ambulance, which in turn was flooded by the headlights of a squad car. Beyond the ambulance, about twenty yards distant, Gilchrist could make out the dark shape of another car, with two wraiths that manifested into PCs fussing around it.

"What happened?" he asked Jessie.

"Apparently Janice stopped the car, got out, and was hit at high speed by a passing vehicle, which fled the scene."

"Witnesses?"

"Of course not. That would be too easy."

"Why would she stop here?" Gilchrist asked.

"That's the million-dollar question."

"And the million-dollar answer," he said, "is that her car broke down." He glared into the dark distance. "Magner's up to his neck in this. He has to be. There are too many coincidences."

"Come on, Andy. You've been reading too many crime stories. Janice's car breaks down in the back of beyond, out of sight of CCTV cameras, she steps out, and she's run over by Magner in his Aston Martin?" She snorted. "I think not."

"Not Magner himself," Gilchrist said. "He's too smart for that."

"Even if he had miraculously made her car break down on demand, why would he kill her? He was giving her one. He was probably giving her lots of ones. So if a man's got nookie on tap, give me one good reason why he would switch it off."

"That's the second million-dollar question," Gilchrist said. He had his mobile to his ear. The call was answered on the third ring.

"Whyte here."

Without introduction, Gilchrist said, "DI Davidson said you called him about Janice Meechan. I take it you didn't get a chance to speak to her?"

"No, I didn't. But when I do, I'll let you know. Would you like to come along?"

"She's dead, Billy. Killed in a car accident."

"*What?*"

Gilchrist gave a quick update, then said, "First thoughts?"

A gasp of breath down the line, then, "That's fucking inconvenient. Or convenient, depending on whose side you're on."

"That's what I thought."

When Gilchrist ended the call, he eyed the plastic sheeting by the side of the road, the abandoned car, the police vehicles, the ambulance, the dark fields beyond. He felt his body give an involuntary shiver as fingers of ice slithered over him. He did not believe in coincidences—never had, never would.

Everything was linked.

Believe that, and you would be surprised at what you could uncover.

The downpour was diminishing, no longer beating the ground, just patting it. Jessie peeked out from beneath the umbrella, as if to test the strength of the rain. "I heard most of that," she said. "So you think it's convenient?"

"Could be," he said, tugging her toward the plastic sheet. A shoeless foot protruded from one end, toenails painted an electric blue. He looked around. Janice must have been really distracted for a vehicle to hit her out here. "This way," he said, and they walked toward Janice's car.

Gilchrist showed his warrant card to the first PC and said, "You find her mobile?"

"Not yet, sir. We're about to start searching the grass verges."

"Start close to her car," Gilchrist instructed. "At the edge of the road, maybe in the hedgerow. Better still, have someone get her number and give it a call. Once you find it, check her records. I want to know who she talked to last."

With that, he turned and stared at the body.

A chill slid over him, as if Death had reached out and stroked his skin. He had come up against some nasty creatures in his thirty-plus years with Fife Constabulary, seen cruelty that defied belief, gruesome scenes that could choke the breath from your throat. But at that moment he felt as if he were standing at the edge of a black precipice, his thoughts filled with doubt, afraid to take the next step, with nothing between himself and the devil.

"What's up?" Jessie asked.

"I think Stan's chat with Janice has just flushed Magner out."

19

It was close to midnight when Gilchrist entered the interview room in Strathclyde HQ on Pitt Street, Glasgow. Jessie took the seat to his left, Stan the other on his right. Opposite them sat Thomas Magner and his solicitor, no longer the slick-haired Thornton Pettigrew, of Jesper Pettigrew Jones, but a white-haired man with a deep tan and white teeth that boasted of too much sun or too much money—or probably both.

With the help of Strathclyde Police, Stan had tracked Magner to the Urban Bar and Brasserie on St. Vincent Place in Glasgow city center. He had been enjoying a meal and a bottle of Krug Vintage Brut in the company of an attractive blonde young enough to be his daughter. Gilchrist was convinced she had been hired for the occasion.

When cornered by two detectives from Strathclyde, Magner had dabbed his lips with a napkin, stood up, and held out both hands in mock-arrest to the shocked gasps of other patrons. Then he had excused himself from his blonde companion with all the airs and graces of a knight about to slay a dragon.

A short interview with Magner's girlfriend-for-hire confirmed Gilchrist's suspicions. She had only met Tommy the day before, in Maison Bleue, Edinburgh, spent the night with him at the Balmoral Hotel on Princes Street, and not left his side, or his wallet, since. Well, there he had it. Another perfect alibi.

Magner's solicitor was the first to make a move.

He slid a card across the table to Gilchrist, then another to Stan, and sat back—Christopher Brooks Jones of Pettigrew Jesper Jones.

"Don't I get one?" Jessie said.

Jones's mouth twisted in a what-do-you-think smile.

Gilchrist slid his card to Jessie, who smirked at it, then said, "Right. For the record . . ." She introduced all five present, ending with place, date, and time, and noting that Magner's attendance was voluntary and that he was free to leave at any time.

Then she eyed Magner. "How's your hand?"

Magner turned it over to reveal a fresh Band-Aid. "Getting better."

Jessie returned his gaze. "Who's the bimbo?"

Jones leaned forward, his mouth in a lopsided twist. "Excuse me?"

"Why? Did you burp?"

Jones's eyes failed to blink. "You asked, 'Who's the bimbo?'"

"Good to see your hearing aid works." Back to Magner. "Well?"

Jones leaned forward and said to Gilchrist, "We have a problem here. You are obliged to advise my client why he is being questioned."

"It's a continuation of an earlier interview," Gilchrist said. "We are investigating multiple murders."

"About which my client has already advised you he knows nothing."

"Correct," Jessie said. "But now we have another one to add to the list."

Jones raised his eyebrows in surprise. "And when and where did this alleged new murder take place?" he asked Gilchrist.

"This evening. Outside Anstruther," Jessie replied.

Jones looked at his client, eyebrows still high, then faced Gilchrist again. "So, how—"

"You're right," Jessie interrupted. "We do have a problem. Usually, when I talk to someone, they answer *me*. You know, I speak to you, you speak to me. That sort of thing. One-on-one. Face-to-face. Understand?"

Jones smiled at her, then turned to Gilchrist. "As I was saying—"

"Let me repeat my question, Mr. Magner—who's the bimbo?"

"This is out of—"

"*Shut it.*"

"I really do have to object—"

"Put it in writing," Jessie snapped. "Address it to him, if you want," nodding at Gilchrist. Then she turned her attention to Magner. "Are you going to answer the question or just sit there looking dumb? Who's the bimbo?"

Magner returned Jessie's look but said nothing.

"To clarify, I'm not talking about your solicitor," she added. "Even though bimbo could be an apt description. I'm talking about the blonde bombshell you picked up last night to establish your alibi."

Magner shifted in his seat, as if about to speak, but Jones turned his head and leaned in. "You don't have to say anything, Tom."

Magner nodded at his solicitor's wise words, then said, "I've a busy day ahead of me, Chris. Besides, I've got a blonde bimbo to get back to tonight."

Jones chuckled, then sat back with a smile. "As you will, then."

Magner's eyes burned at Jessie. "I don't know the bimbo's name."

"So you pick her up, wine and dine her, spend the night with her, and don't have the common decency to ask her name?"

"Is that a crime?"

"Not yet. Was she expensive?"

"She's not a prostitute, if that's what you're asking. But I've spent a couple of thou since we met, so I guess you could say—"

"All that money, and you haven't even bought her a going-away present yet."

"I don't believe she's intending to leave anytime soon."

"I wasn't talking about her."

Jones chuckled, put his hand to his mouth, and winked at Gilchrist.

Magner smiled, although Gilchrist caught the tiniest hint of annoyance.

On the drive to Glasgow earlier that night, they had discussed their interview strategy and agreed that Jessie should lead, try to wriggle under Magner's skin, get him to say something he might regret. She was doing well, but Magner looked as cold as stone.

"How did you meet Miss Anonymous?" Jessie asked.

"I walked up to her in a bar and said, 'Hi, gorgeous, I'd like to fuck your brains out.'"

Jessie laughed. "With a face like yours? That's chancing your arm."

Magner kept his composure.

Jessie pressed on. "More like you flashed her a few hundred quid and told her there was plenty more where that came from if she stuck by your side for a night or two. Of course, you wouldn't tell her she was going to get dumped before the end of the weekend."

"Is there a question in there?" Jones complained.

"Why don't you ask him?" Jessie said, nodding to Gilchrist.

"Got a mobile phone?" she asked Magner.

"Of course." He removed it from his jacket and slid it across the table.

"I didn't ask to see it. But I understand why you're keen to let me check it out—to prove you never made any calls to or received any calls from Janice today." The mobile was a top-quality Samsung. She worked her way through the menus to the call log, then said, "I must say you've surprised me."

"Why?"

Jessie stared hard at Magner. "You never asked who Janice was."

"I assume you're talking about Janice Meechan, although I fail to see why that's an issue."

Gilchrist had to admit that Magner was good. Great, even. Give Jones his due, too—he hardly twitched. Of course, Jones would have been kept in the dark, fed only scraps Magner deemed safe to hand over. How could you lie if you didn't know the truth?

"She's your late business partner's sister-in-law," Jessie continued. "Or, to be more precise, your late business partner's late wife's sister. And the woman you've been screwing since Christmas."

"I've heard that rumor," Magner said. "So is that what this is about?"

"This?"

"This interview."

"Do you deny having an affair with her?"

"Of course I deny that. Janice is a lovely woman, and a wonderful wife to Perry, and a fine mother to Jane and John. Is this how you speak of someone who's in mourning for the brutal death of her sister and her family?"

Gilchrist noticed the present tense, and for the first time that night he felt the tiniest of nips worrying his gut. So far, all they had to go on was instinct alone. But they were nearing the point when they needed to uncover some hard evidence.

And at that moment, it felt like there was none to find.

Jessie eyed Magner's phone. "You didn't ask why we were interested in you contacting her today."

"I couldn't give a shit about why you're interested in Janice. Something to do with the tragic death of her sister and her family, no doubt."

"I'm interested in why *you* contacted *her.*"

"She's an employee. She's been with our company for the last ten years. She's also my partner's . . . sorry, my *late* partner's sister-in-law. What's so strange about me contacting her, today or any other day?"

"Did *she* call *you* today?"

"I haven't spoken with her since yesterday, when I called the office."

"Did she call and leave a message today?"

"If she did, I didn't get it." Magner held out his hand, palm up. "You've got my phone. Check it and see."

"Can you be reached on any other numbers?"

Magner slid a hand into his pocket, retrieved his wallet, and opened it. "Here," he said, and removed a business card. "These are all the numbers I have."

"Do you know Janice is dead?"

Magner blinked once, twice, then said, "No. I didn't. How . . . ?"

"Hit-and-run."

"*What?*"

"You heard."

Jones reached for Magner's hand and squeezed.

Gilchrist thought he had seen it all, but this was playact-
ing at its worst.

Magner nodded to his phone. "I'd like to make a call."

"Who to?"

"Perry, of course."

"I might have to confiscate this phone," Jessie said.

Jones slid his hand into his suit pocket.

"No calls," Jessie snapped. "They can wait. You can phone
when we're done." She picked up Magner's business card.
"How did Janice compare to her sister Amy?"

Jones frowned.

Magner said, "Now you've lost me."

"Amy McCulloch, a.k.a. Charlotte Renwick?"

Magner's eyes turned to beads of ice.

"You screwed her, too, didn't you? Well, actually, you
raped her."

Jones said, "As your solicitor, Tom, I'm instructing you not
to answer that." Then he glared at Jessie. "If you continue in—"

"I'm not interested in anything you've got to say," Jessie
barked at him. Back to Magner. "I take it that's a no?" She
gave him two seconds, then said, "Thomas Magner has refused
to answer the question under instruction from his solicitor."

Neither Gilchrist nor Stan said a word, just listened as Jessie
continued to fire questions that Magner took in his salesman-
smooth stride—the phrase *perma-smirking bastard* sprang to mind.
And not a tear in sight for Janice or Amy or Brian or the kids.

Fifteen minutes later, Gilchrist felt a ripple of relief as Jones
leaned forward. "It seems to me that you've got nothing on

my client," he said. "You're fishing." He glanced at his watch.
"It's getting late, so I suggest you either charge my client with
whatever the hell you think you can get away with, or we
call it a night." He harrumphed a throat clearing and sat back.

Gilchrist hated to admit it, but Jones had a point. Jessie's best attempts to rile Magner had failed. Not that she
had handled the interview poorly, rather Magner had not
slipped up once, shooting back answers with barely an intake
of breath. You had to be a brilliant liar to do that. Or, more
worryingly, completely innocent.

That thought sent another stab of doubt through Gilchrist's
system. Did he have it all wrong? Was it only coincidence
after all?

Defeated, he turned to Stan. "Anything you'd like to ask?"

Stan shook his head.

He turned to Jessie. "Anything else?"

She glanced at the clock on the wall and stood. "DS Jessie
Janes leaving the interview room at twenty minutes to one."

Jones waited until the door closed, then said, "So, this
interview is over?"

"For now," Gilchrist said. "We're through, yes." He switched
off the recorder.

Magner retrieved his phone from the table.

Jones eased himself to his feet. "I think it only fair to warn
you that I'll be writing a letter of complaint to Chief Constable Ramsay over the manner in which this interview was
conducted. Never in my forty years of professional experience
have I come across anything so outrageous. I'll be seeking to
have DS Janes severely reprimanded, and it would give me
the greatest satisfaction to see her career terminated."

"You're free to file a formal complaint," Gilchrist said. "Do
you have the chief constable's address?"

"I'll find it. Good night."

Gilchrist waited until the pair of them shuffled out and the door closed, then turned to Stan. "What do you think?"

"I watched his eyes every second, boss." Stan took a deep breath, then let it out with a shake of his head. "I have to tell you, he's good."

Not what Gilchrist wanted to hear. "Good as in . . . ?"

"I hate to say it, boss, but good as in innocent." He shook his head again. "I just don't see it. Sorry, boss."

A hoof to the gut could not have winded Gilchrist more. Over the years, he had come to trust Stan's judgment, and their instincts rarely clashed. But this was one of those rare occasions, and Gilchrist was only now beginning to question why he had been so blinkered. He had next to bugger all to suggest Magner was involved in the McCulloch murders, or Janice Meechan's hit-and-run, for that matter. Whichever way he tried to cut it, Stan was right.

A feverish flush rose within him as he struggled to fight off an image of Amy McCulloch's butchered body. He blinked once, twice, to force away the horror. But that left him with the painful realization that his investigation was going nowhere, that he was failing, that over the last forty hours, the most critical period in any investigation, he had come up empty-handed.

As if to offer him one last straw to grasp, Jessie walked through the door.

Gilchrist looked at her. "Penny for your thoughts?"

"Lying bastard," she said. "I'm going to nail him to the mast."

Gilchrist almost said, *That's my girl*. But deep down he felt the debilitating sickness of failure, the burgeoning weight of worry, and at that moment he did not have it in him to contradict her.

20

Gilchrist's alarm rang at 7:00 AM.

He reached for his mobile and switched it off, then struggled against an almost overpowering urge to close his eyes, savor another few minutes of glorious sleep. But he knew that would probably turn into a couple of hours.

He had crawled into bed this side of 3:00 AM, but his mind had ebbed and flowed with sleep—one moment wide awake, the next sucked into its deepest folds—and now he felt exhausted, as good as drugged. He lay there, trying to pull his mind back into the present, shift the remnants of his fading nightmare—humans hanging by hooks through their feet, naked bodies stripped of skin and guts, bloodied meat with nerves still twitching, swaying past him on overhead rollers, an endless line. He knew the imagery would stay with him through the rest of the morning, dragging him down, replacing all sense of enthusiasm with ominous foreboding.

With cursed resignation, he rolled from bed but could not shift the draining sense of failure. He had put too much stock into searching for some connection—*any* connection—between the McCulloch massacre and Magner. But instead of working with the facts, he had let his gut instinct overrule all logic.

A piping-hot shave, followed by a ten-minute shower, managed to clear the fog from his brain but did nothing for his stomach. He felt as if he could throw up on request, and almost did when he entered the kitchen and opened the fridge. Not that any food had gone off; his stomach just cramped at the thought of even a slice of toast.

A jog to the harbor had his heart racing and his breath steaming in the cold March air. A sea haar that shrouded nearby rooftops stirred and shifted around him like thinning smoke as he slowed, then walked the length of the stone pier. By his side, boats sat as silent as hunting beasts. Gulls eyed him from their perches on the stone wall. At the pier's southernmost tip, he stared off to the horizon. Even the ocean seemed stilled, as if it too were struggling with the dismal weight of it all.

He turned and faced the old fishing village of Crail.

Haar obliterated the background. The harbor row could have been all that was left of the world. His breathing had recovered, his heart no longer pumping hard. But instead of jogging back, he decided to carry on walking. Something about the frigid air and the salty smell of the sea and kelp was clearing his mental fog, nudging his mind back to life. A flock of gulls ruffled their wings and strutted along the seawall, as if contemplating flight. A gust of wind brushed in from the sea, and one by one they spread their wings and settled onto it, webbed feet hovering inches above the stone, as if reluctant to set off into the new day.

Then they spilled over the edge, out of view.

By the time Gilchrist reached the shorehead, the haar had mostly cleared to reveal a sky streaked with pinks and reds.

The village seemed to spring into vivid color, too. A shaft of sunlight stroked the harbor walls, and tile-reds, plaster-whites, stone-browns all sparked alive with lightened hues. A door opened and a collie jerked its owner on to Shoregate. A gray Ford cruised around the corner, its engine breaking the silence. Even the boats seemed to be emerging from slumber as they creaked and bumped against their moorings.

Gilchrist pulled out his mobile. He had ordered a review of CCTV footage in Anstruther and Pittenweem in the hope of identifying the vehicle that had killed Janice Meechan. He scrolled down the call log for Glenrothes HQ's number and was put through to the surveillance room and PC Elizabeth Sutton.

"Anything?" he asked her.

"Nothing conclusive yet, sir, but a black BMW 6 series—we're thinking top-of-the-range 650i—fits the time frame. We haven't been able to ID it, because the plates were covered—"

"*Covered?*"

"As best we can tell, sir, it looks like plastic sheets were clipped to both the front and rear plates."

Gilchrist exhaled. They had to find that car. "Were you able to follow it through the town?" he asked.

"It turned left on to the B9131 to St. Andrews, sir. That was the last we saw of it."

Gilchrist cursed. Once out of town, the road network was as good as a rabbit warren. If you kept to the back roads, it was possible to drive all the way to England without coming across another CCTV camera. "What about damage to the car?" he asked.

"The front nearside wing looked dented, and the windscreen appeared to be cracked, but it's difficult to tell for sure at night on black paintwork under streetlamps. We've got our IT guys reviewing footage," she added.

"Witnesses?"

"Not to my knowledge, sir. But we're still asking. So far no one's come forward."

Gilchrist thanked her, told her to notify him the instant they found something, then ended the call. His mind pulled up an image of Janice exiting her car, her attention more on her phone than on passing traffic. After all, most drivers do what they can to avoid pedestrians. The BMW must have hit her hard—judging by the distance her body was found from her car—the impact throwing her onto the bonnet, into the windscreen, then flying over the top to land on the road, probably dead before she hit the ground. An image of electric-blue toenails came to him, and he had to blink hard to shift it.

The driver had taken a calculated risk driving into Anstruther with the number plates covered. But he had to drive somewhere, and on a Saturday night, in the Fife countryside, who would ever have noticed? And if the covering plates were fixed by clips, a short stop at the side of the road, a quick tug back and front, and the car would be legal again.

It struck Gilchrist that the driver probably had another car, so he could garage the BMW until the incident was all but forgotten. A power wash with a pressure jet and soapy water would clear all trace of human impact from the paintwork. Then wait a couple of months, let police interest die down, and take it to any number of bodywork shops out of the county.

By the time Gilchrist reached High Street, he had heard that Janice Meechan's mobile had been found in the hedgerow, undamaged. She had called Magner's registered mobile number twice on Saturday afternoon, but he hadn't answered. Ten minutes after the second unanswered call, she had received a call from an unregistered mobile number that had lasted less than three minutes. When Glenrothes Office dialed the number, the call just rang out. Gilchrist was convinced that Janice's two calls to Magner had prompted him to call her back using a pay-as-you-go phone, and arrange to meet her. But the details of how the hit-and-run on a country road was set up continued to puzzle him.

In the Co-operative, he bought a *Sunday Times*, two soft breakfast rolls, and a packet of smoked back bacon. Just the thought of a grilled bacon and poached egg roll revived him, and as he opened the front door and stepped inside Fisherman's Cottage he had already resolved to refocus his line of inquiry.

He switched on the kettle, fired up the grill and a hot-ring, put a couple of tea bags in the teapot. Then he filled a pan with water and set it on the ring. Next, he slapped four slices of bacon under the grill, set on low. The pan was boiling nicely, so he turned it down to simmer and removed two eggs from the fridge.

And while Gilchrist was preparing breakfast on autopilot, his mind was working through the logistics of how Magner could have killed three people—Amy McCulloch and her daughters—four, if Brian McCulloch's death was not suicide—or even five, if you included Janice Meechan's hit-and-run.

But it just seemed so improbable.

Magner had the perfect alibi for Janice's hit-and-run—a date with a blonde bimbo—and the perfect alibi for the McCulloch murders—a conference in a hotel in Stirling. Given that Magner could not be in two places at one time—on two separate occasions—was it possible that he had an accomplice, someone who did as he was told?

Should all efforts now focus on trying to find that connection?

Or should they concentrate on Stratheden Enterprises, the business common to all five who had died, and the one irrefutable and direct link to Thomas Magner?

Gilchrist flipped the bacon over, added a couple of drops of vinegar into the simmering pot, and gave the water a stir. Then he cracked an egg and slipped it in, and did the same with the other. He peeled the rolls open, slapped some low-fat butter on them, then checked the time—8:21.

He called Mhairi.

"Did Jackie get back to you with details of Stratheden's first major contract?" he asked.

"She did, sir, yes. I don't have it in front of me, but if memory serves, it was a three-year maintenance contract with Fife Council's Department of Housing. They really hit the mother lode in the first year, the winter of 1990–91. Three months of snow, high winds, heavy rain, and sub-zero temperatures had them working double crews round the clock."

"Anything contentious about the contract award?" Gilchrist asked.

"Jackie's not come up with anything yet, sir. But if it was contentious, it's hardly the sort of thing the council would broadcast."

"Meaning?"

"Meaning we probably need to talk to someone."

"Anyone in mind?"

"Let me get back to you, sir."

"Make it soon." He ended the call and replayed the conversation in his head.

If they found any evidence of Magner handing over brown paper bags stuffed with cash to crooked council officials, at least they would have *something*—an indication that his business life was as dubious as his personal life. But if Magner and McCulloch had lucked out by landing their first council contract at the perfect time, then where did that take his investigation?

No closer to solving the case as standing on Mars, came the answer.

He was so far off target, he could have been shooting at the wrong bull's-eye. He had absolutely nothing, and the odds of finding something were worsening with each passing hour. If the investigation was in the same sorry state a week from now, they might as well send the lot straight to cold storage.

His mobile rang—Mhairi again.

"It doesn't look good, sir," she said. "The guy who was director of the Department of Housing when the contract was awarded to Stratheden has since died."

Gilchrist groaned.

"But Jackie's done her usual. Got copies of the minutes of every relevant meeting, highlighted the important sections. You were right, sir. The award *was* contentious. Stratheden was not the low bidder. Three others tendered lower bids, but all three subsequently withdrew."

"Did the council pull their bid bonds?"

"I'll ask Jackie to check it out."

"Who was head of the council when Stratheden won the contract?"

"Hang on, sir." Gilchrist caught the sound of paper rustling; then Mhairi's voice came back with, "Jack Russell."

"Like the dog?"

"Yes, sir. Woof, woof."

You had to laugh, he supposed. But something in the shadows of his mind caused his smile to fade. He had come across that name years before, in a newspaper article about a crime somewhere. Not in Fife. In the Highlands and Islands, perhaps? No, not a crime. *Allegations*. Sexual allegations. Was that right?

"Ask Jackie to look into him for me. He's ringing a bell, but I can't quite place him."

"Will do, sir. Anything else?"

"Yes. Have her get back within a couple of hours," he said, and ended the call.

Next, he called Stan.

"Bloody hell, boss. What time is it?"

"Jack Russell, Stan. Does that name mean anything to you?"

"Russell? Jack?" A gush of breath, then, "Nothing's coming to me, boss."

"When it does, give me a call."

He thought of calling Jessie, but she was from Glasgow. Crime in the north of Scotland probably would not have made it onto her radar. Besides, she would have been no more than a teenager at the time. He heard a spark from under the grill and cursed as he removed the bacon—more crispy than he liked—and placed two rashers on each roll. He drained the water from the eggs—hard-poached, not soft, damn it—and stuffed them into the rolls, too.

He bit into the first roll, heard the bacon crunch, then carried the plate through to the lounge and switched on the computer. Googling the name brought up a host of articles, and as he studied them, his memory cleared.

In the early nineties, Jack Russell had been a rising star in Scottish politics, holding a parliamentary seat in Aberdeen. But his life started to unravel when he began dating Nichola Kelly, an up-and-coming soap opera actress from Inverness, and filed for divorce from his wife of twelve years. When

Jack's wife refused to go quietly, Jack retaliated with fearsome vengeance, accusing her of having a lover of her own.

The press latched on to him and nicknamed him "the Terrier."

He was photographed at all hours of the night in various states of drunken revelry, and always with the photogenic Ms. Kelly on his arm. In spite—or because—of this, his political ratings soared. It looked as if Jack was still heading for the big time, when rumors of drugs and swinger parties made the headlines, and his career took a nosedive that proved terminal. Being no longer the handsome charmer with the aphrodisiac of political power, he was ditched by Nichola Kelly for a younger stud.

Gilchrist read on, remembering snippets of news from way back. He had paid little attention to the scandal at the time, but goose bumps rippled across his skin as the memory of Nichola Kelly's fatal car accident came back to him.

Another search pulled up more articles on the young actress and her tragic death.

Gilchrist read on, intrigued by the similarities between Janice Meechan's hit-and-run and Nichola Kelly's. Except that Nichola's accident had not been a hit-and-run per se; more of a hit-and-stop. Both Janice and Nichola had been the only occupant of the car, and both had pulled over in the quiet of the countryside. The driver of the vehicle that killed Nichola Kelly—Jason Purvis—was not convicted of causing death by careless or dangerous driving, as it turned out that Nichola was over the limit, and witnesses confirmed she had stumbled into the path of his car.

Nothing particularly striking in any of that, Gilchrist thought.

Except for a newspaper photograph of Purvis on the court steps.

Gilchrist noted the long darkish hair, the square face. But if he half-shut his eyes and imagined shorter hair dyed blond, the similarity to Magner opened up more troubling possibilities.

21

When Jessie slid into the passenger seat, Gilchrist handed her the printout of the article, then shifted into gear.

"Nichola Kelly?" she said. "What's this?"

"Anything strike you?"

"She's a looker. I remember watching that program—what's it called?—and thinking I'd love to have hair like hers. And she used to wear these short skirts, and I'm thinking how much I would give to have her legs—"

"Should I be worried about you?"

Jessie barked a laugh. "Try telling Jabba that."

The mention of CS McKellar wrenched Gilchrist back to the present, reminding him that it was deadline day for Jessie. "Have you spoken to him?" he asked.

"Twice this morning. The man's a wonder. Never stops trying."

"Except where dieting's concerned."

"He's never heard of the word."

Gilchrist eased into Bridge Street. "Still giving you a hard time?"

"Fight fire with fire. He wants to play dirty? I'm thinking bring it on, sonny Jim, bring it on." She tapped his leg as he slowed down for the roundabout at the West Port, his indicator ticking for a left turn down Argyle Street. "Straight on. I've not had my caffeine kick yet."

"Starbucks?"

"Got it in one."

Gilchrist clicked off the indicator and accelerated through the mini-roundabout. He turned right at St. Mary's Place, and a few minutes later pulled up against the curb outside Starbucks in Market Street.

When he switched off the engine, Jessie said, "I forgot to mention that Vicky Kelvin called me first thing this morning. Said she remembered something else about that night with Magner, about what he said that frightened her."

Gilchrist faced her. "Go on."

"He said he would gut and skin her alive if she didn't give him what he wanted."

An image of Amy McCulloch's slaughtered body ripped through Gilchrist's mind with an icy chill. "Gut and skin her?"

"Exact words."

"Alive?"

"Thought that would get your attention."

"Contact DI Smith and find out if any of the others were similarly threatened," he said. "And read that article on Nichola Kelly while I get the coffees."

He ordered two tall lattes to go. His mobile rang as he was about to collect them—Stan. "Is this going to be quick?"

"Just off the phone with Anne Mills, boss. Magner's estranged wife."

"What's she got to say for herself?" Gilchrist tucked his mobile under his chin and picked up both coffees.

"She lives in Aberdeen, never remarried, and lives with . . . get this . . ."

Gilchrist maneuvered his way through the shop door onto Market Street, stepping back as two students pushed past him, ignorant of manners. "I'm all ears."

"Tom Junior."

"Magner has a boy?"

"He does indeed, boss."

"So, Tom Junior must be, what . . . in his teens?"

"Try twenty-nine."

Gilchrist frowned as he struggled with the arithmetic. "I thought Magner married Anne Mills in 1986."

"Yes, but she'd had his child long before then."

"Hang on, Stan." Gilchrist sat the coffees on the roof of the Merc, then opened the door. "Was that why he married her?"

"And also why she left him."

Gilchrist handed both coffees to Jessie, slid behind the wheel, then put his mobile on speaker. "You've lost me."

"According to Anne, Magner doted on his son when they got back together again." Stan's voice sounded metallic through the phone's speaker. "But it all began to fall apart after about a year when Magner developed these weird suspicions that his son was gay. Thomas Junior was only nine or ten at the time, so Anne thinks he was just looking for any excuse to get out of the marriage. After that, things got worse, with Magner refusing to have anything more to do with the boy."

"Bastard," said Jessie.

"What's that, boss?"

"Just Jessie airing her views."

A pause, then, "So Anne said she moved out of the family home, back to Aberdeen with her son, and that's the last she ever saw of Thomas Magner Senior. Despite that, he paid for his son's education at Robert Gordon's College, as well as maintenance until Junior turned twenty-one."

"So you're trying to tell us he's a good guy?" Jessie quipped.

"Not according to his wife, he isn't."

Gilchrist caught the change in tone. "We're all ears," he said.

"She said they lived together as husband and wife for about a year and a half, by which time she'd seen enough."

"*Enough?*"

"Drugs, drinks, sex. She was sick of it."

"*Sex?* As in with other couples?" Jessie asked.

"Swingers, wife swaps, full massages, strip shows, nude parties, you name it, in her two years of marriage she'd done it."

"Does she remember any names?" Gilchrist asked.

"She does indeed." The line seemed to die; then Stan came back with, "Would you like me to send them through to you in a text, or read them out—"

"Just get on with it."

Stan recited a list of about ten names that meant nothing to Gilchrist, until he said, "Jason Purvis—"

"Hang on," Gilchrist snapped, and reached for the printout.

"Boss?"

Jessie already had her finger on the image of the man on the court steps.

"I haven't reached the good bit yet, boss," Stan said. "One well-known swinger and drug user was a guy called Jack Russell, a politician with his fingers allegedly in any number of dodgy pies. Which might explain why Stratheden was awarded such a lucrative contract with Fife Council a couple of years later."

"We need to talk to him."

"You can't," Stan said. "He had a stroke several years ago, and been in a coma ever since. But it might be an idea to talk to someone else."

Gilchrist glanced at Jessie. "Who?" he said.

"Another not so well-known swinger was . . ." A pause, then, "Drum roll—"

"For crying out loud—"

"Martin Craig."

"The MEP?" Jessie said.

"And the man behind the drive for Scottish entrepreneurial investment in Europe."

"But all this went on, what, over twenty years ago?"

"About then, boss."

"So this Anne Mills must have one hell of a good memory if she's not been to a swinger party in about two decades."

"Better than that, boss. She's got photographs."

Gilchrist caught the triumph in Stan's voice and could not prevent a smile from stretching his lips. "Blackmail?" he suggested.

"Blackmail. For her son's education and maintenance, boss. But mainly for her own security. She says Magner's the most evil man she's ever known. Her words. So when she left him, she made sure she had something to keep herself safe."

"She had his son," Jessie said. "Surely that would—"

"Magner disowned Tom Junior, remember? That was when Anne knew she had to find some way to protect herself."

"So, what kind of photographs does she have?" Gilchrist asked.

"Haven't seen them, boss. She's now scanned them and keeps them on a memory stick in a safe-deposit box. And she filed a letter with her solicitor, which states that if she ever dies or goes missing, then the box is to be opened and its contents distributed to the press."

Jessie said, "I don't see Magner letting his wife take photographs of him having deviant sex. He might be the most evil man she's ever met, but he's smarter than that."

"Someone else took the photos," Stan replied. "Anne just nicked the negatives before she left," Stan replied.

"Ah," Jessie said.

"But if she releases the photographs," Gilchrist argued, "she'll lose whatever security they give her."

"She's been diagnosed with cancer," Stan said. "She's been told she's in remission, but she suspects she's only got another year or so—three, tops."

It never failed to amaze Gilchrist how people diagnosed with a terminal illness had an innate ability, maybe even a need, to think clearly through to the closing days of their lives, wrap up all the loose ends, as it were. But something was still troubling him.

"Did Anne Mills ever meet Vicky Kelvin?"

"Never asked her that, boss. You think it's important?"

"I'm thinking that if Anne and Vicky know each other, maybe it was Anne who instigated all the rape allegations against Magner."

"I'll ask, boss."

"And let's have sight of these photographs today, Stan."

"Already tried, boss. But she has to wait for the bank to open tomorrow."

Gilchrist almost cursed. "Get them first thing, Stan," he said, and ended the call.

He wondered what sort of depravity Anne Mills's photographs would reveal, although he suspected they would be of more use to Billy Whyte's case than his own. But even so, he now felt that he had turned a corner. He had a connection. In fact, he had a whole series of connections.

Magner's late partner's wife, Amy McCulloch, née Charlotte Renwick, had filed a rape allegation against him, albeit anonymously. Of the other accusers, five had since withdrawn their complaints. And Amy herself had since been murdered.

Magner's bit on the side—his late partner's sister-in-law, Janice Meechan—had been killed in a hit-and-run that bore uncanny similarities to another car accident fifteen years earlier in which Nichola Kelly had died. And Nichola's ex-lover might well have pulled the strings in the award of a major local-government contract to Magner's company.

Magner's first wife, Sheila Ramsay, had died after just four years of marriage and left a hefty life insurance payout that Magner used as start-up funding for Stratheden Enterprises. His second wife, Anne Mills—who left him after only two years—possessed a series of sexually explicit photographs with which she had kept him at arm's length for almost two decades.

The answer to his investigation had to lie somewhere in the midst of all this sexual, political, and familial entanglement. Gilchrist was sure of it. His thoughts crackled through the possibilities, and he removed the printout from Jessie's grip and eyed the photograph again.

The man on the court steps—Jason Purvis.

He pulled the image closer. The resemblance between Purvis and Magner could be coincidence. But if you did not believe in coincidences . . . ?

He slapped the photograph.

"Get on to Jackie for an address," he said. "We need to talk to Purvis."

22

Back in the Office, by 10:00 AM, Gilchrist could not shift the feeling that his investigation was almost stalling again. McVicar had been on the phone to Greaves, who in turn called Gilchrist for an update. But after bringing Greaves up to speed, he received only a snort of derision. He and Greaves had once enjoyed a strong professional relationship, but ever since Greaves missed out on a promotion about a year ago, he seemed to take out his disappointment on Gilchrist at every opportunity. When Greaves ended the call with a curse, Gilchrist was hard pressed not to call him straight back and tell him where to shove it.

Then Stan phoned with the disappointing news that both Anne Mills and Vicky Kelvin had just confirmed they had never met. They could both be lying, of course, but why would they?

The prospect of a break came when Jessie's mobile beeped receipt of an e-mail.

"It's from Jackie," she said.

On account of her disability, Jackie was the only civilian researcher permitted to work mostly from home, as long as she put in a couple of appearances at the Office each week. And no one could ever accuse her of slacking, especially on a Sunday morning.

"Anything?" Gilchrist asked, accessing his own e-mail account.

"Give me a minute." Jessie scanned down the tiny screen as fast as she could, then said, "Listen to this. Purvis has form. In 1980 he was sentenced to twelve years after being found guilty of rape and attempted murder. Spent time in Peterhead and was released after serving six years—"

"So that would be 1986?"

"Where's a calculator when you need one?"

Gilchrist felt a thrill of excitement. Stratheden Enterprises was launched in 1986.

Jackie's e-mail opened up on his screen, and he scrolled down the page. "After his release, Purvis moved to England. First to Newcastle for five years, then York for two, then London for four. In each of these cities he was questioned over the disappearance of three women—in 1990, '92, and '94. But he was not charged for any of the incidents due to lack of evidence."

"He must have returned to Scotland at some point," Jessie said, "if he was involved in Nichola Kelly's fatal accident." She read on. "Born in Aberdeen in 1954. Mother and father both unidentified. Raised in an orphanage. Seems not to have had a normal family life. Worked on the rigs from '74 to '79—"

Gilchrist shot a look at Jessie. "The same time period as Magner. Did they work for the same company?"

"It doesn't say. But I'll get that checked out."

"Here's the address," he said. "We're in luck. Cauldwood Cottage, Ceres."

"Where's that?"

"A few miles outside Cupar," said Gilchrist, clicking the mouse. He was already halfway to the printer as it whirred into action. "Jackie's provided a location map for the cottage," he said, grabbing the sheet and folding it in half.

"She's also provided a mobile phone number."

"Don't call it," Gilchrist said. "Let's pay Purvis a surprise visit."

"On what grounds?"

"On the grounds that I'd like to talk to him. Does that work?"

"That works."

They both took the stairs two at a time.

———

Despite the map, Gilchrist took a couple of wrong turns and had to perform a tire-spinning three-sixty before they arrived at Jason Purvis's cottage about six miles southeast of Cupar. The building sat no more than eight feet from the edge of the road. A parcel of land bordering the side of the cottage appeared to double as waste ground.

Gilchrist slowed to a crawl at a wooden sign fixed to the stone wall—CAULDWOOD COTTAGE—then drove past, noting that the gravel driveway by the gable end was clear of parked cars, although damp tracks where tires had splashed through puddles suggested that a vehicle had only recently driven away.

He pulled off the road and onto the grass verge beyond, and eyed the place.

"Looks like it could use a coat or three of paint," Jessie said.

The cottage looked solid enough, its old stone walls darkened by grit and dirt thrown up by passing vehicles. A hawthorn hedgerow in need of a cut tried to define the front boundary. The property seemed to comprise about fifty yards' roadside frontage and an open area to the back that had to be at least two hundred yards deep.

"Let's see if anyone's in," Jessie said, and opened the car door.

The wind seemed to tumble across the open fields, buffeting hedges and bushes as if trying to shake them down. A row of mature pine trees that bordered one side of the property swayed as if the land itself were rocking. The back garden was nothing more than brown grass flattened by rain and wind, a desolate patch that stretched all the way to the distant back border, where a wooden barn sat in dire need of painting. Even from where he stood, Gilchrist could see that a chain-link fence surrounded the building. He might not have paid the barn any attention, except that he caught movement in the grass in front of it. The hairs on the nape of his neck rose as first one Rottweiler, then another, rose to their feet and stared at them with silent malevolence.

He turned away from the dogs and watched Jessie place her hand to the kitchen window and peer inside. "Looks neat and tidy," she said. "But I don't think anyone's in."

Gilchrist walked to the door, tried the handle—locked— pressed the doorbell. He heard nothing. He rang the bell again, then rapped his knuckles against the wood. He took a couple of paces back, glanced up at a slate roof devoid of skylights, which told him they could search the house in its entirety simply by looking through each of the windows.

He peered through the nearest one. Wooden flooring stretched from the rear to the front of the cottage, as if two original rooms had been knocked into one. Rugs that could have come from an Egyptian bazaar colored the floor in stripes of yellows,

blues, reds. Abstract paintings littered the walls, their indeter-
minate subject matter reminding Gilchrist of his son Jack's
work. Purvis seemed to have a taste for color.

Five minutes later, he and Jessie had worked their way
around the entire building.

"Any thoughts?" he asked.

"He lives by himself."

Gilchrist nodded. The bedside table near the bathroom
held several magazines and books, whereas the one on the
other side of the bed lay clear.

"Should we leave a calling card?" Jessie asked.

"I'd prefer to surprise him."

"He could be gone for the rest of the day." She stared over
his shoulder and said, "What's with those dogs? And why the
security fence?"

A set of tire tracks that ran through the grass in the general
direction of the barn only added to the mystery. "While we're
waiting for Purvis," Gilchrist said, "let's have a closer look."

Jessie squinted at him. "Must we?"

"Scared of dogs?"

"Only big ones."

"Come on," he said. "They're caged in by the security fence."

"How high can they jump?"

"Not high enough," he said, and walked toward the barn,
conscious of Jessie trailing him by several yards. The dogs
noticed their approach and lowered their heads, as if ready-
ing for the attack.

Gilchrist kept his eyes on them, then noticed with a shiver
that they were not tied up. But a glance along the base of the
fence confirmed there were no loose strands near the ground
through which the dogs might squeeze. Nor did he see any
sign that they had tried to dig their way under.

The closer they approached, the more malevolent the dogs appeared, their eyes black beads that had no need to blink. Even their noses seemed incapable of twitching a sniff. As they watched Jessie and Gilchrist approach, white drool swelled from their mouths and dripped to the grass, as if in anticipation of sinking their teeth into fresh meat. Only when Gilchrist changed tack and headed toward the padlocked gate did they move—a slow turning of their black necks. And it struck Gilchrist that they were focused on him alone, not Jessie.

He reached the gate and stopped.

The barn beyond seemed larger than he first thought—maybe twenty feet by thirty—and cleaner, too. What he had taken to be dried wood in a state of disrepair was dark stain on solid timber. The tire tracks, now only faintly visible, led all the way to the barn door.

Jessie came up beside him. "These things aren't tied up," she said, positioning herself so that Gilchrist's body shielded her from the dogs.

"We're OK," he said. "The fence is in good nick."

"I could do with it being another ten feet higher," she said, lifting her eyes.

Gilchrist put the fence in the range of nine to ten feet, too high for any dog to leap over, surely. He tried to ignore the Rottweilers and their vicious stares, and turned his attention to the barn. A heavy-duty padlock secured the door, the same as on the chain-link fence.

He reached out and touched it.

Both dogs snarled in unison and crossed the short distance to the fence in less time than it took to blink. Their bodies slammed into the chain links with a force that should have snapped them.

Jessie screamed.

Gilchrist stepped back, stunned by the ferocity of the attack.

The fence wobbled but held.

The dogs threw themselves at the fence again. Slather spattered from their jowls like spray. Lips drew back in frightening snarls that reached their eyes and revealed canine teeth that could tear a man's neck to shreds in zero seconds flat. Growls as deep as thunder emanated from their throats in an expression of raw animal brutality.

Behind him, Gilchrist heard Jessie whimper, then held his breath as one of the dogs leapt up at the fence, as if attempting to climb it. Its front legs scrabbled to get a grip as its rear claws tore at the chain links, its muscles rippling with frenzied effort.

The other dog had the chain links clamped in its mouth and was shaking its head and tugging with a viciousness that Gilchrist thought must surely rip the fence from its concrete foundations.

"Let's get out of here," Jessie said.

Gilchrist backed away, stumbling as he went, conscious of Jessie already running through the grass. He could not take his eyes off the dogs for fear that they might break loose and attack them from behind.

Then the dogs stopped.

So did Gilchrist. He glanced at Jessie. She was still running. He ran his tongue across his lips, surprised to find his mouth dry. Both dogs faced him, black eyes staring, until one of them turned its attention to the bottom of the fence and started scrabbling at the grass with a ferocious speed that was raw brute force.

Gilchrist turned and followed Jessie. Ten yards from the cottage, he risked a backward glance. The dogs were standing perfectly still, looking at him, as if the frantic activity of moments earlier had been only imagined.

When he reached the car, Jessie was standing by the passenger door, her fingers on the handle. He clicked the fob, and she tugged the door open.

Gilchrist slid in behind the steering wheel and glanced at her. Her face was an ill shade of white, and her hands were trembling.

"You all right?" he said.

"Just drive."

"Are you sure you're—"

"Just drive, for fuck sake," she shouted. "Jesus mother of fuck, will you just drive?"

He twisted the key and the engine fired alive.

Without a word, he accelerated onto the road, away from Purvis's cottage and the black-eyed Rottweilers.

23

Gilchrist stared at the road ahead, saying nothing until he sensed Jessie settling. "Can I buy you lunch?" he offered.

"You think that's going to make me feel better?"

"It's amazing what food can do. And drink," he added.

"Does it have anything with a double whisky in it?"

"It can have a triple in it if you think you need it."

"Jesus, Andy," she said. "These fucking things. I tell you," she shook her head, "just seeing them reminded me of a case I was involved in. Three years ago. In Cambuslang. A wee girl got savaged by a big dog, just like one of these things. A Rott . . . something or other—"

"Rottweiler."

Jessie let out a rush of breath. "I don't suppose you have a cigarette on you?"

"Sorry. No."

"Some knight in shining armor you are."

"Forgot my horse."

Jessie stared at the passing countryside for a quiet mile or two, then said, "You should have seen the mess that wee lassie was in. Her rib cage was crushed, her neck was broken.

She'd been shaken like a doll. Her face was unrecognizable. And if that wasn't bad enough, do you know what really got me upset?"

It took several seconds for Gilchrist to realize she was waiting for an answer. "No, what?" he said.

"The dog's owner. A big fat punter with tattoos all over the place. You know what he said?" She paused for a couple of beats. "He said she shouldn't have been in his garden. That was it. No remorse, no mention of the fact that the wee girl had just been mauled to death." She sniffed. "Caroline, her name was. She'd only pulled herself over the fence to get her tennis ball back. When the fat prick said that, Caroline's father went for him. It took three of us to pull him off. Then the big fat punter stands up, spits blood from his mouth, and says he wants the father charged with assault."

Gilchrist kept his eyes on the road. He had only ever seen one victim of a dog attack, and nothing as serious as Jessie was describing. But he had watched police dog handlers working with their animals, witnessed the brutality of their attacks. Something chilling about the ferocious way they tore into their victims, snarling and slashing with bared fangs, pure animal instinct directing them to the throat, to tear it out, go for the kill. If he was ever attacked by a dog as powerful as a Rottweiler, he knew he could do little to save himself. Few men could. Let alone a three-year-old girl.

"I nearly got fired over that," Jessie said.

Gilchrist jolted in his seat. "Come again?"

"I lost it. Completely." She stared out the window for several seconds, then said, "It must be a woman thing. There were four of us, and I was the only female. Not one of them said anything to the fat prick. I pulled out my baton and said, 'If you want to charge anyone, try charging me.' Then I broke his nose. Out like a light. Of course, when he came to, we all had our stories sorted. And that was the end of that. But I tell you, I was worried for a while."

"Should you be telling me this?" Gilchrist asked.

She shook off a shiver, then said, "When these things battered into that fence back there, it all came back to me. I couldn't stop thinking about that wee girl, the pain she must have felt. I tell you, Andy, I was shitting myself. I can't tell you how scared I was."

"I wasn't exactly trying to scratch their ears and take them for walkies either."

She gave a short chuckle. "I shouldn't have told you any of that," she said. "It just . . . I don't know . . . seeing these things . . . hearing them . . . and the size of their teeth . . . and all that slobbering—"

"Forget it," he said.

The words came out louder than intended, but if the truth be told she should not have confessed to having hit a civilian with her baton. He could make discreet inquiries, maybe even file a report. But on the other hand, how many times had he been confronted with the condescending arrogance of a hardened criminal, someone for whom the law was only to be scoffed at, shoving it in his face, threatening him with vitriol and spittle, ready to take it further than he ever could, because the police, by definition, were constrained by the limits of the law. If one of his own children had been mauled to death by a dog, it would take a far stronger man than he was to turn his back on it and let the law take over. He felt his lips stretch at the unintended pun. Best to let sleeping dogs lie.

"We both got a fright back there," he said. "Let's leave it at that." He waited for Jessie's nod, then added, "We need to talk to this Jason Purvis, regardless of how many dogs he's got. So get hold of Jackie and find out what he drives."

"Hang on," Jessie said, retrieving her mobile. "In our rush I didn't go through Jackie's e-mail completely."

Gilchrist slowed down for the roundabout at City Road, then accelerated into North Street. He had not been in the Dunvegan Hotel for a couple of weeks. Lunch there would make a nice change. Just the thought of warm food had his mouth watering.

First left took him into Golf Place, and he found a parking spot on the Scores.

A hard wind blew in from the Eden Estuary and swept a chill off the Old Course as he helped Jessie across the street, still scrolling through Jackie's e-mail. They had just turned the corner at Hamilton Hall, when Jessie stopped.

"You're not going to believe this," she said. "Jackie's done it."

Gilchrist waited.

"A black BMW 650i is registered in the name of Jason Purvis."

Gilchrist had his mobile in his hand almost before Jessie finished the sentence. He got straight through to HQ control. "Add a locate-and-trace marker on the PNC for a black BMW 650i," he said, then held out his mobile to Jessie. "Year?"

"Two thousand four," she said, then rattled off the registration number.

Gilchrist moved the mobile back to his ear. "Suspected to have been involved in a fatal hit-and-run on the outskirts of Anstruther. Driver, Jason Purvis. Previous conviction for serious assault. Six years in Peterhead. Approach with caution. BMW could have some damage on the front nearside panel. And run the registration through the ANPR and see if you get any hits. You got that?"

She had, and Gilchrist told her to call him with any feedback. Next he called the Anstruther Office and instructed them to initiate proceedings for a search warrant for Purvis's home. They couldn't fool around if a serial offender was in any way involved in a fatal hit-and-run—just get a warrant and go in with maximum force.

He ended the call and slipped the mobile back into his jacket.

Things were now moving. The Automatic Number Plate Recognition system—ANPR—tracked vehicle movements in real time, so there was a good chance of someone pulling Purvis over in short order. On the other hand, it still left time for a quick lunch. But something also told Gilchrist that he was going to need all his strength to tackle a nutcase like Purvis.

"Come on," he said. "My stomach's grumbling. I'm having fish and chips. How about you?"

"Double Glenfiddich, if you're still buying."

"On an empty stomach?"

"On a diet."

"Not for Jabba, I hope."

"Jesus, Andy. You're in a right cheeky mood, so you are. I'll nick some of your chips then, if that'll make you feel better."

They hurried inside, and Gilchrist ordered at the bar, then carried their drinks to one of the corner tables and took a seat with his back to the window that overlooked Auchterlonies. Jessie slumped in beside him, her sullen silence suggesting she was still unsettled by the memory of that wee girl, Caroline.

Gilchrist took a sip of Belhaven, then called Stan to tell him about the locate-and-trace marker for the BMW. "And I've decided that I'm not waiting until tomorrow for the banks to open," he said. "We're working all weekend, but we've to wait for everybody else to get their arse into the office on Monday? I'm through with it, Stan. Get hold of Anne Mills right now, then call her bank manager and tell him we need access to a safe-deposit box *today*. I want to see what she's holding."

He almost slapped the mobile onto the table and powered it down.

"Steady on," Jessie said. "You're scaring me."

"Yeah, well, maybe you should be." He was saved by the arrival of a basket of fish and chips, which he shoved Jessie's way. Then he asked the waitress, "Could we get a side plate and another fork and knife, please?"

"I'll just use my fingers," Jessie countered, and picked a chip from the basket. She was nibbling it when the side plate arrived.

Gilchrist tilted a pile of chips on to it. "Like a piece of fish, too?" he asked.

"You've talked me into it."

He broke off a piece. "Excuse the fingers."

They ate in silence, both deep in their own thoughts, until Jessie angled her whisky Gilchrist's way and said, "Fancy one?"

"Not when I'm on duty," he said, as if beer did not count as alcohol.

"Me neither," Jessie said, bringing the glass to her lips. "Cheers." Her mobile rang at that moment, and she eyed the screen before taking the call. Gilchrist took a sip of beer and felt his heart give a stutter when she said, "So where's Magner at right now?" She tightened her lips, then shook her head. "So, he's nothing to do with it?" She nodded again. "We'll be there in thirty minutes." She ended the call and said, "That was DI Smith. He couldn't get through to you. Linda James has just been found dead in her flat in Cupar."

Linda James: one of the eleven who filed a complaint against Magner.

"And Magner's got a watertight alibi?"

"Spot on." She threw back her Glenfiddich. "DI Smith gave me the address. We're meeting him at Linda's flat." She nodded to his plate. "You might want to put that to the side."

Gilchrist let out a groan. "Don't tell me . . ."

"Got it in one. According to Smith, it's not pretty."

24

Not pretty was an understatement.

The flat was a mess. Linda James lay facedown on the middle of the floor in a pool of blood that had seeped through the carpet and floorboards and dripped into the flat below, terrifying the downstairs neighbors.

As far as Gilchrist could tell, Linda had put up one hell of a fight. Her fingers, hands, and arms were all sliced with defensive wounds. Her right thumb had been severed and was found on the draining board by the sink. From spatter patterns that trailed across walls and through rooms, they surmised that she had been attacked as soon as she opened the door. From there, she had run into the kitchen, where she had scrambled for a carving knife to protect herself. It was found on the floor in the corner, its serrated blade devoid of blood. Smeared handprints low down on the door frame, and streaks of blood on the linoleum, told the grim story of a dying woman struggling to escape her attacker, only to be stabbed to death in the middle of her own living room.

Back outside, DI Smith pulled back his coverall hood, his mouth little more than a white line. CS Whyte was still inside the flat, talking to Cooper and Jessie.

"This isn't doing anything for your case," Gilchrist told Smith. "By my count, there are only four left now."

"And once they hear about this they'll all probably retract their statements."

"And if they don't?" Gilchrist asked.

"Chief Super Whyte has arranged twenty-four seven surveillance on their homes. They'll also each have a uniform with them around the clock."

"Armed?"

Smith nodded.

Gilchrist raised his eyebrows. No matter how serious the situation was, budgets still had to be met and protocols still had to be followed. But Billy Whyte seemed to have control over some major purse strings. "And what about Magner?"

"He's distancing himself," Smith said. "Been in Glasgow all day, shouting his head off, attracting attention, making sure he has a ton of witnesses." He cleared his throat. "Finding a suspect is easy, but trying to prove he's guilty is another kettle of fish."

"How about his phone?"

"*Phones*. Plural."

"Any luck with them?"

"Of course not. We've gone through his records, but SIM cards are ten a penny. He'll have a pile of mobiles with different cards and numbers for every call he makes that he doesn't want us to know about." He shook his head. "We're spinning our wheels."

"How about CCTV footage?"

"Already on it, but the cameras closest to Linda's flat have been deactivated. We're thinking he's got someone on the inside."

Gilchrist told Smith about his search for the BMW, then mentioned Purvis's striking similarity to Magner, and the fact that they'd worked on the rigs at the same time. "Your case and the McCulloch massacre are connected," he said. "I'm sure of it."

Smith nodded. "But how do we prove it?"

"Well, we have a common victim—Amy McCulloch, née Charlotte Renwick. That's a start. By killing Amy, he takes care of two birds with the one stone. Takes out his business partner and one of his accusers at the same time."

"Could be a coincidence."

"No such thing."

Smith stared at him. "It's a thin connection."

Gilchrist waited.

Smith finally understood and shook his head. "I'm sorry, we can't help you, sir. We're stretched to the limit. Resources are committed. ACC McVicar spoke to Billy today to approve the round-the-clock surveillance, but that won't last forever."

"How long?" Gilchrist asked.

Smith gave him a look that said he was just as frustrated as Gilchrist. "The way things are going, sir, not long enough. Nowhere near."

The hard voice of CS Whyte from within the flat had Smith moving away with a quick, "Keep me posted, sir."

"Likewise."

As Jessie stepped from the flat and removed her coveralls, Gilchrist pulled out his mobile and called Stan.

"Boss?"

"Are you with Anne Mills?" Gilchrist asked.

"We're at the bank, even as we speak. They've lent us a computer, and we're just booting it up. I'll be able to plug in the memory stick in a minute or two."

"Hand her the phone, will you?"

"I can't at the moment, boss. She's with the manager, filling in half a dozen forms. Payback for making him work on a Sunday, I imagine."

Gilchrist brought him up to speed with Linda James's murder, then said, "When you get a chance, ask Anne if she knows her. It's odd that she's happy to talk to you about photographs that could nail Magner to the wall, while every other witness is retracting her statement or lying in a pool of blood."

"You think her life's in danger, boss?"

"Don't you?" Gilchrist said. "Or, more to the point, doesn't she?"

"Let me get back to you, boss."

Gilchrist killed the call as a thought came to him. He turned to Jessie. "Any guesses as to why Jason Purvis was not at home?"

Jessie narrowed her eyes. "Out on business?"

"Magner's business?" He glanced at his watch—not yet four o'clock, but it would be dark in a couple of hours. Better to confront Purvis during daylight hours. He knew it was a long shot, probably one of his longest. But it was still a shot.

And Cauldwood Cottage was less than fifteen minutes away.

"Let's go," he said.

———

Rather than park on the grass verge as he had before, Gilchrist drove into the short driveway at the side of the cottage and parked behind a white Ford Focus—just about the most common car on the road. He noted the registration number, called Glenrothes HQ, and asked for someone to check the PNC records and CCTV footage in and around Cupar for any sight of the Focus close to the time of Linda James's murder.

"Oh, and while you're at it, do the same for Tentsmuir Forest on Thursday evening." He turned to Jessie and asked, "You ready?"

"Wish I had my Beretta with me."

"I don't recall you having a firearms license."

"I don't."

He held her steady stare. She'd mentioned her .22 before, but he'd taken it as a quip. Her jerk for a smile told him she was joking again, but just in case she wasn't, he said, "Unless you want your jotters, it's better that you don't."

"You're no fun," she said, and grabbed the door handle.

Together, they walked around the back of the cottage to a lawn–cum–vegetable garden that could have done with a good weeding and mowing, or maybe plowing up altogether. Beyond the rear property boundary, the barn stood in the long shadows of a low sun.

"You see the dogs?" Jessie asked.

"Maybe he locks them up in the barn for the night." He turned back to face the cottage.

The curtains were drawn, but the warm glow of indoor lighting told him Purvis—or someone—was at home. He pressed the doorbell, half expecting to hear the demented barks of a pair of wild Rottweilers. But the house remained silent. He rang the bell again and this time caught its faint chimes from deep within. He counted to twenty before saying to Jessie, "What's that number Jackie gave us?"

Jessie already had her mobile out. She scrolled down the screen until she found it. Two seconds after clicking the number, she said, "It's ringing."

Gilchrist stepped back into the long grass, so he could see all four windows that overlooked the rear of the property. He was hoping to catch the flicker of a curtain as Purvis checked to see who was pestering him on a late Sunday afternoon.

Jessie flapped a hand at Gilchrist to let him know her call had just been answered. "Could I speak to Jason Purvis?" she said.

"What do you want?" a voice answered, but not from Jessie's mobile.

Gilchrist spun round in surprise to face the corner of the cottage.

He recognized Purvis instantly. Not from an old newspaper photograph but from his striking resemblance to Magner. A tad over six foot, like Magner, but with hair more blond than Magner's blond-going-gray, styled short and combed, and still damp from a recent shower. Even though Magner kept himself fit, Purvis seemed stronger, his body bulked with muscle that rippled beneath a white T-shirt. He could be Magner on steroids. This was someone who could hold his own in a battle and was certainly more than a physical match for Gilchrist.

Purvis clicked off his mobile, slipped it into his pocket, then lowered his hands to his sides. When he clenched his fists, the muscles on his forearms flexed like tendons of steel.

Gilchrist held out his warrant card. "We're with Fife Constabulary."

Purvis hissed something that Gilchrist failed to catch, then felt his blood turn to water as the two Rottweilers slipped from the side of the cottage and squatted on their haunches either side of their master. Rumbling growls, as deep as thunder, filled the air. Something hit the grass to Gilchrist's left, and a quick glance confirmed that Jessie had dropped her phone.

Purvis almost smiled. "You still haven't told me what you want."

"To talk."

"About what?"

Gilchrist returned the warrant card to his jacket. "About where your BMW is."

"Don't have it."

"Why not?"

"Lent it to a friend."

"Name?"

"Jimmy Watson."

"When?"

"Last week."

"When's Jimmy going to return it?"

"When he's done with it."

"Done?"

"Finished his holiday. He wanted to drive to Europe."

"Why drive to Europe when you can get all these cheap flights?"

"You'd need to ask him."

"Didn't you?"

"Didn't I what?"

"Ask Jimmy why he wanted to drive to Europe."

"I couldn't give two fucks why Jimmy wanted to drive to Europe. As long as he brings the Beemer back in one piece, that's all that matters."

"Where does Jimmy live?"

A half nod at the cottage. "Here."

"He lives here? With you?"

"You deaf or what?"

Gilchrist let several seconds pass, then said, "We could always arrest you and take you to the Office, if that's what you'd prefer."

"Arrest me?" Purvis grinned. "For what? Besides, you're a long way from home. So why would I *let* you arrest me?"

"In case you haven't thought it through," Gilchrist said. "The Office knows we're here."

"Oh, yeah?"

"Yeah," Jessie said. "Do you think we'd come out to the middle of nowhere to talk to a nutter like you without covering our backs?"

Anger shifted across Purvis's face like a shadow, as if his mind were debating whether to order the dogs to attack. As if sensing his dilemma, the Rottweilers' growls deepened, and for one uncertain moment Gilchrist thought Purvis was about to let them loose. Then Purvis snapped his fingers, and both dogs rose to their feet.

"Been broken into twice in the last five years," he said, as if that explained everything. "So it's good to have these boys around."

"Did you report the break-ins?" Gilchrist asked.

"What's the point reporting anything to you lot?" Purvis said.

Gilchrist stifled a smile. There never were any break-ins. "Get rid of the dogs," he said.

Purvis held his gaze for longer than Gilchrist thought polite. Then he cocked his head and gave a shrill whistle. Both Rottweilers jerked into motion and ran off through the long grass toward the barn. "The door's not locked," he said. "Help yourself to a cup of tea and a biscuit while I lock that pair up for the night."

Gilchrist returned Purvis's cold stare, toying with the idea of cuffing him just for the hell of it. But it would likely take no more than another whistle for both dogs to return to protect their master. Better get rid of them first, he thought. "We'll be waiting for you," he said.

Purvis gave a scowl in response, then strode after his dogs.

Jessie stood with her arms wrapped around her middle, as if on the verge of tears.

Gilchrist retrieved her mobile. "You dropped this," he said.

She took it from him and wiped it clean. "I think I wet my knickers."

"I would've wet mine, too, if I was wearing any."

Jessie tried to smile. Then Gilchrist brushed past her and walked to the back door. He twisted the handle. To his surprise, it opened—unlocked, just as Purvis had said—leaving him thinking he had it all wrong, that Purvis, just like Magner, might be innocent. Or more correctly, when he thought about it, that proving Purvis or Magner were guilty was another matter entirely.

He pushed open the door and stepped into a tidy kitchen.

"Not quite the proper way for a criminal to behave," Jessie said.

He looked around the small room, ready to seize the opportunity. He had work to do while Purvis locked up the dogs. "You any good at making tea?" he asked.

"I'm a mum, you forget, and mums can do anything."

"I'm not asking if you can or can't," he said. "I'm asking if you're any good at it."

"I think you've got verbal OCD."

"Jesus, Jessie. Just put the bloody kettle on, will you? And give me a shout before Purvis gets back." Then he turned and walked into the lounge.

25

Gilchrist worked out that he probably had four minutes, tops.

He walked straight through the living room, intending to start in the master bedroom. The first thing that struck him was how neat and tidy everything was. The bed was made, pillows fluffed up, duvet cover folded over without even a hint of a ruffle. A quick opening and closing of wardrobe doors offered nothing obvious.

He entered the en suite shower room, which was still warm and clammy from Purvis's recent shower. The glass panel had been wiped down with a squeegee, the sink dried with paper towels. The toilet seat was down, and a quick look-see revealed nothing. He launched himself at a wicker basket in the corner and pulled off the lid, only to feel a surge of disappointment on seeing the contents—a white T-shirt, a pair of white underpants, and black socks. If his theory was correct, that Purvis had been involved in the murder of Linda James, then there had to be blood-covered clothes lying around somewhere, or at least some traces of blood.

Purvis surely could not have had time to dispose of them.

A look under the bed revealed nothing, so Gilchrist strode into the spare bedroom.

A quick inspection told him that if Jimmy Watson shared the cottage with Purvis, then he maintained an almost invisible presence. The wardrobe, drawers, and bedside cabinets were all empty, except for two sport coats that looked as if they would fit Purvis, three T-shirts, an unused pocket diary, and a small plastic container. The latter piqued Gilchrist's interest.

He opened it to find twenty-five separate compartments—five by five—with the whole unit perfectly sized for storing twelve-gauge shotshells in the down position. Given Purvis's record, by law he would not be permitted to own any gun. So, did the empty ammunition container belong to Watson?

With a mild flush of panic, Gilchrist realized he was almost out of time. He returned the container to the cabinet drawer and made his way back to the kitchen. The kettle was reaching the boil, and three mugs were lined up on the countertop next to a packet of biscuits. Jessie had the kitchen drawers open, and she was scratching her way through their contents.

"Anything?" Gilchrist asked.

She shook her head. "You?"

"Maybe."

The cottage was too small to have a separate utility room, and Gilchrist opened the kitchen units one at a time to confirm they were fully integrated. A small under-the-counter fridge hid behind a wooden cabinet door. Next to that he found a freezer. He located the tumble dryer and washing machine at the far end of the kitchen.

"You see him?" he asked Jessie.

She eased back the curtain. "He's on his way back. I'll let you know."

Gilchrist pressed the button to open the washing machine's door. It clicked, but nothing happened. He tried again, but the door was either locked or stuck. He kneeled on the floor and peered through the glass.

"Andy, he's back."

Gilchrist jumped to his feet, closed the wooden door that concealed the washer, and stepped toward Jessie as the back door opened.

"Find anything of interest?" Purvis asked.

Jessie said, "Tea's up."

Purvis eyed the mugs on the countertop, the plate of biscuits, the kitchen cabinets one by one, his eyes missing nothing as they shifted from one cabinet to the other. Then his gaze found Jessie and hung on her for a moment, before drifting over her shoulder to settle on Gilchrist.

"Do you own a gun?" Gilchrist asked.

"No."

"I can apply for a search warrant and come back later, if you'd prefer."

Purvis said nothing for a long moment, then walked into the living room. He opened a drawer in a corner table and removed a key, which he handed to Gilchrist.

"What's this?" Gilchrist asked.

"It's Jimmy's." Purvis nodded to a small door on the wall next to the fireplace, which Gilchrist had assumed contained the fuse box. "Look in there," he said.

Gilchrist inserted the key and the lock clicked. He pulled the door open to reveal two twelve-bore shotguns and a rifle.

"Any of these yours?" he asked Purvis.

"I told you. They're Jimmy's."

"You got proof of that?"

Purvis walked to an ornate wooden chest in the middle of the room, which doubled as a coffee table. He released the clip lock and lifted the lid, then retrieved a folder from deep inside.

Silent, Gilchrist waited.

Purvis handed him several slips of paper, and a quick scan confirmed that the rifle and both shotguns were registered to Mr. James Watson of Cauldwood Cottage.

"Satisfied?" Purvis asked, holding out a hand for the key and gun licenses.

"I'd like to see the paperwork for the BMW, too."

"Why?"

"A similar car was involved in a fatal hit-and-run accident last night."

"I was in Edinburgh last night."

"I never said where the accident occurred."

"You're with Fife Constabulary," Purvis replied without missing a beat. "Edinburgh's Lothian, not Fife, so you wouldn't be involved if the accident happened there."

The speed of Purvis's response told Gilchrist he was dealing with someone with a quick mind who was not afraid to challenge police authority. More troubling was that Purvis had a violent criminal record and ready access to a cache of weapons, even though they were purportedly licensed to the mysterious Jimmy Watson, whose presence so far was nothing short of ghostlike.

"Do you have proof you were in Edinburgh?" Gilchrist asked.

"What sort of proof?"

"Restaurant bills, hotel receipts—"

"I do cash. Not credit cards."

"Earn a lot, do you?"

"Enough to get by, yeah."

"Where were you this afternoon?"

Purvis narrowed his eyes, as if a seed of doubt had entered his mind. Or perhaps he had just worked out that Gilchrist must have visited the cottage earlier in the day.

"In Cupar," he said. "Shopping."

"Go there often?"

"Only when I need to buy food."

"What did you buy?"

"Look in the fridge. You'll see. Milk, yogurt, cheese, butter, bread."

"Show me," Gilchrist said, and followed Purvis back into the kitchen.

Jessie asked, "Milk and sugar?"

"Don't push it," Purvis replied, and leaned down to open the fridge.

Gilchrist glanced inside and noted the contents—exactly as described. "What about laundry?"

Purvis closed the fridge door. "What about it?"

"Do any at home?"

Purvis looked at Jessie and said, "Does he always do this? Act the fool?" He turned to Gilchrist. "Washing machine's behind you. You've already had a look. But go ahead and have another."

Gilchrist glanced at the cabinets and, sure enough, the door that hid the washing machine had sprung open just a touch. "What are you washing?" he asked.

"I usually wash clothes in my washing machine. What do you wash? Your dick?"

The question lay between them like foul-smelling smog.

"Do you have a number for Jimmy Watson?" Gilchrist said.

"Off the top of my head, no."

"So how do you get hold of him?"

"He gets hold of me."

"You don't worry that he'll run off with your Beemer?"

Purvis narrowed his eyes, as if seeing the danger in Gilchrist for the first time. His lips pressed tight together, and anger worked across his face. "He wouldn't dare."

Gilchrist decided to press harder. "What do you keep in the barn?" he asked.

"My private collection of classic cars. What d'you think?"

Purvis's answer was intended as a lie, and Gilchrist said, "Not good enough."

"Too true, mate, it's not good enough." Purvis slipped a mobile out of his back pocket and said, "Chat's over. I'm calling my solicitor. You want to talk to me again, book me with something; then we can have a formal talk down at the station." He turned his back on Gilchrist and walked into the living room.

Jessie caught Gilchrist's eye and shook her head. He could tell she was still nervous from the dogs. And Purvis's bullyboy manner had not helped. But that aside, Gilchrist had found nothing to suggest that Purvis had anything to do with the murder of Linda James. The irritating fact—or irritating *lie*—was that the BMW had been lent to a friend. If it was not on the premises—as a reflex, Gilchrist turned his head in the direction of the barn—then it really could be anywhere, and impossible to find.

His mobile rang—Stan. He took the call, aware of Purvis talking to someone—presumably his solicitor—in the other room.

"I've got the photographs, boss." A pause, then, "I think you need to see them."

"Where are you?"

"Heading to the Office. Should be there in about ten minutes."

"We'll meet you there," Gilchrist said, and ended the call. He walked through to the living room.

Purvis was still on his mobile, his voice little more than a whisper, as if not wanting to be overheard. At the sight of Gilchrist, he stopped and pressed his hand to the mouthpiece. "Why don't you come right on in?" he said.

Gilchrist handed him one of his business cards. "We can't stay. Thanks for the tea. Have Jimmy Watson call me the moment you hear from him."

Purvis stared at the card, as if deciding whether to rip it up now or later.

He chose later, and Gilchrist retreated back to the kitchen.

Outside, neither he nor Jessie uttered a word until they were inside the car.

"He scares me," Jessie said.

Gilchrist slipped into reverse and eased out of the driveway. "It's the dogs that are scaring you," he said. "Not Purvis. Without the dogs, Purvis is just another cocky bastard trying to act hard." He knew it was a lie even as he said the words.

Purvis was more than just a nasty piece of work. He was a narcissistic psychopath with obsessive compulsive disorder. The neatness of his home, the assured confidence when under interrogation, the arrogant belief that he was above the law and better than those who served it all told Gilchrist that. But he had not failed to catch the one question that triggered the end of the interview—*What do you keep in the barn?*

"Can you take me home first?" Jessie asked.

"Problems?"

"I need to change my knickers."

Gilchrist glanced at her, but she was looking out the window. "I'm sorry," he said. "Back there, when you said . . . you know . . . I thought you were joking."

"No joke," she said. "And it'll be no joke either if Jabba's waiting for me."

"He hasn't called today, has he?"

"I blocked his number."

Gilchrist's smile turned to a chuckle. "He'll be jumping up and down."

"Not in my house, I hope. He'd go through the floorboards."

———

When Gilchrist pulled up to the curb at Canongate, Jessie said, "It doesn't look like he's here." She opened the door. "Back in a jiffy."

Gilchrist waited until she slipped inside, then called the Anstruther Office and asked if they had managed to secure the search warrant for Cauldwood Cottage. He was convinced the BMW had not been lent out. It had to be in the barn. But when the news came back that the warrant had been denied because of insufficient evidence, he cursed and killed the connection.

Next he called Stan. "We'll be with you in another five minutes."

"OK, boss. I'm back in the Office, at my computer."

Something in the tone of his voice had Gilchrist pressing the mobile hard to his ear. "You sound concerned, old son."

"You need to see this, boss. I'm not sure." A pause, then, "I haven't shown it to anyone else. But I think we've got trouble."

Gilchrist gave Stan's words some thought. "Trouble?" he said. "As in, *el shito* is about to hit *el fano?*"

"Got it in one, boss."

"Good," said Gilchrist. "I'm in the right mood for that."

26

Jessie climbed back into the Merc and slammed the door shut with a force that should have broken its hinges.

"Couldn't find a clean pair?" Gilchrist tried.

She glared at him for a hard moment, then said, "If anyone threatens my son, I swear to God I'll have them. I really mean it. I don't care how high up the police tree they are."

"Or how fat they are?"

She paused for a second. "That fat prick. He's really done it this time." She clicked her seat belt into place, then looked to the upstairs bedroom window and blew a kiss.

Robert looked down at her, gave a wave in response, then slipped from view.

Gilchrist pushed into gear. "Is he OK?"

"He's fine. Now. But he was worried earlier."

"What happened?"

"You know I've blocked Jabba's number. But oh, no, he still doesn't get it. So he came round this morning looking for me. When he found out I was at work, he was not happy. Then he tried to play the big Mick with Robert, show him how good a dad he could be, telling him that he wanted to take him to the new flat that he thinks we're going to move into."

"Does Jabba know sign language?"

"You know, Andy, you can be a right plonker at times."

Well, he wasn't going to argue about that.

"No, he doesn't know sign language. He wrote it down." She had her mobile out and was scrolling through her call log. "Look at this," she said. "Four numbers I never answered. I knew they would be from him, trying to call me from someone else's phone. Maybe I need to block these—"

"What did Robert do?" Gilchrist interrupted.

"Nothing. He just let Jabba know that I would be back later. Then Jabba sees Robert's mobile lying on the table, so he picks it up and tries to call me using *that*. He knows I'll always answer a call from Robert. Anyway, he's fiddling with it and Robert tries to grab it off him. Well . . ."

Gilchrist accelerated onto Bridge Street. "Well what?"

"He pushed Robert away, and Robert tripped and banged his head on the floor."

"Is he all right?"

"He's a bit shaken, but nothing's broken. That's not the point. I can't have that fat prick entering my home and laying hands on my son." She scrolled through her contacts, found a number, and pressed the mobile to her ear.

Gilchrist stared at the road ahead. This was not good. Having an affair—albeit a short-lived one—with a fellow detective was one thing. Harassing her to go out with him, despite being told in no uncertain terms to piss off, was another. But entering her home uninvited, when she was not there, and pushing her son around was beyond a joke.

"Lachie. It's me. No, no, *you* listen. I am not having you—" Gilchrist glanced at her—lips pressed tight, eyes glistening with tears. The tinny echo of Lachie's rattling voice left him in no doubt that *he* was telling *her* off.

"No, Lachie, listen . . . No, that's not true . . . No, no, it's not. Will you listen—"

Gilchrist eased the car onto North Street and accelerated up the hill.

"OK, Lachie, you do what you have to do. But I'm telling you, that's it. You just stay away from me. You hear? Just stay away." She stared at the mobile in her hand for a long moment, then looked at Gilchrist. "He hung up. Can you believe that?"

"Would you like some help?" Gilchrist said.

"If you're any good at dumping body parts in the middle of the ocean, big fat ones, then, yeah, I'd like all the help you can give me."

Gilchrist frowned as he drove on while Jessie glared out the window. Minutes later, he pulled off North Street and drove through the pend into the Office car park. He switched off the engine, but neither of them made any effort to move.

"Want to talk about it?" he said.

She sniffed. "I don't know."

"If he's threatening you or harassing you or bullying your son, you can take legal action against him."

She shook her head. "I don't want to do that to him."

"Why not?"

"What's wrong with me?" She turned to look at him. "I mean, as fat as he is, he's got a good heart, and he'd do anything for me. It's just . . ." She shook her head, then startled Gilchrist by grabbing hold of her breasts and wobbling them. "I mean, look at me. What do I have to offer? Big tits and a deaf son and a family you'd run a hundred miles from."

Gilchrist let several silent seconds pass. "You shouldn't put yourself down, Jessie. You're a good detective, one of the best. And I've seen you with Robert. You're a great mum, too."

Jessie sniffed again.

"In fact, you're probably the best mum Robert's ever had."

She chuckled. "You're a right charmer."

"Other than Jabba, has anyone ever told you how attractive you are?"

Her brown eyes glistened at that, almost pleading, and he saw in their reflection the hurt and pain she had suffered at the hands of others. Her fine nose and clear skin, and lips that could flash a ready smile, could be the dream of any model. But somewhere along the way, she had let herself go, to the point where she no longer had any confidence in her looks.

She turned away and grabbed the door handle.

He reached for her. "Look at me, Jessie."

But she swatted his hand away. "Come on. We've got work to do."

They entered the Office and walked up the stairs in silence.

Stan almost jumped when he caught sight of them approaching his desk.

"Steady on, Stan. You look nervous."

He ran a hand across his lips. "Anne Mills doesn't know I have these."

"I thought you went to the bank and—"

"We did, boss, but then she had a change of heart. She wouldn't say why, but I think someone must have told her about Linda James's murder. So now she's thinking if Magner finds out she's given the police these, then dying of cancer is the least of her worries."

"So you stole them?" Jessie said.

"Copied them."

"I'm not sure whether to say naughty boy or well done," said Gilchrist.

"Don't say anything until you've had a look." Stan clicked the mouse.

Gilchrist watched the screen over Stan's shoulder, conscious of Jessie standing on the other side but keeping her distance. The speed with which her emotions could change—from madder than hell to insecure in a matter of seconds—never failed to amaze him.

"The quality's not the greatest," Stan said. "Our IT guys can try to improve them, but I think they'll be on a loser. Right, here we go."

Gilchrist leaned closer.

The image was of a group of people on a dance floor. Balls of colored lighting in the background suggested it was a disco.

"Recognize anyone?" Stan asked, leaning back.

Gilchrist took hold of the mouse and concentrated on the screen.

"You can zoom in," Stan suggested.

Gilchrist moved the cursor over the dance floor and rested it on a couple caught in a frozen jive. Then on to a woman with a scowl on her face as if she had found half a grub in her maraschino cherry. But he was having difficulty establishing what had Stan so worked up.

"Try the next image," Stan said.

Gilchrist shifted the cursor to the right, clicked on the arrow, and an image slid onto the screen—same dance floor, different couple. This time he recognized Magner, slimmer by twenty years, hair longer, thicker, and less blond. The press of their bodies and his hands on the woman's backside left little doubt about what either partner had in mind.

"Who's he dancing with?" Gilchrist asked.

Jessie chipped in with, "Looks like he's giving her a dry hump."

"Not yet," Stan said. "Try the next one."

A group of eight people seated at a table opened up on the screen, all seemingly oblivious to the photographer's presence. An empty dance floor lay behind them, as if the DJ was taking a break. Gilchrist recognized Magner again—his photogenic good looks and white smile would have him standing out in any crowd. This time he was sitting beside an attractive brunette in danger of her breasts spilling from her low-cut dress.

"Who's she?" Gilchrist asked.

"Anne Mills."

In the seat on Anne's other side sat a man who appeared to have his hand on the left breast of the woman beside him. The remaining four had their backs to the camera.

"Is he doing what I think he's doing?" Gilchrist asked.

Jessie leaned forward. "Jesus," she said. "They're swingers."

Gilchrist glanced at her, then at Stan, who raised his eyebrows.

"Keep going, boss."

Gilchrist was about to pull up the next image when he hesitated. He placed the cursor over the face of the man with his hand on his neighbor's breast and zoomed in. As Stan had said, the images were of low quality, and he zoomed out, then in again, trying to strike the best balance.

"Is that who I think it is?" he asked.

"Have a guess."

"Martin Craig?"

"The Lib Dem MEP, boss."

"Are there more of him in here?"

"Carry on, boss."

"Does he know about these photographs?" Gilchrist asked.

"Oh, he knows about them all right," Stan said. "He's looking at the camera on a couple of them. And I bet he can't
wait to get his hands on them now."

"You think Magner's blackmailing him?" Jessie asked.

"Don't know for sure, but I'd be prepared to put a hefty
bet on that he is."

"You're not a gambling man," Gilchrist said.

"Only when it's odds on."

"If Magner's blackmailing Martin Craig, that might explain
Stratheden's meteoric rise," Gilchrist said.

"Precisely."

Stan's nervousness—or maybe excitement—told Gilchrist
he was still missing something. But nothing he had seen so
far would suggest that *el shito* was about to hit *el fano*.

So he pressed on.

He opened up the next image—the same group of eight,
but shot from the opposite side. Magner and his wife now
had their backs to the camera. The glowing gantry of a busy
bar filled the background. A topless woman shook cocktails.
Back to the group: the groping man was now fondling his
partner's exposed breasts with vigor. No one else at the table
seemed to notice, especially not Magner, who was giving his
full attention to the woman on his right. Anne, to his left,
seemed intent on filling a champagne flute from a bottle of
Bollinger.

Gilchrist placed the cursor on the faces of the opposite
two couples and zoomed in a touch. One woman had a hand
on her smiling partner's lap beneath the table, leaving little
for the imagination. Beside them, the other couple were deep
into an intimate kiss.

But still Gilchrist did not see what he was missing. He
opened the next image.

Same angle, same shot, but maybe five or ten seconds later than the previous image.

The kissing couple were now smiling for the camera, arms around each other, the gleam in their eyes hinting at what was yet to come. As Gilchrist studied the image, he finally thought he saw what was making Stan so anxious. He leaned closer, then said, "I don't believe it. It can't be. Can it?"

Jessie said, "What am I missing?"

Gilchrist zoomed in on the man's face, then shifted the cursor to the woman. "Is that his wife?" he asked.

"Could be," Stan said. "But he's widowed now, isn't he?"

"Would someone please tell me what's got everyone's knickers in a twist?" Jessie pleaded.

Gilchrist leaned back from the computer screen and ran a hand down his face. "You're new to Fife," he said, "so you probably haven't met him yet. But that man there"—he nodded at the screen—"is our boss."

"The head potato," Stan confirmed.

Jessie mouthed a *Wow*, then said, "Chief Constable Ramsay?"

"Chief Constable Michael MacNairn Ramsay, QPM, to be more exact."

"And rumored to be in line for a knighthood at the end of this year."

"And he knows Magner?"

Gilchrist grimaced. "Intimately, by the looks of it."

27

They spent the next hour compiling a list of all the photographs and the people who appeared in them. Seventy images in total, starting at the table, then moving to what appeared to be a private room where the business of free sex and wife-swapping began in earnest.

They were able to identify with certainty only four of the eight: Magner and his wife, Anne; Martin Craig, MEP, and his partner, as yet unknown—Craig had married late in life, the rumor being that he had done so to counter persistent accusations of being gay, but nothing in these images suggested Craig was anything other than a testosterone-fuelled heterosexual; Chief Constable Ramsay with a woman presumed to be his late wife, Jean. The fourth couple, a slim blonde—obviously dyed, or a wig—with dark-nippled breasts and a black bush that trailed in a thin line to her navel, and her partner, who appeared to be more inebriated than the others, remained anonymous.

Jessie suggested the blonde might be a prostitute, as she was the only woman photographed in flagrante with all four men. Stan joked that he wouldn't mind finding out if she was still available for hire, which earned him a fearsome scowl from Jessie.

Of all the couples, Chief Constable Ramsay and his partner appeared the most shy, with Ramsay's effort of intercourse with the dyed blonde being performed with his hand to his face. Ramsay's partner was snapped with Magner's penis in her mouth, and as Gilchrist worked through the images, he came to understand that Magner had been one step ahead of the others, maybe several, the end result of that evening's fun being a file of photographs for future reference—read blackmail.

The problem facing Gilchrist now was what to do with this information.

None of them had any doubts that they had to report this. The chief constable's relationship with the accused in an ongoing rape case—a man who also happened to be a suspect in a multiple-murder investigation—could not be ignored. How it had flown under the radar for all these years was the most troubling question.

"It makes you wonder if Ramsay knows about these," said Gilchrist.

"Maybe it's not him," Jessie said, and when Gilchrist and Stan rounded on her, added, "Maybe he's got a twin brother."

"Let's not try clutching at straws," Gilchrist said. "This is dynamite. But we have a more immediate problem to resolve, which is that all this evidence has been obtained by false pretense, so is inadmissible in a court of law."

Stan scratched his head. "Sorry, boss. I just thought we should—"

"Who else knows you have these?" Gilchrist asked.

Stan shook his head. "We're it."

"Right," Gilchrist said. "We can apply for a warrant to gain access to Anne Mills's safe-deposit . . ." But another troubling thought hit him before he finished the sentence. "The application for a warrant to search Jason Purvis's place was turned down."

"On what grounds, boss?"

"Insufficient evidence," Gilchrist said, as he paced the room. "I was going to talk to Whyte and ask him to reapply for a warrant. But having seen these, I'm not sure I want to do that." He looked at Jessie. "You agree?"

"You're thinking that shit from above drops through the ranks?" Jessie asked.

"From the chief constable, down to God knows who," Gilchrist said. He thought of his recent run-ins with Greaves and tried to convince himself that the chief super was under pressure to meet costs and budgets. In his heart of hearts, Gilchrist believed Greaves to be a man of integrity, but— and here was the problem—considering the decline in their relationship, could Greaves be trusted with this information?

With resignation, Gilchrist thought not. "I don't want to risk a warrant application reaching the eyes and ears of those above us," he said, nodding to Stan. "So you're going to use that charm of yours, and advise Ms. Mills that it's in her best interests to hand the images over to the police."

"But she's scared of what Magner might do," Jessie said.

"No, she's scared of what Magner's *man* might do. So we need to take him out of the equation."

"Boss?"

This was where it became fuzzy for Gilchrist. His instinct was urging him in one direction, while his logic was pushing him in another. He had no proof that Purvis was involved in the murder of Linda James or the McCulloch massacre or anything else linked to Thomas Magner. Purvis had not even made so much as a cameo appearance in the swinger images. But sometimes you just have to go with your gut.

Besides, he had nothing else to go on.

"It's the same four couples in all of these photographs," he said. "But we're missing the man behind the camera."

"Or woman," Jessie said.

Gilchrist ignored the comment. "What if it's Purvis?"

Was that too much of a stretch of the imagination? Purvis and Magner worked on the rigs together, boyhood friends who had carried that friendship into adulthood? They looked so alike they could be brothers, even twins. Could they have played games with people, switched identities for their own benefit?

"Here's what we know," he said. "Purvis has a BMW registered in his name, identical to the BMW that killed Janice. It's been lent to Jimmy Watson, or it hasn't, depending on what you believe. And a pair of Rottweilers guard a barn at the rear of his property."

Just the mention of the dogs had Jessie wringing her hands. Stan returned Gilchrist's look with an unblinking stare.

"So I'm thinking that the BMW's not in Europe with this Watson. It's not even on the road. It's hidden somewhere." He raised an eyebrow and held out his hands. "Any suggestions?"

"Purvis's barn?" Stan said.

"That's what we're about to find out," Gilchrist said.

"Want me to organize a team, boss?"

Gilchrist shook his head. "If Ramsay's in any way involved, and if I'm right about Purvis, we might end up giving someone a heads up. So . . ."

"Don't tell me," Jessie said.

"Yes, dear Jessica. I'm going to check out the barn first."

"Alone?" Jessie asked. "What about the dogs?"

"I'll take care of them."

"Count me in, boss."

"I'm about to break the law, Stan. You've got your career to think of. You said you only gamble when it's odds on. And this is anything but."

"Then it's time I learned how to take a bit of a punt, isn't it?"

Gilchrist groaned. If Purvis caught the pair of them on his property, at night, breaking into the barn without a warrant, it would be the end of both their careers. But if this long shot proved to be correct, then Purvis had a lot of explaining to do.

"That makes two of us," Jessie said.

Gilchrist jerked a look at her. "Out of the question."

"I'm not asking. I'm telling."

"You're forgetting who the senior officer is here."

"And you're forgetting that the pair of you are about to break the law. If you go ahead with your half-baked scheme, I'll arrest both of you."

Stan chuckled with disbelief.

Gilchrist returned Jessie's stare. "You're scared of the dogs."

"You said you'll take care of them."

Gilchrist continued to hold her hard gaze. She didn't flinch. He thought of abandoning the idea and just initiating another formal warrant application. But that would probably be refused or—worse—granted, only for them to discover that his instinct was wrong and the car was not on the property.

He really had only one option. "OK," he said. "But wipe that smug look off your face."

Jessie ran the flat of her hand from forehead to chin to reveal a scowl.

Gilchrist shook his head, but in a strange way he was pleased that Jessie had wriggled in. He could use her as a lookout, or as backup in the event of something going wrong.

"We'll do it this evening," he said. "And I'll take care of the dogs"

"How're you going to do that?" Jessie asked.

"Trust me," he said. "Then Stan will use his locksmith skills to pick the padlocks for the barn."

"Didn't know you were a safecracker, Stan."

"Just plain old locks," he said. "Nothing fancy."

"Then we enter the barn and find the car," Gilchrist said.

"Then what?" Jessie asked. "We call the cops?"

"No, we photograph it. After that, we're home and dry."

"I'll bring my new camera, boss."

But Jessie persisted. "And how do you explain our presence in Purvis's barn?" she asked.

"I'll think of something. But we need you as a lookout."

"Why can't Stan be the lookout?"

"Because you don't like the dogs."

"And Stan does?"

"No one does," Gilchrist said, "but I saw how you reacted last time. And if Purvis steps outside, we need to know about it. Maybe he checks up on the dogs every night before going to bed. Maybe he stalks around his boundary. Who knows."

"Won't the barn have an alarm system?" Stan asked.

Gilchrist had already dismissed that. "It's about two hundred yards from the cottage. It would cost a fortune to run wires all that way to provide electricity."

"Wi-Fi, boss. They have that now. Security cameras and alarms that work off Wi-Fi. No wires, just clip them on and set them up on your laptop. Motion activated. Not sure of the cost, but I'm thinking for less than a few hundred quid you could set webcams and motion sensors all over the place."

Gilchrist felt a hot rush of doubt, then found the answer. "Not with the dogs running around, Stan. They'd set off motion sensors all night long."

"But the sensors might be *inside* the barn. The dogs are locked outside."

"So why does he need the dogs in the first place?"

"As a deterrent?"

"Maybe. But I still think it's a risk worth taking." He looked at Jessie and Stan, and they both nodded. "Right, we head out as soon as it's dark. And no airwave sets. We'll use our mobiles. I'll pick Jessie up from home; then we'll take Stan's car."

"One last thing," Jessie said. "What about the guns? Purvis has access to them."

"What guns?" Stan asked.

"There's a cache in the cottage," Gilchrist said. "A couple of shotguns and a rifle, all registered in the name of James Watson."

"Who's he?"

"Good question."

"Just playing devil's advocate," Jessie said, "but what do you want me to do if I see Purvis walking toward the barn with a loaded shotgun?"

What indeed, Gilchrist thought. Running into the night could be their best option. On the other hand, they could remind Purvis that shooting police officers was still a criminal offense, no matter whose land they were trespassing. Although the fact that there are no trespass laws in Scotland would likely mean nothing to a man like Purvis.

At length, Gilchrist said, "Warn us, then call for backup."

"Want me to organize backup before we go, boss?"

"No. The fewer people who know about this, the better." Which all sounded good and well, except that they would be unarmed. Securing weapons needed the signature of the control room inspector after approval from the Silver Tactical Commander. But if they kept away from the cottage, Purvis would be none the wiser. At least, that was the theory. "Once the dogs are taken out of it, we'll be safe," Gilchrist pressed on. "So dress appropriately. Black everything. And wear body armor."

Stan nodded. "OK, boss. Let's do it."

Gilchrist raised an eyebrow at Jessie.

"I like wearing black. It makes me look slimmer."

"Right," Gilchrist said. "We're on."

But as he watched Stan shut down the computer and remove his memory stick, he could not rid himself of the dark feeling that he had overlooked something.

28

Back in Fisherman's Cottage, Gilchrist was surprised to see his old answering machine blinking. No one other than cold-callers phoned his landline these days, so he switched on the kettle, popped two slices of bread into the toaster, and opened a tin of tuna.

He sat down with his sandwich and a cup of tea and played the messages back.

The automated voice announced the time and date of the first call; then he jumped at the sound of Cooper's voice. "Andy, can you give me a call on my new mobile number?" As she read it out, he thought her voice sounded strained, as if she'd been crying. "I can't talk now," she said, rushing. "I've got to go."

The call ended.

He stared at the machine as the next message kicked in—same number, same date, but two hours later. This time Cooper said, "Just calling to let you know that Max has decided to leave." Maxwell now shortened to Max. "I can't really talk over the phone, but we've tried to work it out, and we both realize that what we used to share we now no longer have."

The distant call of a seagull told him she was probably walking along the beach, which she liked to do to clear her mind. "Of course, if you'd rather not call, then I understand. Maybe this is a chance for all of us to make a clean break." A sniff, then, "But I think you have the right to know."

The message ended.

Gilchrist jolted back to life and found a pen. He replayed the first message and wrote down Cooper's new number. Her voice sounded stronger on the second message, as if she had already accepted a life of separation. But her parting comment brought a frown to his forehead.

I think you have the right to know.

Know what? That Mr. Cooper was leaving? That her marriage was over?

He played the message one more time, but it still failed to make sense.

I think you have the right to know.

At the far end of the lounge Gilchrist peeled back the curtains. Light spilled over the bed of crocuses, now past their best, the hard green stems of daffodils competing for space. A glance at his watch confirmed the second message was already an hour old. But why had she phoned his landline and not his mobile? Because she had not wanted to talk to him, came the answer, just to leave a message to see if he would call back. It was a test, of sorts, to measure the strength of his feelings for her, perhaps.

The sound of the doorbell brought him back to the present.

He opened the door to a skinny man with long hair and a pasty face. Black jeans, worn gray, hid pipe-cleaner legs. A loose combat jacket with holes in the sleeves covered a skeletal frame. Every time Gilchrist met Jakie he was left with the impression that the man did not have long to live. He stood aside to let him in, feeling the rush of cold air as he brushed past into the warmth of the hallway.

In the lounge, Jakie scanned the walls, the floor, even the ceiling, as if surprised to find himself still standing—or maybe alive. "Nice house," he said.

Silent, Gilchrist closed the door behind him.

Jakie sniffed and retrieved a brown-paper package from the innards of his combat jacket. "Twa steaks with enough thiopental to give you at least sixty minutes, Mr. Gilchrist, sir."

Thiopental was a fast-acting barbiturate. Gilchrist took the package. It felt supple, pliable, and probably weighed less than a couple of pounds. "Without killing them?"

Jakie sniffed, gave a nervous twitch. "*Should* be all right."

"I don't want to kill them."

Another sniff. "That'll knock them out, no kill them. But you don't want tae fuck around when it comes to they Rottweilers."

"How quickly will it kick in?"

"It'll shut them up within a few minutes, yeah? Then they'll start going wobbly like and keel over."

Gilchrist raised his eyebrows. "How much?"

Another sniff. "Spot me forty," he said, and looked to the floor.

Gilchrist knew he was being ripped off, but Jakie looked as if he could use the money, maybe food, too. "You cold?" he said, handing over two twenties.

Jakie snatched the money, stuffed both hands into his pockets. "S'fucking freezing."

Gilchrist smiled. "I can give you a sandwich," he offered, "and a cup of tea to heat you up."

"Naw. Got tae go."

Gilchrist opened the lounge door and led Jakie along the hallway.

Jakie pushed past him and skipped across the threshold, then slunk away without a word of thanks or good-bye, or even a backward glance.

Back in the kitchen, Gilchrist peeled open the brown paper to reveal two steaks that glistened with blood. He laid the package on the draining board and separated them. Then he wrapped each individually in cling film and placed them in the fridge.

Next, he called Stan. "Are we good to go?"

"I've got the body armor and torches. And I've just had it confirmed that the Ford Focus you mentioned was captured on Tentsmuir Forest's CCTV on Thursday night."

"When?"

"Entered at 7:50," Stan said, "left at 8:40. It fits, boss."

The times certainly did fit, which opened up another nest of possibilities. But he said, "I'll pick up Jessie, and we'll meet in the Office in an hour," and killed the call. It would take about thirty minutes to collect Jessie then drive to the Office, which gave him time to make a phone call.

He dialed Cooper's new number.

She answered on the fourth ring.

"I got your messages," Gilchrist said. "Are you OK?"

A heavy sigh, then, "My marriage has been on the rocks for a long time, Andy. It's been coming to a head, and we . . . I . . . need time apart, to think things through, work out what I want to do."

Gilchrist let a healthy five seconds pass before saying, "And do you know what you want to do?"

"You're doing it again. Talking in questions."

He tried to find some other way to keep the conversation going, but questions were just about all he had. How could he learn what she meant by *I think you have the right to know* if he was not allowed to ask?

"I can't meet you tonight," he tried. "I'm working on a case."

"That's a bit presumptuous, don't you think?"

He gritted his teeth. "Well, trying to avoid asking requires presumption."

"You sound smarmy."

"It's not intentional."

"Really?"

He almost snapped a nippy response but bit his tongue. Cooper was still emotionally raw. The breakup of any marriage—particularly one as strong as hers had been—was always painful. Instead, he said, "Maxwell is leaving."

"Yes."

His mind was full of questions. When? Is there any likelihood he'll return? Is it over for good? What exactly do you think I have the right to know? Instead, he tried, "When Gail left, and took Maureen and Jack to Glasgow, I felt lost for a while." He paused for a response, but she seemed happy to let him go it alone. "The strangeness of an empty bed," he went on, "an empty house, and quiet weekends that felt all wrong, with no one to talk to during the week, I thought I would never get used to it. It took months before I was able to accept the loneliness."

Still nothing.

"But it gave me time to reflect on my relationship—the failings and successes of our marriage—and that helped me understand that we really were doomed from the start—"

"Are you suggesting my marriage was—"

"All I'm saying is that time apart, time you can use to think things through, is often worthwhile."

"Even if it brings Max and me back together?"

"If the end result is that you manage to save your marriage, and that is what you want, what you *truly* want," he added, just to ensure he was not planting seeds that could cultivate against him, "then, yes, even if it brings you and Max back together."

"And if I felt that you and I needed time apart, too?"

Well, there he had it. He had walked straight into it, with no way out but to wade in deeper. "If that's what you feel you need to do, to help you understand what you want—"

"It is."

Silent, he held on to the phone. During their relationship, he had enjoyed their bantering back and forth, the nip and tuck, the thrust and parry, the spice it added. He had always seen Cooper as his intellectual equal. But he was no match for her now.

"Are you still there?" she asked.

"I'm still here."

A pause, then, "I think I do need some time by myself."

For a moment he was tempted to challenge her, his pedantry telling him that if she only *thought* she needed some time alone, then she was not sure. Instead, he said, "Take as long as you want."

"I intend to."

He was about to ask what she had meant by *I think you have the right to know* when the call ended with an abruptness that left him wondering if she had expected more from him. Should he have offered a shoulder to cry on? Should he have said he would call in a day or two to check she was OK?

Instead he had done none of that and shown no compassion for or understanding of the pain she was suffering.

He thought of calling her back, but a glance at the clock confirmed he really had run out of time. Cooper with her marital problems would have to take a backseat. Meanwhile, he needed a quick shower and a change of clothing before driving to Jessie's.

I think you have the right to know.

He laid his mobile on the table and walked to the bathroom.

———

Jessie place a hand on Robert's cheek and mouthed, *I love you.*

Robert shrugged a nod, then turned back to his computer.

"Come on, Robert," she said. "I said I'll take you to the pictures next week. I promise."

Although he could not hear a word, it felt good just speaking to him. She stared at the back of his head, at his dishevelled dirty-blond hair—morning bed-head, she would call it, although night had already arrived. Even seated, Robert looked tall and lanky. Not like his father, for all she could remember of him. She'd been drunk when he'd shagged her on the floor, with the lights off. She wondered if Robert's physique had come from her own father's side. She had never met him, or even knew his name. She had asked her mother once, but she refused to tell her, which prompted Jessie to accuse her of not knowing which of the hundreds of drunks she'd shagged was her father. There was no love lost between Jessie and her mother.

She had left home shortly after that and joined Strathclyde Police as a secretary at seventeen, after giving birth to Robert. Through a combination of hard work and a favor or two, she worked her way up to detective constable. Her career seemed to be going well, until she met Chief Superintendent Lachlan McKellar. She had dropped her knickers for him just once—too much drink was involved again—but since then Jabba had been obsessed with getting back into them. So Jessie had applied for a transfer to Fife Constabulary.

But moving from Glasgow to St. Andrews was not just about getting Jabba out of her life. Robert was a teenager now, and it would be increasingly difficult to keep her family's criminal past a secret if they remained in Strathclyde.

She kissed the top of Robert's head, but he never even flinched.

In her bedroom, she opened the wardrobe and pulled out a pair of black jeans and a black turtleneck. *Dress appropriately. Black everything,* Andy had said. Did that extend to bra and knickers? She imagined him thinking of her. But she knew she was not his type. Still, it was a nice thought, even if for only a fleeting moment.

Her smile died as her thoughts flashed to the Rottweilers, and a shiver of ice ran through her veins. Ever since she'd seen that wee girl's savaged body, she'd had recurring nightmares. She closed her eyes, took a deep breath, tried to steady her nerves. Christ, just the memory of their demented growls had her hands trembling.

She opened her bedside cabinet and removed a hair dryer, three hairbrushes, a pile of magazines, and, to her pleasant surprise, a silk scarf and a pair of tan leather gloves—so they hadn't been stolen at that party after all—to uncover a polished wooden box. She opened the lid to reveal a Beretta 950B 22 Short.

She had never used the gun, never registered it. How could she, when she had stolen it from her brother Terry, who had probably stolen it from someone else? It was small, fitting neatly into her hand, and sleek. It was Italian, after all.

She could lose her job if she took it with her. But only if somebody found out.

Ah, shit, she thought.

And closed the lid.

———

Jessie slipped into the Merc's passenger seat, dressed all in black—boots, jeans, sweater, anorak, scarf, and gloves, to fight off the bitter cold of a Fife March night. Perfect for carrying out nighttime surveillance work.

"How's Robert?" Gilchrist asked.

"On his computer," she said. "Sometimes I wonder if he even knows I'm his mum."

"I'm sure he loves you."

"But does he know I'm his mum and not someone who just turns up every now and again and makes his dinner?"

"Is Angie sitting for you?"

"Don't know what I'd do without her."

Stan was already waiting when Gilchrist drove into the car park at the East Sands. Without fuss, he parked the Merc and slipped into the passenger seat of Stan's Audi. Jessie jumped in the back.

"Right," Gilchrist said. "Let's go."

29

Stan slowed the Audi to forty as they approached Jason Purvis's cottage.

"Lights are on," Gilchrist said.

"Doesn't mean he's in," Jessie countered.

Stan kept the speed steady as they drove past. A Ford Focus was parked in the driveway at the side of the house. Purvis was home.

"You think he might go out later?" Stan asked.

"That would be too simple," Jessie said.

Gilchrist weighed it up. "We'll enter round the back, from the adjacent field, as close to the barn as we can. But Jessie, you need to get close enough to the cottage to report any activity the instant it happens."

They decided to park well off the road and out of sight of the cottage. From there, Gilchrist and Stan would walk across the fields while Jessie worked her way along the back of the hedgerow that lined the road until she found a spot from where she could monitor the cottage—and remain hidden from the headlights of passing cars.

About a hundred yards along the road, the open entrance to a field was too good to pass up. Stan reversed into it and switched off the lights. The sky was clear, and Gilchrist worried out loud that the half moon might throw too much light on the surrounding fields.

"Where's the Scottish weather when you need it?" Jessie asked.

"We'll be all right as long as we keep low," Stan said.

"What if the dogs hear you and start barking?"

"That's a chance I'm prepared to take," Gilchrist said. "Remember, they kept quiet when we approached them this morning."

"That was in daylight. In the dark it might be different."

"If they start barking and it's obvious they're going to alert Purvis, then we'll abandon it and try something else later."

"Like handcuff and lock him up?" Jessie suggested. "That would simplify things."

They each checked their mobile phones were switched to vibrate. Although the phones' screens would still light up when they received a call, as long as they kept their backs to the cottage, Purvis would be unlikely to see them. And once inside the barn, they could talk freely.

Outside, the crisp night air stung. Stan clapped his gloved hands. "Bloody hell, boss, I'd almost forgotten how cold it can be in March."

"A brisk walk across the fields will heat us up," Gilchrist said.

They set off, Jessie beside the hedgerow, Gilchrist and Stan into the heart of the open fields. The approach to the barn proved more difficult than Gilchrist expected. Hollows and ridges small enough to avoid in daylight were large enough to jar bones and jerk the breath from their lungs in the darkness.

Bands of cloud doused the moon, which helped keep them hidden but made their trek more troublesome.

Keeping the lights of Cauldwood Cottage to their right, they tried to guess the position of the barn. But with nothing in front of them except blackness, they were left with no option but to continue to plod on as if blind.

Gilchrist cursed as he felt his boots sink into softer ground.

Stan whispered, "I think we're coming to a burn, boss."

They agreed to change course, heading farther away from the cottage, and Gilchrist was relieved to feel the ground firming up. His vision was becoming attuned to the dark, too, and he thought he could just make out the silhouette of the high row of pine trees that lined Purvis's boundary close to the barn.

"This way," he said, and changed course again. At that moment his mobile vibrated. He turned his back to the cottage and took the call.

"That's me," Jessie said. "I'm about fifty yards from the back door. The car's still in the driveway. I think he's watching the telly."

"Can you see him?"

"No. But there's a wee gap in the curtains, and I can see a light flickering. Maybe he's watching *Songs of Praise.*"

Gilchrist smiled. "Keep out of sight. And don't use your mobile unless you see movement."

"Can't I call my wee boy?"

"For crying out loud—"

"Only joking. Jesus, Andy, where's your sense of humor?"

"Freezing itself to death, along with my balls," he said. "And I don't want any heroics if Purvis sticks his head outside. All you have to do is alert us. OK?"

"OK."

Gilchrist killed the connection.

"Everything all right, boss?"

"Except for her tongue." He slipped the mobile into his pocket and set off in the direction of the pine trees.

Within three minutes the fence appeared. Gilchrist peered into the darkness beyond, straining every sense for any sign of the dogs. But other than the dark shadow of the barn itself, he could see nothing. "What do you think?" he whispered.

Stan cocked his head and lifted his face to the breeze. "Not a squeak, boss."

"Let me get the meat ready," Gilchrist said, "just in case."

He removed the steaks from his jacket pocket. Still wrapped in cling film, they were cool now, rather than cold. He was pleased to see they were positioned downwind of the barn. He did not want the dogs to catch the scent of raw meat.

"Let's work along the front of the fence," he said.

They eased toward the corner, where the fence turned at a right angle to run parallel with the rear wall of the distant cottage. Its windows were bright squares on the black horizon. Two cars drove past, their headlights briefly illuminating both the building and the Focus in the driveway. Then they passed and the cottage was swallowed by darkness again.

Gilchrist turned his attention back to the task at hand. A memory of both dogs eyeing him in silence until he touched the fence reminded him to keep well back from the chain links.

They were only about twenty yards along when Stan stopped. "Over there, boss."

Gilchrist peered into the darkness and felt a shiver run down his spine. "I don't see anything," he whispered.

"It's standing still," Stan said. "Watching us."

"Only one?"

"So far."

Purvis was not the sort of guy to sit in front of the fire with one of the dogs at his feet. No, both Rottweilers were here somewhere, protecting the barn. Gilchrist was certain of that. "I still can't see it," he said.

"I think the other one might be lying down."

"We need to make sure we feed both of them."

Stan edged toward the fence.

"Don't get any closer," Gilchrist said. "If you touch the fence, you'll set them off."

Stan stepped sideways, like a crab edging along an invisible line, keeping his distance, not taking his eyes off whatever he thought he could see.

Gilchrist followed, his fingers gripping the meat. He was finding it hard to resist the urge to rip off the cling film and just launch both steaks over the fence.

"*There*," Stan whispered. "You see it?" He pointed to the corner of the barn, held it for a couple of seconds, then swung his arm twenty feet to the left. "And over there."

Gilchrist stared hard into the darkness, forcing his eyes to see. Slowly, limb by limb, muscle by muscle, the dogs manifested into view—first the one standing at the corner, then the other—their deep chests and powerful shoulders a raw display of animal strength.

"I need to get closer," Gilchrist said. "The meat's got to land right beside each of them."

"We don't want one of them eating both pieces, boss."

Gilchrist saw that Stan was right. And they had to close the gap between the dogs and the fence, without setting off a barking frenzy. "If we edge a bit to the right," he whispered, "we might entice them to approach."

They'd moved only a couple of yards when Stan let out the tiniest of whistles. Gilchrist felt his throat constrict as both dogs trotted toward them. They stopped about five feet from the fence and ten feet from each other. As steadily as he could, Gilchrist undid the wrappers and held a chunk of raw meat in each hand. He eased his right arm back and lobbed the first piece over the fence.

The instant it landed in the grass, both dogs launched themselves at it with snarling growls, tearing and ripping into it. Within three seconds, the fight turned into silence, except for hard sniffing and grass ruffling as the dogs searched for more food.

In the darkness, from where he stood, Gilchrist could not tell if one dog had eaten the whole steak, or if they had both torn a share from it. He worried that one of them might not have enough thiopental in its system to knock it out. He could throw the other piece over and hope the hungrier of the two managed to prevail. But what if that did not work?

"Bloody hell. Now what?" Stan asked.

"We wait," Gilchrist said.

"For what?"

"For one—or both—of them to drop."

"Good thinking."

As they waited, Gilchrist's night vision improved to the point where he could see the outlines of both dogs clearly. Like before, they stood in silence, head-on, watching him— not Stan, he was sure of that—as if Purvis had trained them not to attack until the fence was actually touched.

In less than two minutes, one of the shapes grunted and shifted, then lowered itself onto its haunches, as if the effort of standing had become too much.

"I think he's going," Stan said.

Gilchrist waited until the dog settled into the grass; then he stepped forward and lobbed the second steak over the fence. This time there was no feeding frenzy—just a rush of power from the other dog, a nasty growl, and a slobbering sound that lasted all of two seconds.

"Did it eat it?" Stan said.

"Swallowed it whole."

"Remind me not to buy one of these as a pet."

They waited in silence.

Gilchrist counted the seconds in his mind. It took less than thirty beats for the dog's legs to totter. Then it tried to move but collapsed to the grass with a grunt and a whimper.

"I think we're good to go," Stan said, reaching into his pocket and removing his locksmith's kit with a tinny rattle— nothing more than a few keys and a set of picks.

Gilchrist approached the fence.

As soon as he touched it he would know if the dogs were out cold.

Or not.

30

Gilchrist kept his eyes on the nearer of the two dogs. The instant he touched the padlock, both dogs growled, and one of them—the first to collapse—rose to its paws. But it managed no more than a couple of steps before its front legs buckled and it fell muzzle-first into the grass. It struggled to pull itself upright again, but managed only to roll onto its side, where it lay whimpering, back legs kicking, as if somewhere in the darkest folds of its subconscious it was galloping over grassy terrain and tearing police detectives to shreds.

"Bloody hell," Stan said.

"Precisely." Gilchrist peered into the shadows for any movement from the other dog but saw none. "OK, Stan. Open sesame."

Stan gripped the padlock, inserted a pick, removed it, and chose another.

With a click, the padlock sprang open.

"Like riding a bike," Stan said.

"Slowly." Gilchrist was conscious of the rattling of the padlock and the creaking of the gate as he eased it open. They stepped into the compound, and Gilchrist sensed movement to his side. The closer of the two dogs was still jerking on the grass, its movements becoming more sluggish with each kick, until its nervous system could no longer fight the drug, and it stilled.

Gilchrist let out a breath and glanced at the cottage. He half-expected to see Purvis running toward them with a loaded shotgun. But the cottage stood undisturbed, a picture-perfect silhouette under a black sky. "You're good to go for the other padlock," he said.

Together they strode to the barn door.

While Stan worked at the padlock, Gilchrist searched for the tiniest flicker of light at the cottage windows. Behind him, the sound of metal scraping on metal seemed as loud as hammer blows, and he jumped when his mobile vibrated. He turned his back to the cottage, expecting it to be a call from Jessie, but felt a flutter of hope when he saw it was a text from Cooper's new mobile number: "I need time to myself because I'm pregnant. Will let you know what I decide. xx"

Something tight clamped Gilchrist's chest. *I think you have the right to know.* Well, now he did. He read the message again—

"That's us in, boss?"

"Right, let's go." Gilchrist pocketed his mobile, took hold of the handle, and pulled the door open for Stan to enter. Then he followed, closed the door behind him, and clicked on his torch.

Stan did likewise, and the barn filled with shafts of light that stuttered around the shadows until both beams settled on the gleaming body of a black BMW. "We've got a result," Stan said.

As he watched Stan make his way to the front of the car, Gilchrist shone his torch over the walls and corners, searching for motion sensors but finding none. But it seemed to him that the barn was smaller inside, as if it should be twenty feet longer. A flick of the torch toward the far end provided an explanation as the beam fell on a door in the left corner, which presumably led through an internal wall to some sort of office or storage area.

"We've got him, boss. Look at this."

Gilchrist joined Stan at the nearside wing. The headlight was shattered and the front and side panels badly deformed. He shone his torch along the bonnet to a cracked windscreen and dented pillar. Road Policing had estimated the car that hit Janice was traveling in excess of sixty miles an hour, maybe as fast as eighty. A human body hitting the BMW at that speed would cause exactly this sort of damage.

Gilchrist studied the crumpled metal, searching for evidence of human contact—fragments of cloth, skin, blood—but the bodywork looked as if it had already been cleaned. Another flick of the torch to the wall by the barn entrance lit up a coiled hose, beside which stood an electric pump, which told Gilchrist that Purvis had power washed the damaged panels. If the car had been cleaned outside the barn but within the enclosed compound, any human remains—slivers of skin and blood—would surely have been sniffed out and consumed by the Rottweilers.

"Stand back, boss."

Gilchrist walked away from the car and shone his torch around the barn while Stan took a number of shots using his digital camera. The barn appeared to be a workshop of sorts, with a concrete floor and strengthened beams overhead for lifting out car engines. All kinds of tools hung from hooks on its walls or stood beside workbenches—drills, chainsaws, power hammers, sump pumps, oxyacetylene torches, welding gear. And other bits and pieces of equipment, too—gloves, camouflage combat jackets, safety helmets, and what looked like a matching pair of binoculars.

Gilchrist dragged his torch beam along an electrical cable and into a corner, where it danced over a mechanical unit. It took him several seconds to realize it was a generator—power for lighting and for the tools, of course. Which had him wondering why all the equipment was sitting out in the open if there was a storage room at the rear of the barn.

Instinctive curiosity had him edging toward the internal door. He tried the handle, but it was locked. In addition, a padlock was clamped over a metal hasp, causing Gilchrist to wonder why a simple office or storage room would demand such security.

"Finished?" he asked Stan.

"A couple more, boss."

Gilchrist shone his torch along the top of the door, then ran his hand over the wooden surface. Nothing. He illuminated the wall to the side and spotted a shelf from which hung a set of keys. From their shape and size, they were all too large to fit the padlock, but the third one he tried in the door's own lock turned it over with a heavy click. The padlocked hasp kept it firmly closed, though.

Then Stan was standing beside him. "Want me to open this one too, boss?"

While Stan worked away with his picks, Gilchrist phoned Jessie.

She picked up on the second ring. "Nothing happening here," she said, "except my tits are freezing off." She made a rushing sound, as if blowing into her hands, then said, "Any luck?"

"We've found the Beemer," Gilchrist said.

"Brilliant," she gasped. "Can I go home, then?"

"We're going to be another few minutes," he said. "Any movement from Purvis?"

"Nada."

"Well, you might as well head back to the car, then." His main concern had been that the dogs would alert Purvis. Now they were out of the picture, there seemed no chance of Purvis making the long trek from the cottage to the barn on such an arctic night.

"And not a moment too soon."

"Be with you shortly," Gilchrist said, but Jessie had already cut the connection.

"Got it," Stan said, and slid the padlock free. "Thought I was losing my touch there for a moment."

Gilchrist pushed the door open and entered a windowless room. His torch beam danced over bare wooden walls and a dusty floor. The room was as long as the barn was wide but no more than six feet deep, leaving Gilchrist with the feeling that some internal space was still missing. He rapped a knuckle against the end wall, and it echoed back at him. Not the rear wall of the barn, then, but there appeared to be no door.

"What's this room for?" Stan asked.

Gilchrist shone his torch over the four barren walls again— no light switches, no power points—then up to a spider-webbed ceiling.

"The SOCOs can look into it, boss. After we get a warrant for Purvis's arrest."

Gilchrist nodded. He didn't want to spend any more time than was necessary in the barn. If the dogs came to, where would they be? He was about to move away when something caught his eye. "What's that?" The beam illuminated a semi-circular scrape mark on the ceiling. He lowered the torch to the floor and could just make out an identical mark. "It's a door," he said, running the beam up the wooden wall panels.

"Here, boss."

Gilchrist kept his torch trained on the edge of the panel as Stan ran his fingers down its length.

"Got it," Stan said as he slid a flat metal lock to the side and pulled.

A section of the wall peeled back toward them.

Gilchrist was first inside. The room was almost identical to the previous one, except that it was fitted with ceiling fans that whirred in a stuttering motion, as if operated by the wind. Even with the limited ventilation, the air carried a thick and musty smell that left an aftertaste of stale meat on the tongue. Something else, too—a hint of soot or smoke.

Stan already had his hand to his nose. "Bloody hell, what is this?"

Their torch beams danced in wild disarray across the walls, then settled in unison on a wooden pallet on the floor.

Gilchrist leaned down and shoved the pallet to one side to reveal a trapdoor. Maybe he was imagining it, but the smell of meat seemed stronger here. An inner voice once again told him they didn't have much time before the dogs came to, but he knew he could not leave now. He slid a metal latch across, pulled up the O-ring handle, and lifted the trapdoor. Then he rocked back on his heels as a stench as thick and ripe as a putrid carcass rose to greet him.

"Ah fuck, boss," said Stan, stepping back.

But Gilchrist was on his knees, his torch lighting a metal ladder that sank into the dark confines below. He shifted on to his backside, his legs dangling into the open space. Then he placed his feet on the rungs and descended into the black hole, his torch beam shivering from side to side. The shaft was short, and he was soon in a cold and fetid basement. He shone his torch at the concrete floor, one hand to his nose to fend off the stench. He coughed once, twice, and fought off the urge to retch.

"Anything, boss?" Stan shouted from the shaft's opening.

Gilchrist's beam danced over concrete walls and columns, and into open doorways that seemed to lead from one empty space to another. The metallic rattle of Stan's torch on the ladder's rungs echoed around the basement as he worked his way down.

"It's some kind of bunker," Gilchrist said. "The barn's been built over it."

Then Stan was beside him, their beams lighting the immediate darkness but sinking into a distant blackness. "It's bigger than the barn," Stan said. "And it doesn't smell as bad down here."

Gilchrist knew that the human olfactory system could stand only so much, and that their sense of smell had been obliterated by the strength of the stench. He remembered old Bert Mackie—head of forensic medicine before Cooper took over—telling him that once you got past the initial hit and your sense of smell was cooked, you just stayed with it until you completed the postmortems. Hell mend you if you took a break and a breath of fresh air, for when you returned to the job you had to go through the whole hellish process of becoming accustomed to the rotten guff again from scratch.

"This way," he said, heading through one of the open doorways.

Dripping water echoed in the dank stillness. The sound of their shoes scratching the concrete floor and the feverish rush of their breath were amplified in the blackness, too.

"What the hell is this?" Stan said.

"Could be an old bomb shelter from World War II."

Their torch beams sliced into walls of darkness, and Gilchrist could only guess at the size of the place. They stepped deeper into the labyrinth, scanning a series of small, empty rooms either side. He could visualize families with sleeping bags and camp stoves, wide-eyed children fearful of the night ahead, huddling together in the cold concrete units.

"I think we should head back, boss."

Gilchrist wanted to agree, but something kept pulling him on. He shone his torch into another room, and the light disappeared down a long corridor with even more doorways. It seemed as if they had discovered a concrete warren. For all he knew, it could run all the way to the cottage.

"This reminds me of the story of Theseus and the Minotaur," Gilchrist said.

"The one with the maze and the thread?"

"Didn't know you read Greek mythology, Stan."

"I read a lot of stuff," Stan said, "But I don't like the thought that we won't find our way back."

Gilchrist turned and shone his torch back to the ladder. But its beam settled into blackness. For one unsettling moment, it hit him that they really could lose their bearings down here, that if their torches failed they could stumble about in total darkness, completely disoriented. But his mind cast that aside as his gut told him they were going in the wrong direction, that they had walked too far into the underground maze. And it struck him, too, that despite the earlier assault on his sense of smell, the air seemed cleaner here, no longer thick on the tongue.

"It's not here," he said.

"What's not here?"

"How does it smell to you?"

Stan turned his head to the left, then the right. "I can't say, boss."

They headed back in the general direction of the shaft. The room above was in total darkness, so the shaft offered not even a glimmer of light to assist them. But Gilchrist breathed a sigh of relief when their torch beams picked out the distant rungs of the metal ladder.

Stan strode toward it, but Gilchrist said, "The smell's stronger over here."

Stan responded by shining his torch in the same direction of Gilchrist's beam, and together they entered another section of the warren. Gilchrist ducked his head as he passed through an open doorway into yet one more chamber. His instincts were telling him he was on the right path this time. The air seemed thicker and not quite as cold.

"Ah fuck," said Stan as his torch clattered to the floor, its beam spinning across the concrete. He bent down to pick it up, but even then the beam continued to quiver.

"You all right, Stan?"

"Boss . . ."

Gilchrist followed the line of Stan's shivering beam as it settled on the metal legs of some kind of workbench, then rose from the floor to rest for a moment before shifting to the side.

Ice flashed through Gilchrist's blood.

The shock forced him back a step, then another.

He stopped, struggled to stay upright.

His legs could be rubber, his lungs dried paper for all the good they were doing.

Then the moment passed, and he gasped, sucked in air, gripped his torch.

And shone it at the hellish scene before them.

31

Gilchrist tried to hold his torch beam steady, but his hands and fingers seemed to have developed a nervous system of their own. The figure . . . the *thing*, because that was what he was looking at—a thing that seemed part human, part alien—was hanging from a hook secured into the concrete ceiling.

Its glazed eyes stared at some point directly over Gilchrist's head, as if it were interested in something beyond him. As he traced the beam down its length, he was struck by the strangest sensation that he was looking at a work of art, a sculpture of sorts, comprising body parts and metal wires and pieces of wood and cloth, which together formed a discernible human shape—a creature that seemed to be captured in the sculptor's snapshot of life . . . or death.

A head sat atop a wire-meshed cage that resembled a skeletal frame covered in strips of skin that curled like dog-ears. Through the gaps in the skin, and beyond the metal mesh of ribs, Gilchrist could not mistake a ruddy lump of meat that had once been a beating heart. Beneath that, in a cavity of their own, coiled intestines lay like a sleeping nest of snakes. Arms stretched out both sides in scarecrow fashion, strips of skin frayed like tattered clothes, ending in wooden fingers tipped with human nails for claws. Lower, too, legs dressed in stripped skin for trousers, and shoeless feet of wire and toes of wood with toenails that glistened in the flickering beam.

Gilchrist was aware of Stan by his side, shocked into momentary silence, their torch beams frozen on the horrific figure before them.

"Is it human, boss?"

An image of Amy McCulloch's gutted and skinned body hit Gilchrist with a force that had him gripping his throat to avoid retching. He flashed his torch to the head, then down to the heart, the intestines, and along one leg to the full set of toenails that had been torn from a once-living human being. "She's human," he said.

"Who is she?"

Gilchrist flicked his beam back to the head to confirm that this was not Amy McCulloch but some other poor soul whose life had been stolen.

So if this was not Amy McCulloch, then where was she?

He shone his beam to the side and gasped. "Jesus, Stan."

Stan's beam flickered alongside Gilchrist's, forcing light into deeper recesses, revealing a row of concrete chambers that housed a series of individually wired figures, as if each were set in its own personal sarcophagus.

Stan was first to recover. "That's it," he said. "We need to get this seen to." The light from his torch flickered around the walls of the chambers as he pulled out his mobile.

Now that the initial shock was past, Gilchrist's instinctive curiosity overpowered all reservations, and he stepped deeper into the catacombs. He counted six other figures and stopped at the first—a young woman with blue eyes glazed like icing and blonde hair as dry as straw. Within her wired body, her lungs and heart reflected his torch beam like the sheen from plastic. Intestines lay curled beneath a bloated ball of a stomach. Her blue fingernails reminded him of Janice Meechan's bare foot dripping with rain.

Who was she? Was she a mother, a daughter, a sister? When was she killed? Had anyone even reported her missing?

"Can't get a signal, boss."

Gilchrist pulled out his own mobile, but the concrete labyrinth was blocking any kind of signal. He was about to ask Stan for the camera when he cocked his head to the ceiling. "You hear that?"

Stan frowned as he shone his torch at the concrete roof. "Sounds like a motor."

At first, Gilchrist thought Purvis must be making his escape in the BMW. But why would he do that when the Focus was parked in his driveway? As the logic tumbled into place, Gilchrist came to understand that the sound was not the revving engine of a top-of-the-range Beemer but something much heavier, more industrial.

"It's the generator," he said.

"Purvis knows we're here?"

Gilchrist caught the alarm in Stan's voice. "Someone does."

"We must have triggered something," Stan said. "Maybe there are webcams down here." He flashed his beam along the corners of the ceiling, then walked toward the entry shaft. "Let's go and get him before—"

"Don't, Stan."

Stan stopped and swung his beam at Gilchrist.

"If it's Purvis, he'll be armed. He's got two shotguns and a rifle in that cottage." *And God only knows what else*, he wanted to say, and almost cursed his own stupidity. He should have insisted on a search warrant and seized the cache of arms before trying anything like this.

"We can't stay down here and do nothing, boss. What if he locks us in?"

Gilchrist saw that Stan had a point. But he also saw that Purvis was not someone who let loose ends lie around. He would not want two detectives sniffing around his underground graveyard. And Gilchrist came to see that if Purvis had caught them on a webcam he would know exactly how many were down here.

Would he lock them in and leave them to die?

Or would he flush them out like rats from a nest?

The noise from the generator gave Gilchrist his answer.

Purvis was going to switch on the lights and come down with a loaded shotgun. His criminal past spoke of a man who was not afraid to take on the law. He would do whatever was necessary to make sure he never spent time behind bars again—including killing two detectives, if he had to.

From somewhere overhead, the sound of a fan starting gave Gilchrist a jolt. He strained to hear footsteps in the barn above, but the concrete roof was as good a sound-damper as any. Even so, Gilchrist knew that he and Stan were running out of time.

He shone his beam over the bare concrete walls—there had to be a light source somewhere. But he could find no switches on the walls, or light bulbs hanging from the ceiling. Then the ringing clatter of metal on metal to his right warned him that someone was descending the ladder. He switched off his torch.

"Lights out, Stan."

Stan did as ordered.

A pitch blackness, thicker than any Gilchrist had experienced, descended on them with the suddenness of a guillotine chop. In the darkness, the heavy weight of the torch felt good. He slapped it into the palm of his hand. Not much of a weapon, but it was all they had.

Or maybe not.

"Purvis is as blind as we are," Gilchrist whispered. "So we'll wait until he switches on the lights, then surprise him." He tried to pull up what he could remember of the basement's layout in his mind's eye, and edged along a wall, his back against the cold concrete. Then he caught the leathery scrape of shoes on the floor. "Lift your feet, Stan. Don't drag them."

In the ensuing silence, Gilchrist heard the steady crunch of someone walking toward them—not creeping like they were, but striding with confidence, as if he knew every twist and turn of the labyrinth.

As if he could see in the dark.

And Gilchrist realized that the binoculars on the workbench in the barn were not binoculars at all but night-vision goggles.

The footsteps stopped, and Purvis said, "Just look at the pair of you. Cowering in the corners."

Gilchrist peered into the darkness, in the direction of the voice, but he was as good as blind. The footsteps shifted, shuffled on the concrete, crackling clumps of dust and fragments of stone. A bit more to his right, Gilchrist thought, but closer, too.

Then silence.

Gilchrist waited, his senses stretched as tight as wire.

Not a sound now, except the hard beating of his heart.

Gilchrist pushed to his feet and stepped into the darkness. "You're under arrest," he shouted, imagining Purvis facing him from about ten yards away.

He lifted his torch and clicked it on.

The beam lit up nothing but a concrete wall.

Stan got the message and clicked his torch on, too.

A cough from somewhere to their right had both beams flashing to the side, where they picked up Purvis smiling at them. The night-vision goggles were high on his forehead, and a shotgun was aimed straight at Gilchrist.

"OK, boys, down with the torches." Purvis shifted to the side and nudged the wall with his elbow. A switch clicked, and the place lit up like Blackpool Illuminations.

Gilchrist grunted and shielded his eyes.

"On the ground. *Now.*"

"We're police officers," Stan said.

"I know you are."

"We've already sent for backup," Gilchrist tried.

Purvis chuckled. "The little bimbo who was shitting herself? Now you've really got me scared." He leveled the shotgun at Gilchrist's face. "It makes no difference to me if you drop the torch when you're alive or if I have to kick it out of your dead fingers." He gave a sideways nod at Stan. "And don't you be getting any ideas, sonny. On the ground."

Gilchrist forced all thoughts of rushing Purvis from his mind. The casual way he handled himself, the ease with which his muscles flexed, told him that he would not hesitate to fire at either or both of them before they took more than two steps. Gilchrist caught Stan's eyes, gave the slightest nod, then released his torch and let it clatter to the ground.

He kicked it toward Purvis, and it skittered across the floor.

Without a word, Purvis turned the shotgun on Stan.

Stan hesitated, then dropped his torch.

"Kick it over here."

Stan nudged it with his foot, and it clattered toward Purvis.

"Turn around, boys."

Gilchrist raised both his hands, palms up. "You can't possibly get away with this. If we don't report back to the Office within the next few minutes a team will be dispatched—"

"*Dispatched?* I like that word. *A team will be dispatched . . .*" Purvis shook his head and laughed, a hard sound that reverberated through the chambers and returned to them in pieces. "You think you're a smart-arse, don't you?" Something settled behind Purvis's eyes. His face tightened, his knuckles whitened, and Gilchrist wondered what was preventing the shotgun from letting off both barrels.

Purvis steadied his aim, pointing straight at Gilchrist's face. "How about I dispatch you?"

Gilchrist closed his eyes and tensed for the blast that would take his head off.

32

J essie clapped her hands and shuffled her feet, trying to force some warmth into her body. Returning to the car had sounded like a great idea, but everyone had forgotten that Stan had the keys. Now her legs were chilled to the bone, her feet lumps of ice.

"Come *on*," she said, calling Gilchrist's number again, then Stan's. Both were still unobtainable. "Shit." She tried to work out what had happened, but nothing made sense. Had they lost the signal? They had drugged the dogs and gotten safely into the barn, Andy had told her that. The signal had been fine then. And they would be only another few minutes. His exact words.

That was ten minutes ago.

She felt a gut-wrenching sickness wash through her at the thought that something had gone terribly wrong, and she fought off the overwhelming urge to call for backup. It would be just like the thing that as soon as she did, Andy and Stan would turn up. Then where would she be? In serious trouble, came the answer. So she stared into the darkness across the fields, straining to pick out the slightest movement.

Her mobile vibrated, and she made the connection without looking at the number. "Yes?"

"So, you've finally deigned to answer," Lachie said.

Jessie gritted her teeth, then cursed under her breath. She was angry, freezing, worried sick about Stan and Andy. She didn't have time to deal with *this*. Her anger surged to fury, and she shouted, "I don't want you ever entering my house again when I'm not there. You hear me, Lachie? And I don't want you anywhere near Robert ever again—"

"That was an accident—"

"And while we're at it, I'm not interested in moving out of our home."

"I've got a nice wee place lined up for—"

"Or having any kind of relationship with—"

"Listen, Jessie—"

"No, Lachie. You listen to me."

"I'll tell you what I'm going to do," Lachie said. "I'm going to—"

"Highland Tam."

Silence.

Jessie waited a couple of beats, then repeated the name. "Highland Tam."

Lachie cleared his throat. "What about him?"

Jessie could not fail to catch the tiniest shiver of uncertainty in Lachie's tone. "You remember him well, I'm sure."

"What about him?" More forceful this time.

"You were responsible for his death, Lachie."

"In case it's slipped your mind, Highland Tam committed suicide—"

"Because you pushed him to it."

"He was as guilty as sin."

"We all knew it. And so did he. But you didn't need to plant the drugs on—"

"Wait a fucking minute."

"You can deny it all you like, Lachie."

"There's nothing to deny."

"There's *plenty* to deny, Lachie. I watched you do it."

"No one'll believe you. It's your word against mine."

"Are you prepared to take that chance?"

One beat, two beats, then, "It could backfire on you, Jessie. Big time."

"It certainly could. But d'you know what, Lachie? I'm up for it."

"Where do you get off, you fucking wee tramp."

"Right here is where I get off. This is my stop. You hear me? I'm getting off right now. Without you. And if you ever come near me again, or phone me again, I'm warning you, Lachie, I'll—"

"You wouldn't fucking dare."

"Oh, I'll dare all right. You'd better believe it," she said, then killed the call and stuffed the mobile deep into her pocket. She took a deep breath and let it out in a sudden gush. Oh, Jesus. She dabbed a hand at her eyes wiped away the tears. Oh, shit. She pressed the hand to her mouth to stop her lips from trembling. Shit and shit again.

What the hell had she gone and done?

No one crossed Lachie McKellar. *Ever.*

Not unless they wanted to ruin their career. Or worse.

Oh, fuck. She shielded herself from a hard gust of wind that shook the hedgerow by the side of the car, as if Lachie were trying to burst his way through to strangle her. She had seen him in action before, knew how vindictive he could be. No one survived an onslaught from him. *No one.* She tilted her head to the black oblivion of the night sky and closed her eyes—shit, shit, shit—and took several deep breaths that did little to settle her nerves.

When she opened her eyes again, she tried to force the worry of what she had done from her mind. She needed to focus on what was important—*really* important—and find out what was going on. She retrieved her mobile and called Gilchrist's number again.

But his phone was still dead.

Then Stan . . .

Same result.

"Right," she said, staring off into the cold night, her breath clouding the air as if she had just run the hundred-meter dash. "If you think I'm going to stand around freezing my tits off, you've got another think coming." She stepped from behind the car and into the full force of a bitter east coast wind. Rather than work back to her hiding spot near the driveway, she decided to walk across the open fields, just as Andy and Stan had done.

That way she had a better chance of bumping into them if they were on their way back.

She entered the field through the open gate and took her bearings from the distant lights of Purvis's cottage. Her feet kicked through damp grass and sank into puddled soil. She cursed, put her head down, and strode on into the cold darkness, struggling to force all thoughts of Lachie from her mind.

———

"I said turn round. *Now.*"

Gilchrist stared into the twin black bores of the shotgun.

Purvis had repositioned himself to bring Stan more into his line of fire, so that he could take out Gilchrist first, then Stan, or the other way around, if he preferred.

Gilchrist caught Stan's eyes and nodded, and together they turned around.

"On your knees," Purvis ordered.

Gilchrist felt something hard catch in his throat. He had seen wartime footage of men jogging to their spot of execution, then being shot in the back of the head, one after the other. He had often wondered why no one ever fought back. But now, as he and Stan did exactly as Purvis instructed, he knew the answer—disbelief and the horrific and numbing realization that there was no hope of survival. Life, for all the good and bad that had been done with it, was about to end.

Stan's eyes were closed, as if he, too, were simply waiting for the blast.

"Eyes to the front."

The closeness of the voice jolted Gilchrist. Then he caught the scratchy shuffle of leather soles on dusty concrete and sensed a subtle shifting of Purvis's body—the lowering of the shotgun toward his head.

He closed his eyes and prayed to a God he did not believe in.

33

It took Gilchrist's silent counting to ten before he opened his eyes, and another ten to twenty before he took a breath and let his hopes cling to the slimmest of beliefs that it might not be his last. Of course, with encaged human body parts in wire-mesh sculptures all around them, logic told him that Purvis was only toying with them and that there could only ever be one outcome.

"You don't have to do this," Gilchrist said.

"Yes, I do."

"Give yourself up."

"And do what? Go back inside?" Purvis chuckled.

"You'll get a fair trial."

"My arse. They'll lock me up as soon as look at me."

Stan cocked his head, risking a glance. "Do you have family?"

"Shut it, you. Don't try to give me any of that sentimental shite. It don't work on psychos."

"Is that what you are, then?" Stan said. "A psycho?"

"I told you to shut it," Purvis snapped, and clipped the side of Stan's head with the stock of the gun.

Stan keeled over, the side of his head gushing blood.

Gilchrist rose from his knees and felt the stock slam into his back with a force that sent him sprawling. He struggled back to his knees, a burning ache telling him that the blow had either torn a muscle or cracked his scapula.

He winced as he turned to Stan. "Let me stop the bleeding—"

"Stay the fuck where you are."

Gilchrist froze, arms by his side, the flat of his hands pressing on the concrete floor. He curled his fingers, managed to scrape some dust into his loose grip. But his logic was telling him something was wrong—they should both be dead by now.

"Why are you keeping us here?" he asked.

"You'll see. Eyes to the front."

Another hit from the stock reminded Gilchrist that Purvis was still calling the shots. What he had learned was that Purvis was waiting for something or, as it was gradually becoming clearer to him, waiting for *someone*.

And if Gilchrist had been a betting man, he might have risked a punt.

But he had also learned that with Purvis you could never be too careful.

———

Jessie reached the compound fence, and a rare break in the clouds gave her a moonlit glimpse of the barn. She stopped, her heart in her mouth as she searched for the dogs.

But she saw nothing.

Something else was niggling at the back of her senses, the noise of a running engine coming from the barn. She edged her way along the compound fence to the corner. In the distance, the lights of the cottage glittered. She turned her back to them and removed her mobile and tried Andy's number, then Stan's, but the connection was well and truly dead. She thought again of calling the Office for backup but reasoned that by the time it arrived, she would likely have found a simple explanation for the lack of communication.

So she decided just to press on.

She resisted the urge to click on her torch but held it tight as she edged onward. She reached the gate to find the padlock dangling open. The night sky shifted again, killing light from the moon, and blackness settled all around her like a cloak. Her senses felt raw to the touch, as if her every nerve was exposed. A hard lump threatened to choke her throat as she strained for signs of movement. She gripped the cold metal and caught her breath as the chain links rattled. The memory of the dogs rushing the fence chilled her blood, and she waited in the darkness, afraid to take another step.

But nothing stirred.

She eased the gate open, all the while staring blindly into the black shadows for any sign of the Rottweilers. Then she stepped inside the compound and pulled the gate behind her. The latch clicked with a metallic ring, and she felt her blood turn to water as something shifted in the grass by her side.

She froze stock-still and peered into the darkness.

Movement.

Black on black.

Then she heard a low growl that rose for a terrifying moment, only to fade to a whine and the cutting song of the wind as it brushed over the grass.

She reached the barn door in fifteen quick strides. The sound of the engine was louder here, drowning out the wind.

She grappled with the loose padlock, her fingers feeling thick, rattling metal on metal as they fumbled for the latch.

Then she found it and tugged the barn door open.

Inside was as black as night, and the noise from the generator deafening. She shut the door behind her, held her breath, and waited for any signs of movement. Then, for the first time since crossing the fields, she flicked on her torch.

Its beam shimmered across the floor and settled on the generator. Her ears had become accustomed to the noise, the beat of its racing engine now less invasive. She shone the torch around the barn, and its beam fell on the BMW.

"Nice one, Andy."

She walked the length of the car, shining her torch through the side windows—to confirm it was unoccupied—noticing the cracked windscreen, the dent in the window pillar. The generator thrummed in the background. Had it been running when Andy called earlier? In the inexplicable absence of two senior officers, she knew she should phone the Office and report the discovery of the BMW, call in the registration number and ask them to check the VIN.

She laid her torch on the barn floor, removed her mobile, and started to scroll down.

"Cut the call."

Jessie jolted and spun around to face the darkness from where the voice had come.

"I said cut the call."

In the black of the barn, Jessie could see nothing. She looked down at the torch on the concrete floor, its beam shining aimlessly under the BMW, which stood between her and the source of the voice. She shifted her feet . . .

If she could only . . .

She slowly bent her knees, lowered her hand—

"Don't even think about it," the voice said. "I have a gun, and I *will* shoot."

The man had moved around to the front of the car, and Jessie realized with a stab of fear that he must be able to see her clearly, even though she could see nothing.

"Cut the call," he repeated, his voice taking on a steely tone that left Jessie in no doubt that the last warning had just been issued.

She killed the connection.

"Now drop it."

The voice had crept closer, although still some distance away—maybe ten feet. Jessie thought she caught some move-ment—shadow on shadow—but she could not be sure. One part of her wished she had the strength and the courage to put up a fight, just go for it. Another part reminded her that Robert needed her, and what would he do if she was not around for him?

"I'm waiting."

Jessie dropped her mobile to the floor.

"Step to the side and turn around."

Something in the cold finality of his words caused Jessie to picture the man steadying himself and aiming the gun straight at her head. She raised both hands in the air. "I'm unarmed," she said to the darkness. "Don't shoot."

"Turn around."

Jessie wondered why he was so insistent when he could see her clearly. The only logical answer was that he was going to shoot her. She tried to reason with him. "My son's deaf," she said. "He needs me."

"I said turn around."

"Please."

"Last chance."

Jessie swallowed the lump in her throat and shuffled around. Every nerve in her body was jumping, while her mind tried to reassure her that she was not about to die. The sound of shoes—or boots—crunching over the dust and dirt sent a wild flash of panic through her. Her heart launched into overdrive, thudding in her chest like some caged animal kicking to free itself.

She did not want to die.

Leather scraped concrete.

Closer now. Too close. As if . . .

The footsteps stopped.

Silence, save for the rush of her breath and the frenzied beating of her heart.

She could feel his presence now, sense he was leaning closer.

Making sure he could not miss—

Her world exploded in a blast of white light.

34

Gilchrist tilted his head to the ceiling. To his side, Stan stirred from unconsciousness with a long groan, as if he had caught it too—the momentary stutter of the generator's engine in the barn above, which caused the lights in the basement to flicker.

"We have company," Purvis announced.

Gilchrist risked taking another hit from the shotgun's stock by turning his head and saying, "Magner?"

Purvis smiled down at him. "Clever you."

As Gilchrist's mind flashed back to that first interview with Magner, and the cut on the base of his right thumb, he saw where he had made the most basic of errors, stunned into silence that not one of them had picked up on it. CCTV footage of the Highland Hotel—on the night Brian McCulloch was seated in his Jag in Tentsmuir Forest, supposedly committing suicide after having murdered his entire family—and Magner standing in the hallway outside the conference room, about to enter, mobile phone in hand, powering it down—and all of it done with his mobile in his left hand, while he prodded at the keyboard with his right.

"You stood in for him," he said.

Purvis cocked his head, a silent question in his eyes.

"The conference in the Highland Hotel. It wasn't Magner. It was you that night."

Purvis grimaced as he stared down at Gilchrist, as if deciding whether to hit him with the stock of the shotgun again or blast him with both barrels. It took him two seconds to choose the former, and he stepped forward and thudded the gun into Gilchrist's face.

Gilchrist had time only to turn away, take the blow to the side of the head. Even so, the hit sent a flash of light through his brain, and he grunted with surprise as the concrete floor rose up to meet his face with a grit-laden slap.

———

The next second—well, it felt as if it was the next second, although he failed to see how he had missed Magner's entrance—Gilchrist rolled onto his back, confused for a moment as to where Purvis had gone. The skin by his left eye felt thick and sticky to the touch, as he struggled to focus. Another dab at the side of his head had him wincing with pain, trying to gauge the extent of the wound through hair clotted with blood and dust. And Jessie was here, too, seated on the concrete floor beside Stan, their backs to the wall. He struggled to push himself upright, which caused Magner to stride toward him and glare down at him.

"You're a silly man," Magner said. "Persistent, I have to give you full marks for that, but silly."

If Gilchrist could have spoken, he would have agreed. Silly sounded about right. He had been silly not to arrest the bastard sooner, silly not to see how the resemblance between

Magner and Purvis was crucial to the case, silly to have led Stan and Jessie into this basement. He would have agreed with all of that, but his tongue had glued itself to the roof of his mouth, and all he could do was shake his head in silent acknowledgment of his abject silliness.

Magner held up a mobile, which Gilchrist recognized as his own. "Been looking through all your call logs, and it's good to see that not one of you called for backup."

Oh, that, too. He was silly for not calling for backup, silly to think they could have gone it all alone. But not silly, really, when you think about. Just stupid.

Downright fucking stupid.

"We didn't need to call for backup," Gilchrist said, working spittle into his mouth, "because they already know where we are."

"Really?"

"If we don't check in, they'll send uniforms to the cottage. They're probably already on their way."

"On a Sunday night?" Magner sounded incredulous.

"Never heard of twenty-four seven?" Jessie said. "That's the constabulary for you."

"Every day a working day. Is that it?" Magner's smile evaporated the instant his lips curled.

The clanging of metal on metal had everyone turning their heads toward the access ladder. Light shone through the shaft, revealing Purvis working his way down, rung by rung, into the basement.

Gilchrist counted twenty-seven steps from the foot of the ladder to Purvis standing in front of him and noticed for the first time that he was dressed in camouflage gear. Magner, on the other hand, was wearing a dark blue suit and a white shirt with a red tie. A matching handkerchief poked from his top pocket.

Purvis took one step closer to Gilchrist.

The kick to his chest took Gilchrist by surprise, the power behind it staggering. For one frightening moment his world turned black again, and he thought his heart had stopped.

"*That's* for killing Bruce," Purvis gasped.

Gilchrist's system came to with a grunt. He sucked in air and winced from the fresh pain.

"Bruce was one of Jason's dogs," Magner explained.

"I thought psychos didn't like pets," Jessie quipped. "Cruelty to animals, and all that."

Purvis gave her a look that could have boiled the air between them. But Magner raised his hand and Purvis took a couple of steps back, distancing himself from Jessie, as if not trusting his right boot. If looks could speak, Purvis was telling Jessie just how high over the crossbar he was going to punt her.

"You've put us in a dilemma," Magner said. "What should we do with you?"

"I know what to fucking do with them," Purvis countered. "Turn them into dog food."

Another raised hand from Magner shut Purvis down and told Gilchrist who was in charge. But he also knew that no matter who was pulling the strings, the situation could end only one way, with one of them—likely Purvis—pulling the trigger.

He glanced into the darkness, where the lights failed to reach, at sarcophagal chambers that resembled square mouths to dark caves, in each of which dangled skeletal wire-mesh cages that housed human artefacts. Or, as Gilchrist's numbed mind came to understand, symbolic tokens from each kill, prizes to be treasured or fondled, through which the killer—read *killers*—could relive that glorious moment of ultimate pleasure, when they watched the light of life in each of their victims flicker, then die.

Purvis turned to the workbench and reached for something. When he turned back, the sight of the shotgun turned Gilchrist's blood to ice.

"My son needs me," Jessie pleaded.

"You should've thought of that before you became a cop," Purvis said, shouldering the gun.

This time, Magner did not raise his hand. Instead, he reached for the gun and pushed the barrels down so they pointed at the floor. "There's plenty of time for that," he said.

Purvis almost sulked, like a child being told he could not watch TV, and Gilchrist realized that Magner wanted to talk. He needed to know how much they knew, how close they had come to nailing him for the McCulloch massacre.

Of course, asking questions could work both ways.

"How's your hand?" Gilchrist asked.

Magner frowned but said nothing.

"How did you kill Janice?"

Magner narrowed his eyes. "Interesting question," he said. "*How?* Not *why?*"

"I know why," Gilchrist said. "She had seen too much. She was going to talk. She was the weak link between you and McCulloch. And after we questioned her, she called you up in a panic."

"And . . . ?"

"Well, I have to admit I'm guessing here, but I'd say you arranged to meet her, maybe even drove behind her and gave her a last-minute phone call to tell her to pull into the side of the road so you could talk where no one could overhear you.

Maybe you opened your car door to invite her to cross the road, but you were really just timing it right so your guard dog there"—Gilchrist nodded at Purvis—"could run her down. And that makes you an accessory even if—"

"Who the fuck're you calling a guard dog?"

Again, Magner raised his hand. "Sticks and stones, Jason. Really, you must learn to control that temper of yours."

"Ah, fuck." Purvis stepped back, raised his shotgun, and aimed it at Gilchrist's face.

Jessie screamed.

The sudden noise of both barrels releasing thudded through the basement like a solid wave that shocked Gilchrist's body like a punch. If Magner hadn't swatted at the shotgun, Gilchrist's head would have been blasted from his shoulders. As it was, the tight formation of pellets made a ten-inch crater in the wall to the side of his head, scattering fragments of concrete over his hair and shoulders like confetti.

The noise reverberated through the basement like a war beat.

Magner took hold of the shotgun and jerked it from Purvis's grip.

They faced each other in a silent standoff that seemed to last minutes but was no more than a few seconds. If the shotgun had still been loaded, Gilchrist was convinced one of them would have blasted both barrels at the other.

Then he caught a hint of movement by his side and turned his head to catch Jessie fumbling with an ankle holster.

Purvis shouted, "Ah, fuck," and pushed Magner to the side. He was on Jessie in four athletic steps, just as she retrieved the Beretta from its holster and pulled the trigger.

In the tight chamber, the shot from the .22 echoed like a cannon firing.

Purvis cursed—a guttural grunt that sounded like a wild animal being hit—but his momentum carried him forward, and he lashed out at Jessie's arm, sending the gun flying.

Gilchrist was on his feet at the same time as Stan, but his world had the disconcerting feeling of having its axis tilted in the wrong direction. He stumbled to the side and landed on the concrete floor with a heavy thud that punched the wind from him.

And Stan, as if realizing that the shotgun was now out of ammunition, tried to catch Jessie's gun as it bounced off the wall. He almost had it but fumbled trying to take hold of the grip, and it skittered to the floor.

Purvis toppled over Jessie, his hands scrabbling for her gun, too.

But Stan was too fast for him. He reached Jessie's gun, which seemed to go off without him pulling the trigger.

Stan froze, eyes white.

Magner said, "The next one won't miss."

Purvis groaned, pushed himself to his knees, his face twisted in an ugly grimace that could have destroyed any suggestion that he and Magner, with his pretty hardman looks, were in any way related. He stretched for Jessie's gun.

"Leave it."

Purvis glared at Magner.

"You can't be trusted with guns, Jason," Magner explained. "Now get to your feet and let's have a look at that arm of yours."

From his position on the concrete floor, Gilchrist watched the scene unfold before him as if in slow motion . . .

Purvis reached up to Magner, hand outstretched for help to his feet, leaving Jessie's gun abandoned on the floor; Stan, still on his knees, glanced at Gilchrist who, even in that fleeting moment, read the intention from the desperation in Stan's eyes and tried to warn him off by shaking his head. As Purvis was pulled upright, Stan reached for the Beretta, his fingers working around the grip and through the trigger guard.

Magner aimed his pistol and shot him.

Stan hit the floor like a dead weight.

Jessie gasped a scream, then pressed a hand hard to her mouth, tears squeezing through clenched eyelids.

Gilchrist groaned and tried to say, "Stan," but the word came out flat and lifeless.

Magner said, "I told him the next one wouldn't miss."

35

Gilchrist struggled to his feet, aware of Magner's eyes on him, his every move covered by a gun—a SIG Sauer P250, he thought, although he never had been the best at identifying pistols.

"You've killed him," Gilchrist said.

"I have indeed," Magner agreed. "So why don't you sit next to Miss Piggy while I attend to Jason here?"

Gilchrist felt too exhausted to resist. His body could have been drained of blood. He sat beside Jessie—more collapsed than sat—and placed an arm around her shoulder in a vain attempt to still the tremors that jumped through her body like electric shocks. Her head seemed to fall onto him, and her breath jerked in shivering sobs until he placed a hand over her eyes and turned her face to his chest, away from the morbid stare of Stan's sightless eyes.

Stan lay less than six feet from them, body motionless, blood pooling around his face. His blond hair above his right temple glistened with a mixture of brains and blood.

Gilchrist had to close his eyes, but images of himself and Stan flickered through his mind in stroboscopic strikes. He struggled to blank them out, but his mind fired through the logic, until a sudden realization hit him.

"You're shutting up shop," he said.

Magner looked up from Purvis's arm, which was leaking blood.

"That's why you're here," Gilchrist continued. "You're getting ready to leave."

Purvis glanced at Magner, who shook his head as if to suggest Gilchrist's conclusion was pure fantasy.

"Didn't he tell you?" Gilchrist said to Purvis.

Silence.

"Was it meant to be a surprise? Sorry. Have I ruined it for you?"

Silence.

"You knew it was only a matter of time until we found this place," Gilchrist pressed on. If he could have raised his arm and cast it around him in an expansive gesture, he would have. But his head ached with a pain that had his left eye wincing and his logic firing in fits and starts. Even so, ideas flickered and held for a moment before fading away, none of them bringing him any closer to finding a way out of their hopeless predicament.

Except one, maybe . . .

He forced himself to concentrate on the interaction between Magner and Purvis, the way they spoke to each other in muted whispers. But he also thought he picked up an unnatural closeness in the way Magner wrapped a make-shift tourniquet around Purvis's arm, his touch soothing the fire in the wound, the sound of his voice seeming to salve the heat of Purvis's anger. "If you were ever to be connected to this place, then you'd both be finished, wouldn't you?" Gilchrist said.

No reaction, other than a casual glance from Magner and a quick shift of Purvis's eyes to confirm the Beretta was still lying on the floor, inches from Stan's dead fingers but out of Gilchrist's or Jessie's reach. Gilchrist suspected it had been left there deliberately, as some sort of test, failing which, they would be shot.

Rather than go for the gun, he went for the throat.

"That was why you were intending to leave Jason down here," he said, "to rot with all of his sculptures."

Purvis tried to free his arm, but Magner held tight and said in a voice loud enough for Gilchrist to hear, "He's talking nonsense, Jason. Forget him."

"So, you still haven't told us what this place is for?" Gilchrist said, probing for a greater reaction.

Purvis grunted as he slipped from Magner's grip and reached with his uninjured arm for one of the torches that sat lens-down on the workbench. He slapped it into the palm of his hand, as if testing its usefulness as a weapon with which to beat Gilchrist's brains to pulp.

"Don't indulge him," Magner said.

But Purvis shrugged Magner's hand away with a "What the fuck can they do about it," then clicked on the torch and pointed it into the black warren of chambers until it rested on some point beyond the reach of the single overhead bulb.

Gilchrist followed the torch's beam and felt his breath catch.

"You see it now?" Purvis asked.

Magner seemed almost embarrassed.

"It's my studio," Purvis explained. "This is where I work."

He shifted the beam across trestles, workbenches, rolls of wire mesh of different gauges, and an array of tools—both carpentry and surgical—all neatly organized on hooks on the walls. Something heavy flipped over in Gilchrist's stomach as his gaze settled on a pair of heavy-duty pruning shears with two stubby flanges eighteen inches apart welded to one length of handle. He realized with a shudder that the tool could be used to hold open a ribcage while the victim was disembowelled. Jessie seemed to sense his unease and stirred beside him, pushing herself upright.

The beam of light danced to the roof of the chamber, then rested on a metal beam that spanned one of the open doorways. Purvis laughed, a hard sound that echoed through the basement like the cackle of a madman. "My sculpting studio." The beam shifted along a signboard and, like a teacher reading aloud to his pupils, Purvis said, "The Meating Room."

Jessie put her hand to her mouth and whispered, "Holy fuck."

Purvis redirected the beam into the heart of the studio, playing the light across skin stretched on a wire-mesh frame, as if to dry it. Other lumps of meat and rolls of intestine sat in glass jars in an opaque liquid. "Formaldehyde solution," Purvis explained as the beam reflected off the glass. "Slows down decomposition. Like varnishing wood."

Magner seemed to have had enough of the morbid display. He retrieved Jessie's gun from the floor, then stepped up to Purvis and, like a doctor to a patient, gave a gentle tug at his arm. As if in some kind of hypnotic state, Purvis let Magner remove the torch from his grip, and Gilchrist realized that Purvis was not suffering from shock but was drunk, plain and simple.

Without warning, Jessie tried to struggle to her feet.

"Sit," ordered Magner.

She ignored him.

Purvis turned, his eyes blazing fury.

Gilchrist managed to grip the tail of Jessie's jacket and gave a hard tug. She slumped back down beside him, then tried to push herself free. But Gilchrist kept his grip firm.

"Leave it," he said.

Purvis stood before them, looking down. Gilchrist was certain that if the man had any kind of weapon in his hand, he would finish them both off without a second thought. As if sensing that possibility, too, Magner shouted, "*Jason*," then added a softer, "Jason."

Purvis's eyes seemed to settle—like watching fever lift, Gilchrist thought—and he retreated to Magner's side once again.

Gilchrist waited until Magner looked his way, then asked, "What were you going to do with the dogs?"

Magner narrowed his eyes, as if seeing the trap.

"You weren't going to take them with you, were you?" Gilchrist continued. "You're not a doggie person. They would spoil the image—slobbering all over your nice white shirts. What were you going to do? Shoot them?"

Purvis looked at Gilchrist, then at Magner, who shook his head and said, "You ask far too many questions." The SIG Sauer reappeared in his hand as if by magic.

Gilchrist felt his heart stutter as the pistol turned his way until all he could see of it was the black hole of its barrel. Survival instinct forced him to say, "We're worth more to you alive. You know that."

Magner smiled. "I see you know how to play your cards." He waited, as if for Purvis's nod of approval, then asked, "Are you a gambling man?"

Gilchrist knew he was being toyed with, but he also knew the longer he kept Magner talking, the longer he and Jessie had to live. Of course, finding some way to overcome two armed killers posed another problem, the answer to which eluded him utterly.

"I have the odd punt," he said. "Never really took to it, though. Always lose more than I win, which kind of numbs the thrill of it, I suppose. But I bet you know how to play the odds." Another twitch from Purvis gave Gilchrist his cue. "Once you'd shot the dogs were you going to drag their bodies down here and leave them to rot?"

Magner raised his hand to stop Purvis from stepping forward and beating Gilchrist to death. Oddly, that simple action worked, for Purvis stood still, lips drawn in a white line, eyes no more than slits too narrow for blinking. And, as they stood side by side, looking down at him, Gilchrist was struck by how similar yet different they were.

Purvis was smaller, stockier, and broader than Magner—not by much—but with less sense of sophistication. Of course, the camouflage outfit did not compare well with a pristine suited collar and tie. And where Magner could no doubt command attention by the simple act of making an entrance, Purvis would always prefer anonymity. Purvis's face, too, had less of a defined jawline, more rounded than square-chin sculpted, and Gilchrist came to see that Purvis had always stood in Magner's shadow—like checking in and out of hotels manned by rotating staff and attending conferences in the dim light of an audience, while Magner was off somewhere hunting for another victim for Purvis to turn into art, which only compounded Purvis's sense of the underdog.

And where Magner possessed the confidence and presence of mind to attend to the grisly with a sober mind, Purvis sought strength from alcohol. But more importantly—and Gilchrist thought he saw an opening here—where Magner remained cool under fire, Purvis could be the proverbial loose cannon.

"The dead one was called Bruce," Gilchrist said. "What's the other one called? Lee?"

"You can ask him yourself when he comes round," Purvis said with a twisted smile. "But you'd better be quick. He's got an appetite on him first thing. He likes to have a ball. Or two." He let out a manic cackle at his own joke.

Magner found nothing funny in Purvis's antics. His attention was focused on something flickering on the workbench—a monitor that Gilchrist had not noticed until that moment.

"Bring him here," Magner snapped.

Purvis obliged by leaning down, gripping Gilchrist by the collar, and lugging him to his feet. For a moment, Gilchrist felt as if his central axis was going to let him down again, but the moment passed as Purvis pulled him beyond Stan's body, to face the monitor.

"Who's that?" Magner asked, pointing at the screen.

The monitor was divided into four sections, with each quarter showing a view of the exterior of Purvis's cottage from a different webcam. Someone was standing at the back door, a woman Gilchrist recognized as PC Mhairi McBride. He felt a stab of pain pierce his heart and had to fight off the urge to glance at Stan's body. He and Mhairi had just been settling into a deepening relationship.

And as Gilchrist stood there, Magner watching him, Purvis just itching for the order to gut him, Gilchrist came to see why he and Jessie had not been killed right away. Magner needed to know if anyone from the Force would turn up at the cottage, before he gave Purvis the instruction to take their lives.

Gilchrist grunted as Purvis poked him with a hand as hard as wood. "Recognize her?"

Gilchrist shook his head. "I don't know who she is."

Purvis punched Gilchrist's side with a force that could crack ribs—and probably did—which caused Gilchrist to sink to his knees as pain as sharp as a knife strike overwhelmed him.

"We need him," Magner growled.

Purvis nodded to Jessie, who was still sitting on the floor, her back to the wall. "We can use her."

"We've got *him*," Magner replied. "Now get him up."

Gilchrist gasped as Purvis grabbed a clump of hair and tugged him to his feet. He managed to remain upright, a bit shaky, but he was getting the hang of it. "I told you," he said. "I've no idea who she is."

"Why is she here, then?"

"How would I know?"

"Have a guess," Purvis suggested.

"Well, it's Sunday. Maybe she's selling Bibles."

A punch to the side of the head bowled Gilchrist over. He hit the floor with a thud that almost knocked him unconscious again. He lay there for a few beats, struggling to fight off the almost overpowering urge to let his eyes roll back and settle under his eyelids. Then the moment passed. He spat out a mouthful of blood and pushed himself to his knees.

Purvis's grip had him standing to attention in zero seconds flat, as well as wondering if he had any hair left. His scalp was stinging, but at least he was still alive—well, for the time being.

"Let's try this one more time," Magner said.

Gilchrist stared at the monitor. Mhairi had walked from the rear door to the kitchen window and was tilting her face to peer through a gap in the curtains. Then the monitor flickered to display another quartered screen—views of the outside of the barn. Another flicker, and this time the quarters turned a hazy green—images from infrared webcams located within the basement warren itself. Each showed what looked like a door—four exit points. He realized that the monitor's electrical supply was being provided by the generator, via some sort of transformer, and probably powering a Wi-Fi transmitter too, so images could be beamed from the cottage.

Another set of four images showed two screens in which the three of them stood facing the monitor from different angles. He turned his head to search for the webcam in the ceiling and received a slap to the side of the head for his effort.

"Eyes to the front," Purvis said.

Gilchrist obliged and said nothing while the screen shifted again to show four images of the inside of Purvis's cottage, which Magner studied as if to ensure no one had broken in. The next screen brought them back to Mhairi at the rear of the cottage.

"OK," Magner said. "One last time. Who is she?"

"I'm telling you, I don't know."

Magner stared hard into Gilchrist's eyes. "I don't believe you."

Gilchrist shook his head.

"You three turn up," Magner said. "Then someone else shows up. I don't believe in coincidences."

Neither did Gilchrist, but he was not for agreeing.

Magner looked at Purvis, then nodded at the screen. "Get her."

Without a word, Purvis retrieved the shotgun from the workbench, inserted two cartridges, and snapped the barrels back with a click that sent a shock through Gilchrist's system. Then he picked up the night-vision goggles and marched toward the entrance shaft—an eager hunter hungry to shoot his quarry.

Gilchrist risked another glance at the monitor. Mhairi had moved to the corner of the cottage and appeared to be making her way round to the front, but she was taking her time. Gilchrist knew with absolute certainty that if he did not do something within the next few minutes, Mhairi would end up as dead as Stan.

As if reading Gilchrist's mind, Magner pointed the SIG Sauer at him. "Over there."

Gilchrist thought of risking all in one crazed attempt to overpower Magner.

But sense prevailed and, defeated, he walked toward Jessie.

36

ilchrist had enough sense left in his battered brain to know that to have any chance of overpowering Magner, he had to wait until Purvis cleared the entrance shaft. On the other hand, the dilemma he now faced was that if he was forced to sit down, he could not attack Magner without making it obvious, and Purvis would be free to murder Mhairi.

If he could find some way to . . .

"I need a pee," he tried.

"Sit down next to Miss Piggy, and do it in your pants," Magner said.

The ringing sound of metal on metal as Purvis clambered up the exit ladder echoed through the chamber, and Gilchrist veered to the left. "Shoot me in the back, if you want to," he said, "but I'm having a pee in private."

"How about I shoot *her* instead?" Magner replied.

Gilchrist stopped. Magner had leveled the gun at Jessie's face, leaving Gilchrist in no doubt that he would pull the trigger in a heartbeat. "I'll hold it in," he said, and shuffled back to stand beside Jessie.

"Sit."

"I'd rather stand."

Magner lined up the barrel on Jessie again. "Your choice."

Defeated, Gilchrist slid down the wall, then looked over in surprise as Jessie pushed herself to her feet.

"Trying to make it easy for me?" Magner said.

Jessie nodded at the monitor. "You never asked if *I* could identify that woman. It might be Aggie."

"Who's Aggie?"

"Head of Special Ops."

Magner's mouth twisted into a lopsided grin. "You're at it," he said.

"You'd better hope I'm at it," Jessie said, "because if I'm not, you and your dickhead for a partner won't be going anywhere soon, dog or no dog."

Magner glared at her as she stepped toward him.

"Let me have a look," she said. "What've you got to lose?"

"Stay put." Magner's knuckles whitened on the grip of the pistol.

Gilchrist felt a thud of fear in his gut. Whatever Jessie was up to, she was pushing Magner to the limit. It would not take much more pressure on his trigger finger to stop her in her tracks. "Jessie," he said. "Sit down."

Jessie snapped a look at Gilchrist, then back to Magner. "A big strong lad like you? Afraid of little old me? I don't even have a gun," she said, and held out her hands to prove her point. "What're you afraid of? That I might scratch your eyes out?" She chuckled. "You should see your face," she said. "Why don't you show me? I'll keep my distance, I promise. I can't be fairer than that."

As Jessie edged closer, Magner backed off, a puzzled look on his face, as if undecided whether to shoot her or hear what she might say if he let her look at the monitor.

Then he stepped aside, still pointing the gun at her forehead. "Go ahead then."

Jessie reached the monitor, pressed a key, and the screen shifted to a new quartet of webcam images. "I don't see her," she said.

"Step back," Magner ordered, and waited until Jessie backed up a couple of paces.

If Jessie was going to do anything, Gilchrist thought, she would do it now.

But Magner tapped the keyboard, said, "There she is," and stepped aside to let Jessie have another look. He glanced at Gilchrist and received a blank stare in return.

"Where's that dickhead partner of yours?" Jessie said.

"Get on with it," Magner snapped.

Jessie peered at the screen. "I'm not sure," she said. "How do I zoom in?"

"You don't."

Jessie shrugged. "Can't help you then." She turned to walk away, but then stopped and returned to the screen. "Oh, now I think I know who it is," she said.

Gilchrist saw that Jessie had tricked Magner into half-trusting her. He was standing a little closer to the monitor, and as Jessie leaned toward the screen she slid a hand into her jacket pocket. By instinct, as if Jessie had explained it to him in advance, Gilchrist knew what he had to do.

"Help me up," he shouted.

Magner glanced at Gilchrist, who had a hand outstretched for a pull up to his feet. The SIG Sauer wavered for a moment, as if Magner was undecided who to shoot first—Gilchrist or Jessie. And in that split second of indecision, Jessie moved.

With a speed that surprised Gilchrist—and Magner, as it turned out—she slipped her hand from her pocket and squirted something into his eyes while her other hand struck out at his gun arm.

Gilchrist winced as Magner pulled the trigger—once, twice—the bullets ricocheting off the concrete wall over Jessie's shoulder. Another couple of shots blasted at the ceiling, as Magner squealed in pain, one hand at his eyes, the other waving the gun.

The echo of the explosions reverberated back to them like rolls of thunder as Magner collapsed to the floor with a grunt and a thud that spread-eagled his body—Jessie had just hit him full in the face with one of the torches from the workbench. In a second she stood astride him, trapping his gun arm under one boot. But instead of cuffing him, she swung the torch at his face again. The splash of blood and the sound of tearing cartilage told Gilchrist she had broken Magner's nose. One more hit for good measure cracked his jaw and knocked him unconscious.

"Jesus, Jessie," Gilchrist gasped.

She turned to him then, and he saw nothing but raw fear in her eyes. Before he could reach her, she had both hands to her face and the torch clattered to the floor. Her shoulders shuddered, breath heaving, as she sobbed, "Oh Christ oh Christ oh Christ—"

Gilchrist took hold of her, pulled her to him. "It's OK," he said. "It's OK." But he knew he had to act fast, and he pushed her away. "It's Mhairi," he said.

That stopped Jessie midgasp. "What?"

"At the cottage. That's who Purvis is going to shoot."

"What about *him*?" she said, glaring at Magner.

"He's not going anywhere," Gilchrist said, removing a pair of Flex-Cufs from his jacket. He cuffed Magner's hands behind his back, and an ankle to the steel leg of the workbench.

Next, he retrieved all three mobile phones from the bench and handed Jessie her Beretta. "I never saw that," he said, "and you never brought it." Then he picked up the torch from the floor.

"We don't have time," Jessie gasped. "We'll never catch up with Purvis."

"We do, and we will." He powered up his mobile, nodded at the pepper spray in Jessie's hand, and said, "Remind me never to fall out with you." Then he ran toward the entrance shaft.

He reached the metal rungs and clambered up, praying he was not too late. He pulled himself out of the shaft with a speed that surprised him—adrenaline will do that—and crouched on the floor of the anteroom. He clicked on the torch and shivered its beam over the bare walls and floor.

"Give me a hand up, will you?"

He grabbed hold of Jessie's hand and tugged her from the shaft.

"Shit," she said. "I'm all puffed out."

Gilchrist knew that Jessie was still in shock, that her heart and lungs would be working overtime to settle her system, which would take time. But they had no time. He eyed his mobile and saw he now had a signal.

He found Mhairi's number and pressed the phone to his ear. "Come on come on," he said, following Jessie from the anteroom, through the next small room, and into the barn. The noise from the generator was loud enough to shake bones, and he pressed a hand over his ear to block off the sound. The air smelled fresh and felt cold enough to cut skin. He breathed it in as his sense of smell returned to him. "Come on, Mhairi, answer, for crying out loud."

For one insane moment, he thought of stepping outside and running across the fields to warn her. But Purvis was armed with a shotgun and wearing night-vision goggles. Gilchrist could do nothing for Mhairi unless he reached her by phone. He watched Jessie's beam dance across the walls as she searched for a light switch. "Call for backup," he shouted and killed the call. He was about to try again when his blood froze at the snarling growl.

He tried to turn, but his legs seemed to have lost all connection with his brain.

By the light from his torch, his peripheral vision picked up movement as something dark rose from the shadows and powered toward him.

Just in time, reflexive instinct jerked his arm up to protect his face as the Rottweiler slammed into him with the momentum of a prop forward. His forearm felt as if a mantrap had snapped onto it, and he grunted in pain as his back hit the floor.

He could smell the dog's hot breath, hear the primeval savagery in its snarls as its drool splattered his face, its jaws gnashing and tearing through his leather jacket and into the meat of his arm. Its back legs were scrabbling, claws tearing into his thighs, as it tried to surge forward for the kill. With his free arm, Gilchrist managed to grip the dog's neck, fingers sinking into its short fur, and he tugged for all he was worth. But against the wild strength of an enraged Rottweiler he was barely holding off the attack, only delaying the inevitable.

If it released his arm and went for his throat, he stood no chance.

Then the barn lit up like a lightning strike.

The Rottweiler never noticed.

Gilchrist gasped, "Jessie," as he caught the firework crack of a gun and felt the thud of the bullet. The Rottweiler released his arm and turned its head to its flank, as if something had irritated it. Then it returned its attention to the task at hand and, with lips pulled back in a snarl that bared canines long and hard enough to crush bones, went for Gilchrist's throat.

He had time only to cross his arms in front of his face.

Another firecracker popped.

The Rottweiler's snarl turned to a pained whine.

Another pop.

Gilchrist felt the strength drain from the beast as its whine changed to a burbling growl, and its splattering drool turned pink.

Then Jessie's boots were by his head, and he could only gasp for air as she pressed her Beretta to the dog's head and pulled the trigger.

Not even a whine that time.

Gilchrist pushed the Rottweiler off him, rolled to his side, tried to catch his breath. His trousers were bloodied and ripped where the dog's claws had dug in. The sleeve of his leather jacket could have been put through a shredder. He felt the warm stream of blood running the length of his forearm to drip from his fingers.

"I'm scared to ask," Jessie said.

"I'm scared to look." He gripped the torn sleeve and tried to staunch the flow of blood. From the amount dripping from his fingers, he knew the attack had not severed his radial or ulnar artery. He was losing blood and in pain, but it could have been much worse.

"Did you manage to call for backup?" he asked.

"Battery's flat," she said. "Forgot to charge it."

Gilchrist glared at her. "Tell me you're kidding."

"Sorry."

"Right. OK. First things first. Are you any good at tourniquets?"

"I used to be a Girl Guide."

He pulled off his jacket to reveal a torn shirt sleeve soaked in blood, grabbed the material, and ripped most of it off. At first glance, his arm looked a mess, but he rubbed his hand over it and confirmed they were mostly flesh wounds. Just one, deeper than the rest, was pulsing blood.

"OK, Florence Nightingale. You're on."

Jessie did a fine job of making a tourniquet out of the remnants of his shirt sleeve. She assured him she did not want it too tight in case it stopped the blood flow to his fingers; just tight enough to stop the worst of the bleeding.

"Where did you learn that?" he asked.

"You forget, I'm a mother, and mothers take care of their sons."

He flexed his arm. It felt stiff and tight, but at least the tourniquet was doing its job. He pulled on his jacket, then said, "Let's find my mobile."

Jessie located it in less than thirty seconds—under the BMW, where it had slid from the impact of the Rottweiler's attack. She handed it to him just as it rang.

He eyed the screen—Mhairi—and breathed a sigh of relief.

He made the connection and said, "Where are you, Mhairi?"

"She's with me," Purvis said. "Safe and sound."

37

Gilchrist felt his strength leave him. The thought of what Purvis might do to Mhairi shocked him to the core. "We've cuffed Magner," he said. "It's over. Don't make it any worse for yourself."

Purvis let out a demonic cackle. "Do you know what I'm going to do with her? With the lovely Mhairi?" he said. "I'm going to set up a new studio, and Mhairi's going to be my very first model."

"Listen to me, Jason," Gilchrist said, hoping that using the first name might help him get through to the man. "You can't—"

"She'll make a fine model, too. She's got lovely bone structure. And such a lovely face. I think she'll look good on my—"

"Listen to me. It's over. You can't escape." But words or reason were meaningless to a man like Purvis, so he changed tack. "Put Mhairi on. Let me speak to her."

A pause. Then, "Say please."

Gilchrist struggled for control, toying with the idea of just hanging up. But Mhairi's life was at stake. "Please put Mhairi on," he said. "I won't believe you haven't harmed her until I speak to her."

"Well, believe this. The lovely Mhairi will make a perfect model, yeah?"

Purvis killed the call.

Gilchrist had no time to waste. He dialed Glenrothes HQ, requested ARVs—armed response vehicles—and gave the address of the cottage. "It's an emergency," he said. "We have one officer dead"—his throat choked as he gave Stan's full name—"and PC Mhairi McBride is being held captive. The target is armed and will kill if cornered." He provided more details, requested an ambulance, then ended the call.

"How long until they get here?" Jessie asked.

"They'll send officers from Anstruther and North Street to close off the roads, but we're looking at an hour—at the earliest—for the ARV. So, until then, it's just the two of us." Gilchrist shouldered open the barn door.

Together, they stepped outside.

The night air felt bitter cold and smelled clean and fresh. In the distance, the lights from the cottage could have him believing all was well. Nothing stirred. Even the wind had died. Passing headlights momentarily lit up the Ford Focus parked to the side of the cottage.

It could be any normal Sunday night.

"Do you think Mhairi's tied up inside the cottage?" Jessie asked.

Gilchrist stared into the night. It seemed a logical suggestion.

Where had Purvis been when he answered Mhairi's mobile? Gilchrist thought back to the call, tried to remember what he had heard in the background. Nothing. Just Purvis's voice, laughing like a lunatic, that demented cackle, and the echo on the line.

He searched for any movement in the cottage. The warm glow from the windows beckoned him inside.

But it was too calm, too natural, too still.

The echo on the line . . .

"What's up?" Jessie asked.

"I'm not sure," Gilchrist said as he dialed Mhairi's number. He continued to stare at the cottage while the connection was made, only for the automatic recording to kick in: "The person you are calling is unable to take your call."

He tried again. Same result.

He slipped the mobile into his pocket and walked back inside the barn. The sight of the dead Rottweiler startled him. It lay on its side in a pool of blood, eyes open, tongue lolling. He stepped around it and headed for the internal door.

"Want to tell me what's going on?" Jessie asked.

"Mhairi's phone's not receiving."

"Purvis must have switched it off."

"Why would he do that?"

"So the sick fuck doesn't have to talk to us?"

"Then he wouldn't be able to tell us all about his new studio. He's an egotistical psycho. He wants us to know what he's going to do."

"Flat battery?"

"Mhairi's reliable," he said.

"Not like some of us?"

Through the first room, the air thickened with the stench from the basement warren. In the second room, Gilchrist slid both legs into the shaft, found the rungs, and gripped the handrail.

"I don't think he's in the cottage," he said.

"Well, the car's not moved. So where is he?"

"That's what we're about to find out."

———

The foul smell of the basement had Gilchrist covering his nose. He worked his way through the chambers to the lit main room. Magner was still cuffed to the workbench but was now conscious, with blistered eyes and a face to match. He swung his free leg as Gilchrist entered the room, a weak attempt at a kick, and spat blood at Jessie as she followed.

"Not so suave now, are we?" she said.

"Fuck you."

She showed Magner her torch and said, "Believe me, it won't take much pissing me off to make me give you another one with this. So why don't you shut it."

Magner glared at her but got the message.

Gilchrist reached the monitor, still set on the four views of the exterior of the cottage. Two quick clicks had him looking at the interior from four different angles. Then he brought up another quartet of interior images, only to confirm that the cottage was deserted.

He turned to Magner. "Where is he?"

Magner did his best to look confused.

Gilchrist was not up for beating the truth from the man. Instead, he clicked through the webcam images until he found what he was looking for—the screen that showed four doors within the basement warren.

The Ford Focus—still parked in the driveway—had sealed it for Gilchrist. Mhairi would not have parked her car any-where near the cottage—Stan would have warned her about that—and Purvis could not risk being seen dragging a captive woman across the Scottish countryside.

So they still had to be on the property.

But not necessarily at ground level.

"Where do these doors lead to?" he asked Magner.

Silence.

Jessie stepped toward Magner, clenching the torch.

"You can hit me all you like," Magner said to her, his words slurred through a broken jaw. "But I can't answer something I don't know." He spat another mouthful of blood at her.

"Forget him, Jessie. I think I see which one."

Jessie turned to the monitor and frowned. "They all look the same."

"But they're not."

Gilchrist stepped back and stared at the opening to the main room. Dim light from the entrance shaft gave him his bearings. The basement warren mirrored the rectangular barn above it—meaning that one axis pointed in the direction of the cottage, with the other at right angles to it. He reasoned that as there were four doors, each had to exit in one of four directions, the four sides of the basement. His rationale also told him it was difficult enough to build an underground warren, without having to construct a maze leading from it. And what would be the point?

So, logically, only one of those doors led to the cottage.

He clicked on his torch, said, "This way," and stepped into the shadows.

Soon, they were stepping over blockwork rubble and rusted rebar, as if the contractor had left the structure unfinished. The steady drip of water seemed to surround them, and the walls glistened wet as they splashed through puddles. Gilchrist flashed the torch left and right, penetrating deeper into the maze, as they stepped from chamber to chamber.

"What *is* this place?" Jessie said. "Maybe it was constructed during the war. Some sort of bomb shelter?"

"Bit big for a bomb shelter," Gilchrist said.

"Are we anywhere near the Secret Bunker?"

Now opened to the public, the Secret Bunker had been constructed after World War II to house the regional government in the event of a nuclear or biological attack. A guardhouse, constructed to resemble a farmhouse, was the main entrance to the reinforced-concrete subterranean control center. It was not too much of a stretch to imagine this warren formed part of some similar government scheme.

"We're miles away from it," he said. "But who knows what the government gets up to."

Something scrabbled over stones in the dark to his left, and he swung his torch to reveal a wall crawling with rats big enough to take on cats. A crack in the concrete near the ceiling, caused by years of settlement, seemed to be the point of ingress. The exposure to an unexpected torch beam caused not even a ruffle of fur as the rats sniffed the air and brushed around and over each other, oblivious to their presence.

"I hate these things," Jessie said.

"They eat them in the Far East."

"Remind me never to dine out there."

"But it makes sense now," Gilchrist said.

"What does?"

"The wire mesh in the sculptures. So the rats can't eat the meat."

"Like squirrel-proof bird feeders?"

"Exactly."

"Fuck sake," Jessie said. "We anywhere near that door yet?"

Gilchrist directed his torch ahead and thought he saw an end to the warren. "Getting close," he said.

They stepped through another opening, which seemed to be the last of the chambers, and shone their torches to the left, then the right. A narrow corridor peeled off to either side, each echoing with the sound of dripping water and the whispering scuffle of rodents.

"The corridor probably runs around the entire perimeter of the basement," Gilchrist said.

"You see a door?"

His beam picked up a darker shadow on the wall about ten yards to their right, and he strode toward it.

The door was inset about six inches or so into the wall. Gilchrist felt his heart sink as he shone the torch over it. Layers of rust curled from its metal panels like sheets of burned paper and swelled around the hinges like peeling blisters. A black slit for a keyhole suggested it was locked. But the corroded handle tempted him to try it anyway. He pressed down hard and heard the lock click. Then he gritted his teeth and pulled. The hinges creaked in resistance, but the door eased back half an inch.

"We're in," he said.

38

Cracking the door open was one thing. Forcing it wide enough to let a body through was another. And Gilchrist's injury was not helping. When he gripped the handle with both hands and flexed his muscles to pull the door open farther, his left arm burned with a fire that had him gasping in pain.

"It's no use," he said. "I can't open it."

Jessie shone her torch at the door to reveal a gap of no more than three inches. "Let me try," she said, but gave a squeal of disgust when she took hold of the handle. She shone her torch at her hand. "You're still bleeding," she said.

"Trying to open rusty doors will do that."

"Want me to take another look at it?"

"Let's open this first."

"That's what we'll inscribe on your headstone," she said. "'I should have kept the door shut.'" She turned back to the door, gripped the handle, and closed it with a grunt. Then she jerked it open, closed it, jerked it open again.

"I think it's working," Gilchrist said. "Keep going."

"Where's a man when you need him?"

After thirty seconds of heaving the door open and shut, Jessie released the handle and gasped, "Got to stop. I'm knackered." Her breath clouded like ectoplasm in the gloom.

Gilchrist's beam showed the gap was now some ten inches. If he could just squeeze his shoulder into it, he might be able to use his body to prise it open a touch more, maybe even slip through. He pushed his right arm in, then managed to get his shoulder in, too. He pressed and pushed and flexed his shoulder but could not open it any wider.

"Ah, shit," Jessie said. "My torch has just died on me."

"I'm not going to say a word."

He shone his torch at her face and saw fear in her eyes. He had partnered her long enough to understand that her bravado and cocky talk were no more than a shield she put up to protect herself. Being underground in a psycho-cum-artist's studio was enough to scare anyone witless. And witnessing Stan's cold-blooded murder had rocked Jessie to the core—himself too.

"Take mine." He flinched from the pain as he slipped off his leather jacket.

"What're you doing?"

"Squeezing through."

"Christ, Andy, you're on your own. One of my tits is bigger than that gap."

"I thought you were taking karate lessons and losing weight."

"I'd need to get down to four stone before I could squeeze this lot through."

Gilchrist pressed his face hard against the wall and pushed his right arm and leg into the opening. Squeezing his head through the gap almost cost him an ear, and his backside kept him locked in place for a good two minutes, until he wriggled and turned and managed to break through. He twisted his body, then pulled his left leg into the darkness of the tunnel and took great care doing the same with his left arm.

"I know you're slim," she said, "but that must have hurt."

"A bit tight."

"How are your balls?"

"Fine."

"You counted them?"

"Jacket," he said.

She passed it through.

He removed his mobile from the pocket and powered up the screen. Not the best torch in the world, but at least it let him see where he was going. He stretched out his arm and did a one-eighty sweep but could see no more than a few feet, the light from the screen casting a glow rather than a directional beam.

"Anything?" Jessie asked.

Her torch beam was blinding through the gap in the door. "Not yet," he said. "But I'll press on." He turned round, shielded his eyes. "Make your way back. You can't go wrong. It's only one of three directions. Left, right, or straight on."

"As long as I don't have to read a map."

"I need you to take charge, Jessie," he said, serious now. "Read Magner his rights, then organize a team to take him to the surface. Start the ball rolling for search warrants of Purvis's property, the works. And call Chief Super Whyte, too. Let him know what we've got."

"Meanwhile, you're going for a stroll?"

"And arrange for someone in Family Liaison to notify Stan's parents," he said.

A pause, then, "Will do, Andy." She shone her torch through the gap, and he had to turn away. "How's that arm doing?"

"Sore," he said. "But I've got a spare one."

She chuckled at the lame attempt at a joke. "You don't have to do this. We can get cutting equipment down here and send in a team."

They could also try searching Purvis's cottage for a trapdoor. There had to be one, if his theory was correct. Instead, he said, "We don't have time. Not if we want to save Mhairi." With that, he turned from the door and stepped into the darkness of the tunnel.

The going was not easy.

The tunnel floor was not concrete but hard angular stones over which Gilchrist's feet slipped and twisted. Moss glistened on the walls and floor. Water dribbled between the stones, reflecting the light from the phone like a mirror. The constant echo of drips and splashes accompanied the crunching of his boots as he worked his way forward.

His progress was much slower than he'd hoped. About two minutes in, he stumbled, lost his balance, and only just managed to keep hold of the phone as his knees crashed onto sharp stones, causing him to cry out in pain. The fire in his left arm flared, and he wondered if he should just do as Jessie had suggested—return to the surface and let the experts take over. But the echo of Purvis's laugh, and the thought of what he might do to Mhairi, forced him to ignore the pain and struggle to his feet.

Upright again, he took some time to recover.

The ceiling seemed lower here, the walls closer, too, as if the tunnel were narrowing on all sides. He looked over his shoulder but saw only pitch blackness beyond the weak glow of the phone. He could be a bubble of light in a black tunnel in space. In his mind's eye, he pulled up an image of the barn and where it stood in relation to the cottage. Then he shifted that image underground and tried to figure out how far he had come.

Moving on with that mental map, he reckoned he must be only about fifty yards from the cottage. But however near he was, he knew it would be slow going from here.

He held his mobile in front of him and pressed on.

———

Jessie surprised herself by finding her way back to Magner without any wrong turns. Once she had stumbled her way through a series of empty rooms, the distant glow of light from the main chamber drew her forward like a moth to a flame. She intended to leave Magner lying in his own blood and snot for another thirty minutes—the more extreme his discomfort, the better, as far as she was concerned.

Her first task would be to organize a team to search the cottage for the trapdoor to the tunnel. And she needed a team down here, too—to cut through the metal door and follow Andy. Just the thought of creeping through the dark like that caused a shiver to run the length of her spine.

As she entered the last of the chambers before the main room, she shielded her eyes from the macabre anterooms that housed Purvis's sculptures. She could hear the heavy throb of the generator in the barn above, and the light was now bright enough to permit her to switch off her torch. She braced herself for the imminent sight of Stan's body on the floor.

She entered the main room.

Her breath locked. Her heart stopped . . .

Then restarted with a kick that pulled a gasp from her.

Magner was gone.

Survival instinct and raw fear dropped her to the ground like a rock.

Beyond Stan's body, by the leg of the workbench to which Magner had been cuffed, a hacksaw lay discarded on the floor. Even from where she crouched, Jessie saw that Magner had somehow managed to haul the heavy bench across the floor, pull a shelf from the wall—pliers, saw blades, screwdrivers, hammers, lay scattered—and cut his way through the Flex-Cufs.

She tried to still her pounding heart, stop her lungs from panting, as she placed the torch to one side, undid the ankle holster, and removed her gun. She shuffled across the floor, her back to the wall. If Magner made an appearance, she would shoot him stone dead. She tried to remember what Andy had done with Magner's pistol, and her mind drew a blank.

As her eyes probed into the darkness beyond the light of the main room, she realized that the entrance shaft was no longer illuminated. And as she worked out that Magner had escaped from the basement and closed the hatch, she heard the stuttering sound of the generator powering down.

The lights flickered, then died.

Jessie let out an involuntary whimper as darkness landed on her like a heavy weight. All of a sudden, her sense of direction evaporated. Was she staring blindly at the workbench, or was she looking off at an angle? And where had she left the torch?

She patted the concrete behind her. If she retraced her steps along the base of the wall, she would surely stumble across it. But she cursed herself for leaving it behind in the first place. Inch by careful inch, she edged her way back to the main room's entrance. She caught the faintest shuffle of tiny claws on stones, the distant rustling of rats, the soft thud of fur on concrete as they tumbled from the wall and made their way into the blackness.

"Dear God, help me," she whimpered.

———

Gilchrist reached the end of the tunnel—another metal door.

If it was locked, he could do nothing but retreat. He reached for the handle—identical to the one at the other end—and pressed it down.

The lock clicked.

To his surprise, this door opened wide enough on the first pull for him to slip through without difficulty and step into what appeared to be another tunnel. He held his mobile out in front again, worried that the screen might fade any time— how long did these things last anyway? He had already taken longer than expected.

This tunnel was wide enough for one person. It had a concrete floor, but the low ceiling made walking upright impossible—

The walls lit up like an explosion.

Gilchrist's body jerked as if shot. He managed to hold on to his mobile but had to squeeze his eyes against the sudden brightness.

"Don't move."

The voice came from behind and hit him like a rabbit punch to the neck.

He spun around.

Magner crouched at the foot of a wooden ladder that reached to the tunnel ceiling and the inviting opening of a cottage trapdoor. His face was bloodied and bruised, his jaw twisted at an odd angle. His bloodshot eyes glared at Gilchrist, twin slits of red. If utter vitriol had a look, this was it. And it struck Gilchrist with a flutter of surprise that Magner could handle a shotgun every bit as smoothly as Purvis did.

"Drop the phone." The shotgun barely twitched.

Myriad questions blasted through Gilchrist's mind with the power of a tornado. How had Magner broken free? Where was Jessie? Was she alive? Where were Purvis and Mhairi? Had the backup arrived? And how the hell had he fucked up so badly?

"The phone," Magner reminded him.

Gilchrist threw it toward Magner's feet, where it landed with a clatter.

As nonchalant as you like, Magner lowered the shotgun and let off one barrel. The mobile exploded, sending pieces of plastic and metal ricocheting off the tunnel's walls and ceiling. Somewhere a light bulb popped, and the tunnel dimmed as glass tinkled to the floor. Gilchrist shielded his eyes as the shrapnel stung his face. Still, if he could take any heart from the moment, it was that Magner had only one shot left.

As if to confirm Gilchrist's thoughts, Magner dropped his left shoulder and slipped a strap off it, which materialized into a rifle that he pointed at Gilchrist's head. A quick check confirmed that Magner had only the rifle and shotgun, although from where Gilchrist stood it was impossible to tell if he had his SIG Sauer on him.

The barrel wiggled—an instruction for Gilchrist to move.

"Turn around," Magner ordered, his voice slurred through his broken jaw.

"You're only making matters worse," Gilchrist said.

Magner kept the rifle steady. "I'm thinking they can only get better from now on."

It looked to Gilchrist that Magner would smile if he could, and he slowly turned his back to him, knowing that any second now he would be shot through the back of the head.

"On your knees."

Gilchrist did as instructed, taking his time, his survival instinct fighting to eke out every last second of his life.

"I should have killed you back there," Magner said. "Killed all three of you."

"Don't do this—"

"*Shut up.*"

Gilchrist held up his hands, shoulder high. "I'm unarmed."

"I said shut *the fuck* up."

Gilchrist closed his eyes and took his last breath.

The rifle shot snapped like a whip crack.

39

Jessie struggled to fight off a searing flare of panic that engulfed her like a boiling wave. Her breath pulled in and out in sharp hits that burned her throat. In the pitch black, and hyperventilating, she lost all sense of direction and found herself struggling even to determine what was up and what was down.

Without the wall at her back, she was certain she would have toppled over.

She crawled through the darkness, her shoulders brushing the concrete, one hand sweeping the floor—dust, stones, fluff, hard bits of something that had her throat gagging at the thought of what they might be. She reached the point where the torch should be and swept her arm in a wide arc, fingers tapping, probing, until she touched—

She screamed, withdrew her hand with a primal gasp, and wiped the stickiness of Stan's blood from her fingers. Her lungs choked then, and she could do nothing to stop the surge of bile that erupted from her mouth in spluttering vomit that threatened to take her breath away for good. But she sucked in air and sat there in blinded horror as a spasm shuddered through her system to compete with her sobbing.

She did not know how long she sat there crying—one minute? twenty?—but she finally forced herself to take deep breaths and tried to steady her nerves. Her night vision, too, had improved to the point where she could make out shadows—dark on black—but nothing more definitive. Gray walls stood next to darker openings. Things on the floor seemed to scuttle and shift. The workbench, with its monitor and butcher's tools, was a lighter shade of black.

Jessie shuffled onto her hands and knees, reached forward, keeping away from the dark shadow she knew was Stan's body, and swept the floor again with one hand. She patted around in a methodical manner, a one-eighty in front of her, then extended her arm through another arc. On the third sweep her fingers touched the rubber casing of the torch, and she let out a cry of relief.

With shivering hands and clumsy fingers, she clicked the switch.

The pitch blackness evaporated into grays through which the beam cut like a knife of light. Shadows shrank away to reveal walls, workbenches, open doorways, and beyond . . . her escape route to the entrance shaft.

She rose to her feet and tightened her grip on both torch and Beretta.

Each unsteady step forward took her closer to the ladder and away from the Meating Room, with its horrific sculptures, away from Stan's stiffening body, away from a pervading fear that had squeezed the air from her lungs and shaken her to the bone.

With each step, she felt as if she were shedding another layer of terror.

By the time she reached the ladder, her hopes were soaring.

She put the torch in her pocket and the Beretta back in its ankle holster. Then she gripped the handrail and pulled herself up rung by rung until she reached the closed trapdoor. She felt for the hinges, then pushed up at the other edge. Locked. But she recalled what the lock looked like—nothing more than a sliding metal latch—then reached down to her ankle and retrieved the Beretta.

She pressed the muzzle hard against the hatch, turned her head, and pulled the trigger.

Wood and metal tore apart with a splintering bang.

A thump upward with the heel of her hand and the trapdoor crashed open.

Jessie pulled herself out, grabbed her torch from her pocket, and walked through the anteroom into the barn. The Rottweiler lay dead on the concrete floor in front of the BMW— Magner had not driven off. She stepped around the dog's body, brushed past the car, and switched her torch off as she neared the door.

Outside, the cottage's windows shone like a line of beacons, as if all was in order.

"Right, you fucker," Jessie whispered. "You've asked for it."

———

Gilchrist felt the hot buzz of the bullet zip past his left ear, heard it ricochet off the tunnel's wall in the distance. Then his stomach spasmed at the clicking sound of the rifle's bolt action behind him and the metallic tinkle of the empty cartridge as it bounced off the floor.

It took all of his willpower not to wet himself.

The first shot was to scare him. The second would kill him.

He thought of just getting to his feet, putting up a fight.

"That was a warning," Magner said. "To stay put."

Relief flooded through Gilchrist. Without both hands on the floor, he would have collapsed. He flexed his fingers, tried to calm his nerves, and forced his mind to work beyond the fear. His ears pricked at the sound of feet on wood behind him, then the electronic beep of a call being made.

"Got him," Magner said. "Be with you in fifteen," followed by a grunt and a heavy echoing thud as the cottage trapdoor slammed shut.

Gilchrist struggled to work through the rationale.

Magner had said he should have killed all three of them back in the Meating Room, yet had just passed up the perfect opportunity to execute Gilchrist.

Which meant?

The situation had changed in some way . . .

With Stan dead, and the police closing in, Magner's whole game plan had changed.

He would not be going to court to defend himself against the rape charges. Having killed Stan, he would now have to flee. And his best chance of doing that was to keep Gilchrist alive and use him as a bargaining tool. Gilchrist could only hope that Purvis had captured Mhairi for the same reason.

"Get up," Magner said.

Gilchrist struggled to his feet, bumped his head against the low ceiling, and hunched his shoulders in a stooping stance.

"Start walking."

Gilchrist placed one unsteady foot in front of the other. The rifle barrel prodded his back, instructing him to speed up. So he did, but not too fast. Magner's call to Purvis told Gilchrist he had fifteen minutes to try to work out how to prevent himself and Mhairi from being killed, as well as finding the answer to a few puzzling questions.

So he started with, "It took me a while to figure it out."

"Shut it."

"Walking helps me think, and thinking makes me talk," Gilchrist tried. He knew he was taking a chance, but no response suggested that Magner might let him continue, just for the hell of it. But the echo of Magner's voice—*Be with you in fifteen*—told Gilchrist that as long as he was walking and talking, he was safe. Well, as safe as you could be with a loaded rifle and shotgun two steps behind you.

He took another chance with, "It always amazes me how the smallest things bring you down. The one thing you overlooked."

Silence.

"It was the cut on your hand that gave you away. At the initial interview. You're left-handed. But your partner in crime isn't, you see?"

Magner gave a noncommittal grunt.

"So it got me thinking that maybe you'd cut yourself hacking poor Amy to bits."

The rifle jabbed the nape of his neck, more instruction to speed up than stop talking, and made Gilchrist think it might be more prudent to be less direct.

"No one remembers talking to you on Thursday afternoon at the Highland Hotel," he said. "Because Jason was standing in for you. You look alike, but not close up, so he had to stay in your room for most of the afternoon, then swap places when you returned some time during the conference that night." He stopped, took a breath. "It's hard going down here. Not much air." He waited for another prod from the rifle, but when it never came, he knew Magner was finding the going just as difficult.

He pressed on, walking and talking. "And here was me thinking Jason was the one who cut up the bodies, disemboweled them, chopped off their heads, ripped out their hearts and guts—all the stuff he needs for his artwork. But it was you all along—"

"You know the square root of fuck all."

"And artwork?" Gilchrist said. "I mean, that's pushing the boat out. But it does make for an interesting concept. Whose idea was it to protect your tokens with wire mesh?"

Nothing but the hard rush of deep breaths behind him.

Gilchrist counted thirty steps until they reached a ninety-degree corner. They rounded it, and he worked out that they must be under the main road that fronted the cottage. The ceiling was even lower here, and he had to stoop and shuffle forward with bended knees and thigh muscles that burned with pain. Magner was as tall as Gilchrist—six-one—but not as slim, so Gilchrist knew he must be finding it difficult, too. He slowed down a touch, but another prod in the back assured him that Magner was handling progress in the cramped space perfectly well.

"We checked CCTV footage of the park," Gilchrist said. "Tentsmuir Forest. It's busy, even at this time of year. Dog-walkers, hikers, fitness fanatics, and the like. We have a Ford Focus that matches the one parked outside Cauldwood Cottage entering at ten to eight. But by then, you'd already killed Amy and the kids, and I'm guessing you had Amy's body parts wrapped in towels in the boot.

"I'd also guess that Amy told Janice that she'd filed a complaint against you for rape under her maiden name—Charlotte Renwick. Or maybe their other sister, Siobhan, told Janice.

Either way, you'd reached breaking point. The game was up. When Janice phoned you yesterday, that sealed her fate, too. So you and Purvis killed her—just as you'd killed Nichola Kelly, all those years ago."

Gilchrist listened for some response that might confirm his theory. But Magner's breathy silence gave nothing away, only that he was starting to find the going tough.

The tunnel dipped for a short stretch, taking them deeper. The sound of dripping water was closer too, the floor damp enough for their boots to slap the odd splash. Without any ventilation system—nothing to pump air in one end and suck it out the other—just the effort of walking had sweat running down his face, tickling his neck. His lungs labored to pull in sufficient air to breathe.

But he knew he had to keep talking.

"Most suicides put the tube from the exhaust through the rear window. It's easier to open the door to sit in the front seat if you do it that way. And stuffing the scarf in from the outside was a bit sloppy, I have to tell you. Didn't I tell you that it's always the smallest things?" The memory of Jessie's words that morning sent hope surging through him.

He was not done and dusted yet. Just keep talking.

"And I'm guessing it was maybe midafternoon when you killed Amy. Which gave you plenty of time to hack her up, shower yourself clean, and make it to Tentsmuir Forest that evening. But what did you give the kids when they got home from school? A soft drink from their favorite uncle? Spiked with enough drugs to have them unconscious within minutes, ready to be smothered?"

Nothing.

"They were *children*, you murdering bastard. What harm could they do to you?"

Still no response—not even a grunt or an angry prod in the back to remind him to shut up.

"And what did you give Brian? A celebratory spiked Grey Goose?" Gilchrist stopped to catch his breath. "What did you have to celebrate? A new business deal? Another million quid in your bloated bank account? I don't think so. I'm guessing Amy told Brian about her rape complaint. Or maybe Janice did. And Brian was going to—"

Shock fired through Gilchrist from a jolt of pain in his left arm.

"You're doing a lot of guessing," Magner said, his tone giving the impression that the cramped walk through an ever-tightening tunnel was like a stroll in the park. But he was fooling no one. He prodded his rifle at Gilchrist's arm again.

Gilchrist let out another cry of pain.

"Maybe that'll teach you to shut it."

Gilchrist fought back tears as the pain in his left arm subsided. But the sound of Magner's heavy breathing assured him that Magner was faring no better and that his facial injuries and physical bulk were working against him in the confined space.

"Keep going," Magner grunted. "Nearly there."

Gilchrist did as he was told and clasped his left arm with his right hand, trying to stifle the pain. His fingers throbbed with a pulse that ticked to the beat of his heart. But that was the least of his worries. They were nearing the end of the tunnel, and more than likely the end of his life. The air seemed too thick to breathe, the cramp in his legs too strong for him to continue. But he pressed on.

Another fifteen steps brought them to another bend where the tunnel turned through forty-five degrees. When Gilchrist squeezed round the corner, he faced what he thought was a dead end, until he realized it was door.

He stopped.

The door was metal, not as corroded as the others, but lacking a handle. He pushed it and heard the metallic rattle of the deadbolt against the latch plate.

Locked.

It puzzled Gilchrist why this door was locked and the others not, until he worked out that this must lead to the open, and Purvis could not risk someone stumbling across the tunnel entrance, then walking all the way underground to the cottage trapdoor, or even to the Meating Room.

"Use this." Magner passed a heavy key over Gilchrist's shoulder.

He took it, slotted it into the keyhole, and turned.

The lock eased open with a heavy click. Using the key as a handle, Gilchrist pulled the door open, having to back into Magner as he did so.

Which gave him his chance.

He leaned forward to push through the door opening but struck out with his leg in a back-heel kick. He felt the satisfying thud as his foot hit something hard; then he scurried through the opening, key in hand. As he closed the door he glanced at Magner, his broken face contorted into a grotesque mask of surprise and anger and pain, his rifle swinging Gilchrist's way.

The first bullet struck the edge of the door and ricocheted past Gilchrist's face with a sizzling whine. The second hit the door full on with a dull crack, almost at the same time as Gilchrist slammed it hard into its frame.

He slotted the key into the keyhole and turned.

Three more bullets thudded into the metal with frightening force.

Gilchrist scurried along yet another tunnel, worried that Magner might find some way to shoot him through the keyhole. He also worried that blood was once again dripping from his fingertips—his wounds reopened by the sudden exertion. By the time he had gone ten steps, the silence behind told him Magner was already making his way back to the cottage, from where he could use his mobile to warn Purvis.

How long would that take?

Fifteen minutes? Ten? Less?

Gilchrist gritted his teeth and pressed on.

40

Jessie reached the cottage's rear lawn and stopped in the shadows.

If Magner was inside the cottage he could not see her. She was sure of that. Unless he was wearing night-vision goggles, of course. But she managed to convince herself she had nothing to fear—she was supposedly trapped in the Meating Room, after all. Even so, as she crept forward, her gaze darted from the windows to the door, to the driveway, to the Ford Focus, and back to the windows again.

Nothing stirred.

Without her mobile, she could not call for support. Andy had said up to an hour before the ARVs arrived, but she had expected police presence to be already here, to have blocked off the roads by now.

The smell of smoke hung in the air. Somewhere off in the distance, she caught the fading sound of a departing car. Everyone could have been settling in for an early bed on a Sunday night. She crept forward, Beretta gripped firmly, nerves stretched as tight as piano wire—Magner could be anywhere, she thought, although if he had any sense he would be well on his way to the Far East by now.

She reached the back door and tried the handle.

To her surprise, it was unlocked.

She pushed the door open and pressed her body to the cottage wall in case Magner tried to blast his way to freedom from inside. After five seconds of silence, she risked a look, then rushed through the doorway to crouch on the floor.

Nothing.

She moved through the small dining area and into the living room.

Again, nothing.

She eyed the phone on the coffee table, resisting the urge to call the Office and tell them to be on the lookout for Magner—"You can't miss him; pepper-sprayed face like a baboon's arse." But first she needed to establish that the cottage was empty.

A quick look through the two bedrooms, main bathroom, front hallway, and visitors' bathroom confirmed that the building was deserted. She slid the Beretta back into its ankle holster with a sigh of relief. A second, more thorough search of cupboards, wardrobes, undersides of beds, and a tight attic space assured her that both Magner and Purvis had fled and taken every weapon from the gun cupboard with them, too.

But she failed to find a trapdoor, which led her to conclude that Andy had been wrong, that the tunnel he thought led to the cottage must terminate under one of the outbuildings—disused greenhouse, garden hut, coal shed, maybe even some manhole cover.

Back in the living room, she moved to the phone and caught a glimpse of herself in the mirror over the fireplace, shocked to see the pale drawn face of someone who could have been a stranger staring back at her. Her reflection stunned her. She seemed to have aged ten years since putting on her makeup that morning. Shadows as deep as bruises lined her eyes. Her hair looked as if it had been blowtorched, then washed in dirt. She looked at her hands and gasped at the black grit under her fingernails, two of which were broken. Dried blood on her fingers had her rubbing her hands hard against her trousers.

From outside, she heard the first signs of police activity—sirens in the far distance—and caught the flickering light from a helicopter's spotlights brushing over the grass in the back garden as if the pilot were trying to land. Someone had pulled out all the stops.

She picked up the phone's receiver and dialed the Office. "DS Jessica Janes," she said. "I'm at Cauldwood Cottage and I—"

She froze.

Cocked her head at the noise.

A scraping sound in the kitchen. As if a sackload of gravel was being dragged across the floor.

Then a dull thud.

She dropped to her knees, eased the phone back on the table, and pulled the Beretta from its holster. If anyone walked into the living room, she would have them in her sights.

She waited.

Ten seconds passed in silence. Then twenty.

She thought of calling out, but that would only alert whoever was there.

She tried to still the pounding in her heart. Overhead, the helicopter roared like a hurricane that flattened grass and blasted the window with light. Through a gap in the curtains she saw a collection of blue and red flashing lights draw up on the road outside. Their presence gave her strength and hope, and she stood up, Beretta held out in front of her, and walked toward the kitchen door.

She kicked it open, her mind struggling to make sense of the confusing scene before her—the kitchen table up in the air at an angle of some sixty degrees, along with an entire section of wooden flooring, beneath which the dim opening to a smaller hatch beckoned like the dark entrance to Hades. Instinct screamed at her to back off, but she had time only to turn to the side as a hard crack hit her with a force that thumped her backward.

As she fell, glass exploded all around her to the echo of two more cracks. She flinched from flying splinters, her mind already working out that the first shot had thudded into her body armor, while the next two had missed altogether and shattered the crockery in the cabinet. Even before she hit the floor, the scene before her slowed down, as if she were watching it one frame at a time, her own actions as sluggish as moving through treacle.

A couple of clicks and a grunted curse told her the gun that had fired at her might have jammed.

From the hallway, Magner staggered into the kitchen, the rifle already cast aside and on its way to the floor behind him, while a shotgun seemed to slither from his shoulder into his grip with expert ease.

Jessie's Beretta seemed paltry by comparison—its barrel short and stubby, compared to the long double barrels swinging her way. She squeezed once, felt the kick, then squeezed again.

But still the shotgun zeroed in.

Another shot from the Beretta, and the twin barrels shuddered for a millisecond, then continued on their search until they settled on her.

She fired again to a hard click—the sound of an empty magazine—and felt her lungs empty in a scream as Magner's finger squeezed the trigger.

She jerked to the side in a quick roll that cracked her face against the edge of a cabinet door. The shock as the shot thundered through the wooden flooring felt like a kick that hit the full length of her body. She lay still, afraid to move in case she found she could not, that she had been hit full bore, and had only seconds to live.

Magner had stilled, too, as if stunned by the shotgun blast.

He stood for two seconds before his body followed the command from his brain. The shotgun dropped from his hands; then his legs buckled, and his knees hit the floor with a hard thud that should have broken bone. His continuing collapse was inevitable, as he fell forward, eyes already blinded by death, his broken face smacking the floor in a full-blooded head-butt.

Jessie squeezed her eyes shut—

"*Armed police.*" A hefty kick to the back door burst it open to a riot of screaming voices. "*Drop the gun drop the gun drop the fucking gun. Now.*"

Jessie let the Beretta slip from her fingers.

She wanted to come back at them with some memorable quip like, "You missed a great party, guys," but a sob choked its way out of her throat with a dry gasp, and it was all she could do to raise her hands and place them behind her head.

———

Gilchrist reached the end of the tunnel.

A set of wooden steps and a handrail ascended into a shaft in the roof—no more than four feet in depth—and appeared to end at a wooden trapdoor, distinguishable only by a thin rim of light that ran along the hinged edge.

Gilchrist's options were severely limited. Injured and without any weapon, he was completely defenseless. An image of Magner climbing up the wooden steps to the cottage warned him that he had no time to fuss over any plan of action. The sensible thing to do would be to return back the way he'd come, try to escape that way, maybe even head down the tunnel to the Meating Room, emerge through the barn, and work his way back to the cottage from there.

But that would be no use to Mhairi.

As he stared at the trapdoor at the top of the shaft, he came to see that the only way forward was up. He gripped the handrail, placed one foot on the first step. It felt flimsy, as if it might collapse under his weight. The shaft seemed decrepit, too, as if no one had been here for years, maybe decades.

He placed a foot on the next step.

All his weight was now supported by the rickety ladder. But he pressed on, one careful step at a time.

He reached the top, tilted his head, and placed an ear to the trapdoor. He thought he caught the faintest hint of someone talking—a man's voice, deep, not angry, more like talking to a pet, teaching it tricks, teasing it with biscuits.

His heart froze at the thought of another pair of Rottweilers. If something like that was waiting for him, then it really was game over. The memory of gnashing teeth and snarling growls had him closing his eyes and saying a silent prayer. He would need more than one arm to fight off a pair of dogs. Even two arms would not be enough. A baton gun might help level the odds.

An Uzi would give him an advantage.

He studied the underside of the hatch, placed both hands flat against the wood, but the fire in his left arm warned him to try something else. He readjusted his position, eased up another step so that his right shoulder pressed against the wood.

He held his breath and flexed his muscles.

The trapdoor eased open.

The man's voice was clearer now, closer too, and Gilchrist risked a quick look through the gap at floor level. As best he could tell, he was in another barn, and the voice was coming from a lighted area to his right. He had to shuffle his feet on the creaking steps before he could see the source of it clearly.

Purvis was standing with his back to the trapdoor, hunched over what looked like a wooden table, maybe a workbench. All his attention was focused on whatever was lying in front of him, but Gilchrist could not tell what. He risked opening the hatch a little wider but had to readjust his feet.

He shifted his weight, and his right foot slipped.

He just managed to prevent the trapdoor from slamming shut, more by luck than design, as it snapped down on his right hand. But that was enough to cause Purvis to lift his head and pull himself upright.

Gilchrist tried to tear his hand free, but the rim of the hatch had his knuckles trapped. To free himself, he would first have to open the trapdoor. He held his breath as he peered through the gap and prayed that Purvis would not see him.

Purvis reached out and picked up something off the table.

Then he turned to face the trapdoor.

Gilchrist's blood turned cold at the sight of the shotgun in Purvis's hand. Then it boiled in a hot surge of disgust and anger when he saw Mhairi's bare thighs parted on the table.

Purvis grinned as he walked toward the hatch.

"Come on in, Mr. DCI," he said, "and join the party."

41

Gilchrist pushed the trapdoor wide open and let it flop over on its hinges.

It landed with a wooden slap that sent dust flying.

He stepped halfway out, then glanced down into the shaft and shouted, "All right, all right. No need to whine about it." Then he pulled himself up and out, to stand on the edge of the opening with his hands shoulder high. "Your pal needs help," he said to Purvis, who leveled the shotgun at him.

"Do what?"

"His jaw's broken."

"Get back," Purvis snapped, and walked toward him.

Gilchrist obliged, shuffled one step away, then another.

Purvis reached the open shaft and looked into the empty space below. Then he turned back to Gilchrist. "What the fuck're you up to?"

Gilchrist put on a puzzled look of his own, shrugged, and nodded to the opening. "He's the one who needs help."

Purvis leaned farther over the opening. "Tom?" he shouted. "Hey, Tom?"

His voice echoed back at him.

"He can't talk," Gilchrist assured him. "His jaw's broken."

Purvis glared at him. "How'd he break his jaw?"

"Tripped."

Something settled across Purvis's eyes at that comment. He stepped back from the opening and pointed the shotgun at Gilchrist. "Get him," he said.

Gilchrist held out his left arm, still dripping blood. "I need both hands."

Purvis stared at the tattered sleeve, then jiggled his shotgun. "Go down there and get him."

Gilchrist lowered both arms.

He was about to step forward when Purvis said, "Drop the jacket."

Gilchrist dipped his right shoulder, pulled his arm free, then did the same with his left, grimacing with pain as he eased the sleeve down his bloodied forearm.

"I hope it hurts," Purvis said.

Gilchrist was about to drop the jacket to the floor when the tinny sound of Rod Stewart singing "Maggie May" stopped him.

Purvis stilled, too. His gaze darted to the shaft. He stepped to the edge again and removed a mobile from his pocket, shotgun in one hand, trigger finger curled within the guard. His puzzled shout echoed down the shaft. "Tom?" Then he took the call and placed the mobile to his ear. "Talk to me, Tom."

Gilchrist watched surprise crease Purvis's forehead, then shift wide-eyed through the shock of realization to full-blown anger.

Purvis dropped his mobile and lifted his shotgun to give Gilchrist both barrels in the face, but Gilchrist was already on the move, whipping his leather jacket at the muzzle.

Purvis squeezed the trigger.

The blast sounded like cannon fire.

The shockwave slapped Gilchrist's face as the pellets ripped past his head.

Somewhere behind him, wood exploded, metal clattered.

With Purvis not gripping the shotgun in both hands, the recoil sent the barrels pointing roofward. Gilchrist saw an opportunity. He swung his jacket at the shotgun again, the tattered sleeve wrapping around the barrels, almost ripping the weapon from Purvis's grasp. Then he lunged forward and tried to grab the stock.

But Purvis was too quick and stepped to the side.

Except there was no floor to step on.

Only the open shaft.

Purvis noticed his mistake too late, as one ankle twisted on the edge, shock and pain firing across his face. He tried to recover, but his leg buckled and his sideways momentum sent him toppling into the shaft.

Even then, he tried to save himself by turning his body as he fell, like some devilish acrobat. But as one hand refused to release the shotgun, the other clawed nothing but air. The opening, too, was not large enough to take him full length, and the back of his shoulders hit the frame of the trapdoor with a force that shivered the floorboards.

Gilchrist jerked his jacket, snapping the shotgun from Purvis's grip as he slumped through the opening, fingers dragging across the wooden floor like claws as he tried to stop the inevitable. The single handrail caught Purvis's right leg for only a moment, but long enough to change his angle of descent and send him in a headfirst dive down the shaft.

By the time Gilchrist stood at the trapdoor opening, Purvis lay at the foot of the ladder, his head pooling blood and lying at an impossible angle that told Gilchrist his neck was broken.

Gilchrist staggered back from the opening and turned to the workbench.

Mhairi was lying on her back, naked, her ankles and wrists strapped to the four corners with duct tape. Her body jerked in spasms from the force of her sobs.

Gilchrist threw his jacket across her body, then reached down and ripped the tape from her mouth. "You're safe now," he said. "It's OK, it's OK."

Tears streamed down Mhairi's cheeks, her lips shivering, lungs gasping with sobs that made speech impossible. The tape securing her wrists proved difficult to unwrap, but Gilchrist found a piece of broken glass lying in debris in a corner, and freed Mhairi at the cost of several cuts to his fingers. When he helped her to her feet, she clung to him as if her life depended on it, her body shuddering with a force that made him think she might never recover.

The sound of a helicopter overhead told Gilchrist they had tracked Purvis to the barn from the call to his mobile. He helped Mhairi hobble toward her clothes, then turned his back to give her some privacy as she struggled to put on what was left of them.

He retrieved Purvis's mobile from the barn floor, but the connection was dead. He dialed the last incoming number and the call was answered on the second ring.

But the line remained silent.

"This is DCI Andy Gilchrist," he said.

"*Andy?*" Jessie shouted. Then, much quieter, "Are you . . . ?"

"I'm OK," he said. "And so's Mhairi. But we need an ambulance." Then he added, "I don't think she's been harmed, but she needs to be checked out."

He listened in silence as Jessie brought him up to speed, and found himself squeezing his eyes and giving a silent prayer of thanks when she told him Magner was dead.

When he ended the call, he walked toward Mhairi.

She had dressed as best she could, but her clothes were little more than torn strips that she was now trying to hold together. Gilchrist grabbed his jacket from the floor, held it open, and helped her put it on. She tried to zip up, but her fingers were shaking with a tremor that worked all the way to her teeth, and she was forced to give up with a chattering attempt at a smile.

Rather than zip it for her, Gilchrist folded one side over the other.

Mhairi crossed her arms in a shivering hug, then said, "Stan?"

Gilchrist shook his head and placed an arm around her shoulder, his silence telling her all she needed to know. She fell against him then, her sobs taking her breath away, and he could do nothing to stop his own tears welling. He stared into the darkest recesses of the barn, hugging Mhairi closer, as much for himself as for her, while images of Stan flickered in the shadows of his mind.

When Mhairi's sobs finally shuddered to a stop, she managed to say, "I loved him, you know."

"I know," Gilchrist whispered.

He had loved Stan, too.

He just wished he'd had a chance to tell him that, and to say good-bye.

Together they turned and walked to the barn door.

42

Mhairi was driven to Memorial Hospital in St. Andrews, while Gilchrist was flown by helicopter to Ninewells Hospital in Dundee for treatment to his arm. Despite the makeshift tourniquet, his wounds continued to bleed, and he was given a local anesthetic so the surgeons could repair a torn vein. All in all, his forearm required thirty-six stitches and three pints of blood were transfused into him. The largest of several lumps on his head—where Purvis had clubbed him with the shotgun stock—required four stitches, but he declined to have a CT scan. The consultant advised that he remain in the hospital for observation, but Gilchrist signed himself out and took a taxi straight back to Cauldwood Cottage, his left arm strapped in a sling.

He thought of calling Cooper but instead sent her a text: "call me." By the time he arrived, Cooper had not contacted him, and dawn had broken to a blue sky and stiff winds.

The roads were closed, and the taxi could approach no closer than two hundred yards. Gilchrist had to show his warrant card to a young PC before she would permit him to proceed by foot. He paid the taxi fare, asked for a receipt—

mainly to irritate Greaves—and stepped into the fresh morning chill.

When he reached the cottage, it seemed as if an army had invaded. Purvis's Ford Focus had been towed away for forensic examination, and rows of vehicles—marked and unmarked police cars, SOCO vans, private cars—were parked in the long grass to the rear. Gilchrist had to step aside to let a tow truck ease down the driveway. A car covered by a tarpaulin was on the back, which he presumed was Purvis's Beemer.

The cottage was taped off, and dragonlights lit up its rear wall like a stage. SOCOs busied themselves in silence, flitting through the scene like ghosts. Gilchrist decided to return to the barn, see it in daylight, maybe even go a few steps farther and risk a look in the basement warren—the Meating Room—provided Stan's body was no longer there.

To his surprise, Jessie caught up with him.

"I was inside filling out a report," she said. "Thought I should join you."

"Been up all night?"

"Went home for a couple of hours' kip," she said. "Couldn't sleep, though. Too much going on up here." She tapped the side of her head.

"How's Robert?" he asked.

"Asleep in his grow bag." She shook her head. "I sometimes wonder if he remembers he's got a mum."

"You should go home," he said. "Spend some time with him. You look knackered."

"Thanks a bundle. You're looking not too bad yourself." She sniffed, turned her face into the wind as if to shift her irritation, then returned with, "You're standing there like a one-armed bandit. How's the arm?"

"Getting better," he said.

"And the mess on your head?"

"That, too," he said, then lowered his voice. "What about the Beretta?"

"I handed it over. Told them I found it."

"They'll check the registration."

"It's stolen."

He mouthed an *Ah*, and said, "Right."

They continued in silence toward the barn. The compound gate was open, and they stepped through.

A SOCO Transit was parked to the side, its engine running, doors open, as if it had been abandoned on arrival. Ahead, the barn doors were open, too, revealing a tidy interior. All sorts of tools glistened on metal Peg-Board racks. Stacked shelves lined the walls, holding plastic containers, boxes, tins, filters, even books.

Jessie stopped at the entrance, as if reluctant to step inside. She nodded to a bloodied spot on the floor. "They took the dogs away," she said. "These things shouldn't be allowed. They should be drowned at birth."

Drowning sounded good, but he nodded, and said, "What about Stan?"

In the blink of an eye, Jessie's anger vanished, and she stared off to some point over his shoulder. Her eyes glistened from the cold, or from memories of Stan, Gilchrist could not be sure. "That's why I couldn't sleep," she said. "Every time I closed my eyes, I saw that bastard shoot him."

Silent, Gilchrist waited for her gaze to return to him, then said, "You should make an appointment and talk to—"

"I'm not talking to any psychiatrists," she said, then ran a hand under her nose. "Did that once before. Spilled out my heart to some prick who never uttered a word. He just sat there like a doo-wally and listened to me rattle it off. All he did in the end was offer me sleeping pills. I was so pissed off, I nearly took them." She shook her head. "I couldn't trust myself. Thought I might take the lot. Lights out, and all that."

Gilchrist frowned. "When was this?"

"Years ago. Before your time. Before Robert's, too." She stared at him. "Does Mhairi know about Stan?"

He nodded.

Jessie's breath clouded in the morning chill. "I really thought they were going somewhere, you know? Stan seemed happy. Mhairi too. It's so bloody sad."

Gilchrist could think of nothing to add, and said, "What about Magner and Purvis?"

"What about them? Cooper and her lot have already been here and done their stuff. Photographed the bodies ad nauseam, then transported them to Bell Street. Cooper'll be doing her best to cut them up. I hope she slices their balls off. That might cheer her up."

He caught the emphasis, and said, "Cheer her up?"

"She didn't seem her usual self, you know? Miss Woman-of-the-World looking down in the dumps. Didn't suit her." She shot a smile at him. "Think I might even have seen a hair out of place."

He tried to cover his emotions with a smile of his own. "Well, it would have been early on a Monday morning," he offered.

He thought Jessie returned his gaze for a moment too long, as if searching for something behind his eyes—the truth about his relationship with Cooper, perhaps, or some explanation as to why she might not have been herself. But what could he tell her? That Cooper was suffering from morning sickness? Or depressed over the imminent end of her marriage? Or—and this was even more troubling—that she had already decided to have a termination? Which he knew would be heartbreaking for her.

"What happened across the road?" Jessie said.

The non sequitur confused him. "When?"

"When I called Purvis on Magner's phone."

"That was *you?*"

"The IT guys were only trying to get a trace on his location, not set off a shooting match."

The memory of the change in Purvis's expression sent a chill down Gilchrist's spine. If not for that chance call, he would not be standing there now. "You saved my life," he said. "Your call distracted Purvis and I took a chance. His shot still nearly took my head off, though."

"It nearly blew my ear out," she said, and glanced over his shoulder. "Uh-oh. Here's trouble."

Greaves was approaching them with his eyes fixed on Gilchrist. Not quite as bad as a Rottweiler eyeing his throat but close enough for Gilchrist to brace himself for the onslaught. But Greaves surprised him by shaking his hand and almost cracking a smile.

"How's the arm?"

"Still sore but getting better."

"It'll take time to heal," Greaves said. "Fortunately, that's something you'll have a lot of."

"Sir?"

"Your maverick approach has caught up with you at last, Andy. Big Archie wants a word." Greaves's eyes sparkled with pleasure, or victory—it was difficult to tell. "Nine o'clock. His office," he added.

Gilchrist pursed his lips. Assistant Chief Constable Archie McVicar, a fair man, but a tough man to deal with if you ever crossed him. Not that Gilchrist had, or so he thought, but he could not shift the worry that McVicar's urgent call would result in his being suspended. No matter how he tried to cut it, the facts were that Stan had been killed, and Gilchrist had been the senior investigating officer. The more he thought about it, the more he came to see that suspension was the least of his troubles. Greaves's grimace for a smile almost confirmed it for him.

"I'll give ACC McVicar a call, sir," Gilchrist said.

"He's expecting you in his office within the hour."

"Sir?"

"I told him you would be there."

Well, there he had it. Ordered about like a dumb puppy. He let several seconds of silence pass before he nodded to Jessie, then turned and walked back to the cottage.

He thought of trying to postpone the meeting with McVicar by pretending he had another hospital appointment. But Greaves would revel in the prospect of drilling him a new arsehole if he tried that. Still, he had too many unanswered questions in his investigation just to be pushed to the side, and in the end he decided to tackle the devil head on.

He wangled a lift to Glenrothes HQ with Nora Wells, a young PC from the Anstruther Office. On the drive there, he was struck by her resemblance to his daughter—dark hair, brown eyes, smooth skin, slim to the point of skinny.

"Are you all right, sir?"

"Sorry? Yeah. I'm fine. Why?"

"You keep looking at me."

"I didn't mean to," he said. "It's just . . . you remind me of someone."

They continued the journey in silence, with Gilchrist sinking ever deeper into gloom. He did what he could to shift the specter of suspension from his mind, but it refused to budge, so he tried to look on the bright side. It would give him time to help Maureen do up her flat—papering, painting, tiling, even tackling the new kitchen flooring he'd promised to lay for her. He shifted in his seat from a stab of pain, as if his body were reminding him he had only one arm in working order and handyman jobs required two.

He sank back into misery.

PC Wells pulled up in the car park at Glenrothes, then sped off before he had time to thank her, leaving him with the feeling that he was upsetting everyone that day. He pushed his hands deep into his pockets and walked toward the meeting with McVicar.

He could always strike first, he supposed, and just hand in his notice.

43

McVicar remained seated as Gilchrist entered his office. "Take a seat, Andy," he ordered.

Silent, Gilchrist obliged, pulling out one of two chairs set in front of a polished desk devoid of clutter. Just like the man's thinking, he thought—clear, concise.

McVicar pressed himself into the back of his chair, as if trying to distance himself from something unhealthy. Then he eyed the hospital sling, giving Gilchrist the impression that he was trying to work out if it would heal before or after his suspension was over. When he shifted his gaze to one of his fry-you-in-your-seat stares, the answer was *before*.

Gilchrist found himself struggling to return the look.

"Fiasco," McVicar said, his voice booming in the small room. "Unmitigated disaster." He shook his head, causing his jowls to shudder. "I've lost count of the number of times I've heard these words from Chief Superintendent Greaves this morning."

Gilchrist chose silence.

"You have an unhealthy habit of alienating those above you, Andy. And this . . . this . . . maverick attitude of yours—another phrase I've heard far too often today—lands you in trouble time and time again." He growled, cleared his throat. "But you know all that, of course."

"Of course." Agreeing seemed as good a response as any.

McVicar lowered his head, as if to study Gilchrist over a pair of imaginary specs. "And we lost a good man last night," he said.

Gilchrist felt his lips tighten, his eyes nip. He blinked once, twice, then let out a heavy breath. "Yes, sir. We did. Stan was unarmed when he was shot in cold blood by Thomas Magner, more or less at point-blank range."

"You were there?"

"Yes, sir. DS Janes, too." He worried all of a sudden that Jessie might not recite the same story—that Stan had done nothing to instigate his death—and made a mental note to brief her as soon as he could.

McVicar's eyes seemed to have lost their ability to blink. He stared at Gilchrist, as if trying to will his thoughts to his lips. "Detective Sergeant Jessica Harriet Janes," he said, as if reading from a script. "She said you saved her life."

Gnashing teeth and snarling growls flared into Gilchrist's mind with a flashback that shook him. It took the memory of Purvis dropping his mobile phone to the barn floor and raising his shotgun to force the image away. "I think she has that the wrong way round, sir."

"And you saved PC McBride's life, I hear."

Gilchrist returned a blank stare while he worked out that Jessie must have mentioned all of this to Greaves, who had passed it on to McVicar. But that didn't seem right. Why would Greaves put in a good word for him? He was missing something. Nine o'clock on a Monday morning and his head was already spinning.

"We were fortunate," Gilchrist said.

"She phoned me."

"Mhairi?"

"DS Janes. Just got off the phone with her about ten minutes ago." McVicar leaned forward, rested his arms on the desk, as if no longer afraid of contamination. "She said Chief Super Greaves informed you that I wanted to talk to you. So she thought she should give me, as she put it, the correct version of events."

Gilchrist mouthed an *Ah*.

"Ah, indeed." McVicar said. "You're long enough in the tooth, Andy, to know that I'm going to have to take you off the case until a full investigation into Stan's murder is carried out."

Gilchrist gave a defeated nod. "Define off the case, sir."

"Well, if Greaves had his way, you'd be asked to hand in your notice. The least he wants is to demote you to tea boy." McVicar shook his head. "I sometimes wonder if the job is all too much for us anymore."

Gilchrist felt a stirring of hope. Greaves had done himself no favors by coming down so heavily. McVicar had seen through his complaints and taken them for what they were—a personal vendetta. But before he dared breathe a sigh of relief, Gilchrist thought it best to say nothing.

"I don't see any benefit in forcing one of our top detectives to sit on the sidelines. We're short staffed as it is, for crying out loud."

Gilchrist risked a thoughtful nod.

"However, given the overlap between your investigation and Chief Superintendent Whyte's, I'm arranging for him to take over. I want you to debrief him personally, Andy, bring him fully up to speed. Give him everything you've got. Hold *nothing* back. Then step away. Understood?"

"Yes, sir."

"And let me take care of Greaves for you," McVicar said. "I'll point out the error in his thinking . . . in a manner of speaking."

"Thank you, sir."

Then McVicar's look darkened—a reminder to Gilchrist that he was still walking on thin ice that could crack at any moment, and that McVicar was still the man in charge. "I understand we have some video evidence that could turn out to be rather embarrassing."

Statement, not a question, but Gilchrist said, "We do, sir."

"I don't want the waters muddied by the media getting wind of any breach of protocol in the manner in which you handled this investigation."

Gilchrist knew the breach was that they had broken into Purvis's property without a search warrant. The fact that they subsequently stumbled upon the Meating Room and discovered evidence of a string of murders was neither here nor there. It should all have been done by the book, without which Gilchrist strongly suspected that Stan's murder could come back to hit him big-time.

He was not out of the woods yet. Not by a long shot.

"I understand, sir."

"I've already been in contact with Chief Super Whyte," McVicar said, glancing at the clock on the wall. "He'll be along any minute."

Gilchrist mouthed another *Ah*. It seemed as if he was being made privy to the other side of McVicar, a man who had not reached ACC by walking around admiring the scenery but who could make decisions and march into the heart of hell to see them through, if he had to. Rumor had it that he was a shoo-in for chief constable next year.

As if to nail that point home, the door rapped, and Whyte entered.

"Come in, Billy," McVicar said, then lowered his head to Gilchrist. "Now, I'd like to hear your side of the story, Andy."

———

It took Gilchrist the best part of two hours to bring Whyte and McVicar up to speed. McVicar listened with his hands steepled to his lips, not missing a word, not saying a thing. Whyte was more inquisitive, and smart, firing off a series of pertinent questions. But when Gilchrist came to Stan's cold-blooded murder, both men listened in silence, their faces grim, their moods solemn.

Only when Gilchrist had brought his debriefing to a close did McVicar nod to Whyte and ask, "Any other questions?"

"Just the one, sir." Whyte faced Gilchrist. "Was PC Mhairi McBride part of your original covert team?"

"No, sir."

"Just the three of you? DS Janes, DI Davidson, and yourself?" Which were two questions. "Yes."

"So, how did PC McBride know where you were?"

Gilchrist had asked Mhairi the same question, only to learn that Stan had phoned her prior to setting off with him and Jessie. When Gilchrist explained that, Whyte asked, "But why would Stan call *her*?"

"Extra backup from someone he trusted."

"Really?"

"Really."

"I think you need to elaborate, Andy."

"Mhairi and Stan were in a relationship."

"I see."

"Of course, she was particularly upset when she found out that Stan was dead."

"As we all were," McVicar assured him.

Whyte narrowed his eyes. "You told her?"

"I did."

"And did you tell her *how* DI Davidson died?"

Gilchrist thought back to comforting Mhairi in the barn. "No, sir."

Whyte returned his stare with an unsettling steadiness, and Gilchrist had the strangest feeling that he was trying to work out whether to believe him or not. Then Whyte offered a tight smile and sat back.

Gilchrist said, "I'm happy to assist in any way I can in the continuing investigation, sir. If Chief Super Whyte and yourself approve, of course."

McVicar narrowed his eyes. "Not sure I do, Andy."

"It might send the wrong message to the media if I'm hauled off the case, sir. If I continue to be involved, then we could simply say it's a reassignment. Particularly as one case appears to be solved—in terms of identifying the culprits."

McVicar glanced at Whyte, who gave the tiniest of nods. "Very well, Andy. The official word is reassignment. But unofficially you're taking a backseat. Understood?"

"Understood."

"Right. I'll make sure Greaves gets the message." McVicar rose to his feet to bring the meeting to a close.

Gilchrist was about to leave the room when Whyte said, "I'd like to talk to DS Janes, if you could get her to give me a call." He held out a business card.

Gilchrist eyed the card. A call to the North Street Office would put Whyte straight through to Jessie or transfer him to her mobile.

He declined to take the card and said, "I'll ask her to call."

44

Forensics spent the rest of the week working through Cauldwood Cottage and the property across the road, as well as the barn and basement warren that the media invariably termed "the Meating Room." In turn, Magner and Purvis were christened "the Butchers."

A CD of scanned images found in the cottage offered early glimpses of the crazed wildness that drove the Butchers to kill time and time again. As a teenager, Purvis had been a keen outdoorsman, excelling in mountaineering, cross-country trekking and, more ominously, hunting. A photograph of a stag's head—with a magnificent set of antlers—superimposed on an image of a naked Purvis ejaculating appeared to be the defining moment when his sexual preferences and perverted demands took a much darker path.

Magner featured in that collection of photographs, too, attending swinger parties and caught in full penetrative mode with a series of female partners. Strangely, or so it was noted by more than one forensic psychologist, none of the photos ever showed Magner and Purvis together. To Gilchrist's thinking, the simple answer was that one had always photographed the other. But with neither Magner nor Purvis alive to cor-roborate that theory, he might as well have been pissing into the wind.

And Jerry McGovern came clean, once he heard that Purvis was dead. His brother, Malky, had been selling hardcore porn on the black market. Although Jerry could not confirm who had supplied the original material to Malky, the presence of a Ford Focus at Malky's house from time to time had led him to believe that Purvis was the supplier—the same Ford Focus he saw turning into the McCullochs' driveway after he had stolen Amy's jewelry that Thursday.

To McGovern's thinking, the McCullochs had been slaugh-tered by Purvis, and it was the frightening prospect of retali-ation by Purvis that had scared him into silence, believing Purvis had recognized him as he fled the McCullochs' after his robbery. Of course, he had failed to notice that Magner was driving the Focus that day, and not Purvis.

As Jimmy swore that he made his exit around midday, Gilchrist determined that Magner must have lain in wait in the house until Amy returned with the girls a few hours later.

Although the boot and interior of the Focus had been scrubbed and vacuumed, a couple of fibers were identified as being from an M&S Egyptian cotton bath towel, identical to the set Amy McCulloch had purchased a fortnight earlier. The assumption was that Amy's body parts were transferred from her home to the Meating Room in the towel. More damning evidence was a hair recovered from the weave of the boot carpet, which matched Amy's DNA.

A brazier was found in one corner of the barn, with a con-nection for a propane gas bottle on its underside. Although the bottom grating had been scrubbed with a metal brush, forensics managed to confirm that traces of ash were fabric remnants. Scrapes on the floor of the first anteroom, along with soot and scorch marks on the walls and ceiling, confirmed that all traceable evidence—bloodied bath towels, clothes, shoes—had been incinerated there.

A search through the cottage's domestic bins for evidence of ash from the brazier uncovered nothing more, and it was concluded that Purvis had bagged and removed the ash off-site. CCTV teams were instructed to review recordings from Thursday morning through Sunday afternoon for activity related to the Ford Focus, to find out where Purvis might have dumped the bags.

The BMW in the barn was positively identified from the position and angle of the tax disc on the front windscreen. A minute chip on the paintwork next to the offside headlight further confirmed it was the vehicle captured on CCTV driving through Anstruther on the night of Janice Meechan's fatal hit-and-run. Finally, traces of Janice's blood were recovered from the damaged nearside wing, which removed any lingering doubt about the car's involvement in her murder.

James Watson—the registered owner of Purvis's Remington 700 bolt-action rifle and the Holland & Holland Royal and Purdey 12-bore shotguns—proved to be fictitious. The Purdey was traced to a Mr. Peter Cuthbertson, a Lancashire sheep farmer, who identified Purvis from a photograph and confirmed he had sold him the gun for cash about seven years earlier. Prior owners of the Remington and the Holland & Holland had not yet been identified, but it was only a matter of time.

Amy McCulloch's head, heart, lungs, stomach, and some seven feet of her intestines were found in a tub of formaldehyde solution in one of eight sarcophagal chambers in the Meating Room. Strips of her skin—including her finger- and toenails—were found on wire-mesh frames in the shapes of arms, legs, and torso, like a dismantled tailor's dummy.

Seven complete female human sculptures were found in the other chambers. One had already been identified as a thirty-one-year-old mother of two who vanished three years earlier while driving from her home in Airth to Falkirk; another as a twenty-year-old shop assistant from Alloa who disappeared while walking her dog the previous March; and three as the Stirling University students who had gone missing during a camping trip in the Cairngorms back at the start of the century. DNA tests on the remaining two flagged up nothing on the Police National Computer, and Fife Constabulary widened their search by requesting the assistance of Scotland Yard and Interpol.

Brenda McAllister, the procurator fiscal, insisted on having round-the-clock forensic examination of the Cauldwood Cottage properties and was granted extended search warrants to include Stratheden Enterprise's offices and Magner's private residences in Edinburgh, London, and Marbella.

Chief Constable Ramsay was interviewed by a team from the Scottish Crime Squad, who presented him with photographs of his alleged participation in a number of swinger parties in the 1980s. Through his solicitor, Ramsay stated that, although the person in the pictures bore a slight resemblance to him as a younger man, it was not him, and he had never been in the company of either Magner or Purvis, nor had any dealings with them privately or otherwise. Within two days of the story breaking, he took himself and his wife on a four-week holiday to an unknown destination in the Caribbean.

Ramsay's story verged on the plausible, frustratingly strengthened by the fact that no photographs of his first wife, Jean, seemed to exist. But Gilchrist suggested they investigate the death of Magner's first wife, Sheila Ramsay, only to discover that she was Chief Constable Ramsay's sister. With a personal link to Magner irrefutably confirmed, Ramsay's lies were exposed. Two detectives from the Scottish Crime Squad tracked him to Saint Lucia and flew over to arrest him, only to be informed by the Royal Saint Lucia Police Force that his wife had filed a missing persons report with Port Castries Police Station that morning. Her husband had left their holiday villa before midnight, claiming that he needed to walk some thoughts through, and had not returned. A few hours later, Chief Constable Ramsay's fully clothed body washed up on the shores of Rodney Bay.

Martin Craig, MEP, resigned from his post two days after the story broke and flew to New Zealand with his secretary. It then emerged that they'd been having an affair for the last four years. The Bureau of Investigative Journalism latched on to the story, and by the end of the week had persuaded the European Parliament to initiate an internal audit into Craig's office.

All computer equipment had been removed from Stratheden Enterprises, and forensic specialists were contracted to search all files. Although early days, one file provided a link to a Royal Bank of Scotland account in the Channel Islands, from which BACS transfers to a number of personal bank accounts in Scotland and England were exposed, varying in size from £200 to a staggering £420,000.

Jessie had been willing to put a bet on with Gilchrist that they would uncover a payment trail that would lead them straight to Martin Craig. "Have you seen the house Craig lives in?" she said. "You couldn't afford that on a normal salary."

"Have you seen the house his *family* lives in," Gilchrist replied, reminding her that Craig had done a runner with his secretary and was an MEP no longer.

"Minor detail," she said. "How about twenty quid, then?"

"I'm not a betting man. But if I was, I'd be betting with you, not against you."

"Coward."

"Just canny."

And the canny Gilchrist verified through Stratheden Enterprises' records that Magner attended conferences in Edinburgh, Stirling, and Glasgow on each of the days the three Stirling University students and the women from Airth and Alloa went missing. In a bid to identify the last two victims, he suggested that they concentrate on searching for women reported missing on days when Magner had attended other conferences. Twenty-three separate conferences over a period of eight years provided key dates, and although no positive IDs had yet been made, Gilchrist felt confident that it was only a matter of time.

Forensic accountants were hired to examine Stratheden's books, but by the end of the first week a preliminary audit uncovered nothing of interest. The PF's office terminated the auditors' contract with immediate effect and initiated a selection process for another firm. Brenda McAllister, it seemed, was determined to bring down the whole empire.

A search of the Land Registry confirmed that the Department of Agriculture had owned both Cauldwood Cottage and the property across the road in the mid-1930s, and that plans for a communal bomb shelter and interconnecting tunnels had been approved during World War II. Construction had begun under a veil of government secrecy—"Department of Agriculture, my arse," said Jessie—but was abandoned a year later, amid proposals for a new project that eventually became the Secret Bunker. Rather than demolish the shelters and return the property to its original condition, the land was sold to a Mr. John Purvis—Jason Purvis's grandfather. Purvis inherited the properties when his own parents passed away.

Disturbingly, a number of unmarked graves were discovered on the other side of the road from Cauldwood Cottage, adjacent to the barn where Purvis had taken Mhairi. Cooper was working with CAHID—the University of Dundee's Centre for Anatomy and Human Identification—to identify the remains. Whether these bodies were related to the Butchers' killings had yet to be confirmed, but Gilchrist was sure another hit was about to be registered.

45

S tan's funeral was held on the Saturday. As a mark of
respect, all forensic work on the investigation was halted
for the weekend.

A church service was held in St. Leonard's Parish Church,
where Tom Greaves surprisingly revealed a compassionate
side with a poignant speech. Later, at the burial service in
Western Cemetery, Gilchrist recognized Stan's parents, Bill
and Rita, who seemed to have aged twenty years since he
had last met them eighteen months ago. Stan's sister, Janet,
was there too, looking broken and frail, as if she had given
up on life altogether. With the graveside service over, all
three departed without a word or backward glance, as if they
wanted nothing more to do with Fife Constabulary.

Gilchrist could not shift the heartrending thought that
while the constabulary was not at fault for Stan's death,
he was. Even so, he tried to reach the family before their
limo drove off—to offer his condolences, and maybe even
arrange to visit them sometime. But he was too late. As the
car brushed past him, he caught a tearful glance from Janet

who, for just that pained and fleeting moment, could have been Stan's double.

Only when the crowd started to disperse from the cemetery grounds did Gilchrist notice Cooper. She was dressed in black, with her hair tied back in a swollen bun that seemed to accentuate her features and only add to her radiance. By all accounts, she should have been exhausted. She and her team had put in long hours in the Bell Street Mortuary, in addition to working with forensic experts from CAHID first on the sarcophagal sculptures—"the devil's artwork," as one paper had dubbed them—then on the remains of six more bodies found in the garden across the road. On top of that, of course, she was pregnant. Throughout the week, she had reported to Billy Whyte, and so avoided all direct contact with Gilchrist.

Although not openly admitted, the worry was that more bodies would be uncovered. No one knew, or even dared to guess, just how many women Magner and Purvis had killed together.

Gilchrist noted Cooper's Range Rover at the edge of the car park, as if she had not wanted anyone to notice her attendance. She seemed to be alone, although as he walked toward her he found himself searching for Mr. Cooper, just to be sure.

The Range Rover's lights flashed as she beeped her fob.

"Weddings and funerals," he said to her.

Cooper paused, the driver's door half-open, and looked at him in silence.

"It's where people our age always seem to meet," he explained. "If they haven't seen each other for a while. At weddings and funerals." He felt as if he was gabbling.

She gave a tight grin. "I got it first time."

Gilchrist was struck by two things: one, that she looked more beautiful than he ever remembered her to be—her blue eyes, flawless skin, sculpted face, and strawberry blonde hair could be the envy of any model—and two, that she seemed painfully distant, as if she was disappointed to see him.

"So, how are you?" he asked.

She nodded. "You?"

He knew from the way she held on to the door handle, from the angle of her body, from her refusal to turn and face him, that she wanted to step into the Range Rover and drive away. But he had to ask the question.

"What I meant was: how's your pregnancy?"

"No morning sickness yet, if that's what you mean."

No, that was not what he meant. And she knew it. But in the three short months of their intimate relationship, he had learned that Cooper could be the devil herself when she put her mind to it. He had no option but to go straight to the heart of it.

"Have you made a decision?" he asked.

She seemed to give the question some thought, then said, "About my pregnancy?"

He said nothing, just waited for her to continue, refusing to be toyed with in whatever game she thought she was playing.

"Don't you think you're being presumptuous?" she said.

Now it was his turn to look dumb. "Presumptuous?"

"My personal choices are none of your business."

Her comment stunned him, but he said, "I think you being pregnant *is* my business. After all, I'm the—"

"No, Andy. You're not."

He might have said *What?* But he could not be sure and had to close his mouth while his mind fired through the rationale. Even though he knew the answer was wrong, he found he still had to say it. "Mr. Cooper?"

She shook her head. "No," she whispered.

Well, there he had it. Cuckolded once again. He thought of asking who she had been seeing behind his back but thankfully remembered he had been seeing Cooper behind Mr. Cooper's back. He had believed Cooper to be a one-man woman—well, a one man at a time woman. How wrong could he be? What goes around comes around seemed to be the order of the day. Silent, he took a step back as she pulled the Range Rover's door wide open and climbed in.

Even when the door closed and the engine fired up and the gearbox slotted into drive with a hard metallic click and the Range Rover pulled away from the parking space, engine burbling, exhaust laying down a trail of white as if enticing him to follow, he found he could say nothing. Not until the sound of the Range Rover's engine faded into the March chill did he realize that he was standing in the middle of the travel lane.

He shoved his hands deep into his coat pockets and walked back to his car.

He thought by now that he should have become inured to the pain of jealousy. But it hurt, burrowing deep into his heart, twisting his gut, the pain sharp and blunt at the same time, as if his body could not work out how best to attack him.

He had told her he loved her. Well, he had, he did. He did love her.

Had he said that only two weeks ago? When had he last uttered these words to another woman? He could not remember. Not even when he had last told Gail he loved her. How many years ago had that been?

Ten? Twenty?

Surely no more.

And Cooper had reciprocated—"I love you, too, Andy."

It seemed to seal their relationship.

Had none of it meant anything? Had she just said that to keep him contented?

He thought he had known Cooper, thought he had understood her, had known when to press, when to hold back, when to tease, and when not. He had known her better than anyone else with whom he had been intimate, known her better than he had known his own wife.

He had known Cooper better . . .

Better than anyone else . . .

Then he thought he understood.

He reached his car, turned his head to the end of the car park. Another cortege was entering the cemetery grounds, a hearse leading three sparkling black limousines, trailed by carloads of mourners.

He slipped out his new mobile and dialed her number.

She picked up on the second ring but said nothing.

He pressed the mobile to his ear but could not hear any background noise.

"You've parked," he said.

"Talking on the phone while driving is against the law."

She had been waiting for him to call, he thought he understood that much. Because he knew her better than he had known anyone else. And she knew him, too.

"You're going through with the termination."

A pause of one beat, two beats, then a sad, "Yes. I am."

He took a deep breath and stared at the gray-brown branches of the trees. Starlings flocked and fluttered in a flurry of wings, then swooped to the ground in feathered unison. In the far distance, a skein of geese pierced the sky in a perfect arrowhead. Life is all around, he thought. And life goes on. No matter what.

"I'm the father," he said at length.

"You are," she said. "I'm sorry. I shouldn't have lied to you."

"You didn't want me to interfere in your decision," he said. "You thought I would walk away."

"Isn't that what men are good at? Isn't that what they always do?"

He had no answer to that. Was that not what he had been prepared to accept moments earlier? He had justifiable reasons for doing so, of course, but even so . . .

Neither spoke for what felt like thirty seconds, until Cooper said, "I have to make my own decision."

He could tell she was crying. What mother-to-be would not in these circumstances? She had no children of her own through her marriage to Mr. Cooper, and now she was pregnant by Gilchrist. No doubt she had lain awake at night torturing herself over the unfairness of life. If she'd had a child by her husband, would they have remained married? Well, if Mr. Cooper had been allowed to continue to spread his seed to all and sundry, then maybe he would have been happy to continue with the status quo. But Gilchrist knew that for Cooper it was not about just being married but about commitment, trust and, above all else, love.

Which seemed to bring him full circle.

"I'll help in any way I can," he offered.

She sniffed but said nothing.

"You don't have to do this, Becky. Go through with it, I mean. We can—"

"There's no *we* in this, Andy. I thought you understood that." She sniffed again, cleared her throat, as if regaining her strength. "I have to do this by myself."

"You don't have to do anything by yourself anymore. I'm here for you." He expected her to snap back at him, but her silence told him that she was not ruling it out. At least for the time being. "Where are you?" he asked.

"Not far."

"I'll be with you in a few minutes," he said, and opened the Merc's door.

The connection died.

He slid behind the steering wheel and fired the ignition. Then he drove off to meet her.